W9-AYS-958

FORWARD ME
BACK TO YOU

PROPERTY OF PRINCETON PUBLIC SCHOOLS
BOARD OF EDUCATION

FORWARD ME BACK TO YOU

MITALI PERKINS

Farrar Straus Giroux • SQUARE FISH • New York

SQUARE
FISH

An imprint of Macmillan Publishing Group, LLC
120 Broadway, New York, NY 10271
fiercereads.com

FORWARD ME BACK TO YOU. Copyright © 2019 by Mitali Perkins.
All rights reserved. Printed in the United States of America by
LSC Communications, Harrisonburg, Virginia.

Square Fish and the Square Fish logo are trademarks of Macmillan and
are used by Farrar Straus Giroux under license from Macmillan.

Our books may be purchased in bulk for promotional, educational, or business
use. Please contact your local bookseller or the Macmillan Corporate and
Premium Sales Department at (800) 221-7945 ext. 5442 or by email at
MacmillanSpecialMarkets@macmillan.com.

Library of Congress Cataloging-in-Publication Data

Names: Perkins, Mitali, author.
Title: Forward Me Back to You / Mitali Perkins.
Other titles: Boy Wonder and Kat Girl
Description: New York : Farrar Straus Giroux, 2019. | Summary: Told in separate
    voices, Kat and Robin leave Boston on a church mission to help combat human
    trafficking in India while Kat recovers from a sexual assault and Robin seeks his
    birth mother.
Identifiers: LCCN 2018038352 (print) | LCCN 2018044414 (ebook) |
    ISBN 9780374304935 (ebook) | ISBN 9781250619907 (paperback)
Subjects: | CYAC: Friendship—Fiction. | Voluntarism—Fiction. | Human
    trafficking—Fiction. | Adoption—Fiction. | Kolkata (India)—Fiction. |
    India—Fiction. | Boston (Mass.)—Fiction.
Classification: LCC PZ7.P4315 (ebook) | LCC PZ7.P4315 Boy 2019 (print) | DDC
    [Fic]—dc23
LC record available at https://lccn.loc.gov/2018038352

Originally published in the United States by Farrar Straus Giroux
First Square Fish edition, 2020
Book designed by Cassie Gonzales
Square Fish logo designed by Filomena Tuosto

10 9 8 7 6 5 4 3 2 1

LEXILE: HL690L

For Anuj and Tanuj

AUTHOR'S NOTE

As readers and writers, we bring our whole selves—past, present, and future—to a novel. We also come with a history of relationships, both sweet and painful. As I crafted the story you're about to read, some things were tough to imagine for my characters—especially exploitation, abandonment, and assault—even though they happened in the past before the book begins. Imagining somebody else's suffering can bring up memories of our own, or sadness over wounds experienced by those we love. My hope is that trauma never gets the last word. Healing requires tenderness, and sometimes even tears, as my main characters, Kat and Robin, both discover. I wrote this novel from my heart to yours, with the prayer that we all receive the grace we need to move forward.

FORWARD ME
BACK TO YOU

PART ONE

BOSTON

KAT

INT. KING APARTMENT, EAST OAKLAND—NIGHT

Canine. Feline. Avian.

Zoologists use taxonomy to separate predators from prey.
Backs to a wall, dogs bite. Felines scratch. Birds peck.

Katina King classifies herself as a mountain lion.

She might have become a tame cat in a safer world. But
when she was eleven, her body changed so fast it turned her
into prey. Nothing she could do to stop luring canine eyes, so
she'd put on a feral mask since then to prowl the hills of
Oakland.

Fangs, claws, snarl.

They should have kept wolves away, but they didn't.

Later, she realizes she should have called the cops. But she
doesn't even tell her mother what happened until she's caught
throwing up in the middle of the night. Kat's so tired from
three nights of no sleeping that the truth comes hurtling out
before she can stop it.

"He did *what*?" Kat's always seen her mother as a pigeon.
But if someone comes after her daughter, look out for beak and
talons. "I'm calling Saundra right now. Oh, honey!"

The two of them are on the sofa sitting so close it sounds
like Mom's best friend is in Kat's ear. "Let me talk to her,"
Saundra says.

Mom hands over the phone. It's wet with tears. Disgusting Wolf. Kat hates him even more for making Mom cry. *Not me,* she thinks. *Never me.*

"When did it happen, Filhote?" Saundra asks. She's in Panther mode—even uses Kat's Brazilian jiu-jitsu nickname. Kat's been *Lion Cub* since she started training with "Pantera" at eleven; this is the same growl that's coached her to victory over other aggressive jiu-jitsu opponents.

"Three days ago. In the stairwell. At school."

"Security cameras?"

"Don't think so." *Probably why he picked the place.*

"Any bruising—apart from what you got at practice? Scratches on your skin?"

"Nothing new." Kat's scrubbed so hard in the shower it feels like she doesn't have much of her own DNA left on her skin.

"Still got the clothes you were wearing? Did you wash them?"

Kat hesitates. "No. I put them in the trash."

"When's garbage pickup?"

"Yesterday." *Stupid, stupid me. Should have known to keep the clothes.* But her mind's been a blur.

Saundra doesn't yell like she does when Kat makes a dumb jiu-jitsu move. "Be there in ten," she says instead.

Mom's crying hard now. Kat puts an arm around her shoulder and pulls her close. This is exactly why she didn't tell her mother right away. *Don't let him do this to you, Mom. Don't give that Wolf power over us.*

Saundra gets to their apartment so fast Kat wonders if

she used the siren on her patrol car. "You okay?" she asks, scanning Kat's face.

Kat has her fiercest fighting expression locked into place. "I took care of him."

Mom sits up. "How? Saundra, he tried to—"

"He didn't, though." Kat turns to Saundra. "I couldn't think at first—it didn't seem real—but then the instincts kicked in. Used a Kimura to break his hold."

"Good job," says Saundra. "Any injuries for him?"

"Broken pinkie, rotator cuff sprain." Kat takes a breath. "He's saying it happened during a pickup basketball game."

"We'll report him to the police," Mom says. "It's not too late, is it, Saundra?"

Saundra sighs. "No hard evidence, Mary. It would be her word against his. But I'll drive you to the station if you want. Take a moment, Kat; think hard."

That's what she shouts when an opponent's got Kat trapped on the mat. Take a moment, think about your next move; think hard. And so Kat does. Cops or no cops? What would she gain if she reported him? Nothing, really. Just more time on the mat with that Wolf. *I'm not wasting one more ounce of energy on him. I left him in pain. He tapped out. I'll get over this; I know I will.*

It's second semester of junior year. ACTs are coming up. She works twenty hours a week at the zoo. Jiu-jitsu practice and matches. Chores and paying bills. Honors classes. College applications staring her in the face.

"No cops," she says.

"He assaulted you, Kat!" Mom says.

3

"I stopped him."

"But—"

"Nothing happened!" Kat stands up. "I'm FINE. *He's* the one who's injured—not me!"

"Then why were *you* the one throwing up?" Mom asks. "We have to tell someone. The school, at least."

Kat scowls. "Nobody'll believe me."

Why would they? He's a basketball alpha. They rule the school. On top of that, he's charming, handsome enough to be a local social media celebrity, high GPA. Grew up in the hills in one of those big houses with two lawyer parents who donate big bucks to Sanger Academy.

And Kat? She overheard a whispered conversation once in the bathroom.

"That King girl has a tiny white-trash mom."

"Really?"

"Yeah. She's 'biracial,' I guess, but just brown enough to win a scholarship."

"Filhote, this isn't just about you," Saundra says, interrupting Kat's thoughts, and her voice is gentler now. "What if the next girl can't fight him off?"

Dang.

She hadn't thought about him trying that stairwell stunt again.

Saundra's right. Kat's going to have to speak the truth at Sanger Academy.

ROBIN

INT. THORNTON HOUSE, OUTSKIRTS OF BOSTON—NIGHT

On Robin's eighteenth birthday, the Thorntons eat takeout Indian lamb biryani as usual. It's an annual tradition. Nobody is sure if March fourth is his actual birthday, but they've always celebrated it on this day.

"We know you were born sometime in early March," Mom says.

"Anyway, you 'march forth' into the future every year," Dad adds.

It's just the three of them this time. Robin's grandparents don't leave Florida much. And he didn't feel like inviting Brian, Ashley, Ms. Vee, PG, Martin, or even Gracie, even though some or all of them had been at his previous birthday celebrations. Gracie sent a card that said "Cristo es mi superhéroe." The rest of them texted, called, sent cards. Except Brian, who probably forgot.

"Glad we have privacy, actually," Dad says, handing Robin a square ivory envelope. "Here you go."

Robin doesn't open it right away. He already knows what's inside. The expensive envelope is embossed with raised letters: EDWARD THORNTON III. That's his name, too. He's been Edward Thornton V for fifteen years, but he never introduces his brown, Indian self as "Edward." That name belongs to his tall, blond father, who looks exactly like a younger version of Edward Thornton III.

The mirroring stopped there.

In the orphanage in India, he'd been "Ravi"—a name he secretly likes—but his parents nicknamed him "Robin" when he started school. And for some reason that stuck. He's never told anyone how much he hates it. A sidekick's name. Even his online gamer tag is a version of it: boy*wonder_7. He didn't get to pick that, either. Brian—dark*knight_7, of course— chose it when they were seven. The only thing worse is "Little Guy," which is what Brian calls him in real life.

"Aren't you going to open it, Robin?" Mom asks.

Robin pulls out the matching stationery inside the envelope—it's embossed with his official name, too—and silently reads Grandfather Thornton's spidery handwriting.

Dear Robin,

Happiest of birthdays to our one and only grandchild. You're turning eighteen this year, which means you now have access to your charity trust fund. We have been blessed with wealth in our family, but as you know, my dear Robin, the Bible tells us that "the love of money is the root of all kinds of evil." One way to moderate the negatives of having money is by giving it away generously. I won't tell you what to support, but here's a bit of advice if you'll bear with me: Find some cause or work that you care about, and be a thoughtful, informed donor. Give with passion and joy. "God loves a

cheerful giver," the Bible also says, and I trust (pun intended)
you'll find that to be true.

> Sincerely,
> Your loving grandfather

Robin has known for years that a charity trust fund was
coming his way. His parents have given through Dad's fund
to many different causes. What he hasn't known, though, is
the amount—now fully in his care—that Grandfather Thornton
scribbled as a postscript.

"Wow," Robin says aloud, putting the letter back into the
envelope. "That's . . . a lot."

"A big responsibility," Mom says.

Her words make Robin feel like he's wearing a heavy suit
of armor engraved with the family crest. No wonder he's
always wanted a sibling—to help shoulder the weight.

"Did your grandfather tell you his two requirements for
giving?" Dad asks.

"Yep. Passion. And joy," Robin mutters. *Neither of which I
have.*

There's a silence.

"The shelter could always use a donation," Dad says
brightly. His "job" as president of the family's jewelry business
is mostly a figurehead role, so he works for free at a nonprofit
in Boston that serves the homeless.

Mom has a real job—public defender for the County—but
she's also on the board of an organization that helps resettle
refugee families. "Our fund-raising gala's coming up," she
says. "You can consider that, too."

Geez. It's been three minutes since he opened the letter, and already they're making decisions about how to give away his money. "I'll think about it. I'm kind of tired. Got homework, too."

His parents exchange looks.

"What about your cake, honey?" Mom asks. "I picked up those big candles—a 'one' and an 'eight'—for you to blow out."

"You guys eat it. We aren't even sure it's my real birthday, anyway. Good night."

During cake time, he knows Mom will say a prayer of thanksgiving for Robin's "first mother, who gave him the gift of life." For some reason, this always makes Robin squirm. It feels like she's giving thanks for a bad accident or a big mistake. Or even a wrong decision.

He doesn't want to think about the past. Not when he's trying to survive the present, and everyone seems to be worrying about his future.

KAT

INT./EXT. OAKLAND—DAY

Turns out Sanger has a judicial process to handle this kind of "claim." Each "party" gets to share their version of what happened, separately. While Mom cries quietly beside her, Kat recounts what happened to an ombudsman committee. *He pushed me against the wall, held me there by the throat, tore open my shirt, and tried to pull down his pants. I had to fight him off.* Her voice is flat and controlled. No tears. She answers follow-up questions the same way—no frills or emotion.

Afterward, she and Mom get a transcript of what he said. *SHE attacked ME*, he told them. *For no reason at all.* When someone asked if he did anything that might have provoked the "other party," he said: *No. Nothing. Maybe she's just a violent type. Grew up in an abusive home? Who knows?*

Kat's fury swells as she reads this. *Come after me, Wolf. I'll beat you again. But stay away from my mother.*

The committee's verdict comes by email. No cameras in the stairwell, so Saundra was right: All they have is his word versus Kat's. His doctor's report: broken finger, sprained shoulder. Her? The school's used to the ongoing jiu-jitsu bruises on her jawline, temple, arms, legs. They can't be sure these are new marks from him. And nightmares don't count as evidence, it turns out. Final decision: counseling for both of them and an unofficial "restraining order" to stay away from each other.

Should have trusted my instincts, Kat thinks as Mom rants about the decision. *Shouldn't have said anything. What good did it do? Dragged us back into a fight, and now I'm the one losing. And so is Mom.*

After the restraining order, he doesn't come near Kat. But Kat keeps an eye on him from a distance. Sees him strutting down the halls of Sanger, day after day.

Brittany and Amber say they believe Kat, but she avoids them. *Don't need anyone on the mat with me.* She's Katina King, the reigning middleweight under-seventeen Northern California Brazilian jiu-jitsu grappling champion. *I've got this*, she tells herself, just like she does in the middle of a BJJ fight.

Problem is that this time, she doesn't.

Still can't sleep.

Nightmares bring back the memory of what happened, night after night.

Rumors spread through the school like a California wild-fire—

She wanted him since her first day at Sanger.

She's mad he didn't like her back.

She's jealous.

Lies, lies, all lies.

But that's not the worst of it. She vomits so often she starts dropping pounds. Loses a BJJ match. Loses another. During practice, she steps on the mat only if a female sparring partner is waiting there.

Checks five times to make sure a public bathroom stall is locked. Even then, pushes her heel against the door while she uses the toilet.

Lines up for female cashiers at the grocery store.

Asks Mom to switch to a dentist who's a woman.

Canine eyes checking her out—which she's always hated— now send her straight into panic mode. Their touch—?! No way.

No man is going to lay a finger on her again.

INT. KING APARTMENT—NIGHT

The school counselor calls while Kat's watching *Batman Returns* for maybe the tenth time. Dr. Mitchell's name pops up on Mom's phone in the middle of Michelle Pfeiffer's brilliant milk-drinking, costume-sewing scene.

Kat sighs. She knows what this is about. Earlier today, she skipped yet another "mandatory" session with the dude.

"Hello, Dr. Mitchell," Mom says, taking the phone into the kitchen.

The apartment's tiny; Kat presses PAUSE to overhear her mother's end of the conversation.

"I'll talk to her. Yes, I'm going ahead with my plan."

Plan? What plan? Pfeiffer-as-Selina-Kyle is frozen on-screen with a crazed expression as she stitches up her mask. Kat presses PLAY again to pretend that she wasn't eavesdropping.

Mom comes back and powers off the television. "You stopped seeing the counselor?"

"I don't need his help."

"That's where you're wrong, Kat. You do. It's been two months, and it's getting harder instead of easier. Dr. Mitchell thinks you might need a break from that environment." She pauses and glances toward the living room window. Somewhere up the street, a car alarm has gone off. "He asked if you wanted to transfer to another school, just for the rest of this semester."

No. Definitely not. Leaving Sanger means Kat loses. "The school in our neighborhood sucks," she says. "No biology honors classes. No free ACT prep. I'm not letting this hurt my college chances."

"That's what I thought." Mom moves closer, and Kat gets a whiff of that hospital antiseptic smell on her uniform. "We've been like sisters, right, Kat darling? Grew up together, you and me."

Kat doesn't say it out loud: *Except I take care of you.* Does the laundry, brews Mom's tea, picks up around the house, keeps track of bills and the budget, and makes them both turn off the television when Mom has an early shift. Kat's mother doesn't even check to make sure the apartment's locked at night. Kat does that.

Mom rests a hand on Kat's short, curly hair and takes a big breath. "But I'm pulling rank this time. Saundra suggested spending some time with her great-aunt in Boston. You leave in a week. I booked your ticket."

Kat jumps up. "BOSTON? No way, Mom! I'm not going to stay with some stranger! Besides, we can't afford a plane ticket. Cancel it. Right now."

Her mother stands up, too. Bends her skinny arms and plants her small fists on her hips. Tips her pigeon head back and stares right up into Kat's snarl. "I'm not changing my mind. Ticket's nonrefundable. You'll finish out the semester there."

Kat can't believe this. "What about school? I'm not letting him—what happened—wreck my life! I need a full ride to USC or Davis! What about my job? And I've got to win my next few BJJ matches—"

"Jiu-jitsu and the zoo aren't worth the pain of staying in that toxic environment. Ms. Jones is an excellent teacher; she'll homeschool you until the middle of June. I've already cleared it with Sanger. Your teachers agreed to send you assignments and keep track of your papers and tests online."

"WHAT? You didn't ask ME first? I'm SIXTEEN!"

"I know. That's how old I was when you were born. But you have a real mom; all I had were a bunch of foster parents. For once in my life, I'm going to be a controlling mother, whether you like it or not."

Mom's voice sounds fiercer than Saundra's. She and Kat glare at each other for a long moment.

Controlling mother, huh?

Cue bratty teenager, then.

Kat stomps off to her bedroom and slams the door.

ROBIN

INT. ROBIN'S BEDROOM—NIGHT

Robin stretches out on his bed and decides to watch *Batman Returns*, the 1992 flick with Michael Keaton as Batman. It's been a while since he's seen it. He forgot that it starts with the Cobblepots throwing Oswald—the baby who grows up to be the Penguin—into a sewer. Poor Oswald. No wonder he becomes a villain. Who wouldn't? Robin turns off the movie and switches to the soundtrack from *Guardians of the Galaxy*, which usually helps him unwind.

"I feel stuck, Ms. Vee," he told his friend at church just last Sunday. "I'm tired of people asking what I'm doing after graduation. 'Figure out your passions, Robin,' they tell me. 'Find your talents.' What if I don't have any? I'm a C student."

"Some people are better at studying faces than books," she said. "And you have a talent for loyalty. Those are gifts many never acquire."

Remembering her words cheers him up a little, but he figures she's biased. She, Gracie, PG, Mom, Dad, Martin, Ash—they love him too much to see him clearly.

Downstairs, his parents are arguing again. "I'm Not in Love" by 10cc is too soft a song to block them out. He hits PAUSE, takes off his headphones, and listens.

"He's sure to get into at least one or two schools he applied to, Ed! Okay, so they're not the best colleges, but he *has* to get a degree, right?"

Same old, same old, Robin realizes. Mom should just pick a college. At this point, he'd go anywhere just to get her to stop worrying.

"A gap year might be better, Marjorie. If you ask me, he needs to see a counselor. It seems like he's been low for months."

The thought of talking to a counselor makes Robin even more tired.

"I don't think he wants counseling, Ed," Mom says.

"Who knows what the kid wants?" Dad answers. "Every now and then he tells us what he *doesn't* want, but that's not a good way to live. It feels like we're always making decisions for him."

"He likes working at Mike's," Mom says.

"*You* lined up that job for him, remember? He enjoys cars now, but he didn't want the job at first. He doesn't *want* anything, Marjorie."

There's a silence in the kitchen.

Dad's right, Robin thinks. Now that he's eighteen, "not wanting" is a habit. His father used to ask questions to help him figure out what he wanted: *What are you feeling?* When Robin couldn't answer, Dad would offer multiple-choice options: *Happy? Sad? Angry?* Even picking from a list was a challenge. *Think about it*, Dad would encourage the younger version of Robin. *Take time. Listen to your heart. And once you identify an emotion or a desire, act on it. Be thoughtful and careful, of course. But act on it, son.*

Easy to say, hard to do. When Robin tries to "listen to his heart," all he hears is the static of numbness. That constant whirl of white noise accompanies him everywhere—home, school, church, small group, work. He's used to the dampening.

He puts on his headphones again. A song by the Jackson 5 is next on the soundtrack. Robin knows the words by heart, but he doesn't sing along.

> *Oh baby, give me one more chance,*
> *To show you that I love you.*
> *Won't You. Please. Let. Me.*
> *Back in your heart?*

KAT

INT./EXT. AIRPLANE—DAY—TRAVELING

Before Kat goes through security, Saundra kisses her cheek. "I know it's your first time, Filhote, but you're going to fly like a pro. Head straight to the gate and wait for them to announce your boarding group."

Mom's teary-eyed but manages a shaky smile. She won't risk a hug—Kat's still too furious. "You'll be coming back in June, sweetheart. It's just three months." Sounds like she's talking more to herself than to her daughter.

Kat keeps her scowl in place. She knows her mother's eyes are following her, but she strides through security without looking back.

"Text when you land, Kat!" Mom's voice calls out.

Kat waits by the gate, like Saundra told her to, keeping her distance from canines. Blue, brown, hazel, behind glasses, peering over a laptop, it doesn't matter—they all look the same when they're hunting.

When it's time to board, Kat chooses the window seat, lifts up the armrest, and spreads out her long limbs. The plane's not full so nobody else sits in her row. One good thing on this otherwise lousy day. The day Katina King's tapping out and letting the world know that her opponent won.

"Our estimated flight time to Boston will be five hours and

fifty-seven minutes," the pilot announces over the intercom. "Sit back, relax, and enjoy the flight."

Kat figures out how to buckle her seat belt just as they take off. The plane climbs high, leaving behind the sparkling blue bay and green hills. By the time she gets back, the grass will be brown again. Somewhere down there, nestled in the Oakland hills, school's in session. The place where he's alpha-wolfing through the halls, as if what happened didn't cost him at all—beyond injuries to that finger and shoulder, which healed quickly. He's back to being a basketball star, winning games for Sanger.

Kat pictures him cornering Brittany and Amber: *See? Your crazy friend WAS guilty. That's why she left. Hope you believe me now.*

The airplane climbs above the clouds and she can't see anything but sky above and white billows below. Kat closes the window shade, puts on her headphones, and turns on the screen embedded in the seat back in front of her. The Celtics game comes on. They're winning; people scattered around the plane are cheering. She switches the channel to women's tennis.

Why does everything have to remind her of him? Smack in the middle of concentrating on a biology test, taking train tickets at the zoo, or grappling with an opponent on the mat, she'll flash back to memories of that stairwell.

Tongue jamming into her mouth.

Fingers tearing buttons.

The zipper of his jeans slicing down.

Kat's stomach lurches like it always does when she remembers.

"Want something to drink, honey?" The flight attendant is leaning across the empty seats with a smile.

"Ginger ale, please. No ice."

Sipping the fizzy drink, Kat manages not to throw up this time. As they leave California behind, she finds the free movie channel. *Oh, thank God.* Wonder Woman. *If she can't get me through this flight without puking, nobody can.*

It does the trick. And so does Black Widow in *Avengers: Age of Ultron*, which comes on next.

The plane lands at Logan. Kat doesn't text her mother. Instead, she leaves her phone on airplane mode, gathers her things, and follows the signs to baggage claim.

As suitcases start hurtling out of the chute, a stately, silver-haired, sun-weathered woman pushes her walker over. Her skin is as black as an ibis beak. She's wearing an ankle-length, flowery dress and embroidered slippers that match her embroidered head scarf.

"You must be Katina." Her voice reminds Kat of Wakanda. "I am Viola Jones. Welcome to Boston."

ROBIN

INT. METROWEST HIGH SCHOOL
CAFETERIA—DAY

Robin is waiting in the line for sandwiches and wraps. All around him are people he's known for years, people who never seem to see him unless he greets them first.

The line inches forward. Finally, it's his turn to choose his food. Picking up a tuna wrap as usual, he slouches over to the cashier. This line, too, is long and slow. *This cafeteria is what hell might be like*, Robin thinks, surveying the familiar scene.

Metrowest High students of different races don't break bread together. Apart from Martin's table of musicians and actors, the large, sunny room is filled with tables of only white kids and tables of only Asian kids. Black students eat lunch outside on the stairs, and Hispanic kids gather in the gym. Robin's history teacher once asked her class to discuss whether this self-selected, divided eating arrangement was a legacy from Boston's racist past. They'd had a fiery debate, with Robin silently agreeing each time one of his classmates used a swear word to put down the cafeteria.

Someone brushes by him. It's Sona Patel, a transfer from another school. Bangles clink on her wrists as she cuts right in front of Robin. He steps back, but not too far. Her waist-length black hair is silky and smells like coconuts.

"That kid behind you was next," the cashier tells Sona.

"Sorry," Sona says, turning and spotting Robin. "I didn't see you."

Of course she didn't. He shifts back again to give her more room. "It's okay," he says.

Lots of interested eyes have been checking out Sona's curvy figure and nose-ringed, friendly face ever since she arrived last year. But to Robin, a girl like this is as far out of his league as Gamora is from Quill at the start of *Guardians of the Galaxy.* Okay, so in the sequel they get together, but that's fantasy, not real life.

Sona pays for her lunch, and Robin watches her hair shimmer as she carries her tray to the desi table by the windows. That one's reserved for the dozen or so Indian kids at Metrowest, but Robin's never felt desi enough to join them. Case in point: When he first heard the word, he had to search online to learn that it meant "people of Indian descent who live outside of India."

Technically, this is true for Robin, but nobody else at that table has two white parents. Desis grow up learning Tamil or Hindi or some other Indian language, taking Indian dance classes, worshipping in a temple or a mosque, visiting India to see relatives. Robin speaks only English, dances in church when Ms. Vee grabs his hand and swings him out to the aisle, and hasn't been back to India in fifteen years, even though his parents ask regularly if he wants to go. They've suggested Bangla lessons, attending Bengali Association events, or joining one of the Indian adoptee organizations in the Boston area, but Robin always says no.

Trying to be a Thornton is tough enough.

Trying to be a Bengali Thornton feels like an impossible mission.

"Got your card, kid?" the cashier growls.

He hands her the payment card that Mom loads for him at the start of every semester. Scooping up his tuna wrap, he trudges across the room to sit with Brian. Robin's eaten lunch for the last three and a half years at this table of white jocks. Another mind-numbing habit from childhood—sticking close to Brian's side.

He slides into an empty chair.

"Hey," Brian says.

"Hey."

A couple of other guys at the table greet him, but sitting here makes him feel more invisible than ever. *Like Shorty in* Indiana Jones and the Temple of Doom, he thinks. A small, Asian foil, only in the scene to prove that the main character's a decent guy.

He remembers overhearing a new football player asking—okay, in a lowered voice, but still—why the Indian kid was sitting at their table.

"We've been friends for fifteen years, jerk," Brian answered loudly. "We go to the same church. So shut the hell up."

As he peels the plastic from the tuna wrap, Robin wonders who's going to take his role when Brian's at college. Meanwhile, what's an abandoned sidekick supposed to do on his own? There's not enough material for a full-length feature, that's for sure.

KAT

INT./EXT. LOGAN AIRPORT, BOSTON—NIGHT—TRAVELING

Sacred Ibis, Kat thinks as she extends her hand to Saundra's great-aunt. The Ibis's ancient body is slim, elegant, and strong. She's tall, too. Almost as tall as Kat. She grips her walker with one hand and shakes Kat's hand firmly with the other. "Is that your only coat, Miss King?"

Kat looks down at her leather jacket. Big, black, and loose, like her T-shirt and jeans, to camouflage her figure. Along with her don't-mess-with-this scowl, black clothes are her armor to keep canines at bay.

"Early March might signal spring in California, but not here," says the Ibis. "Don't worry. I have an extra down jacket and gloves and a hat."

There's a traffic jam exiting the airport, and although Saundra's great-aunt argues with the cab driver over the best route, they both end up laughing. She tells him to call her "Ms. Vee" ten minutes into the ride. When they finally emerge from a long tunnel, Kat gazes at the city lights on the horizon. The Boston skyline seems compact compared to her sprawling City by the Bay.

They stay on the highway for a bit, with the Ibis and the driver—Abdul, from Nigeria—swapping stories about their villages "back home." Even though she's lived in Boston for years, Saundra's great-aunt is originally from Sierra Leone. The cab pulls off an exit to wind through a dark, quiet suburb. By now, the driver's turned off the meter.

"This is it," the Ibis says, gesturing at an older building with two front doors. "It's a two-family. A medical resident lives next door. I water her plants; she keeps an eye on me. Fine arrangement for both of us."

Kat climbs out of the car. Moonlight is shining on the snow-covered patch of lawn. The old avian is trying to make the driver accept a twenty, but he's refusing to take it. Kat shivers on the icy sidewalk. Early March in Boston is definitely not springtime.

The driver wins the tussle over the cash and hauls Kat's suitcases up the stairs to one of the doors.

"You stop by for lunch anytime, young man," the Ibis tells him. "I make the best jollof rice this side of Freetown. And if you're in a hurry I can send you off with takeout."

Kat's stomach clenches. *What is she doing? This dude's a total stranger, and she's inviting him over? Maybe she's changed since Saundra's last visit. Gotten dementia or something.*

The driver grins and runs down the stairs to his cab. Meanwhile, the Ibis is fumbling through keys to unlock the door. After a few minutes, it swings open. "Be it ever so humble. Come in, Miss King. Have a look around. It's not big, but it's home."

Kat waits until the deadbolt turns and the door chain is secured. Then she drags her suitcases into the small entry, takes off her jacket, and hangs it in the front closet. The half a building is small and old-fashioned. The kitchen adjoins the living room, and the appliances look like they're from the 1980s. Red flowers in clay pots bloom on every windowsill.

"Admiring my begonias? They're worth the cost of the heat they need to thrive. Speaking of that—we start school as soon as you settle in a bit. Will this machine help us stay in touch with your teachers in California?"

Kat takes the slim, silvery laptop from her and looks it over. It's not new but it's a much faster model than the one she's brought from home. She hopes it costs less than two hundred bucks because that's all the spending money she has. Even that was a parting gift from Saundra; Mom's more broke than usual after that last-minute plane ticket.

MY last two zoo paychecks were in our account, Kat remembers, getting angry all over again. "It's a good one," she says out loud. "How much do I owe you?"

"Not a penny. The last time I taught, my students didn't use computers. When my friend Marjorie heard that I'm planning to teach again, she insisted on giving us this one. Now come along; you can unpack and settle in while I heat up our dinner."

Kat pulls her suitcases into a small guest room off the kitchen—bed, chest of drawers, wooden floors with fluffy white rug by the bed, nightstand with a vase of fragrant white roses. White sheets, white towels, white blanket, white soap. Everything in the tidy little room is white. Everything except Kat, her clothes, and her new teacher, whose eyes take in all the black stuff Kat starts arranging in the empty drawers.

"I'll give you a shout when dinner's on the table," she says, and leaves Kat to it.

Kat finishes unpacking before she turns on her phone. Immediately, texts swoop in from Mom.

Did you make it, darling?

Kat?

Did you land?

Text when you get this.

How's Ms. Jones?

Come on, Kat. Are you going to stay mad the whole time you're gone?

And from Saundra: *Text your mom, Filhote. Cut her some slack.*

Kat sighs and answers both of them at once: *Made it. Tired. Good night.* She puts her phone back on airplane mode before they can answer.

Nothing from Brittany or Amber, but they're not daily-contact friends. They text only when there's a biology assignment due or an ACT prep session to attend. Kat's never visited their homes and they certainly haven't come to her apartment. She's not sure they know she's in Boston, or whether she'll even tell them. By now, Sanger students have probably heard something from a teacher or a staff member like "Katina King will be taking a break until the end of the semester." She can imagine Dr. Mitchell telling everyone to "give her space and honor her privacy."

Vomit. Puke. The entire school is lifting that Wolf's fist high in the air. *And the winner is—*

"Katina! Dinner!"

The table is set with two bowls of piping-hot stew. Tender, sautéed greens and black-eyed beans. Steaming rice. Chocolate cake, too, from scratch, with WELCOME, KATINA in icing swirls across the top.

"Can you call me Kat? That's what Mom calls me. Katina's what they call me at school."

The Ibis scrapes the INA off the cake with a spoon and pops it into her mouth. A smile scratches dozens of new crinkles into her old-lady skin. Kat can't help smiling back.

"I hear it's been a fiery season for you, Kat."

Kat shrugs. Doesn't want to talk about it. Not here. Not with that know-it-all-will-fix-you counselor with a beard. Not with anybody. Not ever.

The Ibis reaches over and pats Kat's hand. "Do you think you can call me Grandma Vee? I've never had a grandchild; Saundra's my only living relative, so you're the closest thing to a granddaughter I have."

There's only one answer to give a woman who's agreed to feed, shelter, *and* teach her for three months. "Sure. Definitely."

Kat, too, has only one blood relative of her own. Her mother. No aunts or uncles. No grandparents; they died. Her "father" didn't want to stick around to raise her. All she knows about her paternal side is this: When she came out of her petite, white mom, she was a long, strong baby with brown skin and black hair.

Now she's grown into a tall, strong woman with brown skin and black hair.

A bit like the person smiling at her across the table.

Saundra said this place was rented with pension checks. She asked Kat to help out—grocery shop, shovel the walk, change light bulbs. Whatever. Kat's ready. She knows what room and board costs. And besides, "Grandma Vee" must be in her eighties.

27

"I want to do some chores for you while I'm here," she says after they finish eating. "I do everything for Mom at home—cook, clean, shop, do laundry. Just tell me what you need."

"You can do the dishes starting tomorrow. But you must be tired tonight. Why don't you head to bed?"

In the small, spotless guest room, before Kat lets herself shower or brush her teeth, she hits the floor for her usual series of planks, crunches, push-ups, and squats, pushing herself to do a couple more with each set. No training while she's in Boston—she'd need sparring partners and a professor to replace Saundra—but she's not about to lose her strength.

After she showers, she slips into the flannel pajamas that were Mom's going-away present. The mattress is soft. White sheets smell like lavender. Pillow fits Kat's head like it was sewn for her skull. Three thousand miles from home, Kat sleeps fourteen hours straight.

ROBIN

INT. METROWEST HIGH SCHOOL
CAFETERIA—DAY

As he chews and swallows another bite of the tuna wrap, a message makes Robin's phone buzz. *Meet me in the library in five minutes.* It's from Martin, Robin's only other church friend at Metrowest High. They've scheduled a review session for Robin's chemistry test.

Robin's eyes go to the theater table. Unlike Robin, Martin knows exactly what he's doing after graduation. He's already accepted early admission to Brown in the fall. Wants to be a teacher. And he'll be a good one, too. He's helped Robin all the way through high school, quizzing him about Shakespeare's plays, unlocking the mysteries of geometry, marking up his draft essays with a red pen like a professional editor.

Martin grins and waves, and Robin stands up.

"Done with your lunch, Little Guy?" Brian asks.

That nickname. It's as old as their friendship. And maybe as stale.

Robin grits his teeth and slides the rest of his tuna wrap to Brian without a word.

"Thanks," Brian says, smiling. "You'll drive me home after small group, right?"

Robin's been planning to skip small group this week. All he wants to do is crash in his room and watch *Finding Nemo* or some other movie he's seen so many times he knows the lines by heart. "Sure, I'll drive you home," he tells Brian.

He heads for the library, where Martin will probably scold him again for sitting with Brian. *You could come join us instead*, he'll say, *or find some of your Greased Lightning buddies from auto shop. I have no idea why you endure that agony. Every. Single. Day.*

But Robin knows exactly why. It's because of a memory. One of his rare memories from childhood. Fifteen years ago, during a Sunday school class, a big, blond toddler grabbed a terrified newcomer by the hand and pulled him into a game of ring-around-the-rosy. Robin can remember every detail, even though he and Brian had only been three years old.

Maybe losing your earliest, most important memories makes you hold on to other ones longer than you should.

KAT

INT. GRANDMA VEE'S APARTMENT—DAY

After her first long sleep in weeks, Kat wakes up feeling rested but anxious. Will she be able to keep her GPA high enough to win a scholarship? How are admissions committees going to understand her so-called decision to leave Sanger mid-semester? Brittany and Amber can afford after-school tutors and hire private college counselors, but not Kat. She's on her own. Mom never went to college—she'll try to help, but she doesn't know much about navigating the applications and financial-aid maze.

Saundra promised that her great-aunt's a terrific teacher. Kat hopes that's true. No way she's adding "academic scholarship" to the list of things that wolf is making her lose.

"I'm looking forward to seeing what they teach eleventh graders in California," Grandma Vee says after breakfast. "What's your area of interest, Kat?"

"Biology's my favorite. I work at the zoo part-time at home."

"Don't worry—you'll stay on target," Grandma Vee says. "I see the brains in your eyes. Let's take a field trip this morning, shall we? It's your first day in Boston so you should see some sights."

A field trip already? Kat thinks. *I missed a day of school yesterday for travel. I don't want to fall behind from the start.*

"We're going to the Franklin Park Zoo," Grandma Vee announces, smiling as if she's sure Kat will be delighted. "It only takes two buses to get there. Your task is to find three animals that you don't have in the Oakland Zoo and tell me all about them."

It sounds more like a fifth-grade homework assignment than honors biology, but Kat can't bring herself to dim that bright smile. "Okay. But I'll have to get started on my school assignments when we get back."

INT./EXT. FRANKLIN PARK ZOO, BOSTON—DAY

Kat looks out the bus window at the unfamiliar scenery. Boston is full of skeleton trees with bare branches, formless bodies bundled in down coats, meandering, narrow streets, rotaries instead of stoplights, and signs at borders announcing a town's long New England history: BROOKLINE. ESTABLISHED IN 1638.

Meanwhile, her companion launches into a conversation with yet another stranger. Kat tunes them out. *Does she have to talk to everybody?* She looks down at her borrowed outerwear—long brown coat, men's so it fits, topped with a red-and-green-striped hat, gloves, and scarf. She feels like a Christmas tree.

At the zoo, the wind is cold and there's ice in some habitats, but the smell of dung and the caws, hoots, roars, and trumpeting are familiar to Kat. Grandma Vee sends her off and waits at a warm table inside the cafeteria. As she walks through the exhibits, Kat identifies animals she already knows and takes photos of three that she doesn't—a pair of tawny frogmouths and an Indian blue peafowl in the bird building, and a red panda in the children's zoo.

She returns to find her new-but-old teacher surrounded by a pod of five kids and five nannies. All eleven of them are eating cotton candy.

Grandma Vee hands Kat a big bag of soft blue sugar and moves over to make room at the table. "Meet my granddaughter," she says.

Kat lets the sweetness of the candy melt into her mouth as she listens to Grandma Vee trying to learn how to say *granddaughter* in the five different languages spoken by the nannies— Spanish, Khmer, Portuguese, Arabic, and Sinhalese.

A light snow starts to fall, and Grandma Vee gets up to go. Kat waits while *Grandmother* in five languages receives multiple goodbye hugs from nannies and kids.

Once they're outside, Kat lifts her face, and snow lands on her cheeks and tongue. It's the first time she's seen snow in real life. She catches flakes on her borrowed gloves and watches them melt.

"Bostonians stop liking snow around January," says Grandma Vee. "But go ahead—marvel. I remember the first time I saw snowflakes. Made by angel's hands, I thought."

Kat slows her pace to match the old woman's. To outsiders, they must look like a tall brown grandmother and a tall brown granddaughter. Even canine passersby don't leer the way they do when Kat's on her own or with her mother, who draws her fair share of unwanted attention. A few jerks still check Kat out, of course, but their leers don't linger—not with those ibis eyes staring them down. It's like Grandma Vee has an invisible shield that protects them both.

INT. GRANDMA VEE'S APARTMENT—NIGHT

After a homemade supper of tomato soup and grilled cheese sandwiches, Kat notices the slumped shoulders of her companion. That was a big outing on a chilly March day—especially for an old woman who agreed to take Kat in only one week earlier, thanks to Mom's last-minute planning.

Kat jumps up to start the dishes. "I'd really like to help you out. I can do more than just wash dishes."

"No dishwashing machine in this place, you know. So it might be more work than you're used to."

"The dishwasher in our apartment's been broken for months," Kat says, leaning in to give the saucepan a good scrub. "I'm used to washing dishes by hand. But what else can I do to help you?"

"There *is* one thing," Grandma Vee says.

Kat stops scrubbing to listen.

"Won't you visit the small group for youth at my church tomorrow? It's right down the street from us, so you can walk. I want you to meet my friend Robin. Something's been troubling that dear child lately. I have a feeling you might be good for each other."

Kat stacks the plates in the drying rack, back to back, making perfect parallels. *A small group meeting? At church? And some needy girl to take care of?* This isn't part of the deal. Besides, friends don't come easy for her. Amber and Brittany are the only two she made at Sanger. And Kat isn't even sure she can call them "friends."

"Will you go, Kat?"

Kat looks over at Grandma Vee painstakingly rolling down her compression socks, one leg at a time. "I guess I can give it a try."

"Wonderful. Pastor Greg leads the group. He's a good man. I'll let him know you're coming. I could tell him a bit more if you'd like—"

"No. That's my business. No thanks, I mean." Kat pauses. "Now go rest. I'll get started on my assignments."

"Oh my. I like the sound of that, Kat. I'll review your work in the morning. Don't worry, students don't fall behind in Ms. Viola Jones's classroom."

Later, Kat powers up the new-used laptop. Its default name is "Robin Thornton," so Kat's pretty sure it used to belong to the friend Grandma Vee wants her to meet. The memory's been wiped clean of any past history.

ROBIN

INT./EXT. METROWEST PRESBYTERIAN CHURCH
YOUTH ROOM—NIGHT

Robin is parking the Corvette in the church lot when a text makes his phone shriek like a siren. Brian's sound effect. What now? *Don't need a ride home, Little Guy. I'm letting the Porsche pick me up for once. Mom's idea.*

Another last-minute cancellation. After Robin's driven over here only because he promised to drive Brian home. Well, maybe it isn't too late to skip out on small group. His parents won't be expecting him home for an hour or so. He can take a long drive instead.

He's about to send a text to PG when he notices a voice call has come in from Ms. Vee. She only calls when she really needs something.

He listens to her message. "I have a house guest visiting from California," her lilting, low-pitched voice informs him. "I'm sending her to your small group, Robin. She needs a friend. Could you make her feel welcome?"

They haven't had a visitor since PG organized the group six years ago. A new person turning up at small group? Robin replays it to make sure he's heard it right. There it is again—she has a house guest she's sending over. Now he *has* to go inside.

Robin sighs and climbs out of his car. He'll do anything for Ms. Vee; it's a good thing she asks for so little. He zips up his coat, shuts the door, and rests his forehead for a second on the roof of the Corvette, as if the leftover energy generated by the vehicle's peppy engine can fuel him.

As he enters the high-steepled brick building, he catches sight of a figure walking carefully across the snowy lawn and then faster across the plowed parking lot.

It's a girl. Light is pouring out of the double glass doors, and Robin can see her stomping her feet on the front step to shake the snow off. Is this Ms. Vee's guest?

He opens the front door just as she spots him. Frown lines deepen as she stalks past him, and she turns sideways so they don't make any contact. She takes off her coat to hang it on the coatrack, revealing a long, black blouse that drapes loosely around her body. It almost, but not quite, disguises the curves. Long legs and neck, head held high, black jeans tucked into spike-heeled boots. Short, curly hair pulled back with a wide band. Smooth, satiny skin, almost the same shade as his. She reminds Robin of a young Halle Berry, one of his on-screen crushes. Even more out of his league than Sona Patel.

Crap. She's caught him watching her. Now she's lifting a corner of her lip and planting her fists on her hips.

"You stalking me?" she asks.

Robin takes a step back. "No, no," he says. "I was just—"

"Then why are you lurking around? Do you belong in this building or should I call 9-1-1?"

That sure escalated fast, Robin thinks. "No, it's okay. I—I worship here. I've been coming to this church since I was three."

"Great. A religious stalker. The worst kind."

"Wait, are you—?"

But she's striding away, as if she doesn't want to waste one more second talking to him.

Robin sighs again. This isn't worth it, not even for Halle fantasies. But if she's looking for high school small group, she'll never find the basement on her own. The twists and turns in this Gothic building are impossible for newcomers to navigate. How much does he love Ms. Vee? Must be a lot. He hangs up his coat and walks down the hall. Ms. Vee's guest—or at least that's who Robin thinks she is—moves fast, taking long steps, each foot landing firmly as if those spiked heels do know where they're going.

Nefertiti, Robin thinks, remembering a poem his mother used to read aloud. *Spin a coin, spin a coin / All fall down / Queen Nefertiti / Stalks through town.*

She's passing the toddler room now, and she pauses by the open top half of the door to glance at the cluster of kids playing inside. Robin takes the chance to study her again. Long purple earrings. Strong nose, diamond chin. Angled eyes. Long, muscular arms that he can tell are toned, even under the loose black fabric of her blouse. A leading lady for sure. Maybe even an antihero, like young Halle's version of Catwoman. He's never understood why people pan that film; he's watched it at least a dozen times.

Inside the toddler room, the ring-around-the-rosy circle must have tumbled to the ground because Robin can hear everybody inside cracking up. Even he can't help smiling at the sound.

Then, to Robin's amazement, Nefertiti chuckles, too.

The fierce, tight angles of her face melt into curves.

A dimple makes a sudden appearance.

Robin can't believe the power of that dent in her cheek. At least over his own mind. It displaces adjectives like *fierce* and *sexy* and replaces them instead with *shy* and *scared*. He leans forward to see her whole face. He's a pro when it comes to reading nonverbals and facial expressions, especially of people he cares about. He's been doing it with all his might since he was three years old. Yes, now he can see what's there—worry, vulnerability, a hint of sadness?

But once again, she's caught his gaze.

The dimple disappears.

She narrows weapon-eyes and shoots amber missiles of hate in his direction before turning her back. Then, spike by spike, she strides on.

Over the pavements / Her feet go clack, / Her legs are as tall / As a chimney stack.

But Robin isn't fooled.

KAT

This isn't the first time Kat's been inside a church building. She and Mom join Saundra in her big church near Lake Merritt every Christmas and Easter. Kat usually tunes out during the service; she's never had much faith in God. So many bad things happen on earth that if a divine being does exist, she's pretty sure he's a canine.

And even before the stairwell incident, she hated all that hand-shaking and hugging that went on, especially between men and women.

Too.

Much.

Touching.

No dude better try to hug me at this "small group," she thinks. If only I can lose this weirdo. Good thing he's so small—I'll have him on his back in ten seconds flat if he tries anything.

ROBIN

"Excuse me! Are you staying with someone named Ms. Viola Jones?"

She stops. Turns to face Robin. "You know Grandma Vee?"

How can Ms. Vee be her grandmother? Robin's met Ms. Vee's only niece, Saundra, about thirty years old, a deputy sheriff somewhere out in California. Not married. No kids. So who is this fake extra relative? "She told me you were coming. I can show you where we meet. It's in the basement."

She raises her eyebrows. "Okay, then. Lead the way, Church Man."

He opens a small wooden door in the wall that's so easy for newcomers to miss, and they climb down narrow, winding stairs. He listens to her heels clicking and clacking behind him. It feels like she's herding instead of following him. *Say something*, he tells himself as they walk along the dark, musty hallway. *Make her feel welcome*, Ms. Vee said. But he can't think of anything.

The door is open. His friends are sitting in their usual circle of two squashy floral sofas, two armchairs, and one loveseat. Standing at the threshold of this room where he's spent so many Thursday evenings, Robin takes stock of the scene with outsider eyes.

Pudgy, balding PG, their youth pastor, is arguing about an Oscar-winning film with redheaded, gangly Martin. Tattooed, purple-haired Ash is strumming on her guitar. The tune's in a minor key; it sounds sad.

Brian's feet are splayed across the spot where Robin usually sits. White T-shirt. Jeans. Six foot three. As usual, immersed in his phone.

And then there's dark-haired, doll-like Gracie. Robin feels himself relax at the sight of her kind face.

Nefertiti clears her throat. To remind him that she's there, maybe?

"Hey, guys," Robin says feebly. "We have a visitor. This is Ms. Vee's . . . granddaughter."

The conversation inside stops like someone presses a mute button. PG, though, doesn't look surprised. He stands up with his signature kind smile. "Welcome, welcome," he says, striding over and reaching out a hand.

Nefertiti doesn't take it. The hand plummets after an awkward pause in midair.

"Er . . . I'm Pastor Greg. Everybody calls me PG, though. Ms. Vee told me you might be coming. You're from California, right?"

"The Bay Area."

Gracie jumps up. "My abuelita lives in San Diego. I've never been to San Francisco, though. Do they speak a lot of Spanish there?"

"Maybe," answers Nefertiti. "But I don't."

"Well, welcome anyway! I'm Graciela Maria Rivera, but

everyone calls me Gracie." She skips past Robin and throws her arms around their visitor.

Robin braces himself for his best friend to be flung aside like a tissue, but it doesn't happen. Nefertiti keeps her arms crossed but allows herself to be hugged.

Eventually, Gracie lets go. Even a master embracer knows you can't sustain a one-way hug for long. "What's your name?" she asks.

"Kat."

Robin can't believe the coincidence. Who's writing this script, anyway?

"Oh, Robin," Gracie says, turning to him with arms open. "I was so happy to see Kat that I forgot to welcome *you*!"

She gives Robin the same hug she gave him during her first visit to small group. Gracie was in sixth grade; Robin in seventh. He was startled by her affection that day, but now it feels totally normal. He pulls her close and leans his cheek on her hair. Hugging Gracie is one of the only times his body feels big; she's barely five feet tall to his five foot seven.

Meanwhile, Kat's turned to face them, her eyes wide. "*You're* Robin?" she asks, once he's let go of Gracie.

"Yep," he says.

As Gracie heads back to the loveseat, Martin waggles his fingers at Kat from his armchair. "I'm Martin. Can you sing like your grandmother? She holds the high notes like a diva."

"Don't sing," answers Kat.

Another silence. Robin stays beside Kat, even though she's

still outside the door. *She hasn't made up her mind about us yet*, he thinks.

And then Brian flashes one of his social media smiles. "How ya doin'? That's the way we say hello in Boston, in case you hadn't figured it out yet. I'm Brian Cleery."

Robin watches Kat closely. When Brian turns on the charm, some girls respond by sucking in a stomach, planting a fist on a hip, fingering hair, lowering eyelids and raising them again. But Kat's body language doesn't change. She isn't even looking Brian's way.

"Won't you come in and sit down, Kat?" PG pats the space beside him on his sofa, which usually stays empty.

With another flash of insight, Robin knows that not a single cell in Nefertiti's body wants to accept the invitation. *Come in*, he urges the girl with the dimple. The one hiding behind the scowl. *You're safe here.*

As if she can read his mind, Kat draws a deep breath. Uncrosses her arms. Slowly, one heel at a time, her boots carry her across the threshold and into the room.

KAT

Youth group turns out to have three people Kat classifies as avian, two as feline, and one, most definitely, as canine.

The hugging girl is a Paloma. Kat actually does know a couple of words in Spanish. Mostly animal ones. She has to, for her job, to point people in the right direction for exhibits. Anyway, this girl's arms feel like dove feathers encircling her. It's been a while since Kat's been hugged by a stranger her age.

Their leader's a Goose. Not much of a fighter when it comes to canines, but won't do any harm himself. PG, they call him. Guess Kat can, too.

The guitar-strumming girl's a Cheetah. Kat gets her, feline to feline. The redhead's a Tabby, Kat's favorite kind of house cat. If their landlord let her have a pet, that's exactly what she'd get.

And then there's the German Shepherd. The Brits call them Alsatians. Domesticated but still dominated by wolf-like tendencies. Kat spots the alpha in his eyes the moment he lays them on her.

Last, Grandma Vee's friend. Kat was surprised when Robin turned out to be a guy, but he's an avian, of course. Bird Boy. What else could he be with a name like "Robin"?

And Kat can't help seeing that Grandma Vee was right; there's something sort of . . . wistful about this kid.

I want you to meet my friend Robin, she'd said.

It's Grandma Vee's request that makes Kat stay.

Ignoring PG's pat, she makes her way to the other sofa. Cheetah puts down her guitar and shifts to make room, and Kat takes a seat.

ROBIN

Robin waits by the sofa until Brian swings his size twelves to the floor. Then he sits down in his usual place.

"Phone stack," PG says.

Robin's the first to obey. It's another conditioned habit, one that always kicks off small group. Everyone turns off their phones and piles them on the coffee table. Even Brian. Last comes Kat's.

PG clears his throat. "Why don't you each give Kat a quick rundown on your basics—grade in school, families, hobbies?"

"I'll start," says Gracie. "I'm a junior at Saint Perpetua's Catholic School for Girls. Two parents, four younger sisters, another Baby Rivera on the way. Hobbies? Babies. That's all I've got so far for college apps. 'Describe a contribution you've made to the planet.'" She sighs. "My essay's going to be about diapers and burping."

Ash is picking at the newest tattoo on her arm—a haiku in Japanese characters, which doesn't seem to be healing well. "I'm Ash," she grunts, catching PG's expression. "Also a junior at Saint Perpetua's. Not Catholic, though."

"Hobbies?" PG prompts.

"Songwriting, guitar, body ink."

PG nods at Martin. "Your turn."

"My younger brother and Mom are here in Boston, but Dad's in New York," Martin says. "Choral music, theater, young-adult novels. I'm graduating this year, thank God, and trying to convince the housing guy at Brown that my cat is a necessary academic accommodation. Can't imagine succeeding at college without Mr. Boots."

"I'll vouch for your need," PG says. He nods at Robin. "Your turn."

"Robin Thornton. Senior at Metrowest High. Two parents, no siblings." He doesn't mention the adoption. She'll figure it out when she sees his parents at church.

"Interests?" PG asks.

None, Robin thinks. "Cars. Movies."

"Robin's seen every superhero movie ever made," Gracie adds. She sounds proud, as if film-watching is an actual accomplishment.

Kat lifts her eyebrows. "*Superman IV: The Quest for Peace*?"

Wow. Nobody knows that one. Robin nods. "Three times."

"*Howard the Duck*?" she asks.

Stop. No way. He sits up. "Once. You?"

"Twice."

"Which one?" he asks. "Chip Zien or Seth Green?" Both actors voiced the character. This is the real test; Zien's the right answer.

She doesn't hesitate. "Zien all the way."

"Okay, enough movie trivia for now," interrupts PG. "Brian, your turn."

Brian's vanilla teeth show up again in his chiseled face. "Already told you my name. It's Brian, in case you forgot. I'm an only child. Live with my mom and her husband. I play football and hockey at Metrowest High. Heading to Texas this summer to start playing for Baylor. Hobbies?" He ruffles Robin's hair before Robin can yank his head out of reach. "Mostly I keep an eye on Little Guy."

That stupid nickname again. And the gesture, which he's endured dozens of times. Robin is sick of them both. He glances at Kat. Has she noticed Brian turning him into a side-kick? Well, she's sneering. And those eyes! They rake across Brian so quickly they erase him. Poof, it's like he disappears and Robin's alone on the sofa. He's never seen anyone make Brian vanish like that.

"It's good to have you with us, Kat," PG says. "What about your family? School? Any hobbies or interests you want to share?"

She shrugs. "I'm a junior. I'll be studying with Ms. Jones for the rest of this semester, and heading home to Oakland in June. Hobbies? Taxonomy. Brazilian jiu-jitsu. Family? My mother."

There's a finality to the way she says *mother*, as though it's all anyone needs. To Robin, the word lands with a thud.

"What's taxonomy?" Ash asks.

"What's jiu-jitsu?" Gracie asks at the same time.

"Taxonomy is the classification of organisms," Martin recites. He's deep into studying for his AP biology exam. "Domain, kingdom, phylum, class, order, family, genus, species. Right, Kat?"

"Right," Kat says. "I have a part-time job at the zoo, so that's where I learned to classify. And Brazilian jiu-jitsu is a martial art. I just got my adult blue belt but—" She stops, and Robin wonders how the sentence might have ended. Kat turns to Gracie. "Actually, the kind I practice is sometimes called Gracie jiu-jitsu."

"Maybe I should learn it," says Gracie, smiling. "I might have to beat someone up one day."

"I think it's more about nonviolence," PG says quickly. When they were studying the part about "turning the other cheek" in Jesus's Sermon on the Mount, he got all passionate about the peaceful resistance of Mahatma Gandhi and Martin Luther King Jr.

"Yes and no," Kat says. "Jiu-jitsu teaches a smaller person how to twist, spin, thrust, throw, pin, choke, and lock a more powerful opponent."

Sounds to Robin like she could be a stunt double in a fight film. Twist. Spin. Thrust. Throw. Pin. Choke. Lock. The verbs ricochet in his mind.

PG takes a big breath. "Interesting," he says, but Robin can tell he means the opposite. "Well, let's get started, shall we? I've got big news to share with you guys. It's a dream come true. I've been waiting for this kind of an invitation for years."

He's beaming, Robin notices. "What's up, PG?" he asks. "You getting married?"

"No way," PG answers. "You think I'd marry someone who hasn't met you guys yet?"

"Well, what is it, then?" Ash asks. "I hate surprises."

"Two days ago—are you guys ready for this?—my old friend from seminary, Arjun Bose, invited me to visit him in India. Turns out the guy who teaches Greek and Hebrew at Kolkata

Bible College is taking a ten-week sabbatical, so Arjun asked if I can substitute."

"You're leaving us, PG?" Gracie asks.

"Well, sort of. The *other* good news is that he also invited any of you to come, too, and learn about his organization. It's called the Bengali Emancipation Society. They fight human trafficking and rescue children who are being bought and sold. We'd leave mid-June and stay in Kolkata through July and August. What do you guys think?"

PG swivels his head and looks right at Robin.

Kolkata. Robin's birthplace. His first home.

The place where he, like Oswald Cobblepot, was discarded.

The place he's told his parents time and time again he doesn't want to visit.

He still doesn't.

So why is his heart pounding?

KAT

"Sign me up," says the Paloma. "That sounds like a win for the college applications. 'Worked with an anti-trafficking organization in another country . . .' Great essay material. Unlike 'helped my parents out with their babies.'"

She's got a point there, Kat thinks. Brittany, Amber, and so many other Sanger Academy kids take "summer service trips" to foreign places like Thailand or the Dominican Republic. Even if they stay in Oakland, rich people's kids can pad their college applications by volunteering as "interns" at the zoo to work directly with the animals. They don't have to sweat all summer long at minimum wage, taking train tickets from sticky little kids, squeezing in time with animals on short breaks.

"Not everything's about college applications, Gracie," says PG. "Sometimes we're called to good work for reasons we can't see. And human trafficking's happening right here in Massachusetts, so if we really cared, we'd be fighting it year-round. We won't be going to India to do any 'rescuing.' Just learning. I'd love to have any or all of you come along."

"Wish I could, PG," the Cheetah says. "But my parents are making me visit colleges this summer."

The Tabby sighs. "Why didn't you tell us before, PG? I promised my dad I'd spend the summer with him."

"I only got Arjun's invitation two days ago," PG says. He hesitates, clasps his hands, and leans forward. "What do *you* think, Robin? After all, Kolkata's your birthplace."

Grandma Vee's friend hasn't moved. He doesn't answer right away, and the question hangs like a baton that nobody's taking. *If a person doesn't want to answer a question,* Kat thinks, *they should be able to plead the fifth.*

After a few more long seconds of silence, Bird Boy shrugs. "I told Mike I'd work at the shop full-time starting in June." His voice is so low Kat can hardly hear it.

"What do you do for work?" she asks, before PG can ask a follow-up question.

He doesn't answer that, either; it's like he's in a daze. After another awkward pause, Paloma answers the question. "Robin works at an auto repair shop," she says. "He can fix anything when it comes to cars."

"That's a good skill," Kat says.

Paloma flashes her a quick side-eye. *Interesting,* Kat thinks. *Guess even a dove gets her feathers ruffled up when it comes to protecting her territory.* She's starting to like this Gracie girl. *I wasn't flirting,* Kat wants to tell her. *Or being sarcastic about his work.*

Bird Boy's eyes flit in Gracie's direction and then Kat's, but he still doesn't say anything.

"Robin can't go to India, PG," the Alsatian growls. "He's driving me down to Baylor in July, remember?"

Cheetah rolls her eyes. "Just fly to college, Brian. You'd

better start getting used to not having your personal chauffeur around."

The Alsatian's scowl deepens. "We mapped our road trip. If we leave on the fifteenth of July, the Corvette gets me to Waco just in time for training."

Why is this mound of macho making summer plans for both of them? Kat thinks.

"Why don't we let Robin decide for himself?" PG asks, echoing her thoughts. "Or at least talk it over with his parents? You can all let me know by tomorrow. I know that's not a lot of time, but we're going to have to move fast to make this trip happen."

ROBIN

Robin feels like he's been sucker-punched by PG's invitation. Something inside him is rising to the surface, breaking through the static, demanding that he pay attention. *Think about it*, Dad would say. *Take some time. Listen to your heart.*

"Gracie, will you ask God to give us wisdom about this India trip?" PG asks.

As Gracie bows her head and starts to pray, Brian leans closer to Robin so that PG won't overhear. "Your new friend's kind of hot, Little Guy."

Suddenly, a jolt of energy surges through Robin like an electric shock. He leaps to his feet, leans over Brian, and looks him right in the eye. The truth about what he's feeling cannons out of his mouth: "I HATE THAT NAME!"

All motion in the room stops, as if the director of the scene has called for a cut. You'd think he hit Brian with a two-by-four. Because Robin never shouts. He never stands up to Brian. Or to anyone else, for that matter.

"Wow, Robin," PG says. "What just happened?"

Robin doesn't answer. His gaze meets Kat's.

"Yeah," Brian says. "What happened, Little Guy?"

Robin's fingers curl into a fist. He's never decked anyone,

but he isn't sure he can stop himself if he hears that name one more time.

"Never. Call. Me. That. Again." Robin glares down at Brian's upturned face until Brian looks away.

"Take it easy," Brian mutters. "I didn't know you hated it so much. I'll stop."

There. Message received. Finally.

Robin unclenches his fingers. He can't stand being in this room another minute. Someone else is going to have to take care of Ms. Vee's guest.

"Have to go," he says, and then grabs his phone and dashes out the door.

INT. CORVETTE—NIGHT—TRAVELING

Robin's always done his best thinking while driving. It's an in-between time, moving from something in the past to something in the future. No pressing demands, even if just for a short while.

Not too many cars are out on this icy night. The Corvette picks up speed as it whips around the traffic circle and down Saint James Street toward the Charles. Robin's been driving it for two years, since his father gave it to him for his sixteenth birthday. Dad doesn't even own a car himself; he commutes on the T and borrows Mom's if he needs it.

As Robin drives along Soldiers Field Road, feelings are crashing through him like chunks of ice after the first thaw. What are they? *Why* are they? *Try to name them.* Robin starts with the emotion that made him yell at Brian. That one's easy. Anger. He's felt it before, rarely, but never acted on it.

Blessed are the meek, PG taught them from Jesus's Sermon on the Mount. Robin has been meek ever since he can remember. He's naturally meek. He's done things out of duty; he's obedient. But tonight, for the first time, acting on anger felt *right*.

Robin replays the scene in his head. "Little Guy" finally Hulked out. Now he feels *victorious*. But neither of those—anger or triumph—explain how he felt when PG invited them to go to Kolkata. His knee-jerk reaction to returning there has always been "no way," but tonight that wasn't the case.

He *wanted* to go.

Because some other emotion's clamoring for attention.

Is it guilt? Shame?

No. It feels like the polar opposite of those.

But he still can't see it. He can't name it.

He crosses the river and heads back in the other direction on the Pike. He'd better get home. By now, Mom will be worried.

"A brown boy driving a red sports car is a ticket waiting to happen, or worse," he overheard her saying once. "What were you thinking, Ed? He could have had an eco-friendly, practical car, like mine."

"Robin couldn't decide," Dad had answered. "When he told me to pick, I just got him the car I wanted when I was sixteen. *My* father said no; it felt good to buy it for my son."

The transponder beeps as Robin passes through the tolls. He loves driving the Corvette—only an idiot wouldn't—but he can't bring himself to tell his dad about the car he truly wants.

A vintage, broken-down Volkswagen Beetle has been rusting in the back of Mike's shop, losing parts right and left to other cars that need them. Robin visits it at the end of every shift and rests his hand on the curved roof for a minute or two, daydreaming about the first steps he'd take in fixing it up.

The Corvette zooms off the familiar exit, times the green lights perfectly, and transports Robin to the only home he can remember. This blue, three-story Victorian was built by his grandfather's grandfather. His father inherited it as an only child. And now, Robin is next in line.

He parks the car he didn't want in front of the house he isn't sure he wants and turns off the engine. *Help me, God*, he prays. *Show me what I'm feeling.*

And then he sits in the darkness and waits.

KAT

INT. GRANDMA VEE'S APARTMENT—NIGHT

Grandma Vee's in the kitchen when Kat crunches back across the snow to her house. "How was small group?"

"Strange," Kat says.

"Strange? Why?"

Well, for one, there's a girl there who actually talks to God like he's real. Gracie's prayer was probably the oddest part of the whole evening. Closing your eyes and asking somebody invisible to help you make a decision? Weird. Weirder than weird. "They're thinking of going to India this summer," she says out loud.

Grandma Vee looks at Kat, eyebrows almost reaching the white hair she keeps trimmed against her skull. "To *India*? But that's where Robin was born!"

"I know. But he didn't seem too excited about it. He and his big friend had some kind of blow-up and he stormed out of the meeting early."

"Robin? *Stormed out?* Well, something *is* definitely going on with that boy. Tell me more about this India plan."

Kat explains the invitation from PG's friend and his organization while Grandma Vee listens closely.

And then: "You want to go along, Kat?"

"Uh . . . no, thanks. I'm going home in June." Saying yes

to visiting a small group of religious weirdos is one thing. But spending a whole summer with them? In a foreign, faraway country? No way.

"Taking a risk can bring healing to your soul," the old woman says.

Kat's phone buzzes and she glances at it. "Excuse me. Text from Mom. I should probably read it."

"Go ahead, child. Mothers come first. I'd actually like to send a text myself. I usually call, but this time I think I'll try the written word." Grandma Vee puts on her glasses, picks up her own phone, and slowly begins tapping the screen with her pointer finger.

Kat turns away to read Mom's message. It's longer than usual. No emojis. *Hope you're starting to feel at home there, Kat. I miss you. I'm sorry to tell you, though, darling, that when I went to the zoo and asked them to hold your job for this summer, they said they couldn't. They need someone now to fill your hours.*

Kat can't believe it. So now that Wolf's making her lose her job, too. Just when she was about to start making more than minimum wage. Forty hours a week this summer could have shored up their bank account.

Another text comes in from Mom. *I know you'll be mad when you hear this, but I still think sending you to Boston was the right decision. You'll see that soon, I'm sure.*

I'll see that never, Kat thinks, scowling at the screen in her hand. A surge of anger—just as Mom predicted—makes her feel like throwing the phone across the room. Right now, all she wants is to make her mother feel some pain.

ROBIN

INT. CORVETTE—NIGHT

No divine answer comes zinging instantly after Robin's prayer. He's talked to God for as long as he can remember, repeating the Lord's Prayer with one or both of his parents at bedtime, bowing his head at church and agreeing with other people, or shooting up simple, quick prayers on his own.

God's not a vending machine, PG warns them when they discuss prayer at small group. Still, up to now, Robin's mostly asked for stuff, and his parents answered instead of God—no to a puppy at eight, yes to a gaming system at twelve, no to a motorcycle at fourteen.

This is the first time Robin's asked God to illuminate his soul. He has no idea how long an answer might take.

He spots his mother peering out of the front window. He knows exactly what she's been up to—watching for him to come home. Even though Dad's always telling her to leave Robin alone, she's probably texted five times.

That reminds him—his phone. He switches it off airplane mode. Sure enough, the texts come flying in like birds to a feeder.

Mom's only sent two messages. Good for her.

#1: *Where are you, honey? Small group got out an hour ago.*

#2: *Text or call soon, Robin. I'm getting worried.*

He texts back: *I see you, Mom. I'll be there in a bit.* He flashes his headlights, and she waves from the window and disappears.

Gracie's sent five.

#1: *Hey, Robin. You left so quickly. You okay?*

#2: *What do you think of Kat?*

#3: *She looks a little like Storm in those X-Men movies you like, don't you think?*

#4: *I'm glad you told Brian to stop using that nickname. I didn't know you hated it so much.*

#5: *Are you there? Is your phone on? Text as soon as you get this.*

Robin smiles. These are so typical, so caring.

I'm fine, he texts back. He's better than fine, actually. He hasn't felt this energetic in weeks, maybe months. Anger's good juice. *At first, I thought Kat might look a little like Halle Berry, but then after a while she didn't anymore. Talk soon.*

Gracie replies with a row of pink hearts with stars slicing through them.

PG's texted Robin twice.

#1: *I know you haven't wanted to go back to India with your parents, Robin, but how do you feel about going back with me? And maybe Gracie, too? Talk it over with your mom and dad. I'd sure love your company.*

#2: *Also what happened tonight? Glad you finally stood up to Brian but I've never seen you so angry.*

Robin decides to answer this one. *Jesus overturned tables. Don't you read your Bible?*

A laughing-hysterically face from PG shows up in two seconds.

And then, to Robin's amazement, there's a message from

Ms. Vee. She never texts. She hates making grammatical and spelling errors, and she can't type or thumb very well. But here it is, mistakes and all. One of her pithy quotes, written this time instead of voiced.

RObin. Kat told me about INDIA. my 2 cents: Some t imes you have to go Back to the PASt to move forWARD into the FuTURE.

What's she talking about? He reads it again. And then once more.

Suddenly, Robin pulls down the visor and looks in the lighted mirror. He sees cheeks and chin that need a daily shave to be stubble-free, brown eyes, wavy hair, dark skin, angular face.

He inherited all of this from strangers.

People he doesn't know. Or remember.

Like his "first mother," as Mom always calls her.

With a jolt, Robin suddenly recognizes that hidden emotion. The one that's behind his strange desire to return to Kolkata.

Hope. It's hope.

If he goes back to his birthplace, by some miracle, after all these years, maybe, maybe he can find her.

He wants to see her again.

Hear her voice.

Even discover something, anything, about why she couldn't keep him.

KAT

INT. GRANDMA VEE'S APARTMENT—NIGHT

Grandma Vee's muttering at her phone. "How do I send this text, Kat?" she asks.

Kat leans over and taps SEND on the screen. "Maybe I will go to India this summer, Grandma Vee. How would I pay for a trip like that?"

"Really? You think you'd like to go? The church raises money for this kind of thing."

"They'll cover the cost? Even for me?"

"Usually. Yes."

Okay, then. This trip to India could be an all-expenses-paid "volunteer summer service trip" for Katina King. Take *that*, Mom. And take *that*, college admissions committees.

"But will your mother allow you?" Grandma Vec asks. "She thinks you're coming home in June."

"She sent me here, didn't she? She must not care too much about mc bcing far away."

"I'm sure she does. Why not call and ask? That three-hour time difference comes in handy at times like this."

Fine. I'll tell her RIGHT NOW.

Mom picks it up on the first ring. "Kat! I'm so sorry about the job—"

"Yeah, well, it frees up my summer. I'm going to India instead."

"WHAT? With whom? To do what?"

"To fight child trafficking. Or to learn about it, at least. Now that I'm fired from the zoo, I need something for my college applications. Plus, the church pays for the whole thing. Which is good, since you broke our bank account."

"You're just doing this because you're mad at me, Kat. I had to force you to go to Boston. And now you're asking to be away from home even longer?"

Mom has it on speakerphone so Kat can hear Saundra offering her opinion in the background.

"Saundra says there's plenty of trafficking right here in Oakland," her mother tells her. "She could set you up with some volunteer work this summer. Wait, what?" Saundra's adding something else now. "It's tough stuff, she says. Hard for a lot of people to handle. You still need time to heal, she thinks."

"Taking a risk like this might help me heal." Out of the corner of her eye, Kat sees Grandma Vee trying to hide a smile.

"If you'd kept seeing the counselor, maybe I'd believe you actually want healing," Mom retorts. "I don't think any counselor in their right mind would agree that running away to another country would be good for you right now."

Grandma Vee holds out her hand for the phone.

"Here," Kat says. "Talk it over with Grandma Vee. She thinks it's a great idea."

Another second of silence. "You're already calling her

Grandma? *I'm* your mom, I don't care—Wait, what?" Saundra's saying something. "I *know* you said she was amazing, Saundra, but *I'm* making decisions for Kat, not—" She stops, listens to something Kat can't hear. "Okay, Katina, put Ms. Jones on the phone."

Grandma Vee takes the phone and disappears into her room. Kat waits, trying to figure out if she wants her mother to say yes or no. She remembers that night on the bathroom floor a few months ago. Maybe Mom's right. Maybe Kat shouldn't travel even farther from home.

When Grandma Vee reemerges, she's smiling.

Kat puts the phone back to her ear.

"I guess you can do this if you want, Kat," Mom says. "Ms. Jones thinks it might be the opportunity of a lifetime. I'd like to send some money to help pay for the trip. We've got a fifty tucked away in our 'spa day splurge' jar. I'll send it with your passport. And thanks for being such a good sport about losing your zoo job."

After Kat hangs up, she turns to Grandma Vee. "What did you tell her? I can't believe she'll let me go." *I can't believe she doesn't want me to come back in June.*

"Just that healing can come in many forms—even through serving others. And that a trip like this *might* be a once in a lifetime chance. So—do *you* want to go? Take a moment, Kat; think hard."

Saundra's coaching words. Kat obeys them.

What else is she going to do this summer? If she stays in Oakland, even if Saundra sets her up with "volunteering," she'll have to earn *some* money to help out with rent and food.

That means a job at a fast-food joint, probably. Where the only animals in sight are leering customers. Besides, if she's gone for six months instead of three, maybe her mother will figure out how to separate colors from whites in the wash.

Time for you to grow up, Mom.

She takes a deep breath. "Guess I'm going to India this summer."

"Wonderful. I'll call PG and tell him."

ROBIN

INT. CORVETTE—NIGHT

A new message comes winging into his phone. It's in the long-time small-group text with Brian, Martin, Ash, Gracie, and PG. This one's from Gracie: *Woo-hoo! Just asked my parents and they said I can go!*

PG: *That's great, Gracie! And Ms. Vee called—Kat's going with us, too! She even asked her mother and got permission already.*

Robin looks up at his reflection again.

Hope feels risky. Maybe that's why he so rarely lets himself feel it.

He holds up the phone and recites Ms. Vee's message again, this time aloud, telling it to the face in the mirror. "Sometimes, you have to go back to the past to move forward into the future."

Then he takes a breath, flips up the sun visor, and opens their group text.

I want to go, too, he thumbs.

Pauses.

And then hits SEND.

Almost immediately, a notification pops up: *Brian Cleery has left the group.* This six-member group has been in place for five years. How can Brian exit so suddenly?

If they notice his departure, the others don't comment.

PG: *YOU DO? I'm so glad, Robin! Have you cleared it with your parents?*

About to tell them now, Robin replies.

Martin sends a fist. *Awesome!*

Ash sends the praying hands emoji, which is so unusual from her that it's weirdly encouraging to Robin.

Gracie delivers five more rows of pink starry hearts, along with this: *Your parents have always been 100% supportive. I'm sure they'll say yes.*

INT. THORNTON HOUSE—NIGHT

Robin's mother and father are perched on stools at the kitchen island, sharing a bottle of red wine. He takes stock for a minute before they see him—two tall, smart, white people. Ever since he was three years old, they've been like those zany mirrors in amusement parks that are supposed to reflect you but don't. It isn't their fault.

The door closes behind him, and they stop talking and turn to him with smiles. Robin knows they've probably been discussing him again. *They care so much,* he thinks. Gracie's right; they're utterly supportive. He walks over so he's standing between them.

His mother studies his expression. "What happened? You look . . . different. You're not smoking anything, are you, Robin?"

"No, Mom. You've got to stop worrying so much. Look at all this gray," Robin says, fiddling with the short curls on his mother's head. He used to do this when he'd sit on her lap to look at a picture book.

"Okay, okay. I've got my salon appointment tomorrow, so hush up about the hair."

His father's also scrutinizing him. "Mom's right. You *do* look different. Something good happen at small group?"

"It did," Robin says, putting a hand on each of their shoulders. "Mom. Dad. I'm going back to Kolkata."

His mother knocks over her wineglass. Good thing it's empty. "Really, Robin? I'm so excited!"

She probably thinks they're all going. That would make sense. Every now and then, they still bring up the possibility. And offer to help him search.

Better to try sooner than later, Dad always says. *People get harder to find as time passes.*

Maybe someday you'll change your mind, Mom adds after Robin says no. *We're always ready to go back with you.*

Well, someday is now, but he isn't going back with them.

He reaches for the wineglass and puts it back upright. "PG's taking a few of us this summer for a service trip. And . . . well, I think I want to try and search while I'm there."

He watches his mother register that he's not asking them to go along. Something flashes across her face for a split second—is it sadness?—but then she jumps up and hugs him. "Oh, Robin. That's amazing! Edward, Robin's going back to search!"

"Let's keep the search part quiet for now, okay, Mom? I'd like to share that with people in my own way."

Robin looks at his father's face over his mother's shoulder.

Are those tears in Dad's eyes? Is he, too, feeling hurt that their son is planning to go back without them?

But Dad stands up and throws his arms around both of them. "There are wonderful gifts waiting in Kolkata, son. Your mother and I sure came back with one."

KAT

INT. GRANDMA VEE'S APARTMENT—DAY

Now that "going to India" is the plan, Kat doesn't change her mind. That's how she wins on the mat. Plans a move and sticks to it until her her hold gets broken. Then Filhote readjusts. Comes up with a new plan. Sticks to that, until her opponent manages to get loose again, or—preferably—surrenders.

It's going to take a while to come up with a good Kolkata Plan A, so Kat's glad she has more free time here than in Oakland. The butt-in-chair classwork takes only about three hours instead of six like it does at Sanger. And Saundra was right; Grandma Vee *is* a brilliant teacher, telling down-to-earth stories to illuminate abstract concepts, unlocking the mysteries of honors biology and chemistry with a sparkle of joy in her eyes. Kat might actually have a shot at finishing her junior year with all As.

After "school," Grandma Vee puts on a bright orange apron and hands Kat a blue-and-white one. "I'd like to show you how to make a few of my grandmother's recipes. Let's cook a big pot of groundnut stew and some jollof rice, shall we?"

As they chop the onions, tomatoes, and hot peppers for the stew, Grandma Vee reminisces about harvesting nuts in her village and making the red palm oil from scratch. "Now I have to go to a West African grocery store in Waltham to get my supply," she says. "I can't seem to break my childhood addiction."

Kat takes a big whiff of the savory smells rising from the skillet. *Not the worst addiction in the world,* she thinks.

Turns out what Grandma Vee's really addicted to is Boston sports. The Bruins are playing, so she listens to the hockey game while they cook.

Kat's not sure why they prepare such big portions, since it's just the two of them, but it doesn't take long to figure it out. The doorbell starts ringing in the afternoon, and some lady named Joann who works at the pharmacy down the street and Min-Seo, the medical resident from next door, both join them for supper. It rings two more times, but to Kat's relief, the dudes who show up don't get invited to stay. They get Ibis-embraced at the threshold instead, and leave with takeaway plastic tubs of stew.

"You don't let men inside, Grandma Vee?" Kat asks, once everyone's gone.

"Until you're okay with it, I don't."

This worries Kat almost as much as it eases her mind. She isn't "okay with" not feeling comfortable around strange men. Or any dudes at all, if they try and touch her. Last year, she hung out a bit with another jiu-jitsu student they'd nicknamed Pinguim—"penguin" in Portuguese. She even held hands with him and they kissed a couple of times. But the attack changed all that. She stopped returning Pinguim's texts and avoided him at the academy. Now she isn't sure she'll ever be able to let him, or any guy for that matter, touch her again.

When the dishes are washed and Grandma Vee turns on the Celtics game, Kat disappears into her room. She picks up her phone and texts her mother. *Did you send my passport?*

Mom's reply arrives in what feels like a nanosecond. *Yes. Remember that "beach resort" I booked for us in Tijuana?* She adds a laugh-till-you-cry emoji.

How could Kat forget? Driving the Mazda across the border to a cheap motel was the only family vacation they could afford last year. It was miles from the ocean, but they made their way to the beach every day. The two of them took salsa-making lessons and faked their way through salsa-dancing lessons. But she doesn't answer Mom's text.

As if she can read Kat's mind, though, Mom sends a GIF of a salsa dancer tripping and falling. Kat feels a sharp twinge of homesickness, but she's not about to let Mom know that.

She switches over to her social media. Brittany and Amber aren't posting much—probably focused on the ACT practice exam this weekend that Kat's not taking—but the school accounts are raving about yet another championship for the Sanger Hawks varsity basketball team. With you-know-who as the lead scorer. Her thumb punches the app to shut it down.

"*Sound of Music* is on!" Grandma Vee yells from the living room.

"Coming!" Kat calls.

Just as she's about to power down, Saundra texts a photo. She and Mom are out dancing at some club in the city. In that slinky dress and those stilettoes, you'd never guess Saundra's a kick-ass cop and the top jiu-jitsu fighter in her age bracket in

California. Mom's hair is dyed red to match her miniskirt, and she's got both hands in the air.

Without a teenager around to worry about, they're having the time of their lives.

Meanwhile, the teenager's about to watch *The Sound of Music* with an old woman who's out there singing "the hills are alive" at the top of her lungs.

The crazy thing is that once she joins Grandma Vee on the couch, Kat ends up having fun herself.

She recites a few of the lines in the movie from memory— "When the Lord closes a door, somewhere he opens a window," and "I am not finished yet, Captain!"—while Grandma Vee belts out all the songs. The two of them demolish a jumbo-sized bag of plantain chips from the West African grocery.

ROBIN

INT. METROWEST HIGH SCHOOL
CAFETERIA—DAY

Everything seems different to Robin now that he's decided to go back to Kolkata. *He* feels different. Hope is revving him up, accelerating his thought processes.

In the cafeteria, ignoring the wraps, he grabs a salad. After he pays the cashier, who looks surprised at his choice, he strides right past Brian's table.

"Robin! Where are you going? Come sit down!"

At least "Little Guy" isn't making a comeback. Maybe this is progress.

Slowly, Robin turns, but he doesn't head back to the place where he's spent so many lunches. Instead, he waits until Brian stands up and walks over to him.

"You're really going to India?" Brian asks, keeping his voice low so the people around them can't hear. "What about your offer to drive me to college?"

I didn't offer. You asked, and I said yes. As usual. "I changed my mind."

Brian frowns. "How am I supposed to get to Baylor if you don't drive me? You know how amazing it would be to pull up in that red Corvette?"

Because you'd be driving. As usual, in that car. "I'm not your only ride, Brian. Your stepdad can take you down. He has a Porsche; that should be cool enough."

"No way. I'm not spending all that time with him."

Robin shrugs. "You'll figure it out."

He starts to walk away, but Brian grabs his wrist. Not roughly, but enough to stop him. "Wait. Can you at least pick me up after practice today?"

Robin knows this is his last chance to prove nothing's changed between them. That what happened at youth group was a weird blip.

He twists out of Brian's grasp. "Sorry. No."

Strange how much easier it is to overturn a table after you do it a first time.

He watches Brian's nonverbals morph fully into anger. Then, as if Robin has suddenly vanished, his longtime buddy turns, strides back to his table, and sits down. "The Celtics got robbed, man," Robin hears him saying. "I couldn't believe that call, could you?"

Martin's been watching the entire interaction from across the room. He raises a fist in the air, and Robin replies with a quick chin lift. Martin answers with a come-sit-with-us wave, but Robin shakes his head. He looks around for any of his auto shop buddies but none are in sight. And then he sees the desi table.

People of Indian descent living outside of India, Robin thinks. Well, he deserves that label, too, doesn't he? Clutching his salad, he makes his way over to them.

Once again, Indian music's playing at the table. Six or

seven kids are leaning into each other, watching music videos on a shared tablet.

"Hey," Robin says. "Room for one more?"

Someone presses PAUSE on the video. "Sure, Robin," Sona Patel says, shifting over.

She knows his name. That surprises him, but why should it? He glances around at the rest of the people sitting with her—he knows most of them. Three are seniors, like him. Vinod, Sanjay, and Chitra.

"Hey," says Vinod. He and Robin played Little League together back in the day.

"What's new, my man?" Sanjay asks. He'd sat next to Robin in second grade, and in their middle-school art class, too. "What do you have planned for after we leave this prison?"

What's new? What does he have planned? "I'm going back to Kolkata this summer." Then, for some reason, he adds, "That's where I was born."

"My parents are from Kolkata, too," says Chitra. Robin crushed on her from afar in the seventh grade; this is the first time he can remember her speaking directly to him. And— wait! Is she twisting her hair?

Sona didn't grow up in their town. "Are *both* your parents Bengali? Isn't your last name Thorning or something like that?"

"It's Thornton. I'm adopted." He's never said it this boldly before. With no hesitation.

"Oh," Sona says. "I'm sorry, I didn't know."

Robin looks her right in the eyes. "No apology needed. I'll

bet I'm the only Bengali dude named 'Robin Thornton' on the entire planet."

"Cool," she says, smiling. "I'll do a search on the internet to make sure."

Vinod puts an arm around Sona in a she's-mine kind of way, which makes Robin feel great. He doesn't want Sona, even though she's gorgeous, but at least someone thinks he's a contender.

KAT

INT. METROWEST PRESBYTERIAN CHURCH
SANCTUARY—DAY

Kat's sitting alone in a back pew in this large, old-fashioned church. Do they make churches like this in California, with stained-glass windows, wooden pews, organ pipes, and high, high arches and pillars bearing the weight of the soaring ceiling? She's never seen one.

The few times they visited Saundra's church in Oakland, it felt like being inside a warehouse. There, Mom's was always one of the only white faces in a big crowd. Kat looks around as people take their seats. This church has only about a hundred or so people scattered here and there, but she sees black, white, and brown faces. It's "racially ambiguous," like some idiot at Sanger once described her, trying to sound smart.

Grandma Vee's smiling down at Kat from the choir. Martin's singing up there, too. He waggles his fingers when he catches Kat's eye just like he did last Thursday, and she lifts a hand in reply. There's a stained-glass window behind Martin. It's of a bearded man surrounded by children. HINDER THEM NOT, says the caption below it in big letters. *That must be Jesus*, Kat thinks. *Doesn't look canine at all. Looks more like a Sparrow.*

Other windows continue along the walls, each one telling another chapter in the story of the Sparrow's life. The two in the very back show his body hanging on a cross, and then draped across his mother's lap. Dead. Didn't have a chance. No way a Sparrow can single-handedly fight off wild dogs.

"You must be Viola's grandchild from California," an old man says, shaking her hand.

Kat doesn't correct him. She likes how nobody seems to question her kinship with Grandma Vee. When Mom, Saundra, and Kat are together, strangers usually assume that Saundra's Kat's mother. Brittany and Amber did a bad job hiding their surprise when they met Mom at a Sanger college prep night.

"What are you, Kat?" Amber asked once, hesitantly. "Racially, I mean? I hope you don't mind if I ask." She's awkward about race, like a lot of white girls at that school.

"No idea," Kat answered. "What are you?"

"I'm . . . white, I guess."

If she got to be a color, so did Kat. "I'm brown, then."

Kat spots Gracie, sitting next to Ash in the front pew. Ash is ignoring the woman sitting on the other side of her. Must be her mother, because she reaches over to straighten Ash's collar. Ash shifts her butt along the pew, yanking her shirt out of reach. *If that was me and Mom*, Kat thinks, *it would be me fixing Mom's outfit, not the other way around. Wonder what time the two party girls got home from their party night?*

She tries to push away her thoughts of home and keeps scanning the pews. No sign of the Alsatian, but she sees Bird Boy squished between two tall white people.

Suddenly, the drama the other night around the trip to Kolkata makes sense.

The kid's adopted.

Nosy strangers probably ask if they're in the same family, just like they do with her and Mom. Kat always answers with a mind-your-own-business glare, but Mom does something silly—throwing an arm around Kat's waist, leaning her head on her daughter's shoulder, saying, "We're twins, can't you tell?" Kat's always liked Mom's banter. It keeps the King women in charge of classifying themselves.

The service starts with an African-sounding hymn about "walking in the light of God" and Grandma Vee goes to town. Even from a pew in the back of the church, Kat can hear her voice rising above the others. For some reason, the off-key pitch of her new grandmother's voice cheers Kat up.

After the song, the Owl sitting beside Ash's mom goes up front. *Must be Ash's father,* Kat thinks. She listens to his announcements about the upcoming sermon series and Bible study options. *Guess he's a pastor, too. Along with the Goose.* This congregation might be mixed, but both pastors are white. And balding. And wearing glasses.

Ash's father sends the kids off to their Sunday school classes. "Come up here and tell us about our youth group's summer service trip to India, will you, PG?" He gives PG a clap on the shoulder and sits down again next to his wife.

"Any kids left in the sanctuary?" PG asks.

"Nope," a voice calls. "You got a PG-13 audience in here, PG."

The congregation groans. To Kat, they sound like one very loud person.

"Good one, Ed, but we may need an R rating for what I'm about to share," says PG. "We'll be going to India this summer to work with the Bengali Emancipation Society. Slavery still exists, both for labor and for sex. And they work to free trafficked children. But guess what? India's not the worst country in the world when it comes to selling humans for profit. It's got a Tier 2 rating, which means it's 'making significant efforts to come into compliance with Tier 1 standards.' Tier 3 countries are places where trafficking is on the rise, with Russia, China, Iran, Belarus, and Venezuela often ranked as the worst five."

Ignoring the congregation's surprised murmurs, PG keeps going. "And don't think we're off the hook here. Human trafficking is big money in our own country. I read somewhere that it's the fastest-growing part of organized crime. The average age for a girl who is sold for sex in our country is thirteen."

"THIRTEEN's the AVERAGE?" a woman calls out. Was that Bird Boy's mom? Kat thinks it might have been.

"That's right," says PG. "And when it comes to children as victims of *online* sexual abuse, many live in Colombia, India, Mexico, the Philippines, Thailand, and—guess where?—right here. The United States of America."

How did Kat not know this? Saundra probably did; why hadn't she educated Kat more? There's not a sound in the sanctuary. Even the Sparrow on the stained-glass window—the one with children surrounding him—seems to be listening.

"I want to share a short film with you," says PG. "My friend Arjun sent me the link; it's password-protected but he gave me permission to show it to you."

PG asks for the lights to be dimmed, a screen comes down in front of the stained glass window, and the film starts playing.

At first, all Kat sees is a green, lush meadow. Indian-sounding music is playing in the background. Then a title appears. *RESCUE: IN HER OWN WORDS.*

More words scroll up the screen, almost like they do at the beginning of a Star Wars movie. *The Bengali Emancipation Society's mission is to fight people who sell and abuse children for profit. Please listen to one such child's story.*

The music fades and the meadow disappears. Kat sees some kind of balcony or veranda behind low-growing bushes that are dotted with small white flowers. Birds are singing. The camera pans in. A girl dressed in yellow is sitting on the veranda, rocking back and forth in a white chair. Her face is blurred out and so is the building behind her, but Kat can see a yellow ribbon woven into her long black braid. *Canary*, Kat thinks.

The girl starts speaking in a language Kat can't understand, but an English translation is appearing across the bottom of the screen. As Kat reads what the calm, sweet voice is telling them, her heart begins to pound.

I was twelve years old when my mother sent me from our village. I don't blame her. She needed money to buy rice for my sisters and brothers. I was the oldest. It was my duty. I went with a madam, thinking I would earn money working in a factory sewing clothes. I am very good at sewing. But when we arrived in Kolkata, the madam sold me to the brothel.

Kat's mouth feels like she's swallowed a fistful of flour.

The Canary in the film keeps talking.

They locked me in a room and bound me to the bed. A man came in. And then another.

Someone in the congregation calls out: "Oh!"

That first sour taste of vomit is rising in Kat's throat. It's been a few days since she's had to swallow it down.

The brothel owner's men beat me. Sometimes they gave me drugs, and I would wake up bleeding and bruised. After many days and weeks, I stopped fighting. I started wondering if I might have deserved this terrible treatment. Maybe I was being punished for some evil I had done in a life before this one.

Kat swallows and swallows, managing to keep her stomach in place. But every muscle in her body is tensed, as if she's about to battle an opponent twice her size. The girl keeps talking.

For months and months, I suffered like this. They didn't let me out of that room, except to go to the bathroom. Soon, I lost count of time. But one day a man came who didn't touch me. He quietly told me he was working for the police. He asked my age; I said I thought I could be fourteen by now. He said they would try to rescue me and told me to trust the police who would come, they would get me out of this prison and take me to a safe place. She pauses, as if she's remembering a girl waiting in the darkness. *And they did.*

She escaped. Somehow, they got her out of there.

But where did she go?

It's almost like the girl on the veranda, far away on the other side of the planet, can hear Kat's unspoken question here in Boston.

The police took me back to my village . . . but my mother would not allow me inside our house. She was afraid. I could hear my brothers and sisters crying. The madam had warned them that if I came home, they had to send me straight back to the brothel. If they didn't, the brothel owner would have me killed and take my two little sisters as payment.

The girl in the film stops talking. Brushes the back of her hand over the upper half of her blurry face.

Fury rips through Kat like a California wildfire. It's so fierce it makes her forget her nausea. What kind of Wolves do this to children? The most rabid, repulsive canine of all. The kind you fight to the death.

ROBIN

Sandwiched between his parents, Robin watches the video, horrified and spellbound at the same time. The blurry-faced girl in the film bends over and picks a white, starry flower. Holding it gently by the stem so her fingers don't damage the petals, she shows it to the camera. And then she starts talking again, as if the flower gives her courage to finish her story.

In all that time when I was a prisoner, I thought if I could see my mother's face again, I would know I wasn't forgotten by God. That my punishment was over. Now I had seen her face, but still I was suffering. I cried to God. Help me! Don't you see me? I am your child.

Robin finds himself praying the words along with the girl on the screen.

God heard my prayer! She throws her arms open. One yellow sleeve to the left. One to the right, fingers still holding the stem of the tiny white flower. *The police brought me to Asha House. Here, I am safe. I am improving in sewing so I can get a job and send money to my mother. And I am getting counseling. So that I can heal on the inside.*

The girl in the film drops the white flower into her palm. *I am starting to feel better. Like myself again. But also new and fresh. Like this flower in my hand. Best of all, I am getting better at speaking English. Listen!*

The translated words stop scrolling across the screen.

"I am better at speaking English!" her lilting, chirpy voice says. "Do you see my beautiful flower?"

Robin can hear laughing somewhere in the background as the music begins to play again. The flower weaves and dances closer to the camera until the girl's open palm fills the whole screen. The dancing flower is five-petaled and pearly white; Robin can almost smell the fragrance of it.

It's over. The lights come on. The screen goes up.

Mom's dabbing her cheeks with a tissue and Dad uses another one to blow his nose.

PG asks the members of the service team to come up front.

That's me, Robin realizes with a start. He follows Kat up the stairs.

KAT

Going to India for college essay material? Going to India to pay Mom back for sending her to Boston? Those are trivial, selfish reasons to Kat now. She wants to meet the Canary. She's going to help her fight Wolves.

As she follows Gracie up the stairs to the pulpit, Kat automatically shifts her body into BJJ mode—tall, strong, and fierce. Suddenly, she notices that Bird Boy is behind her. So he's definitely going to India. Interesting.

Behind the pulpit, she towers over both of them and PG, too, feeling like the Salesforce building in the San Francisco skyline. Curious stares check out her hair, skin, body, and clothes, and she quickly secures her Lion face in place. What do these Jesus-y people think of her?

"You all know Robin and most of you know Gracie, but this is Kat, who's visiting Ms. Vee for a while from California," says PG. "We're thrilled she'll be joining us for the trip. Let's show her some love, shall we?"

The congregation bursts into applause.

For Kat.

They're applauding her. One hundred or so faces are smiling up at her like she's a gift sent to them from heaven above.

There's even a "woo-hoo" shouted in her direction and a loud hurrah or two.

Filhote disappears. She can't help it: Kat, the real Kat, smiles back.

Ash's father comes up again to join them. "I think we were all moved by that film, PG. How can we support you guys?"

"The usual," answers PG. "Money."

Laughter. "Tell us something new," a voice calls from the pews.

"At least I'm consistent," PG says. "But, seriously, we do need your prayers. We don't want to do any harm to these already hurting children. Pray for us to have humility and wisdom. As I told you before, we're going to learn and serve, not to 'fix' or 'save.' I'll be teaching Greek and Hebrew, and I'm sure my friend Arjun will help these three find their own acts of service."

"Wonderful! It's going to be expensive, so dig deep, people," Ash's father tells the congregation. "These folks are traveling all the way to India."

"The money's mostly for air tickets," PG adds quickly. "Once we get there, we'll be living with the locals as guests. No touristy five-star hotels or fancy restaurants, we promise. We'll probably be eating rice and lentils most of the time." He pats his stomach. "I might even lose a few pounds."

"You're just right the way you are, PG!" An older man calls out his affirmation in a shaky voice.

The congregation laughs again.

"That's good to hear," says PG. "But we're all flawed, aren't we? Will you promise to pray for us?"

"Yes!"

"You bet!"

"We've got your backs!"

"We're on it!"

When the congregation finally settles down, Ash's father flings an arm around PG's shoulders. "Let's pray for Pastor Greg's waistline and the team's other needs, shall we?"

He closes his eyes and starts talking as if God's face is on the inside of his eyelids.

Gracie reaches out to take Kat's hand.

Kat doesn't pull away.

ROBIN

INT. THORNTON HOUSE—NIGHT

While he's brushing his teeth, Robin's phone plays the harp music that signals a message from Gracie: *That film! I'm still crying.*

Powerful, he texts back. That's an understatement. For some reason, hearing that girl's story felt like someone poured petroleum on Robin's hope. It's now on fire.

Another harp chord. *I'm so excited to see the place where you were born. You might even have relatives there, right?*

He guesses that she's sub-asking if he's decided to search, but for now he doesn't want to share that with anybody other than his parents. Not yet. Not even Gracie.

Maybe, he texts. *See you Thursday. PG wants to start some "training" he's got planned.*

KK. Twenty pink hearts. She doesn't push it. Robin loves that about her. Three flashing dots tells him she's still thumbing, so he rinses out his mouth and waits. Here it comes. *Your church is so friendly. I'd come more often on Sunday mornings but I don't like to miss Mass.*

So's yours, he answers. He's visited the big Catholic cathedral where the Riveras worship; it *is* welcoming. He adds a cross and a waving brown face. He's not an emoji kind of guy, but when it comes to texting Gracie, sad, confused, happy, laughing, or shocked tiny face symbols flow out as if they have minds of their own.

KAT

He's pinning her to the wall with a hand on her throat. She tries to break his grasp, but she doesn't have enough strength in her body. She's prey to the predator.

Kat sits up screaming, drenched in sweat.

In no time, she hears the sound of Grandma Vee's walker rolling down the hall.

Oh, no. I woke her up. And now she's going to find me like this. She's sitting on the edge of the bed, taking breaths to try and slow her heart rate.

The door opens. Leaving her walker outside, Grandma Vee treads softly inside and sits on the bed beside her houseguest. She turns on the bedside lamp. Kat braces herself for questions, but they don't come. Instead, Grandma Vee puts an old bird arm around Kat's shoulder and they sit side by side in silence.

It's the unspoken aura of love that does Kat in. Breaking away from the embrace, Kat throws herself facedown on the bed and buries her face in her pillow.

And then she starts to cry.

Somewhere in the back of her head, the dispassionate feline version of herself watches in disgust. Katina King never cries.

Not during or after the attack. Not when she faced the committee and told them what happened in that stairwell.

But she can't stop, no matter how hard the Filhote inside fights for composure.

What a loser, she thinks. She can hardly breathe, crying into the pillow, but she doesn't want to move it.

Suddenly, she's aware again of Grandma Vee's quiet presence. One hand starts stroking Kat's hair, the other is patting her shoulder. The old woman is humming in a low, deep voice, off-key as usual. She sounds like she's strolling in a garden, not trying to comfort a sobbing, shaking wreck of a human being.

But . . . it's working.

The Ibis's deep, low breaths, soft humming, and gentle touch are steadying and calming Kat. The true Kat. The hidden one.

Soon, it feels like she can breathe again. After a while longer, the tears slow and then stop altogether. Kat pulls her face out of the pillow, sits up, shifts herself to the edge of the bed, and looks into eyes that are as dark and soft as the weathered skin on Grandma Vee's face.

"Tell me about it, darling?" Grandma Vee asks, taking her hand and pulling it into her lap.

And then, before any version of Kat can stop herself, the truth comes pouring out.

Her companion listens, clasping Kat's hand inside both of her own worn palms, as Kat blurts out everything that happened, from start to finish.

When Kat's done, Grandma Vee still doesn't say anything. At least not to Kat. She starts talking to the Sparrow instead. Out loud. Eyes open. Head up, looking straight ahead. As if he's standing in the room in front of them.

"Jesus, enter the memory in this child's soul. Heal her pain. Jesus, hear our prayer." She stops, waits. Then prays that again. Stops. Waits. And again.

After a third time through this strange routine, she turns to Kat. "Go back to sleep, child. All is well."

Suddenly, Kat's so tired she can't sit up anymore. The pillow feels soft and cool under her cheek. Her eyes close.

Grandma Vee tucks the sheets around Kat's curled-up body.

Drops a kiss on her cheek.

After switching off the lamp, leaves the room.

Kat's not sure if it's the kiss or the prayer, but her heart feels cleaner, lighter, like some unseen vomit's been flushed away. She drifts off into a deep, dreamless sleep.

ROBIN

INT. METROWEST HIGH SCHOOL AUTOMOTIVE ENGINEERING DEPARTMENT—DAY

Robin enters the warehouse where he's taken every automotive elective the school offers. First period of the day and he's early as usual, like all the car-loving students enrolled in Mr. Grant's advanced automotive engineering class.

Aaaahh. Bliss. Hydraulic lifts, loud air compressors, and the smell of brake fluid. Scattered around the room are other Metrowest High students he's known for years.

Kumiko the exchange student waves at him from the back. "Robin! Come and learn how we change a battery the Tokyo way."

Robin glances around. There's as much mixing and mingling across boundaries in here as at Martin's lunch table. Maybe that's why he likes it so much.

Along with the cars, of course.

Kumiko adores big American pickup trucks. Darnell knows everything about German engines. There's also "Luxury" Louis, who's broke but plans to own a Tesla one day. Katie with the small, deft fingers likes complicated rewiring.

And Robin Thornton, who's been secretly longing for two years to bring a 1974 Volkswagen Bug back into commission. He pictures the car: small, rusting, hiding so much potential.

"What do you guys think about me buying an old Beetle?" he calls out. "I'm about to do it."

They stop what they're doing and gather around him, wiping their hands on already greasy rags and placing spark plugs and screwdrivers on the table.

"Dubs are great cars," says Darnell. "Nothing like the sound of that air-cooled, four-cylinder engine once it's running at peak."

"Are replacement parts expensive?" asks Katie.

"What about aftermarket parts?" adds Kumiko. She likes extra decor like elaborate silvery hubcaps.

"The '74 Beetle was Volkswagen's highest production model of all time, so parts aren't a problem," Robin tells them.

"Why not a Tesla?" asks Louis. "Your family could afford one of those, right? That Corvette you drive is worth a ton."

Their auto teacher saunters into the warehouse. "What's up, people?"

"Robin's thinking of restoring a '74 Beetle," Darnell says.

Mr. Grant shakes his head. "That's a HUGE project. You're going to be cutting metal, sourcing replacement parts, doing welding, hammer and dolly work, moving steel. Plus, mechanical and electrical work. Oh, and paint. Maybe even upholstery."

"Sounds like a lot of money," says Louis. "Told you, Robin. Might end up being more expensive than a Tesla in the long run."

"Plus, a lot can go wrong every step of the way," says Mr. Grant. "Use too much heat when you're working on the steel, and you'll warp the panels. Rotten floorboards under the battery tray, rust in the bottom of the A-pillar where it attaches to the channel, rust in wheel wells, badly repaired damage from collisions. Why in the world are you thinking about this car, Robin?"

"I want it," Robin answers, keeping it simple. "I love it."

KAT

INT. MUSEUM OF FINE ARTS, BOSTON—DAY

Kat's next "field trip" is to the Museum of Fine Arts, where Grandma Vee buys postcards of eight reproductions and waits in the café for Kat to track down the real pieces and write her responses to them on the postcards. When Kat gets back, she's not at all surprised to find Grandma Vee chatting with the barista, who has to wipe away tears before shaking Kat's hand.

"Making strangers cry again, Grandma Vee?" Kat asks as the woman turns away to fill their order.

"Nobody's a stranger after they cry. Let's see those post-cards."

"I never cry," Kat says, handing them over.

Grandma Vee gives her a side-eye.

"Or at least I never used to. Before I met you."

"Tears are from God, Kat," Grandma Vee says. "When the time's right—even if you do cry some more—you might want to share your journey with a couple of friends. Gracie's a quality girl. And you and Robin could be a great encouragement to each other. He's had his losses, too."

"Maybe." *And maybe not.* Telling a grandmother is one thing, but letting people her own age know about her surrender? That demographic's never been a safe place to hold Kat's secrets.

Grandma Vee's reading Kat's three-line response to artist Kara Walker's mural *The Rich Soil Down There*. That was a tough one for Kat, but she stayed in front of it for a long time, taking the story in. *Women carrying women who don't see them,* she wrote. *Devil man reaches to grab, take, pillage, loot. Suffering of my sisters, building the American South.*

"Take me to see this one, Kat," Grandma Vee says, looking up. "You really think I make people cry?"

"You're a master."

"I'm not sure that's such a gift."

"If I put you in a superhero movie, I'd name you something mystical like 'Keeper of the Inner Springs.'"

This makes Grandma Vee chuckle. "Makes me sound like a mattress seller."

Kat giggles, too. "Your character could sell *really* uncomfortable mattresses. Anyone who sleeps on one starts sobbing."

Grandma Vee's guffawing now. "Bedbugs no charge," she says, between gasps.

The barista comes up with their cappuccinos, and even though she's not in on the joke, she starts laughing, too.

ROBIN

Mike sells Robin the Beetle for what it will cost to transport it to the Thornton house.

"Doesn't have too many working parts left, anyway," he says. "I haven't had the heart to send it to the dump. It used to be a beautiful car. You sure you want it now, before your trip?"

"Send it over in a few days. Thanks, Mike."

Robin stops by the grocery store after work. He knows how to cook only one meal: spaghetti with sauce from a jar. Garlic bread. And a Caesar salad for dummies that comes with all the ingredients. He also buys a gift bag and tissue paper.

Mom comes home first. "Yum," she says, lifting the lid off the skillet where the sauce is simmering. "This is just what I need. I'm going to shower and wash the court germs away. Dad just texted; he's at the station now."

Robin sets the round teak table in the dining room with heirloom china, crystal candlestick holders, linen napkins.

Dad comes home and raises his eyebrows. "Fancy. Reminds me of my grandmother. We always ate here when she was in charge. More big news to tell us?"

"I guess you could say that. Plus, I just wanted to . . . say thanks, I guess. With graduation coming and all."

"You're growing up, kiddo."

Dad adds wineglasses to his and Mom's settings and turns on some jazz. Mom comes down, smelling like lavender soap, and she and Dad kiss. Robin watches them as he tosses the salad. His parents have provided a great life for him—happy home, everything he needed materially, unconditional love, a church family that supports and adores him. He's grateful for all that. He loves them. And he still wants to search. For him, it's a both-and, not an either-or.

He loads up their plates, and Mom says grace. Dad takes a big bite of spaghetti and fakes a bad Italian accent. "Tastes a-just-a like-a they useta make-a in the old country."

Mom's one-quarter Italian. "Ugh! Stop," she says, but Robin can tell she's trying not to smile.

Robin takes the gift bag from under the table and hands it to his father.

"For me?" Dad tugs out the tissue and gapes at the keys to the Corvette.

"I bought another car today, and I want you to drive the Corvette. It's your dream car, right?" *Not mine*, he adds silently.

"Wait . . . really?" For a second, Dad looks exactly like the sixteen-year-old version of himself grinning in the frame on the grand piano. "What do you think, Marjorie?"

"You bought a new car, Robin?" Mom asks.

"Sort of. It's a fixer-upper, a VW Bug. Mike's giving it to me for the cost of delivery. I'll do most of the labor myself, if I can, and find cheap parts online."

His parents exchange looks.

"Sounds like something you're looking forward to," Dad

says. "I have to admit, I'm going to love driving that Corvette to work. You can borrow it back any time you want."

"It's all yours, Dad."

"Thanks, Robin. Thanks."

"I'm the one who's grateful." He clears his throat and sits up. "But there's something else I need to say. I want to withdraw my college applications. I'd like to take a gap year when I get back from India. I'll work full-time at Mike's, take a few classes at the community college, and figure out if a four-year school is for me." He takes a deep breath. "Sound okay?"

His parents are looking at him as though he's a shape-shifter. Has he sent them into shock by revealing too many "wants" at once?

"Hear that, Marjorie?" his father finally says. "Robin wants to take a gap year."

"Yes, and maybe then he'll choose to go to college," she retorts.

That's the fighting spirit Robin knows and loves.

KAT

INT. GRANDMA VEE'S APARTMENT—NIGHT

Late at night, after her homework's all done, with the Canary's yellow dress and ribbon flying through her mind, Kat is still trying to figure out her Plan A. It feels closer now. At small group, they've been watching videos about the global problem of trafficking, Bengali culture, modern-day Kolkata, India's history. Kat's been researching all that on her own, too. But she also asked PG for the password to the Bengali Emancipation Society film they saw that day at church, and now she watches it again. And again.

During her third viewing, an idea starts to form in Kat's mind.

Do girls know much about jiu-jitsu in India?

Saundra says that self-defense is one of the best ways to empower young women, she remembers, after her fourth time through.

Maybe, Kat thinks after her fifth replay, Plan A can be to teach this brave girl in the film a few BJJ moves.

She actually gets goose bumps thinking about it.

But she'll have to be flexible.

Quick-thinking.

Ready to move to a Plan B in an instant, if need be.

She has no idea if the Bengali Emancipation Society will let her meet the girls, let alone try to teach a martial art to them.

For now, as always in a solo match, she keeps Plan A to herself.

ROBIN

INT. ROBIN'S BEDROOM—NIGHT

After Mike has the Volkswagen towed over, Robin posts a picture of his new-old car in his feed. He captions it with *Goodbye, Corvette. Hello, Bug.*

The first response comes from @dark*knight_7. *You traded your sweet ride for this hunk of junk?!? Huge mistake.*

Robin takes a moment to figure out what he's feeling. There it is again. Anger. What right does Brian have to demean his decision, and publicly? He feels like swearing and yelling, but instead he's simmering it down to a moderated-for-other-eyes reply—*Wait until you see it on the road before you judge . . . I can school you about cars*—when he notices the comment's gone.

He tries to go to Brian's home page, and sees the small lock symbol that indicates a private account.

He checks Brian's other social media accounts, one by one. *This user has blocked you.*

You are not allowed to send a message to this account.

He tries the online games they play together. No access. It's like @dark*knight_7 has disappeared from the virtual world. At least *Robin's* virtual world.

Robin tries sending the carefully worded reply by text message. He sends it ten times over ten minutes. No DELIVERED or READ notifications show up there, either.

Last resort: He calls.

Goes straight to voice mail.

@boy*wonder_7's been deleted.

INT. METROWEST PRESBYTERIAN CHURCH—DAY

It gets worse over the next few weeks. Not only has Brian stopped coming to small group, he isn't answering anybody's texts or calls, not even PG's. Robin tells himself not to worry, not to miss him, but he can't help it. He definitely doesn't want to go back to old patterns, but can't they make some tweaks to the friendship and start again?

On Sundays, Robin keeps an eye on the door. Brian's stepdad and mother sit in their usual pew. But Brian never walks in.

This is how little kids handle conflict, Robin thinks. But if Brian's the one acting like a child, why is Robin the one who feels like crying?

KAT

EXT. BOSTON—DAY

Winter finally gives way to spring, and Grandma Vee pulls on a cardigan instead of her down coat. She takes Kat to Fenway to watch a baseball game, where the peanut vendor tosses them a bag for free and shouts, "Love you, Ms. Vee! Can't join you for Easter this year—I have a girlfriend now!"

Grandma Vee gives him a thumbs-up, but the Sox lose and she grouses on the T about the "lack of depth in the pitching this year," or something like that.

Their next field trip is a walk along the Boston Women's Heritage Trail. Slowly, because Grandma Vee's rattling the walker across cobblestones, and also because Kat keeps stopping to admire a burst of daffodils or a forsythia bush in bloom. Yellow is exploding in Boston's gardens, and to Kat the whole city looks like someone's colorizing a black-and-white film.

"Boston flowers arrive in a parade," Grandma Vee tells her. "First, the whites of crocuses and snowdrops. Then these beautiful yellows. Just wait for the pinks and purples of lilacs. Oh, the smell! There's nothing like it. Makes me feel like I'm sixteen again."

"Do you mind if I ask how old you are?" Kat asks as they

leave the statehouse and start climbing the hills around Beacon Street.

"On the inside or out? Lilacs will tell you my soul's the same age as you are. But my body's saying, 'Viola, you're turning eighty-four this year, my dear.'"

Kat can't believe it. She's spry, this Ibis. Pushing her walker, she tells stories about Rebecca Lee Crumpler, the first black woman doctor, the poet Phillis Wheatley, and Harriet Tubman, who was a regular visitor to Boston. As she listens to Grandma Vee, Kat can almost see shadowy feline figures prowling along these winding, narrow streets.

INT. METROWEST PRESBYTERIAN CHURCH SANCTUARY—DAY

Kat and Grandma Vee go to an extra service on Good Friday, and Kat hears how the Sparrow died. She knows the story, but it hits her this year. The music is somber, the service ends in silence, and Kat leaves feeling tired and drained.

But on Easter Sunday, fragrant white lilies are everywhere in the church, and Grandma Vee, Martin, and the rest of the choir belt out a song of victory.

As Kat listens, she feels exactly like she does after a win and the referee hoists her wrist up in the air. *Good for you, Sparrow*, she thinks. *You stayed on the mat. You kept fighting.*

ROBIN

INT./EXT. METROWEST PRESBYTERIAN CHURCH—DAY

Ms. Vee approaches Brian's mom after the service. About ten people follow her, including Robin and his parents, Ash, Martin, PG, and even Kat.

"Where's that boy of yours been, Emma?" Ms. Vee asks gently. "Is he coming back soon?"

Brian's mother shakes her head. "I don't think so, Ms. Vee. Goodbyes are hard for Brian. He might be making an early break so it's easier to leave for college."

He's not the only one who hates goodbyes, Robin thinks.

"Oh, dear," says Ms. Vee. "Do you mind if we pray for him? And you?"

"I'd love that," says Brian's mother.

As his parents and friends gather around Brian's mother and stepdad, Robin slips out of the church.

KAT

Kat stands at a distance, watching people pray for the Alsatian. Is his mother crying? That Grandma Vee—she really does make *everyone* cry. Is Kat supposed to join them? She has no idea how to pray, so she stays out of the circle.

When they're done, Robin's mother approaches Kat. "So glad you're coming to our house for brunch. Your grandma Vee always joins us on Easter Sunday."

This tall, elegant blonde woman is a replica of the SUV-driving moms at Sanger, but this one's got a brown son. Somehow, that makes Kat feel differently toward her. "I'm looking forward to it, Mrs. Thornton."

ROBIN

EXT. METROWEST PRESBYTERIAN CHURCH—DAY

Robin sits on the bench near the grass that faces the church building. Easter Sunday came later than usual this year, and tall orange tulips are already making an appearance in the flower beds tended by the ladies' aid. On the sun-dappled lawn behind him, smaller versions of Brian and Ash and Martin and Robin played tag as soon as the service was over.

When did he become Brian's sidekick instead of his friend? It must have happened in middle school—right when Brian's dad took off—because by the time high school started, they'd already shifted into their new roles.

PG comes out of the church and sits next to Robin. "Friendships change, Robin. Nothing you can do about that."

Robin sighs. "Maybe I shouldn't have corrected him that day. Not in front of all you, anyway." He figured out what he'd been feeling *after* he'd acted out the anger. Not the best sequence, maybe.

"It's okay to be passionate. Sometimes you have to overturn tables, right? A wise man texted me that once."

Robin smiles. "PG—" he says. And then hesitates. His parents are starting to worry about the details of his search. What if it requires a lot of time, or he needs to take a journey outside Kolkata to follow a lead? Will the Indian staff who work for the Bengali Emancipation Society support him? Mom and Dad have asked him to tell PG the truth, and he knows he has to do that before they leave for India.

PG's waiting without a word.

"PG—" Robin starts again. And stops.

"Still here," says PG. "Go on."

Big breath. You can do this. "Well, I haven't been totally honest with you. I—I'm excited to go back to Kolkata with you. But . . . I also want to search for my . . . story." He can't bring himself to say the word *mother*. It makes the stakes seem so much higher. "I mean, I want to serve the Bengali Emancipation Society, but I hope they'll give me time to follow up on any leads. You know, stuff that I might want to do after I open my file at the orphanage."

"I'm glad you told me," PG says. "I guessed that was going on. Now I can check off 'have big talk with Robin about his motives' on my to-do list. Have you told your parents this?"

"Of course. They even hired a reunion counselor to help me get ready."

"That's good." And then it's PG's turn to hesitate. He puts his hand on Robin's shoulder. "I've heard that searches don't always work out. Don't let your hopes get too high, buddy."

Too late for that, Robin thinks. "Thanks, PG. And can you keep this between the two of us for now? I don't want the whole church asking questions. I know they love me, but—"

"Yeah, they get in our business, don't they? I've stopped

counting the number of times people have tried to fix me up.
No worries, Robin. I'll tell Arjun to keep it confidential over
there as well. And if you need my help for anything, just ask."

KAT

INT. MRS. THORNTON'S CAR—DAY—TRAVELING

Robin and Kat sit in the back seat with Grandma Vee squished between them. An old man is riding with Robin's father. Actually, it's vice versa, because Mr. Thornton lets his guest take the wheel of his fancy red sports car.

"Isn't that a bit fast?" Grandma Vee asks Mrs. Thornton as the red car takes off, tires shrieking as it turns the corner.

Mrs. Thornton follows at a more sedate pace. "The house is only three miles away. What can happen in three miles?"

"Good job not worrying, Mom," Robin says, patting his mother's shoulder.

As Kat fights through a wave of missing her own mother, Mom texts right at that moment. *Happy Easter, sweetheart. Going to church with Saundra. Wish you were here.*

Sure you do, Kat thinks. She doesn't text back, but that doesn't stop her mother.

158 days till you're home. I'm checking them off on my calendar app.

Kat sighs. After all, it is Easter Sunday. *Happy Easter, Mom,* she texts, and waits for the burst of joyful emojis to appear. Sure enough, they do—six dancing ladies in red dresses, fifteen pairs of applauding hands, and ten yellow faces with hearts for eyes.

"I think this is the twelfth year in a row I've joined you Thorntons for Easter brunch," Grandma Vee is saying. "Last year Dylan came, but this year he's going to his new girl-friend's house."

"Oh, right, that nice kid who works at Fenway," Mrs. Thornton says. "I love having you, Ms. Vee. It makes us feel like we have family around. That's what happens to an only child who marries an only child, Kat."

She parks the car along a tree-lined street full of big houses, right behind the red sports car. The old man is climbing slowly out of the driver's seat. Robin's father is standing on the sidewalk, mopping his face with a handkerchief.

"We made it," Mr. Thornton tells them. "Barely."

While he unloads Grandma Vee's walker from the trunk, and Robin's mom helps Grandma Vee out of the back seat, Kat gazes up at a three-story mansion set behind a wide lawn and tall, strong trees. Looks like a movie set.

She turns to Bird Boy. "They might call you Robin, but you're actually Bruce Wayne."

"Want to see the Batmobile?"

She hesitates. She hasn't been alone with anyone male since the stairwell. But Bird Boy's so completely avian that after only a short time, to her eyes he's become Robin first and a dude second. A distant second, in fact.

She follows him into the garage and looks around. He's standing in front of a rusting piece of machinery that might have been a car once. Kat can't even tell what color it is.

Robin's gazing at it with adoring eyes. "Isn't she gorgeous? They used to call these 'Sun Bugs' back in the day. I'm thinking

117

of restoring her all the way—nut-brown sports seats with matching panels and carpeting, wood-finish dashboard, sports GT wheels, and a sunroof with a wind reflector. Plus, that beautiful metallic beige exterior."

Sounds like another language to Kat. "Will you be able to drive it—I mean *her*—before we leave for India?"

"No way. It's going to take a while to get the engine running again. And I'll start with that first. I'm waiting on some parts." His phone makes a harp sound and he glances at it. "Gracie's back from Mass and now she's at some big feast with all her relatives. I'll tell her you're here."

Maybe you'd better not. "Hey, give me her number, will you? I'd like to text her, too."

He reads it out, picks up a wrench, and disappears behind the raised hood of the car.

Hey, Gracie. Kat here. I'm at the Thorntons', watching Robin make out with his new girlfriend.

She waits. Counts the beats. After five of them, an answer appears in all caps: *WHAT GIRLFRIEND?*

Kat walks around to the side of the car, snaps a photo of Robin with his head under the hood, and sends it.

Two beats later: *Oh.*

He calls it a "her." Can you believe it? There's only one girl in the world that's a better fit for him than this one.

One beat later: *Oh?*

You, burro.

Five faces with hearts for eyes whiz in. *I knew it. You do speak Spanish!*

Not really. Just a word or two. Mostly animals.

Wait. Am I that obvious?

Yep. But this kid's too much of a burro to see it. Want me to tell him for you?

Kat, no! I want him to figure out what HE feels about ME. Maybe India will help.

Okay. No worries. I can keep a secret.

Two brown girl faces with hearts for eyes. *Happy Easter, Kat! I'm so glad God brought you here.*

ROBIN

INT. REUNION COUNSELOR'S OFFICE—DAY

"Been watching reunions online?" the counselor asks Robin. She's an adoptee herself, from China, so Robin's not surprised that she guesses how he's been spending some of his free time.

Korea. China. India. Colombia. Vietnam. Guatemala. Doesn't matter where. He streams through dozens and dozens of them, repeating some three or four times, noticing every nonverbal, every stance, who reaches out for whom, who cries first, how long they hold each other.

"Yep," he answers. "They're sort of addictive."

"I know," she says. "But it's the fairy-tale endings that get a lot of views. That's not usually how most searches end. Are you . . . mentally ready for that possibility, Robin?"

"Er . . . I'm trying to be," Robin says. *That's why I'm here*, he thinks. So far, though, hope won't let him imagine any other scenario than a joy-filled embrace.

She slides a couple of pamphlets over her desk. "Here are some recommendations for post-search counselors. In any case, you'll need some practical preparation, too."

Robin takes notes as she tells him to make copies of documents, prepare questions in advance that won't get his first mother in trouble, and keep a first meeting with any first relatives short and simple.

"If there is a first meeting," she adds, looking at him closely. "You're younger than most of us who search. You have to moderate your hopes, I'm afraid. And I always recommend traveling with a couple of people who can support you."

Robin figures he has the latter with PG and Gracie. About the hope moderation, he isn't so sure.

KAT

EXT. BOSTON AREA—DAY

Patriots' Day in Massachusetts is—as always, Kat discovers—the third Monday in April, and now a few pink trees are starting to bloom. Grandma Vee and Kat get up early and take a cab to Lexington Square, where a bunch of zealous volunteers reenact "the shot heard round the world."

As cannons explode, muskets shoot, and bodies topple everywhere around the grass, Kat glances at her companion. Saundra told her Grandma Vee experienced several military coups in Sierra Leone before coming to Boston. Is this bringing back bad memories? But the old woman's expression is as composed as ever.

Later that morning, they head to the Boston Marathon. As usual, Grandma Vee finds out the driver's name, and Mahmoud drops them off as close to "Heartbreak Hill" as he can manage through all the roadblocks.

"This is mile twenty," Grandma Vee tells Kat once they've joined the spectators along Commonwealth Avenue. "A huge uphill near the end of a grueling race. Wheelchair racers come first. Watch what happens."

Kat peers down the road, which is lined with hordes of fans, vendors, race officials, and volunteers handing out water bottles. In the distance, way down the hill, she glimpses a small, bent figure on wheels moving slowly but coming toward them. The people watching at the bottom of the incline break into a huge roar.

Grandma Vee clutches Kat's arm. "Listen."

JA-SON! JA-SON! JA-SON! All along the uphill part of the race route, different portions of the crowd start chanting for the lead wheelchair racer as soon as he reaches them.

How do they know his name? Kat wonders. As he nears and passes them, she sees that it's written in big letters on two signs—one on the front of his shirt and one on the back of his chair. Drenched in sweat, muscled arms straining, he wheels his chair toward the crest of the hill. The entire way, the crowd doesn't stop chanting his name.

Grandma Vee joins in. Kat can't help it; she does, too.

JA-SON! JA-SON!

This solitary athlete is suddenly everybody's friend, or like a joint first cousin. They're infusing him with energy. The spectators feel closer to each other because they're all rooting so hard for him.

When he finally crests the hill and starts soaring down the other side, Kat can hear people at the top explode into a roar.

"Now THAT's what you need on Heartbreak Hill," Grandma Vee tells Kat, nearly breathless from shouting. "A big crowd of folks, cheering for you by name."

Heads around them swivel to root for the next racer, who's just appearing at the bottom of the hill now. The chanting down there begins: *DE-VON! DE-VON! DE-VON!*

ROBIN

INT. METROWEST PRESBYTERIAN CHURCH
YOUTH ROOM—NIGHT

"You three going to Kolkata need to sign these code of conduct contracts," PG says, handing printed documents and pens to Robin, Kat, and Gracie.

Robin can tell PG's getting anxious about how little time they have left to get prepared, especially for the "service" part of the trip. He's made them watch dozens of videos and read countless articles. The congregation has come through with the money for plane tickets, as well as the small stipend they'll give their host families for room and board while they're in Kolkata. The money they've raised will also cover the cost of a Bangla language tutor for Robin, Kat, and Gracie. Now, with only a couple of weeks left before departure, PG is homing in on expectations about behavior.

Martin looks over Robin's shoulder; Ash is reading Gracie's contract. Two out of the three not-going-to-India youth group members are still coming on Thursdays even though the meetings are so India-focused. Brian, even now, is still the Invisible Man.

Robin starts reading the contract PG's asking him to sign.

#1: I will wear modest, culturally appropriate clothing.

"What does 'inappropriate' mean, PG?" Martin asks.

"What does 'modest' mean?" Gracie looks worried.

#2: I will not drink, smoke, or use drugs.

"Come on, PG, what's wrong with smoking?" Ash asks.

PG rolls his eyes and doesn't answer.

#3: I will not act inappropriately or flirtatiously with any of the Indian staff members or the clients they serve.

"*That's* a no-brainer," says Kat.

#4: I will serve the organization with humility, doing anything they ask, no matter how menial the task.

"Sounds like you're joining the Scouts," says Martin.

#5: I will not post or send any photographs while in Kolkata.

Robin raises his eyebrows. "What? How are we supposed to share what's going on with Martin and Ash? And all the people supporting us?" *Including my parents,* he thinks. He's sure his mother's expecting a steady, daily stream of photos and texts.

"We'll be able to send emails from an office computer," says PG. "And maybe call once a week or so from the office phone, or a borrowed mobile. But we'll have to hand over our own smartphones to be stored in a safe during the ten weeks. It's a security measure for all visitors from overseas."

The room explodes in protest.

"That's unrealistic, PG," Ash says. "We're teens, remember?"

Martin: "Ten weeks without a phone? I'd be brain-dead by August."

Kat: "My mother's not going to like *that* rule at all."

"I need to be available to my parents around the clock, PG," Gracie says. "Mom's not due until September, but what if something happens while I'm gone?"

Robin doesn't say anything. It'll be kind of a relief not to have his phone during his search. More privacy. Plus, it gives him the perfect excuse not to share round-the-clock details with Mom.

PG's got his best unyielding expression in place. "Everyone needs to use email or call during set hours if they want to talk to you. They'll have Arjun's number for emergencies. The Society simply can't risk photos or social media posts that might compromise the safety of their rescued children. Not to mention the police who work with them, putting their lives on the line to battle perps. That's the word for perpetrators in the crime-fighting world, in case you didn't know."

"We're not stupid, PG," Martin says. "We know what a 'perp' is."

"And how to turn off location information on our posts," adds Ash.

"Arjun invited us because he trusts me," PG says sternly. "He doesn't want to inflict damage on kids who have already been abused. This invitation is a privilege. If we do any 'acts of service' at all, they'll be what the Bengali Emancipation Society asks us to do. Otherwise, we're just learners, not doers."

Not much we can say after that, Robin thinks. He, Gracie, and Kat all sign the code of conduct contracts and hand them to PG.

KAT

"Now, about housing," says PG. "I'll be staying in faculty housing at the Bible college. But the three of you will be with vetted host families who've been cleared to house volunteers from overseas. Your parents signed the housing consent forms, I hope?"

Kat swallows. Mom signed hers, but sent it along with an emailed suggestion. *What do you think about asking to be assigned to live with a woman, Kat? I'll leave it up to you, but I'm wondering if being in a house or apartment with men around might be tough for you to handle. Maybe you should let this youth pastor know something about what happened here in Oakland. Want me to call him? Or we could ask Ms. Jones to talk to him.*

No, Mom, Kat replied. *I've got this.*

I'm starting to hate that mantra, Mom emailed back. *Tell him, Kat, please.*

But PG might ask questions, and Kat doesn't want anyone knowing what happened to her. Apart from Grandma Vee, that is. If her Indian host family includes men, she'll just have to power through it. It's only ten weeks.

Besides, she's feeling a little less weird these days. Look at her now, sitting in this circle of couches and armchairs with Robin, PG, and Martin. Okay, so they're not touching her and she always stays close to Gracie and Ash, but she's interacting with all of them like a normal person, right?

Besides, after that cry-fest with Grandma Vee, the nightmares disappeared. She hasn't thought about the Wolf for weeks. Now, when she wakes up in the middle of the night, she makes plans about the summer ahead instead of the past—envisioning how she's going to teach BJJ moves to that Canary.

She hands over her signed housing release form to PG without a word.

ROBIN

PG gives them more pieces of paper, this time with envelopes. At the top of the page Robin reads the words: *On this service trip, I hope to . . .* The rest of the page is blank apart from *#1* and *#2* in PG's handwriting.

"Take this with you to a corner of the room and jot down two hopes you have for the time in India," PG says. "This is private. None of us will see it, so I want you to be completely honest. Fold the paper, put it back in the envelope, and seal it. I'll give them back to you for reflection after we return."

The three India-goers disperse.

Robin hesitates before starting to write. Nobody's going to see this but him, right? *Honest*, PG said. Okay. He picks up the pen and writes the truth.

#1: I hope to . . . find my first mother

#2: I hope to . . . help my first mother.

He's the first to return to the circle carrying his sealed envelope; Gracie and Kat follow a minute or two later.

"I feel so left out by this exercise," says Martin.

"Me, too," adds Ash. "What are you guys going to do without us?"

"Not have half as much fun," says Gracie. "Hey, you guys coming over tomorrow?"

"I may or may not have a date," PG says, starting to pack up his notes and papers.

Everyone ignores him; he never joins them for pizza and movie nights.

"I'm in," says Martin.

"Me, too," says Robin.

"I'll be there," says Ash. "Could be our last movie night for a while."

Gracie turns to Kat. "What about you?"

"I'm . . . not sure," answers Kat. "I might have an assignment to finish."

"On Friday night?" asks Robin. "Come on, Kat. Join us. We can watch something from the DC universe, right, Gracie?"

"Definitely," says Gracie.

Robin watches Kat glance around at their waiting faces.

"Okay," she says. "I'll come."

KAT

INT. RIVERA HOUSE, OUTSKIRTS OF BOSTON—NIGHT

Kat's standing on the threshold of the Riveras' house, holding a plate of homemade fritters that Grandma Vee sent along as a gift. She reads the sign on the front door: PLEASE DON'T KNOCK OR RING BELL, BABIES SLEEPING. Should she walk in? It feels rude, but the sign's pretty clear.

The door flies open before she can decide what to do. Gracie's standing there, smiling. "Come in! Mamá, meet my friend Kat."

It's the first time since grade school that Kat's been introduced to anybody's parent with that modifier before her name. It makes Kat feel like she's been invited into a double-Dutch game or to play hopscotch.

A pregnant woman joins Gracie at the door. On her face is an older but just as warm replica of her daughter's smile. She holds out her hand. "Bienvenida, Kat."

Kat manages to recall the right phrase from her Spanish textbook: "Con mucho gusto," she says, handing the fritters to Gracie to shake Mrs. Rivera's hand.

"You know what? Forget the handshake. How about a hug instead?" Without waiting for Kat to answer, Gracie's mother enfolds her into a Rivera embrace—so close that Kat can almost feel the baby's heartbeat against her own belly. After a few seconds, she lets go. "Maybe I should call your mother and get some tips about how to send a child to a faraway place. Gracie's never been away from me, her whole life."

Neither had I, thinks Kat. "It's hard at first," she says.

Gracie flexes her non-fritter-holding arm. Nothing changes there as far as Kat can tell. "Soy fuerte, Mamá."

Her mother sighs. "I'm glad you'll be there to take care of each other. And my querido Robin, too. Pizza's in the basement. Hand over that plate, Gracie. Ms. Vee's fritters are exactly what this mamita is craving." She rubs her swollen stomach in a circular motion. *Did Mom do that to me sixteen-plus years ago?* Kat wonders.

ROBIN

Martin helps himself to a piece of pizza. "This is truly the life. I might have to drive up from Brown on Fridays."

Robin knows he isn't joking. Coming here has always felt like one of the most relaxing ways to end the week. Only two things feel different about tonight: the absence of Brian and the presence of Kat.

"What do you guys want to watch?" Gracie asks.

"How about the stand-up comedian everyone's been talking about?" Ash suggests. "I can't pronounce his name, but you know who I mean. He's Indian, like you, Robin."

"Yeah, I hear he's hilarious," Martin says.

"No, thanks," Robin says. He's seen the preview. Another nerdy, funny desi guy. *I'd like to see one South Asian badass take down villains*, he thinks. *Is that too much to ask?*

"This always happens," Gracie says. "It takes us forever to agree on something. You choose, Kat. I did promise you something from Robin's comic book world, right?"

"How about the original Wonder Woman movie?" Kat says. "I haven't seen that one in forever."

Vintage Cathy Lee Crosby is as sexy as ever in a red vest, blue tights, black boots, golden bangles, and matching gold belt. Weirdly, Kat knows most of the lines by heart and starts saying them out loud. Of course, so does Robin. They start reciting them together.

He can't help noticing how much Kat has changed in the weeks since she arrived. She reaches for a second slice of pizza without asking. She lets the dimple run wild, without any restraint whatsoever. It's like her heart isn't stiff-arming them anymore.

When the movie's over, nobody seems to want to leave. Gracie flips through more free movie choices.

"Hey, it's the original Superman movie!" Robin says.

"From 1978," Kat says. "Best version ever."

"Christopher Reeve as Clark Kent," he says. "Marlon Brando as Superman's father."

"Let's watch it on mute so these two don't start their chorus again," Martin says.

It's been a while since Robin's seen this movie. The last time was with Brian, in the fifth grade.

"Robin, have you heard from Brian?" Gracie asks, reading his mind as usual. Robin can tell she's trying to keep her voice light.

"Nope. It's like I don't exist for him anymore."

"He's ignoring me, too," Ash says. "It's not just you."

"His mom thinks he's acting out because of his dad leaving," Martin tells Gracie.

"I know," she says. "Ash told me."

"Maybe his mother's right," Martin says. "My parents are divorced, but my dad didn't *dump* me like Brian's did."

"Getting dumped by your parents doesn't give you permission to dump other people," Robin says.

"Well, you don't know how that feels, look at your perfect life—" Martin stops suddenly at the sight of Robin's face. "Sorry. It's weird, but I forget you're adopted sometimes. The three of you fit together in my mind like P, B, and J."

We do and we don't, Robin thinks.

"Anyway, perfect timing," Ash says, pointing to the screen, where Jor-El is making a starry crystal rocket ship to send his baby off to earth. "Check it out—Superman's adopted."

"He's not alone," Kat says quickly. "Spider-Man, too."

"Gambit," Robin responds.

She doesn't miss a beat. "Green Lantern."

"Batgirl. After the 1985 reboot."

As the two of them battle it out, Martin, Gracie, and Ash swivel their heads back and forth like spectators at a tennis match.

"Beast Boy," Kat says.

"Hellboy."

"Iron Man."

Wow, she's quick. Robin takes a moment. And then it dawns on him: "Robin."

"Okay, okay," Martin says. "You'll probably go on for another hour if we let you. Turn the volume up a bit, Gracie."

But on-screen, Jor-El and Lara are putting Kal-El in the spaceship and sending him off just before planet Krypton explodes. For some reason, this makes Gracie turn off the movie altogether. There's an awkward silence.

"Superhero birth parents usually don't get much screen time," Robin says.

He takes one of Mom's big inhales. He's told his parents, the counselor, and PG, but he hasn't talked about his search with anyone else. Not even Gracie. It feels like every time he voices his desire, it gets more intense.

But these are his friends.

They care.

He blurts out the truth: "I'm going to try to find my first mother." And then: "I'm not sharing this with everybody, though. Just my parents, PG, and you guys."

Gracie reaches over and squeezes his hand. Nobody else responds.

"Are you going to look for your father, too?" Ash asks, after a while. "I mean, your 'first' father?"

"Not sure. Finding *her* seems more urgent to me for some reason. Maybe . . . because she got pregnant and he didn't?"

Kat suddenly pulls out her phone and hands it to Robin. "Here's a picture of *my* mother. Having me was way harder on her than it was on the man who dumped both of us."

The photo on Kat's phone is of her standing next to a short, smiling white woman with an upper-arm tattoo—Robin thinks it's of a panther—and a third of her hair dyed pink. Looks to him like this person could be Ash's sister instead of Kat's mom. Which means Kat's father—whoever he is— certainly isn't white.

"May I see, too?" Gracie asks.

Kat nods, and Robin hands Gracie the phone.

"She's as pretty as you are, Kat," Gracie says, and passes the photo to Martin.

"She looks so young!" Martin says.

"She was sixteen when she had me. She's thirty-two now."

Martin hands the phone to Ash. "Is she coming to visit?"

"Nope," Kat says. "We spent all our savings on my ticket to Boston."

Robin's shocked. She's sharing so much—about her mom, and that her birth father didn't want to raise her, and now that her family's broke.

Ash stares at the phone for a few seconds. "I'm guessing your father was black?"

"Maybe," says Kat. "He *was* dark-skinned, at least. Mom told me. They met at a party. Didn't talk much, just . . . Anyway, a few months later, she called him and they did talk. Once. She told him she was having me and he told her good luck."

Again, nobody says anything.

"I'd want to track him down if I were you," Ash says. "Just to punch him. Hard."

"Ashhhhleeeeey, I AM your father." Martin's bad Darth Vader imitation draws a halfhearted air punch from Ash, which he successfully avoids.

"Luke Skywalker," Kat says to Robin.

"Leia Organa," he answers right away.

"Anakin Skywalker."

Martin rolls his eyes. "Okay, already! Every superhero since the dawn of time was adopted. We get it."

KAT

When Robin shares that he's going to search for his mother, Kat instantly thinks of Grandma Vee and the Boston Marathon. Here he is, inviting Kat to join his cheering squad. She's only known him for such a short time.

I'm in, Kat thinks, even though she doesn't fully get why he wants to push himself up this Heartbreak Hill. She's seen his parents and their house. Kid's got a good gig going there. When she pulls out her phone to show him Mom's photo, part of her wants to remind him that *not* finding your blood relatives could be okay, too.

Take the man who got her mom pregnant, for instance. Kat's never felt like she's missing something without him around. But maybe things are different when you lose the person who carried you inside her body. Kat had watched the vet at the zoo bottle-feed a pair of abandoned baby meerkats, tucking them under her armpits to keep them warm. *All newborns need their mothers*, the vet had said.

Thank goodness Kat never lost hers. When Mary King was a pregnant sixteen-year-old and had to figure out a way to take care of both of them, she managed it. Found her way to a transition home in East Oakland. Fed them both with WIC and EBT—*welfare*, Sanger students called it—until she got her first decent job with wages that could cover rent *and* food.

Kat glances at her mother's photo again. Robin's taken the remote from Gracie's hand and restarted the movie. On-screen, Superman is chasing after a missile, grabbing it, and heaving it into outer space. Fighting for good. Saving life. Defending the underdog.

ROBIN

EXT. METROWEST HIGH SCHOOL
STADIUM—DAY

Robin is squirming and sweating on a hard, plastic fold-out chair in the *T* row of Metrowest High School graduates. Somewhere in the bleachers his parents are ready to take photos and videos to send to his grandparents, but they'll have to wait to capture their son's moment in the limelight.

First on the program is awards. Brian—who's still completely ignoring Robin and Martin—wins an athletic award. Martin goes up multiple times for academic honors. Robin knows his name will be called only once, when it's time to get his diploma.

How am I feeling about that? he asks himself. His answer comes quickly—the lack of recognition from the school doesn't sting one bit. All he can come up with is relief. Has he ever really been himself in high school? Maybe in auto shop, but in other places students like him don't get noticed much. He's never gotten in trouble, managed to scrape by in his classes—mostly thanks to Martin—and once overheard a non-auto-shop teacher saying, "that Thornton kid isn't much of a joiner."

Maybe not at Metrowest High, Robin thinks. But he had his after-school job at Mike's and his friends in automotive engineering. He had church and small group. And now, he's leaving for India soon. School isn't supposed to be your whole life, right?

The principal's reached the *M*'s now, and Chitra goes up. She and the other desi seniors went to prom as a group. They invited Robin to join them, but he turned them down. Mom suggested taking Gracie and said she'd cover the costs, but he said no to that, too. Instead, he spent prom night in the garage, where he's been most nights since the Dub came home.

Parts are coming in. He's started rebuilding the engine. They leave in a week, but his car's going to be waiting when he gets back from Kolkata.

That, and a future full of relatives he doesn't know yet.

As he waits for the principal to get through the *R*'s, he notices some of his classmates getting choked up over the end of their four-year stint at Metrowest High. *Am I sad, too?* he wonders. No, he's definitely not sad. When it's finally his turn to walk across the stage and grab the embossed blue folder, Robin feels like pumping his fist in the air and shouting, "FREEDOM!"

KAT

INT. GRANDMA VEE'S APARTMENT—NIGHT

"Straight As, Grandma Vee!" Kat yells down the hall. She's logged in to get her grades after finishing her junior year work ahead of schedule, even in her honors courses.

After the dancing, hugging, and kissing, Grandma Vee asks Kat if they can invite the small group over for a celebratory feast. Kat agrees, and the two of them prepare plantains, greens, fish, and jollof rice for dinner.

Everyone comes. To Kat's surprise, they're even wearing fancy clothes, with Martin and Robin in ties and Gracie and Ash in party dresses. She runs to her room and changes into a long black skirt and heels. Grandma Vee's wearing her Logan Airport outfit, which Kat's realized she saves for the most special of occasions.

Take that, Wolf, Kat thinks as her friends toast her achievement with glasses of sparkling cider.

Grandma Vee's smiling at Robin, her favorite small group member—*her favorite before I came along*, Kat thinks.

"So you're going back to your birthplace, Robin," Grandma Vee says. "That's wonderful. Discovering your culture. We're losing the heritage of our ancestors, all of us in this country. Languages, food, music, clothing from villages around the world melting into separate pots of color—white, brown, black.

People here say I'm black, but that erases the Krio right out of me. Don't know if it's right to be sad over losing the cultures of our ancestors, but I am, somehow."

"Some of us don't forget our ancestors by choice, Ms. Vee," Robin says.

"I know, child. Like those of us who descend from slaves. That's my heritage, too, from back in the day, when my ancestors left Nova Scotia as free people to settle in Freetown. But even so, real people came before us, people who loved and suffered and worked and sinned and repented, all so we could take our first breaths. I'm afraid we'll lose even more if we don't remember them every now and then. It scares me that I'm forgetting how to say some words in Krio, I've been here so long."

"Yeah, all you speak is fluent Boston these days, Ms. Vee," Martin teases. "'How ya doin'?' I've heard you say. And: 'Wicked hot today.'"

Grandma Vee chuckles. "You're right. We can always tell a newcomer by how they say 'Wall-tham,' so I trained Kat first thing."

"Wuh-stah," Kat says, pronouncing "Worcester" perfectly and making everyone laugh.

Grandma Vee makes a move to stand, but Kat jumps up. "Cleaning up is my job, remember?"

Robin follows Kat into the kitchen, carrying a stack of plates.

"You go back and get the rest of the dishes; I'll start washing," she tells him.

He puts the plates down by the sink and goes back out. As

Kat waits for the water to heat up, she thinks about *her* unknown ancestors. This is the first time she's not sure if she agrees with Grandma Vee. For now she's okay with them staying strangers. The past can't matter that much. Sometimes you're better off not being defined by it.

"Do you really care what you are? Culturally, I mean?" she asks when Robin comes back with glasses and silverware.

"I do," he says. "It's a double loss for me. Genes *and* culture."

Kat starts scrubbing the empty stew bowls. "For me, too. Culture from both sides, because Mom's fine just being 'white.' She's never searched for her roots."

"Maybe she should." Robin tosses silverware into the soapy dishpan.

"Why? I love Grandma Vee, Robin, but she's not right about everything. Who cares what village our ancestors are from? What matters is the village we're in now. Like me and my mom and Saundra. And you and your parents, and your church."

"And Grandma Vee, for both of us," he adds, making Kat smile. He picks up the dish towel and starts drying. "Maybe you're right. But other people always ask what I am, and I never know how to answer."

Poor guy, Kat thinks *Nobody around to ask about being a brown kid with white parents.*

"Just do what I do. Say 'I don't know,' look them in the eye, and wait. Most will usually quit right there. You need to make your face look stone-cold, like this." Kat turns to face him with her best scowl in place. It's been a while since she's used it, but it's still operational.

"You're wicked good at that. What do the dumber ones ask next?"

Kat thinks for a second before answering, remembering encounters from the past. "'Why not?' or 'Don't you want to know?'"

"And how do you answer those?"

"With another question. 'Why should I?' works perfectly. Shuts them right up."

"Hmmmm . . . ," says Robin. "I might give that a try. Thanks, Kat."

"No problem."

He flashes Kat a smile and heads out for one last sweep of the dining table.

Kat adds more soap to the brush. *It might have been nice to have someone like Robin around growing up,* she thinks. He'd have had Kat's back, she'd have had his. Maybe she could even have helped him out with girls. *All he needs is confidence. Doesn't he notice how Gracie's eyes track his every move?*

She fishes out a couple of spoons from the dishpan and starts brushing them clean at the same time. Katina King might end up doing a little matchmaking while she's in India.

ROBIN

INT. THORNTON KITCHEN—NIGHT

After they return from a send-off church barbecue for the India team—to which Brian doesn't show up—Robin's parents sit on kitchen stools and begin flipping through his photo album.

On the first page is a picture of a baby so small you can barely see a sleeping face swaddled in a blanket. Tiny feet are poking out in mismatched socks. *Ravi as infant*, the photo is labeled. Robin averts his eyes as his parents study the face of the baby he used to be.

"She must have been in such a bind to give you up," Mom says softly. "I wish we could have helped her. But your file was closed to us."

"I know, Mom."

"*I* wish we could have adopted you right after you came to the orphanage," adds Dad. "Whenever that was, anyway. It makes me so sad you had to wait three years to come home."

"Me, too, Dad."

The next photo is still at the orphanage, but now a brown toddler sitting squished on a sofa between two large smiling white people. This one's just as hard for Robin to look at; he always flinches at the terror that's evident in the eyes of his smaller self.

"You were scared of me," Dad remembers. "I don't think you'd ever seen a white man in real life. It took a lot of peeka-boo games to win your first smile. But oh, was it worth it!"

In another photo, younger versions of his parents are beaming outside an official-looking building in New Delhi. Mom is holding small Robin on her hip; Dad has his arm around them both.

"We were thrilled that day," his mother says now. "We finally got our clearance to take you home with us."

The next one is of the three Thorntons on an airplane. "You were always a good traveler," Dad says. "I can't believe you're heading back there tomorrow, Robin."

But when Robin looks closer, he notices that the eyes in his three-year-old face are open so wide it's a miracle they ever closed again. "I'd better finish packing," he says.

Before he heads upstairs, though, he goes out to the garage, throws a tarp over the Bug, and kisses her goodbye for the summer.

"I'll be back soon," he whispers.

KAT

INT. GRANDMA VEE'S APARTMENT—NIGHT

Abdul, the cab driver who brought Kat here in March, is heading out with a big takeaway tub of jollof rice. When the door closes behind him, Kat turns to Grandma Vee.

"WHY are you so good to strangers? What if one of these weirdos pushes through the door and robs you? I'm leaving tomorrow, and you'll be on your own again. You need to be more careful."

"Careful? Why? I have nothing to lose. And everything to gain." She gives Kat a long, searching look. Then: "Are you packed and ready?"

Kat nods. "I left a few things in a drawer to pick up when I get back. Hope that's okay."

"Of course it is. I'll be counting down the days to see you again. Let's make some tea. I have something I want to share with you."

They sit at the kitchen table with two cups of steaming bush tea. "I married my childhood sweetheart," Grandma Vee says.

Kat's surprised; she thought she was about to hear a pithy saying or two to equip her for her time in India. But she lets Grandma Vee continue without an interruption.

"Theodore was a kind and godly man . . ." The low voice

trails off, and she smiles at her begonias as if she's remembering something sweet. And then her usually proud shoulders sag. The smile disappears. "But we were only married four years. He died in a car accident, and I became a widow. We had one son—"

She stops.

Kat watches in dismay as tears spill over and begin to roll down the old woman's cheeks. If only she were better at comforting. All she's good at is grappling. She spots a box of tissues on the kitchen counter, grabs one, and thrusts it in Grandma Vee's direction. "Don't talk about it if it's too hard."

Grandma Vee takes the tissue, dries her cheeks, and blows her nose. "I don't mind, child. I'm glad to tell someone about them again. They won't be forgotten, not as long as I have breath and listening ears around me."

"I'm listening," Kat says.

"I managed to stay in Freetown and raise our son by the grace of God and the help of a wonderful church. That's when I trained as a teacher. Our son grew up, became a high-ranking politician, fighting for the freedom of our country. He married a beautiful, kind girl. Oh, I was so proud and happy. But then, one day, while I was at school teaching, armed thugs working for the opposition party burst into the house." A few more tears leak out, but Grandma Vee brushes them away.

"What happened?" Kat asks.

"Shot and killed. Both of them." Grandma Vee covers her eyes with her hand.

Crap. "I'm so sorry."

No answer. Kat waits. She knows how hard it is to recover once the tears start coming.

Finally, Grandma Vee swallows hard and removes her hand. "I was shattered by grief. It felt like I had nobody left to love. Saundra's grandfather is my younger brother, so he sponsored my green card application and invited me to the United States."

"What happened after you came here?"

Grandma Vee sits up straight. Takes a swig of tea. "Got my teaching credential all over again. Forgave. Cried. And healed. But it took so many years. Thank God I found my way to that little church you've been visiting. Never would have made it without my friends there."

"And then?"

"I became a Bostonian. A Celtics, Patriots, and Red Sox fan. And then I met you."

As if Kat's the happy ending to her sad, sad story.

"I'd like to hear more about your husband and son if you ever want to share again," Kat says.

Grandma Vee's face lights up. "Really, darling? Oh, that would be marvelous. It helps to talk of them. Theodore Jones was the love of my life. May I show you his photograph now? And one of my beautiful Teddy, and his wife, Haven?"

"Definitely."

Grandma Vee totters out and returns with two framed wedding photos from her room inside the basket of her walker. Kat takes her time studying them. Miss Viola Jones was a stunning bride: tall, queenly, serene. Her groom was dark, strong, and handsome. And their son looked just like him.

"Teddy's wife had dimples," Kat says.

"Deep ones. Like yours."

Kat puts the photos upright on the kitchen table. "I won't forget them."

For some reason, this gets Grandma Vee choked up again. All she manages to do is reach out one hand. Kat takes it, waiting as the older woman struggles to steady her voice. Then: "Kat, I wanted to tell you about my family. But I'd also like to tell you about a practice of mine that helped me survive. May I?"

"Of course." At this point, still holding the shaky, ancient hand in hers, Kat knows she'll agree to anything Grandma Vee asks.

The Ibis looks her right in the eye. "I try to 'Golden Rule' people who *are* around me for the sake of the people who *aren't*. It's a habit I've slowly put into place."

"Golden Rule? What's that?"

"Love your neighbor as yourself," Grandma Vee says. "Jesus said it first. Anyway, there are a few people in my past who are out of reach, for now, at least. I've noticed that when I offer some kindness—something I can't give my dear ones this side of heaven—when I give that instead to another person, it brings a measure of peace to me."

Kat thinks about that for a minute. "Like cooking jollof rice and groundnut stew for taxi drivers? Or taking in a stranger from California?"

"Yes, like that."

"But . . . didn't you get angry when you lost them? At the murderers, I mean? Aren't you *still* angry?"

Grandma Vee releases Kat's hand. "Angry? Oh, yes, I was furious. But anger isn't wrong, child. It's where it takes you that matters. It can lead you back to fight an old enemy, again and again. Or it can move you forward to love a new neighbor. I'm not saying I always choose the second, but I try."

Kat thinks of the Canary in that film PG showed them. Maybe that's why she feels so drawn to that girl in yellow. Could Golden-Ruling—"Love your neighbor as yourself"—also mean "fight for your neighbor as you'd fight for yourself"?

Maybe that, too, can bring peace.

ROBIN

INT./EXT. LOGAN AIRPORT—DAY—TRAVELING

Robin's parents are driving him to Logan. The Corvette only seats two, so they're in Mom's car.

They don't talk much, but as they go through the second tunnel, Mom pulls out a tissue and starts dabbing at her eyes.

Robin stifles a groan. He doesn't want an emotional goodbye. Going back to Kolkata feels intense enough. "Mom! Please. I'll be fine."

"I know, but I'll miss you, Robin," she says. "It feels like yesterday that we brought you home."

"Best thing we ever did, right, Marjorie?"

Great, Robin thinks. Now his father's voice is shaky.

Robin's mother takes a big breath. "If you find her, Robin, give her our love. We owe her so much."

Robin reaches forward to put his hands on each of their shoulders, and immediately Dad's right and Mom's left hands grab his. "I'm coming back, you know," he says as Dad takes the exit to the airport. "It's only ten weeks."

More tears from Mom. "But you won't be the same."

Everybody's clustered near the ticket counter, looking sleepy because it's so early. Martin and Ash hand Kat, PG, Robin, and Gracie each a travel goodie bag stuffed with granola bars, chocolate, and mints. All of Gracie's sisters are there, and the two littlest ones are clutching her legs and bawling. Ms. Vee distracts them by taking Robin's arm for balance and giving them her walker to push around.

PG calls them together to pray. After a loud, shared "AMEN," Robin plants a big kiss on his mother's cheek, and then one on his father's.

Dad hands him a wad of cash. "Just in case. Text when you land, okay?"

"We won't have access to our phones, remember?"

"At least text us once before you hand it over," Mom says.

Ms. Vee is draping a long, red scarf around Kat's neck. It's the first time Robin has seen Kat in any color other than black, and for a second he thinks she might yank it off. But she doesn't.

"Teddy gave it to me," he overhears Ms. Vee telling Kat. *Who's Teddy?* Robin wonders.

Kat pulls her adopted grandmother close. "I love it."

"See you people in the fall," Ash says, trying to sound tough, but Robin can see that she's getting teary, too. Great. This is turning into one enormous sob session.

He figures Gracie's about to try and comfort Ash when, to his shock, Kat beats her to it. "Stay true to you on those college visits," she says, pulling Ash into a hug.

"Thanks, Kat," Ash says. She hugs Robin and Gracie.

"Have fun in New York, Martin," Gracie says. "We're going to miss you so much."

Robin can't believe Martin won't be around in the fall. The two of them have seen each other almost every day for fifteen years. He hasn't heard a word from Brian, and it still stings. Maybe all goodbyes are harder when you can't remember the first, most devastating one.

Martin hugs Gracie and PG, and then Robin. "I'll still be here when you get back. Go be a superhero, Boy Wonder. And you, too, Kat Girl." He throws his arms open in Kat's direction with a big smile. There's a too-long pause as he waits.

Kat does return his smile. "Have fun in New York, Martin," she says, but she isn't moving forward.

"Hug?" Martin invites her, not giving up.

"You bet! I'll be missing you in the choir, beautiful boy." And with that, Ms. Vee hurtles forward. Long dress, embroidered carpet slippers and all, she launches herself into Martin's open arms.

"I'm not leaving for Brown till September," says Martin, enfolding Ms. Vee into a bear hug. "But I'll take extra love from you anytime. See, Robin—told you I was her favorite."

The four travelers finally manage to peel away. Gracie turns at the security entrance to blow kisses to her parents and sisters. Ms. Vee flashes a two-fingered peace sign, and Kat returns it. Robin's parents lean into each other as they wave at him. He waves back. He loves them. Nothing's going to change that.

"Canary, here I come," mutters Kat as she loads her bag onto the security conveyer belt.

Robin has no idea what she's talking about, and he doesn't ask. Instead, he takes a deep breath and walks through the X-ray machine. *Forward me back to you*, he thinks.

PART TWO

KOLKATA

RAVI

EXT. KOLKATA AIRPORT—DAY—TRAVELING

Robin can't remember the last time he was outside Netaji Subhas Chandra Bose International Airport, but as they exit the terminal, déjà vu grabs hold and won't let go.

It isn't that he knows where to go or what to do as the four of them pass through immigration, change money, and gather on the sidewalk. It's something about the smell and feel of the hot, humid air, and the language being spoken around them. In Dubai Airport, where they changed planes, he hadn't understood the Arabic, and he can't understand a word of Bangla now, but the cadence and melody of the language being spoken here are weirdly familiar to his ears. Is he making this up? Or did the three-year-old version of Robin store sensory details deep inside his brain, banking on a return visit?

"How are you doing?" Gracie asks, studying his face.

"Okay." But that's an understatement. He feels like he's in a NASCAR race; his head's spinning with adrenaline as he tries to register everything he's seeing, feeling, hearing. He can't stand still. Sweat trickles down his spine but he barely notices as he paces back and forth along the sidewalk.

Meanwhile, Kat, PG, and Gracie wait in the shade with the luggage. PG pulls out a handkerchief and wipes his forehead and Gracie is fanning herself with her passport as she watches

Robin do his laps. Kat looks the same as she did when she first arrived in Boston—cool, tough, reserved.

"We lost a whole day," Gracie says. "It's Monday, right?"

"Right," says PG. "Monday afternoon rush hour. Terrible time to land."

Cars, mostly Japanese-made, and yellow cabs are stopping to pick up passengers. PG peers into each one, looking for his friend Arjun.

"Indians drive on the other side of the road," Gracie notes.

"And the driver's on the other side, too," PG adds. "Just like in England, thanks to colonialism."

A small, sporty white Maruti pulls to a stop. They don't sell that model in the States, but Robin's guess is that it has a six-speed manual transmission and a diesel engine.

"Arjun!" shouts PG. He bounds to the curb to greet his friend.

A man in jeans and a Red Sox T-shirt jumps out of the Maruti. "Gregory!"

They embrace.

"Sorry I'm a bit late," Arjun says. "Terrible traffic. But it's wonderful to see you again, my friend!"

His *t*'s sound different to Robin—the tip of his tongue taps against the roof of his mouth with each one—but his English is perfect.

"I was so delighted to get your invitation, Arjun."

"The delight is mine, now that I see you again after so many years. But where's your team?"

"Here they are," PG says. "Let me introduce you. This is Gracie."

She gives Arjun a traditional greeting, just as they practiced in small group—palms together in front of her face, a bit of a head dip. "Namaste," she says.

Arjun beams and returns the gesture. "Welcome, welcome. We say 'Naw-mosh-kar' here in Bengal, but namaste is fine, too."

"This is Kat," says PG.

No namaste there. Not even a smile. *The return of Nefertiti*, Robin thinks.

"Welcome, Kat," says Arjun. "Cat, like the animal?"

"No," she answers. "With a *K*, not a *C*."

Thankfully, Arjun doesn't seem to mind the terse answer. He looks back and forth between Gracie and Kat. "I didn't expect you to bring such Indian-looking young women with you, Gregory. That will be a big help as these girls come and go, especially at Asha House. They might not attract as much attention as other foreign visitors we've had in the past. But who is this?"

"This is Robin," says PG.

Arjun's face explodes into a huge smile. "Ah, our Bengali boy! You're home at last!"

Striding forward, he throws his arms around Robin. For a moment, it feels to Robin like the entire country of India is welcoming him back.

"But what kind of Bengali name is Robin?" Arjun asks, releasing Robin and looking closely at his face. "May we call you Ravi while you're here?"

Ravi! His original name, at least in the orphanage. Of all the names this man could offer him! *Ravi Thornton*. He likes the one-of-a-kind sound of that. A lot. "That's okay with me."

"Really?" PG asks. "A new name? Won't that get confusing? He's 'Robin' in all the paperwork I sent you."

"Not at all. We Bengalis love nicknames. We each have at least twenty."

"And the three of them should address *you* as 'Arjun Uncle,'" says PG. "Right?"

"That's easy for me," Gracie whispers to Ravi. "I have to call all adults 'tío' and 'tía,' even if I can't stand them."

"Arjun Uncle at your service," Arjun says. "Throw your bags in the boot and pile in. Mira Auntie and the boys are waiting."

Inside, the Maruti is . . . cozy. PG settles in the front seat, and the three others wedge themselves into the back.

Gracie has to perch one bottom cheek on Ravi's knee and the other on Kat's. "It's good to be short sometimes," she says. But even so, she has to duck her head so it doesn't bang against the roof of the car.

Ravi hardly notices how compressed they are. As long as he can be near a window and keep taking it in. He's never seen so much uninterrupted brown skin at the same time, for so long. It's like the desi table at school gone viral. But at Metrowest High, most of the American-born Indian dudes were bigger and taller than him; here, he might actually be "normal"-sized. Five-foot-seven, one-hundred-thirty-pound Ravi look-alikes are everywhere, walking, shopping, pulling rickshaws, riding motorcycles. He can't wait to walk the streets himself and blend in.

Arjun drives like he's playing a video game, veering around cars, cabs, and black-and-yellow three-wheeled motorized vehicles. Ravi can see PG clutching the door handle. He's heard the term *white-knuckling*, but now PG's hand gives him the pictorial.

"The Bible college is only about an hour from your flat, right?" PG asks, and Ravi can tell he's trying his best to sound calm. "When do I start teaching?"

The Maruti stops at a red light. "Tomorrow, if you can, after a quick tour of the office. Greek in the mornings; Hebrew in the afternoons. The faculty quarters are comfortable, but you're welcome to return to our flat on the weekends. That's where the three in the back will be staying."

"What?" PG asks. "There's no need for that, Arjun. Their parents signed consent forms for your vetted host families. Our church raised the money for room and board. It wasn't a very large amount, I have to say. Hope it covers the expense."

"You're not visitors. You're family. Don't worry, we are on the 'vetted for visitors' list, too. But we won't accept your money. I stayed in your Hamilton flat rent-free for an entire year, remember?"

PG shakes his head. "You didn't bring along three teenagers with big appetites. We came to serve and learn, not make more work for you. Or for Mira."

The light turns green. Arjun presses his horn, making the few pedestrians in a crosswalk scatter like leaves in front of a power blower. "Mira is delighted to host them. And our twins are so excited they didn't sleep a wink last night. The only problem is that our flat has just one bathroom. I know that's not normal for most Americans, but do you three think you can survive it?"

One bathroom. Seven people. Eight on the weekends. Ravi pictures his private en suite at home, with jetted bathtub, heated tiles, and option for steam in the shower. So privileged. So *American*. "We'll be fine," he says.

"I'm used to sharing," Gracie says. "We have two bathrooms in our house—one for our parents, one for the five of us. Six, pretty soon."

Kat doesn't say anything. Her profile's turned away, and Ravi can't see her expression. Is Nefertiti going to dominate again, squelching Kat-the-Dimple for the entire summer? He hopes not.

Arjun slams on the brakes and Gracie's shoulder bangs into Ravi's head. "Sorry," she says.

But Ravi hardly notices the collision inside the car. He's gone back to watching the movement, noise, color, and chaos outside. Most of the bigger vehicles are inching along now, and the Maruti's stuck behind them. *How fun would it be to own a motorcycle here?* he thinks, watching a Honda Twister scoot easily between two trucks.

"Too many ride-hailing apps from your country are employing our auto-rickshaws these days," Arjun says, scowling as he tails one of the motorized three-wheelers.

"I hear everything's about apps here," says PG.

"For better or worse," says Arjun. "Traffickers are using smartphones to arrange transactions in hotels and guesthouses. They even use social media to smuggle girls and children from outlying villages into Kolkata. But *we* use smartphones, too—to coordinate rescues and inform the police."

"When do we meet the Asha House girls, Arjun Uncle?" Gracie asks, and Kat tips her head away from the window as if she wants to hear the answer.

"Tomorrow afternoon. Bangla lessons four mornings a week for all three of you—Monday through Thursday—but you'll have Fridays and Saturdays for free time. In the afternoons, the girls will serve at Asha House. Ravi can't join you, of course, because no men are allowed in that particular facility. It's where our most traumatized girls are housed."

"What do you have planned for me then?" Ravi's been so focused on his search, he hasn't thought much about what he might do here as his "act of service." "Isn't there a shelter for boys, too?"

Arjun figure-eights his head. *Does that mean no or yes?* Ravi wonders. He's going to have to learn the language *and* the nonverbals. "That's where Mira Auntie works," Arjun says. "But we don't let men in that house, either."

Guess it meant yes and no. Ravi notices Kat taking a long look at their driver for the first time since she got in the car. But then she turns back to the view outside.

"We could use some help in the office, Ravi," Arjun continues. "Data entry, mostly. We're inputting details from court records to profile the traffickers. We also track police investigations and any sentences handed down. In fact, thanks to our data, our local anti-trafficking unit recently won some national funding."

Ravi feels a bit of his excitement shift, even though he'd

signed a contract to do any task required. Data entry? He came all the way back to Kolkata to do data entry? *Guess it doesn't matter. Once my search starts picking up, I won't have much time for office work.* "When can I visit the orphanage?" he asks.

Arjun looks at him in the rearview mirror. "I called and made an appointment for Thursday morning. You'll have to skip your Bangla lesson that day, but I know how important this is."

"Thanks. It is." *Three days*, Ravi thinks. It's longer than he wants to wait. "I couldn't go sooner?"

"Mrs. Banerjee, the director, is just returning from her holiday. She's the person you'll need to see to get any information, and Thursday morning is her first open appointment."

Ravi's quiet. Thursday morning. He'll be opening his file on Thursday morning.

Again, Arjun glances at him. "I am also thinking that I might introduce you to Sergeant Shen, one of the finest officers in our police department."

"You're not going to let Robin try any risky undercover rescue work, are you?" PG asks. "I'm really not comfortable with that idea."

"No, he won't be able to do a rescue," Arjun says. "Takes at least a year of specialized training. And it's certainly not work we want foreigners to do."

Foreigners? You just said I was a Bengali.

"See, Robin?" PG says, as if Robin was the one who asked to do a rescue.

"Can you try calling me Ravi, PG? It's pronounced Rah-vee. Actually it's my real name. The one I had in the orphanage."

Gracie twists her head at an awkward angle so she can see Ravi's face. "It is? You never told us that."

"My parents started calling me Robin to make it easier for Americans."

"See? *Ravi* isn't really a foreigner, Arjun Uncle," Gracie says.

Always standing up for me, Ravi thinks. *And reading my mind, too.*

"True, but he is an American," Arjun answers. "That's why this idea came to my mind. But let me clear it with Shen first. I shall let you know tomorrow, Ravi."

KAT

Kat texts her mom one word—*Landed.*

She doesn't want to call yet, like the other two did in the airport. Hearing Mom's voice might make her start crying in front of everybody.

She stares out of the car window and tries to push back her panic. What is she doing in a foreign country with a bunch of people she met only a few months ago? They watched videos of the streets of Kolkata as part of their trip preparation, but being here with all five senses is not the same. It's too loud. Too crowded. Too hot. And too far from Mom.

Why did Grandma Vee think it would be a good idea for Kat to come?

And then she finds out that they'll be staying with this Pheasant man.

No. I can't do that. I should have listened to Mom. I should have told PG I needed to stay with a woman. She was hoping for the best—that she's moving on, feeling better, getting *normal* again. But nothing's healed yet, she can tell already.

The car careens around a corner, and a wave of that old nausea rises in Kat's throat. She swallows, hard.

"Is Asha House far from your apartment building, Arjun Uncle?" Gracie asks.

How easily Gracie slips into using that relational term with this stranger. The only time Kat's done that is with Grandma Vee, and that's because the old woman stopped feeling like a stranger so quickly.

"Not far," the Pheasant man answers. "Only two kilometers. Oh, sorry—that's about a mile. Our office, where you'll have your Bangla lessons, is also only a short rickshaw ride from the flat, five kilometers, three miles. But after a heavy rain, the streets sometimes get flooded. The monsoons last till August, so it might be raining the entire time you're here."

Sweat is pouring down Kat's back. The air-conditioning in this mini-mobile isn't pumping out enough air for five people. She cracks the window. Traffic seems worse than the Bay Area during rush hour, which she didn't think was possible.

Each mile takes her farther from the airport, the plane, Boston, Oakland.

Horns are honking right in her ear and the smell of exhaust makes her even more nauseous. She closes the window again.

Why did she come?

I want Mom.

Finally, the car turns off the main road and into a quieter neighborhood. The traffic eases up a bit, and so does Kat's stomach. They stop at a red light near a building labeled CINEMA HALL with a poster plastered on the marquee.

"What's playing?" PG asks. "I'm sure my movie freaks back there will appreciate seeing a few Bollywood movies."

"You might ask the girls at Asha House for suggestions," answers the Pheasant man with a smile. "They know all the top stars, songs, and movies. But we call them 'fillums' here."

The movie poster features a girl who looks a bit like Gracie. Long, black silky hair, tan skin, big brown eyes with long lashes. Petite, wearing an orange sari and leaning her head back to gaze up at a guy who looks like—Kat squints into the late-afternoon sun—wait, who does that remind her of? She studies the face again.

Yes, the male hero, wearing a white uniform, black belt and boots, with handcuffs in his belt and his shirt unbuttoned a little too far, looks exactly like an older version of Robin.

Or Ravi, which apparently he wants to be called now.

She'll call him that—he's got the right to reclaim his first name.

Gracie leans over to Kat's side of the car to peer up at the poster. "Oh my gosh, that guy on the poster looks just like you, Rob—Ravi. Wow, I need to see that movie."

Ravi can't see it from where he's sitting. "Must be the sidekick," he says. "Or the bad guy. Or the bad guy's sidekick."

"Looks like the leading man to me," Gracie says.

The car starts moving again, winding through back lanes— Kat swallows hard—and finally stops at a high-rise apartment building behind a gate.

"We're on the third floor," says their driver. "Mira Auntie will have tea waiting, I'm sure. Come, bring your bags."

INT. BOSE FLAT—NIGHT

Upstairs, the apartment is small, clean, and cool. Following Pheasant man's example, they take off their shoes at the door, something Mom and Kat have always done at home. She had no idea it was an Indian custom, too. A Partridge with two small, identical Parrot boys peeking out from behind her introduces herself as "Mira Auntie."

"This is Bijoy and Anand," says their father. "Twins. Seven years old as of last week. Boys, greet your Gregory Uncle and your new sisters—Kat Didi and Gracie Didi. And here is your big brother, Ravi Dada."

The boys smile shyly and tip their heads.

"Nobody's last name is Deedee or Dahdah," whispers Gracie in Kat's ear.

The Partridge overhears and smiles. "*Didi* means older sister, and *dada* means older brother. It's a term of respect that younger children use for friends who are older." She takes a closer look at Kat's face and rests a cool palm against her hot forehead. "Did Arjun Uncle's driving make you dizzy? I always feel a bit vomit-y after riding with him."

She leads Kat to the bathroom. It's small. A razor and shaving lotion are perched on the sink, the toilet seat's up, and worst of all, the door has no lock or latch.

Can't do this. Can't stay here.

But she has to. At least for tonight. Kat splashes cold water on her face before rejoining the rest of them in the living room. As they sip hot, milky, sweet tea and munch on biscuits with butter, her stomach settles down. The twins, though, don't. They lose their shyness after a couple of biscuits and glom onto Ravi, handing him their father's smartphone.

"YOU play, Ravi Dada," one says. Bijoy or Anand? No idea. They look exactly alike to Kat.

"I know this game," Ravi says. "Battle of the Champions, right? Brian and I beat it a couple of years ago."

"You BEAT IT?"

"We've been stuck on the third level for SO LONG!"

The Parrot boys lean into Ravi, watching in awe. Meanwhile, Gracie's calling this Indian woman "Mira Auntie" as if they've known each other for years. She's holding up her phone, sharing photos of her sisters and her parents.

"That reminds me," says PG. "I'll need to gather your phones before tomorrow."

"The Asha House girls aren't allowed mobiles, either," Pheasant man says. He lowers his voice so the twins won't hear. "Shireen, our Asha House director, worries about a girl getting lured again into prostitution after she turns eighteen. It's not illegal then, you see, unless we prove she didn't give 'consent.'"

Kat leans forward. "How do you prove that?"

"We go to court. Show evidence."

"Like what?"

"Text records. Medical proof."

"What if the *trafficker* is injured by *her* resistance? Does that count as proof?"

The two men look at her. "Er—I do not think we have seen a case like that," the Pheasant man says. "Not in Kolkata, anyway."

Well, you might soon, Kat thinks. *If only Plan A can work.*

If only she can power through her phobia of sharing that one, unlockable bathroom.

RAVI

INT./EXT. BENGALI EMANCIPATION SOCIETY HEADQUARTERS—DAY

After breakfast the next morning, Mira walks PG and Ravi down to the street and gives the cycle rickshaw driver directions. Arjun left before they woke up, and Kat and Gracie are following shortly. Ravi hasn't seen them yet because PG hurried him in and out of the bathroom early so the girls would have a chance to use it.

PG's muttering words in Greek and Hebrew as they rattle along. He woke up before dawn to review his textbooks.

"You'll be fine, PG," says Ravi. "You're a great teacher. Why don't you just enjoy the journey?"

"You're right," says PG. "My first rickshaw ride. Slow and breezy."

Ravi's enjoying it, too, but he can tell somehow that it isn't his first. The whirring of wheels, the bumpy feel of ruts in the muddy road, the touch of the warm, light rain on his elbow that's not under the canopy, the slippery leathery seat—they all feel strangely familiar. It's constant and unrelenting, this engagement of five senses. He fell asleep as the circling fan on the ceiling made the mosquito net ripple around him, woke to the cawing of the crows outside and rain slapping against the banana leaves, and relished the sweet, hot taste of that morning's chai. Kolkata's making his eyes, ears, nose, tongue, and skin remember things that his brain can't recall.

Today's Tuesday. Two more days and he'll open his file. He might know her name then. Maybe even have an address in the city or in a nearby village. If those places aren't too far, he can plan a trip on Saturday. He pictures himself hiring a car to take him to a small house or apartment somewhere, knocking on the door, and telling the woman who lives there that he's her son. Will she recognize him? Will they laugh? Cry? He doesn't know. All he wants is for that moment to come soon.

INT. BENGALI EMANCIPATION SOCIETY—DAY

The Bengali Emancipation Society office is hidden in a drab-looking building with no signage identifying it as the head-quarters of an anti-trafficking organization. PG pays the rickshaw driver, Ravi presses a bell, and they wait as a camera makes whirring noises.

"Face recognition," says PG. "Arjun had them installed for extra security. He had his tech guy process those photos I sent him."

They hear a buzz and PG pushes open the door. A blast of air-conditioned air greets them as they enter a small reception area. Beyond is a carpeted path leading through a maze of cubicles. Phones are beeping and buzzing. People are talking in Bangla and English. Printers are drilling out documents and keyboards are clicking.

Arjun is there, waiting. "Everyone—my friend Gregory is here!"

His announcement is loud, and he claps his hands three times as well. There's a sudden silence—at least when it comes to voices—and about forty or so Indian faces pop up from behind cubicle dividers.

"Meet my good friend Pastor Gregory," Arjun says, and PG does a namaste.

"And his companion isn't really a visitor," Arjun announces, resting a hand on Ravi's shoulder. "It's a homecoming, really, because Ravi's a Bengali. Born right here in Kolkata."

A woman's voice pipes up. "Bap-re-bap. This young man looks exactly like that film star . . . what's his name?"

"Amit Biswas," says someone else.

"That is what I was thinking!"

Smiles and nods join the verbal chorus.

Arjun's phone goes off. "Excuse me while I take this, will you?" He disappears into a room off the reception area.

An older woman in a pink sari joins them. She has iron-gray, short hair and lighter skin. She's a few inches shorter than Ravi. "Enough distraction, back to work," she says crisply. The heads admiring Ravi's resemblance to some actor disappear behind their cubicles again.

"I am Miss Shireen, director of Asha House," the woman says to PG and Ravi. "It is good you are here, but it is quite likely you won't be seeing too much of me. Absolutely no men—"

The doorbell rings, interrupting her, and Arjun reappears. "That must be Kat and Gracie," he says. "With only one bathroom, we're arriving in shifts. Shireen, will you kindly attend to them? I have a thousand things to do. Come, Gregory, let's deposit the phones in our safe, and then I'll drop you at Bible college."

"Just put me in an auto-rickshaw, Arjun, and tell the driver the destination," PG says. "I'll be fine. Have fun, Rob—Ravi. Sorry. It's going to take me a while to get used to that."

PG's leaving already? They just got here. "You'll be back Saturday night, right?" Ravi asks.

"Actually, I'm coming back to the Boses' tonight to get my bags," says PG. "We'll say goodbye then. Or maybe we'll say, 'Apotassomai!'"

Ravi figures that's goodbye in either Greek or Hebrew. Sounds like Greek.

"I'll find you after lunch, Ravi," Arjun says. "Shen agreed to see you at two o'clock today. I have an appointment in town, so I can drop you at the police training center on my way."

I have to talk to this Shen guy on my own? Ravi thinks. *I have absolutely no idea why I'm meeting him.*

As PG and Arjun disappear into the maze of cubicles, the facial recognition program processes Kat and Gracie. Miss Shireen buzzes the door open, and the girls enter the reception area. This time it's up to Ravi to do the introductions.

"This is Miss Shireen, director at Asha House. Miss Shireen, this is Kat. And Gracie." Thankfully, the forty heads don't reappear; he doesn't know any of their names yet.

"Welcome to the Bengali Emancipation Society, ladies," says Miss Shireen.

"Namaste," says Gracie, putting her palms together.

Kat has her Nefertiti face in place, so a small head tip is all she offers.

Gracie comes over to Ravi for their usual hug of greeting, and he leans his cheek on her hair. *Wow, this feels good,* he thinks. *I didn't realize I needed some Boston love right about now.*

But Miss Shireen is frowning. "That won't do, you two," she says. "It's not appropriate for girls and boys your age to embrace in public here. You will have to hide your affections while in Kolkata."

Gracie drops her arms and backs away, and Ravi can tell she's mortified. His cheeks feel warm, too. Good thing only Miss Shireen witnessed the hug.

"I'm sorry," Gracie says. "It's fine in my culture. We're always hugging and kissing."

Miss Shireen looks skeptical. That's what Ravi thinks, anyway. Nonverbals are so confusing here. "Nonetheless, you're in India now," she says. "So it's good to do as we do."

Ravi tries to explain. "We've known each other for years. Gracie's sort of like a sister to me."

"That's what you think," Kat mutters.

Ravi doesn't have time to ask what she's talking about. Miss Shireen scrapes the air with her hand, palm down. "Come, girls. I brought along some Asha House uniforms for you to try. Not sure I have one in your size, Kat, but my brilliant tailor is always ready to make alterations. You come, too, Ravi, and I shall show you where you can wait."

Miss Shireen opens a door to a large room. "Your Bangla lessons will be here, inside our prayer and worship room.

Take your shoes off and go inside, Ravi, while the girls try on the uniforms."

Ravi slips off his sandals and leaves them under a sign that says SHOES HERE PLEASE. The room is spacious, and unlike the office outside, it feels serene. He sees a Bible and a prayer book on a lectern at the front, along with several unlit candles and a simple cross. Foam mats are arranged across the floor to the right and left, leaving an aisle down the middle. A small, rectangular table is set up near the door with three chairs on one side of it and one on the other. Three textbooks are neatly stacked on the table, along with three notebooks and three pencils.

Ravi sits in one of the three "student" chairs and flips open one of the books. The Bangla alphabet is totally different from the ABCs he's used to seeing. Will he need to know how to read Bangla when he opens his file? Maybe someone at the orphanage can translate if the papers aren't in English.

A short, tarry-skinned older man comes in carrying four cups of milky chai on a tray. Tea, tea, tea. Ravi's been back to Kolkata twenty-four hours and has been served six cups of it already. Good thing it's delicious. "Thanks," he says.

"No mention," the man says, smiling and bowing after he puts the tray on the table. "I am Gopal, office bearer. You need, you ask, I give."

As Gopal exits, Kat comes in, still wearing her own clothes. She leaves her sandals beside Ravi's and drops into a chair. "Surprise! Nothing fit. Tore two of those tunic thingies trying them on. Pants were a foot too short. They're sending my measurements to the tailor. Meanwhile, I get to stay in my own clothes."

Ravi risks the question. "Did you bring anything along that isn't black?"

"Just this." She readjusts Ms. Vee's long red scarf around her neck and takes a sip of tea.

Gracie comes in, wearing the exact uniform they saw on the girl in the film—loose yellow pants, flowing tunic, matching scarf. She, too, stops just inside the door to slip out of her sandals.

Miss Shireen is standing behind her. "I'll see you two at Asha House after lunch," she tells Kat and Gracie. "We have a few things to discuss before you meet the girls. Goodbye, Ravi."

"She seems tough," Kat says once the door closes and the three of them are alone.

"Maybe that's what those girls need to feel safe," Ravi says. "Someone tough to protect them."

"Maybe. Doesn't Gracie look great in her Asha House uniform, Ravi? It's a perfect fit. Model it for us, will you, Gracie?"

Gracie struts down the "aisle" in the center of the room on tiptoes as if she's on a runway in high heels. She twirls by the lectern and model-walks back to them with her lips in a pout. Her black, shiny hair is loose and flowing around her shoulders. *It's usually in a ponytail*, Ravi realizes. Kat's right. The outfit fits perfectly.

Gracie gets back to them and sits down. "This long scarf makes me feel so elegant. Miss Shireen says it's called an orna." She takes a sip of tea. "Being a fashionista is thirsty-making work."

Kat nudges Ravi, who's still staring at Gracie. "Beautiful, right?"

They're interrupted by the door flying open.

"Thomader chatri esheche!" An old lady in a white sari and glasses is standing there, palms pressed in a namaste. "I am Mrs. Gupta, your Bangla teacher."

She walks in to join them as proudly as if she were a model herself.

Mrs. Gupta hands out notebooks and pencils. "Outside these walls, knowing a bit of Bangla will open hearts," she tells them. "Bengalis enjoy it greatly when foreigners try to speak our beautiful mother tongue."

I'm no foreigner, Ravi thinks, deciding immediately to learn as much of the language as he can, as fast as he can. After all, Bangla is *his* mother tongue, too.

KAT

Kat's first language lesson passes by in a blur. Mrs. Bengal Tiger looks exasperated, but Kat can't retain more than a phrase or two. All she can think about is how she can't stay at that flat another night.

Sure, the twins gave up their beds so she and Gracie can have a private room, but the front door was unlocked when Kat checked and locked it at midnight. She still feels grimy from travel because she couldn't bring herself to take a shower in that bathroom. And constipated, because it's hard to relax your sphincter with one heel pressed against the door.

What in the world is she going to do? *Stupid, stupid me. Thought I was ready for this but I'm not.* Staying in that flat is like sending a purple belter into a black belt match. Someday she might get there, but that day isn't this one.

The Asha House director's a Bobcat, fierce and feisty. Kat's not sure if she's the one to approach about moving somewhere else but Kat's going to have to figure something out.

And soon.

Before tonight.

"Can you teach me how to say 'son' and 'mother'?" Ravi is asking, making Kat tune in.

"Puth-row and Ma," the Tiger says. "Is your ma Bengali? Do

you wish to write her a letter? I can show you how to spell it with the letters if you like."

Ravi shrugs. "No, thanks. I just want to be able to say the words."

Gracie and Kat look at each other. They both know what this is about. He's visiting the orphanage on Thursday. Probably picturing some fantasy movie reunion that isn't going to happen. And now *he's* reminding Kat of a novice, stepping onto the mat for the first time. She's watched little ones get flattened. A lot of them leave crying.

During lunch break, Gopal leads them to the computer they'll be able to use to send and receive email.

"Mom's been going to church more often," Kat tells Gracie and Ravi, after checking her email. "They offer some kind of course on managing personal finances. Plus she's thinking about night school for her nursing degree. She's finally 'adulting,' she says."

"That's good," says Gracie. "Meanwhile, my mother says the toddlers keep asking why she's so fat."

Reading notes of encouragement from Mom, Saundra, and Grandma Vee makes Kat feel better. She answers them all—without confessing how awful it was to sleep in the Bose flat. Gracie and Ravi take turns at the computer, too.

Another staff member comes in—a young woman not much older than they are. "Ravi, Mr. Bose has instructed me to train you on data entry before you leave for your appointment at the police training center. Come with me, please."

"See you guys back at the flat," Ravi says, and follows her out the door.

Gracie's scowling.

"What's wrong?" Kat asks.

"Does that data-entry person have to be so pretty?"

"Ravi didn't seem impressed. Not like he did when he was watching you. Come on; we'd better get going ourselves."

INT./EXT. RICKSHAW—DAY—TRAVELING

Gopal hails a rickshaw for them and gives the driver the street address of Asha House. It's raining again, so the driver yanks up the flowery, decorated canopy to cover their heads. It's private and cozy back here on this leather seat built for two. *Two Katinas*, Kat thinks. *Probably three Gracies.*

"You look tired, Kat," Gracie says. "Did you sleep at all?"

"Not much."

"Was the bed uncomfortable? Mine seemed fine. We can switch if you want."

Kat glances over at her seatmate. Maybe Grandma Vee's right, and she can risk a *bit* of her story with Gracie. "That's not why I couldn't sleep. It's . . . that I'm not used to having so many guy things around." *Feeble effort.*

"Oh," Gracie says. "It feels weird to me, too. Six women in our house. We 'out-stuff' Dad, that's for sure."

Kat tries again. "It's just that . . . well, I've never spent the night with a man." That sounds even more awkward. "I mean,

I've never slept in the same place where a man is sleeping. I've only shared a roof with Mom, Saundra, and Grandma Vee."

Gracie pats her hand. "I know. But we'll get used to it."

She's still not getting it. "It's just that . . . well, if you've gone through something . . . violent in the past, it's harder to 'get used to' . . . stuff that's easier for other people to 'get used to.'"

Gracie's quiet for a long minute as the rickshaw rattles along. Kat can tell she's processing what she heard. And what she didn't hear. "Oh. I'm so sorry, Kat. I didn't know."

"How could you? Nobody does. That's why I left school mid-semester."

"Does Ms. Vee know?"

"Yep. That's why she encouraged me to come. She thought it might help me . . . move forward."

"Men suck," Gracie says. "At least, gross men do. Like that sleazy no-relative 'tío' who follows me around and ruins every family gathering. He's so scary. Twice my size almost. Maybe that's why I prefer guys who are more . . . compact."

"Like Ravi?"

"Exactly. Although it's going to take me a while to get used to calling him that. I'm so worried about him, Kat. What if he gets crushed on Thursday?"

"I know. I'm worried, too."

"Well, there's nothing we can do for him except be there." Gracie pauses, then turns back to Kat. "But what we *can* do is fix our own housing situation. We'll ask them to move us right away."

"What? You don't have to move! Just me."

"I'm coming with you. I'm happy to ask Arjun Uncle if you want me to. Or Miss Shireen."

"Really? You'd do that?" Kat's throat gets a little tight. Immediate support. Even if it means Gracie giving up being with Ravi.

"We'll talk to Miss Shireen," Gracie says. "And don't worry, I won't say anything about why."

"Thanks, Gracie," Kat says. "Thanks."

The rickshaw stops in front of a peach-colored three-story building behind a high wall. Kat's heart skips a beat. This is the building that was in the background of the password-protected film.

Instantly her focus returns. *Golden-Ruling, Plan A.*

RAVI

INT./EXT. KOLKATA POLICE TRAINING CENTER—DAY

"I'm sorry I can't go inside and introduce you to Shen," Arjun says on the way to the police training center. "But our lawyer asked for a meeting. We may be able to bring a nasty brothel owner to trial if one more girl decides to testify against him. Say a prayer for that to happen, will you? It takes these children great courage to speak up."

"No problem," Ravi says. "Why do you want me to meet this man anyway?"

"It's more that I want him to know you. He told me recently he's agreed to train a nephew of his this summer. The boy's quite unmotivated, but Shen's brother wants his son to qualify as a police officer. Shen has to dedicate his entire afternoon break for this task, but of course, he can't refuse an older brother's request." Arjun pauses, as though trying to word what he's about to say next a bit more delicately. "As soon as I saw you, Ravi, the idea that Shen might also include *you* in that training came to mind."

Saw my unfit body, you mean? Ravi's never been good at PE or sports. His dad never worked out much, so neither did he. But he's had bulging-muscle superhero dreams ever since he can remember. He throws a sideways glance at Arjun, who's built along the lines of PG. "Do *you* work out, Arjun Uncle?"

"Not much; too busy. But believe me, if I had the chance to train with Shen, I would. He's the best of the best. There's something about him—maybe self-denial, courage, discipline—that inspires others. The young people he trains emerge head and shoulders above others. Ready to face anything." He pauses again. "I know you're here to search for your birth family, Ravi. My hope for you is that two hours of hard exercise with Shen might bring some order into your day. And some courage, as well."

Ravi's heard Kat say that working out is a good stress reliever. But is he up for the task? He takes stock of his thin upper arms and sighs. "He'll probably take one look at the shape I'm in and send me straight back to the office."

"I don't think so," Arjun says. "Shen reads people quite well. He sees potential where others may not. Anyway, he owes me a favor. It was our data that won his anti-trafficking unit that big grant. To tell you the truth, I'm also asking *you* a favor. Shen doesn't think highly of American volunteers. We used to send them and potential donors to see his top-notch operation first-hand, but he refused to have any more come after one of them insulted an older officer. I'm hoping this is my chance to prove him wrong about Americans."

They pull to a stop outside a freshly painted, circular building with a sign that reads KOLKATA POLICE TRAINING CENTER, and Arjun hands Ravi a letter and a slip of paper. "Show this clearance letter to the guard. And here is our address; I wrote it in Bangla and English. Give it to any auto-rickshaw driver and he'll transport you back to the flat. I will see you there for dinner. Give this a good try, okay, Ravi?"

Ravi jumps out of the Maruti. "Thanks, Arjun Uncle. I'll see what I can do."

And now he's alone. For the first time. In the city of his birth. He pauses outside the gate and looks around. Motorcycles, auto-rickshaws, trucks, and cars whiz by. People on foot hurry to their destinations. Nobody pays attention to the Bengali young man on the sidewalk.

Ravi imagines himself in this moment as if he grew up with his first mother. He might not be able to afford American-made blue jeans and brand-name sandals. Maybe he'd be a rickshaw puller or one of those hawkers selling bananas and mangoes on the corner. And he'd be thinking in Bangla instead of in English.

How much of himself would remain if he could press REWIND and start life again?

He feels a pang as he pictures his parents' faces. They'd have to be erased in that alternate reality.

Missing them, missing her.

One or the other, that's his life.

All he can do now is press PLAY.

Thunder booms, jump-starting his feet into motion.

"Visiting Sergeant Shen," he tells the guard sitting inside the gate, handing him Arjun's letter.

The guard scans it quickly and returns it. "Inside," he grunts.

Another clap of thunder. This one switches on a torrent of rain.

Ravi bounds through the downpour and bursts into the Kolkata Police Training Center.

KAT

INT./EXT. ASHA HOUSE—DAY

There's a door in the high wall around Asha House, but it's locked from the inside. Gracie rings the bell, and a woman opens it, smiling and saying things in Bangla that the girls can't understand. She locks the door again once they're inside.

Safe and secure, Kat thinks.

They walk into a small garden full of roses and a few trees laden with limes, papayas, bananas. Bushes with glossy green leaves and tiny white flowers are scattered around; Kat recognizes them from the video, too. And there, at the end of the curved pathway, rocking in the same chair on the same veranda that she saw on-screen so many times, the Bobcat is waiting.

Kat's already realized that this woman's the one to convince if she wants to implement Plan A. But she'll have to do it carefully. It takes most people a while to believe that a martial art like jiu-jitsu isn't violent. And that's in California. She's not sure at all how they'll view it here in India.

"What a beautiful garden," Gracie says as they reach the Bobcat.

"My favorite is the night-blooming jasmine. We call them 'Shi-oo-lee phool.' Their white flowers release the most gorgeous smell once the sun sets. They grow right outside the windows of my cottage, also. Come. Leave your shoes on the veranda. I have some guidelines to review before you meet my girls."

She leads Kat and Gracie into a small office, sits in a desk chair, and gestures at the two empty chairs facing her. "Sit, please."

"We have a question for you, Miss Shireen," Gracie says. "We were wondering if—"

An upraised hand interrupts her. "Let me review the guidelines first, please."

"Of course," says Gracie. "Sorry."

The older woman puts on a pair of reading glasses and glances at a notepad on her desk. "Visitors like you should never probe the girls about their past or ask intrusive questions. Yes?" She looks over her glasses at their faces, waiting for a verbal assent.

"Yes," says Gracie.

As if I would, Kat thinks. "Yes," she says aloud.

"Never talk about the girls by name in public places or mention the location of the house in case you are overheard. Yes?"

"Yes," says Gracie.

Kat nods. Sounds good; she likes that safety's a high priority. The Bobcat looks at her. "Yes," Kat says.

"No mobiles allowed. That rule applies to visitors, housemothers, and the girls." She double taps hers, which is sitting on the desk in front of her. "I keep mine with me, but that is only to be in communication with the office and also for emergencies."

FORWARD ME BACK TO YOU

"Ours are already locked in the office," Gracie says.

"Good. The girls go to school in the mornings but return here for training in the afternoons. Your task will be caring for two babies so their mothers may attend a sewing class. Yes?"

Gracie's jaw drops. Literally drops so that her mouth forms a big round O. Poor Gracie has been free of her baby-filled home for just two days and now this. Kat's not excited, either. She's never held a baby in her life. Nor does she want to.

"Isn't there anything else we can do to help the girls?" she asks. *Like teach them jiu-jitsu, for example?*

"You don't like babies?" the Bobcat asks, taking off her glasses and giving Kat a stern look. "This is our biggest need for the summer. You will be doing a good service for those two young women, and giving our housemothers a much-needed rest as well. So, yes?"

Gracie closes her mouth. "Yes," she says wearily.

"Yes," says Kat. "But why are the girls learning to sew? How will that help them?"

"They may get hired in textile factories, or in sari shops."

"Here in the city? What if the men who sold them find them again?"

The Bobcat sighs and leans back in her chair. "That is a worry. Our goal for rescued children is to send them home to their villages, restored to the protection of their families, but my girls have families who didn't welcome them back. We do our best to get their traffickers behind bars, but I would be lying if I told you these girls are not in danger of being caught and sold again."

Kat can see how much she cares about keeping the girls safe. Somehow she has to win this woman's trust.

"Are you finished with your guidelines, Miss Shireen?" Gracie asks.

"For now. I can see you're burning to ask me your question, so proceed."

"The girls all sleep in this building, right?" Kat thought she knew what Gracie was about to say, but the question is surprising. Gracie gives her a trust-me-I've-got-this kind of look.

"Yes, they do," answers Miss Shireen "All twenty-five. With three housemothers. And two babies, for now. Soon, we'll have three."

"Does Asha House have any open beds? If so, maybe Kat and I can stay here. Then we can help with the babies at night, too."

Brilliant, Kat thinks, even though the thought of nighttime baby care is daunting. At least she'll be with Graciela Rivera, Baby Expert. Plus, nobody's feelings will get hurt if they move here to be on baby duty 24-7. No explanations needed. She leans forward, hoping Miss Shireen will say yes.

But the older woman's head is moving in that Indian figure eight that means no. And sometimes yes. *Which is it?* Kat wonders. "I'm sorry, but we don't allow outsiders to sleep in the house overnight."

Kat bites her lip. So disappointing. She gets the reasoning, and supports it, but staying here would have been perfect.

"Isn't there anywhere else we can stay?" Gracie's not giving up. "You said girls and boys aren't supposed to mix here like they do in the States. It's kind of odd to be sleeping in the same flat as Ravi, isn't it? What will the girls think?"

"You have a point there, although everyone knows you're under the eyes of Arjun and Mira." She peers at Gracie over her glasses and takes stock of Kat's expression, too, and then: "From time to time, I have had female guests stay with me in the director's flat. It is a small cottage in the back corner of the property. And I am listed as a 'vetted host family,' too, even though I am on my own."

Kat sits up. "Can we do that, Miss Shireen? I'll clean, cook, do whatever you need."

"We'll keep things so neat and tidy, you won't even know we're there," Gracie adds.

"No need to clean or cook," Miss Shireen says. "But Gracie makes a good point. If you stay with me, you might be able to offer even more service. The little ones will know you since you'll be taking care of them in the afternoons, so perhaps the babies can sleep in my cottage with you for three or so nights a week. At least for the ten weeks that you're with us. That way, our girls and the housemothers can catch up on sleep. And I have good quality earplugs, so the crying won't hinder my rest."

Gracie shoots Kat a what-do-you-think eyebrow raise. This arrangement still means more time with babies. Wailing babies, at night. But if it's a way to get out of that testosterone-filled apartment, Kat will take it. "Perfect!" she says. "You okay with this, Gracie?"

"Guess diapers are my destiny," Gracie says. "I'm in. Thanks, Miss Shireen."

Suddenly, they hear the voices of girls laughing, singing, chatting outside the office door.

"Let me talk it over with Arjun and your pastor," Miss Shireen says. "I think they'll easily give permission for you to shift to my place. Now shall we go and meet the girls? I see them peering through the windows, and I'm certain they are gossiping about you already."

RAVI

INT. KOLKATA POLICE TRAINING CENTER—DAY

Ravi shakes the rain out of his hair and wipes his face with his shirtsleeve. A police officer is standing in the lobby, watching him. The man is wearing a starched, spotless white uniform that includes black boots, a black belt and holster, a pair of handcuffs, and a baton. Ravi doesn't see a gun. The booted feet are firmly planted, arms crossed, stomach flat, and biceps bulging as if this dude's about to enter a boxing ring.

South Asian badass in the flesh, Ravi thinks.

"Thumi ki Ravi Thornton?" the man asks.

Ravi recognizes exactly half the words—his name. "That's me. But I don't speak Bangla. Not yet, anyway. I'm taking lessons."

"No Bangla? It's your mother tongue. Why have you lost it?"

Ravi remembers what Arjun said in the car. "I'm an American," he says.

"I am Sergeant Shen. But my men call me sir. You will do the same." The man looks Ravi up and down. Then he whirls his index finger in the air. "Turn, please."

Ravi obeys, wishing for the thousandth time that he had a different kind of build. Although the officer isn't much taller than he is, he notices as he completes his 360 spin. He's just . . . ten times more fit and strong.

"Follow me."

They enter a musty-smelling locker room, where Shen tosses Ravi a pair of clean athletic shorts and a T-shirt. The building isn't air-conditioned, but fans whirl overhead.

"Come to the gym in five minutes," Shen says. "Did you bring running shoes?"

"No. I mean no, sir."

"Then your bare feet must suffice."

Shen heads to the back of the locker room and a door slams shut behind him. Ravi takes off his sandals and changes quickly. The shorts and shirt fit, although he wishes his bare legs and arms didn't look so scrawny. Leaving his own clothes folded on the bench, he finds the door that Shen must have walked through.

The large, quiet gym is empty except for Shen and a bulky, round-faced young man. Or boy, maybe? Must be Shen's nephew. He's also wearing shorts and a T-shirt, but his are about four sizes bigger than Ravi's.

The boy-man grins at Ravi. "Amar nam Bontu."

They learned that phrase this morning in Bangla class, so Ravi knows how to answer. "Amar nam Ravi."

Bontu looks him up and down. "Even though you're an American, you are resembling a Bollywood actor. Are you a relative to Amit Biswas?"

"That's the second time I've heard that, but no," Ravi answers. At least he doesn't think he's related to that actor.

Shen blows his whistle, making them both jump. "I will evaluate you shortly, Thornton. Join me in five minutes.

Bontu, show Thornton the stretching routine." He lifts a barbell easily and takes it to a corner of the gym, where he starts arranging mats and weights.

"Touch your toes and hold for ten to stretch hamstrings," Bontu tells Ravi, tapping his own shins and straightening up again immediately. "Then do side stretches like this." He moves his hands up and down in front of him like a mime.

Ravi reaches down to his toes, counts to ten, and then shifts to side stretches. "How often do you train?"

"Every Monday through Thursday with Fridays off. This is session number three for me. Thirty-seven remaining."

"Already counting down, huh?"

"I hate it. Let us do twists now." Bontu's slight movements from side to side make him look like he's dancing.

"Why come, then?" Ravi asks, starting to twist his own torso.

"Because every man in our family has served with Kolkata police, and Baba is wanting me to do the same. My weight is over the qualifying limit for application, so he asked Uncle to make me fit. Take your right foot now and pull it up against your bottom."

Ravi balances on his left foot, grabs his right foot, and stretches out his front right quad.

Bontu bends his knee, tries to reach his foot, misses, and gives up. "What about you? Do you want to be here, Ravi? Or is someone making you come?"

"It isn't my idea," Ravi admits, switching feet to stretch

out his left quad. "But I'm here to volunteer with the Bengali Emancipation Society, and they sent me to Sergeant Shen. Why can't you just tell your uncle you don't want to train?"

Bontu sighs. "He knows I have other plans for my life. Big plans. But we both agreed to give it a try for the summer . . . to make my baba happy."

"Bontu, bring the other barbell here," Shen calls.

Ravi watches Bontu struggle to lift the weight that his uncle lifted so quickly. He can already tell that the kid's easy to be around. Maybe they could be friends. It doesn't look like he and Gracie are going to have as much time to see each other as he'd thought. No texting, either, their usual way to catch up during the day. Good thing he'll have the evenings with her; being with Gracie's the ultimate stress reliever. Much better than working out.

Bontu's given up trying to lift the barbell and is rolling it instead to where his uncle is setting up. He trudges back to Ravi.

"Let's get in shape together this summer," Ravi says. "What do you think?"

"I shall watch you get in shape," Bontu answers with a smile. "I am in fine condition just as I am."

Shen blows his whistle.

"One whistle means 'COME HERE IMMEDIATELY,'" Bontu tells Ravi.

"Stamina evaluation first," Shen tells them. "I will time your laps around the perimeter of the gymnasium, Thornton.

Give me eight laps. You might as well try again, too, Bontu, now that you have a training partner."

He blows his whistle twice, and Bontu starts a slow jog.

Beep, BEEEEEEP! "Two means GO, Thornton."

Ravi takes off running.

KAT

INT. ASHA HOUSE COMMON ROOM—DAY

Kat and Gracie follow Miss Shireen into a large, sunny common room lined with sofas, chairs, tables, and a flat-screen television attached to one wall. The speakers are blaring out Bangla music while on-screen a man and a sari-clad woman dance on a beach.

As soon as they walk in, someone switches it off and Kat and Gracie are surrounded by a dozen or so smiling girls. The youngest looks about ten; the oldest about seventeen. They're all wearing the same yellow as Gracie, so she blends in easily. Meanwhile, Kat's the only one dressed in black. And she's a good head taller than everyone in sight.

"Naw-mosh-kar!"

"Hello!"

"Welcome!"

"We were not expecting such *Indian*-looking girls to visit us from America!"

"The tall one is looking exactly like a young Halle Berry!"

Kat's heard that comparison before, but she didn't expect it in India. And they speak English. Thank goodness. Some more than others, and with different accents than she's used to, but Kat can understand them.

"Most of the American visitors who come are white," Miss Shireen says.

This doesn't surprise Kat. That's who usually gets to come from America to volunteer—not three brown teenagers like Ravi, Gracie, and Kat.

"Are you *both* Americans?" a girl asks.

"Yes, but . . ." As Gracie tries to explain her Mexican heritage, Kat scans the circle for a girl who matches the size and shape of the Canary in the film. None of them look like her at first glance.

"Tell your names, girls," Miss Shireen says. "And use Bangla, please. Our visitors need to practice."

They take turns introducing themselves. Kat listens closely to their voices.

"Amar nam Amrita."

Too tall. Deeper voice.

"Amar nam Dipika."

Too short. And younger.

"Ami Charubala."

Curvier than the girl in the film.

"Amar nam Rupa."

Wait.

No. Too skinny.

And then a yellow-clad girl comes through a swinging door, exiting a room that looks like a kitchen. Her face lights up, and she walks slowly over to Kat and Gracie.

"Amar nam Kavita," she says, putting her hands together in a namaste.

Kat's heart jumps at the sound of the distinctive, chirpy voice.

She's listened to it share her story so many times. It's her. The reason Kat is here, so far from home.

Kat manages to keep herself from throwing her arms around Kavita, remembering Miss Shireen's instructions. "Amar nam Katina," she answers instead, using the only Bangla phrase she learned this morning.

"Katina. Kavita. We sound like sisters."

Kavita's English has improved since the film was made. She puts her hand on her back, and that's when Kat notices something else has changed.

Kavita's body.

The shape of it!

Something—some*one*—has been growing inside her womb.

And judging by the size of her belly, it's coming out soon.

The rest of the girls keep introducing themselves, but Kat's stopped listening.

RAVI

INT. KOLKATA POLICE TRAINING CENTER—DAY

Bontu gives up after three laps and is sitting cross-legged on one of the foam mats in the gym. Ravi somehow manages the eight laps. He's breathing heavily by the end.

"Quite slow," Shen tells him. "What have you been doing for exercise to date?"

Working on my car, Ravi thinks. "Er, I walk here and there."

"I can tell. Next, you will do as many push-ups and chin-ups as you can without stopping. And then I shall plan your daily workout from there."

He's never been able to run fast or long, but Ravi did do twenty push-ups by the end of his last required PE class at Metrowest. He hits the floor, eager to prove that he might have *some* badass potential. Sadly, he has to give up after five push-ups. And he can't manage more than one chin-up. *It's been a long time since sophomore year*, he thinks.

Bontu steadies Ravi as he lets go of the bar and drops to the floor. "Good try," he says.

"Good? I'm pathetic." Ravi turns to face Shen. "Is there really any hope to get in better shape this summer? For someone built like me?"

"I am built like you," Shen says. "If you give it your full effort, you might begin to see results within seven or eight weeks. In ten weeks, given a high degree of self-discipline, we can transform any kind of body. But I require mandatory attendance. And full effort. I have only agreed to train you because Arjun asked this of me—I always repay my debts. Do you promise to attend regularly, and try your best?"

Ravi remembers what Arjun said: *The young people he trains emerge head and shoulders above others. Ready to face anything.* "I promise, sir."

"Good. I don't want to waste time and energy on someone with bad character. I train only men and women of integrity and honesty. The poorest and weakest of our citizens suffer most if we have a dishonest police force."

Ravi has grown up hearing that. Sometimes his mother came home from court raving about a brave police officer who had defended someone powerless. But not every time. *We need more good people in blue*, she's always saying.

"My parents raised me to be truthful, sir," he says.

"I'm also looking for duty, loyalty, obedience to elders. These are our Bengali values. Can you manage *those*, Ravi Thornton from America?"

They must be American values, too. Because I've been practicing them my whole life. Ravi glances at Bontu, who nods encouragingly "Yes, I will try, sir."

"Let's begin today's training, then. Fifty crunches, please." Begin? Oh, wow. Ravi had thought they were done.

Beep, BEEP!

KAT

Kat came all the way to India with a decent Plan A.

Or so she thought.

But there's no way on earth she'll be able to teach a Kimura to a pregnant person.

Disgusting Wolves. They wreck everything. Even the Golden Rule.

Kat collapses on the couch, trying to hide her disappointment.

Miss Shireen is sitting on the sofa, scrolling through texts on her phone. The other girls are clustering around Gracie, complimenting her silky hair and smooth skin, but Kavita comes over to sit beside Kat.

"I am fifteen years of age," she says. "You?"

"I'm sixteen," Kat answers. "You speak English well."

"I am continuing to study English here. Before I left the village, I studied up to class six. I stopped after Baba died. That is when Ma sent me to the city."

No questions, Kat reminds herself, even though she wants to find out everything about this girl. Her brain is beginning to recover after the shock of seeing Kavita pregnant. *Now what?* she thinks. *What's Plan B?* "I saw you in the Bengali Emancipation Society film. You were wonderful."

"Oh, thank you. That was before I knew I was having a baby."

Another girl is near Kat now. The one named Amrita. She's squinting at Kat's arm through the billowy sleeve of Kat's loose-fitting blouse.

"We are admiring your height and your strength, Kat Didi," she says, and her English is even better than Kavita's. "May we have a look at your muscles?"

Kat stands. "Of course."

Folding up her sleeve and flinging Grandma Vee's red chiffon scarf out of the way, she makes a fist with her hand and flexes her biceps. A few girls start clapping.

"Bap-re-bap," says Amrita. "Arms like Wonder Woman."

"Wait—you know that movie?" Kat asks.

"It is one of our favorite fillums from your country," says the girl named Rupa. "But I think you have more muscles than her."

Kat has to admit her upper arm is impressive. She doesn't do dozens of push-ups and burpees every night for nothing. Not to mention training for five years to become Northern California's reigning seventeen-and-under middleweight girls BJJ champion.

Dipika says something in Bangla, making the others laugh.

"What did she say?" Gracie asks.

Miss Shireen smiles as she translates: "Muscles like a man!"

"Muscles that can fight off a man," Kat says.

"May I touch?" Kavita asks.

"Please," Kat says.

Hesitantly, Kavita reaches up and taps Kat's biceps with one finger. Then she gives it a squeeze.

"May we *all* touch?" Rupa asks.

"Sure." Golden-Ruling Plan B is starting to form in Kat's head. This always happens if you don't tap out. If you stay on the mat.

"Line up, line up," Amrita orders. To Kat, she seems like the oldest girl in the room, or the bossiest, judging by the way the others obey to wait their turn.

"Miss Shireen, may I borrow your phone for a minute?" Gracie asks.

Miss Shireen looks up. "I don't hand my phone over, I'm sorry."

Gracie gives the director her sweetest smile. "Will *you* put on the score from *Wonder Woman*, then?"

To Kat's surprise, Miss Shireen returns the smile. She taps the screen a few times, the movie's kickass music starts playing, and Kat starts to feel like she's about to take Ares down.

One by one, the girls squeeze Kat's arm. She keeps her biceps rock-hard. Last in line are two of the smallest Asha House residents, who look about ten years old or so. Kat bends, and they clutch her biceps at the same time. She raises her arm, lifting them so that their feet dangle a few inches above the floor. Her audience laughs and claps.

But then a baby starts wailing from somewhere in the building. Another joins in. They sound like police cars screaming down International Boulevard. Kat lowers her arm, and the swinging girls let go.

"That is my baby," Amrita says, sighing. "Must be hungry. She's always hungry."

Kavita glances down at her belly. Her smile fades.

"And the other is mine," adds another. Charubala, maybe? She looks about fourteen. Big shadows under her eyes. "Miss Shireen says you're here to help take care of him?"

"Yes, that's what they'll be doing," Miss Shireen says, looking up from thumbing a text. She's forgotten to turn off the music in the background app. "It's time for your sewing class, girls. Kat and Gracie, the babies are waiting in that room."

"We'll take good care of them while you're gone," Gracie promises their mothers. "I helped raise four little sisters, so I have a lot of experience."

"Oh, we are not worried," says Amrita. "We share our babies freely here, just as they do in a village."

The girls head out. The crying gets louder.

"Come on, Kat, that's the sound of hunger," Gracie says.

Here we go. Kat's never even held a baby, let alone fed one. You don't come across too many babies in jiu-jitsu circles. And the kits and cubs and calves and chicks she held at the zoo were probably not the best preparation for humans.

But the *Wonder Woman* score is still playing on Miss Shireen's phone.

Kat follows Gracie into the Room of Wailing.

RAVI

INT. BOSE FLAT—NIGHT

Ravi said yes to Shen's questions, but that was before two hours of nonstop grueling work that includes lifting, jump-roping, crunching, and burpeeing.

Or attempts at all of that, because Ravi sucks at everything.

Shen's whistle is relentless, though, and when Ravi gets back to the Bose flat, he feels like crawling up the stairs. Does he really want to do this all summer?

PG is back, too, drinking tea with Mira and the boys.

"What happened to you?" PG asks as Ravi throws himself into a chair.

"I've been Shenned," Ravi says.

PG and Mira listen to him describe how he spent his afternoon.

"Sounds like a great opportunity to me," PG says.

"You'll at least get a feel for how recruits become rescuers. Arjun said this Shen guy has a great reputation as a trainer."

"I'm not sure I want to do it," Ravi says. He didn't sign up for this extreme training. It's too hot. He'll stay in the air-conditioned office and do more data entry instead. When he's not following up on leads from his search, that is. "Shen's letting his nephew come just to keep his older brother happy, but he isn't seriously training him. And he only agreed to take me on as a favor to Arjun. I'm sure he'll be happy to hear I'm out."

Ravi leans back and closes his eyes. Even recounting his two hours in that sweaty gym is exhausting. He's still sweaty, in fact. He didn't stay to shower because he hadn't brought along fresh underwear.

"But you can't quit now, Ravi," Mira says.

Ravi's eyes fly open. "Why not?"

"If you quit, you'll reinforce what Shen thinks about foreigners," she says. "This is a chance to open his heart again to future visitors. That's why you were sent there, if I know my husband. He's entrusting you with this because he thinks you're capable."

"Arjun Uncle said it might be good for me, too, though. I'm not sure he's right."

"It will be good for you, but also for us." She turns to PG. "Donors from overseas like to visit and learn about our partnership with local police, but Shen recently closed the doors to them. Did he ask you for a commitment, Ravi?"

Ravi remembers the questions. "Yes, I guess he did."

"And what did you say?" PG asks.

"I said I would try."

"Then please don't quit," Mira says. "You'll be proving that Shen—not my husband—is right about working with foreigners."

210

PG gives him a stern look. "This sounds like a good 'act of service' for you, Ravi. That's why we came, remember?"

"Act of sacrifice, you mean," Ravi says, massaging his aching quads.

KAT

INT. ASHA HOUSE BABY CARE ROOM—DAY

The babies are in a room that's so small there's hardly space to walk. It's stuffed with two cots, a small fridge, a sink, a stove, cribs, a changing table, and two rocking chairs.

Good thing Gracie's experienced, even though she's doing a lot of muttering. "Can't believe I came all the way across the world to do what I do at home. You'd think I could learn something new, but no. Babies. Again."

Kat watches her heat a pan of water, mix formula, and warm two bottles by immersing them in hot water. Meanwhile, she sits in a rocking chair and puts her hands over her ears, trying to drown out the sirens shrieking in two of the cribs.

Gracie pulls one bottle out of the pan, picks up a blanketed bundle of scream, and approaches Kat. "Here, bend your left arm just like you did when you were flexing your right one. That elbow's where the baby's head goes. Hold the bottle in your right hand. There you go. Now put the nipple end in the baby's mouth."

The scream bundle is in Kat's arms. She can barely see a tiny, wrinkled face writhing around inside the blanket. She tries to jam the bottle into its open, bawling mouth and misses. Formula trickles out of the nipple and drips everywhere. The small human she's holding wails even more loudly.

"Gracie, help! I can't do this."

Gracie comes back and guides the rubbery tip of the bottle into the baby's mouth.

Crying stops, at least in Kat's arms.

Small lips close.

Sucking begins.

Alleluia.

Kat keeps rocking in exactly the same rhythm. She hardly breathes.

Gracie picks up the other bundle and takes it to the empty rocking chair. As soon as she attaches that baby to a bottle, the room gets quiet.

Kat and Gracie rock and feed in blessed silence broken only by vacuum-y sucking noises coming from the hungry humans in their arms.

"Breast milk is better for babies," Gracie says. "Hope they get that most of the time."

The one Kat's holding is draining the bottle much faster than Gracie's. "Are they boys or girls?"

"I think this one's a boy and that one's a girl. Wow, yours is a guzzler. Mine's barely finished an ounce and she's almost done with six."

Devouring her food like a Filhote. Good for her.

"You'll need to burp her soon," Gracie says. "And then change her diaper."

The baby slurps the last sip of formula. As Kat pulls out the bottle, the suction makes a whooshing noise. She looks up. Kat looks down. Big, bright brown eyes. Squishy little nose.

"Hold her upright with her face over your shoulder," Gracie says.

Carefully, Kat shifts the baby into a vertical position.

"Rest her against your body, so you can pat her back with your free hand. That's how you get them to burp."

Kat pulls the baby a little closer and pats her back a few times.

Nothing.

Pat, pat, pat again.

A ferocious ERRRRGH erupts out of the tiny mouth. Sounds more like a roar than a burp. "Wow," Kat says.

"Good one," Gracie says.

Suddenly, with a mewing sound, the baby's small body goes limp and nestles against Kat. "Does she have a name?" Kat asks.

"I'm sure she does," Gracie says. "We'll ask Amrita and Charubala when they get back. For now, tell you what—you give mine a nickname, and I'll pick one for yours."

Kat looks down at the boy in Gracie's arms. "Okay. We'll call him . . . Logan."

Gracie has to think about that one for a second. "You mean from X-Men?"

"Yep."

"The only reason I know that name is because I watched every single one of those dumb movies with Ravi. Okay, fine. We'll call yours Diana. That's Wonder Woman's name, right?"

"Right. It's perfect. Especially if she keeps feeding like she just did."

In a low voice, Gracie starts singing a lullaby-sounding

song in Spanish. Outside the open window, rain is falling hard, slapping against the banana leaves and drenching the night-blooming jasmine. Baby Diana is warm. Smells of powder. Kat takes a deep breath and inhales the scent of flowers and baby skin.

She pictures the faces of the girls who felt the strength of her arm. Here it comes. Golden-Ruling Plan B, in full form. Twenty-four other girls in this house aren't pregnant. Maybe *they* can learn some jiu-jitsu. But she'll still need to convince Miss Shireen that self-defense is as crucial for them to learn as sewing.

For now, she rocks and Diana gurgles. Gracie's lullaby ends and out of nowhere Kat remembers a song Mom used to sing years ago. She clears her throat and starts it, even though she knows she's probably off-key.

There sit two little birdies on my windowsill, the name of one is Jack and the other one's name is Jill. Summer's nearly over. It will soon be time. For these little birdies, to look for a sunnier clime. Fly away, Jack, fly away, Jill—

EEEHR! A smaller-sounding burp interrupts her song. Gracie's patting Logan's back and smiling at Kat.

Kat smiles back.

They rock their sleeping bundles.

RAVI

INT. BOSE FLAT—NIGHT

The girls are in the flat when Ravi gets out of the shower. "Hey, Rob—Ravi!" Gracie says. "How was Sergeant Shen?"

No hug, he notices. And he'd better get used to answering to Rob-Ravi, because it's going to take PG and Gracie a while to make the switch.

"Tough. He's training me this summer—not for rescues, but to do Arjun Uncle a favor. They both seem to think he can get my body in better shape."

"What's wrong with your body?" Gracie asks. "It looks fine to me."

Ravi straightens his tired shoulders. The words are good to hear after being pommeled all afternoon. And then he sees the girls' suitcases standing by the door. "Hey, why are your bags out here?"

"We're moving to Miss Shireen's place," Kat tells him. "Right after dinner."

What? They can't do that. "For how long?"

"For the whole summer," Kat says.

No. Suddenly, he realizes how much he's been looking forward to having Gracie under the same roof all summer. Even after long days, full of potentially soul-crushing searching and body-crushing workouts, she would be there to hang out with in the evenings. And now she's decided to leave.

Then PG comes out, hauling *his* suitcase, too. That's right—he's heading to the dorms at the Bible college for the rest of the week.

Ravi turns to him. "Are you okay with the girls moving out?"

"I'm fine with it. Turns out Asha House needs some overnight help, and Miss Shireen's place is on the premises, so it's perfect. I'm proud of Kat and Gracie for stepping up."

Ravi's never liked the feeling of being left behind. In fact he hate, hate, hates it. "I thought we were supposed to be a team." Even he can hear the sadness in his voice.

"We'll see you at the office for Bangla lessons in the mornings," Gracie says. "And maybe we can meet on Fridays and Saturdays to sightsee and stuff."

Great. He's probably going to get even less one-on-one time with her than he does in Massachusetts. And no texting, either.

"Maybe we can catch a movie or two on the weekends," Kat adds.

"And I'm coming back on Saturday evenings," says PG, chiming into the "cheer Ravi up" chorus. "We'll go to church together on Sundays. But listen, Ravi . . . I can come back this Thursday to go with you to the orphanage if you want."

"No, thanks, PG," Ravi says quickly. "I'll be fine."

Opening his file is something he wants to do alone. If he wanted someone along, he'd have come back to Kolkata with his parents. Or he'd ask Gracie to join him.

Mira calls them to dinner. She heaps their plates with steaming white rice, yellow lentils, cucumber salad, egg-and-potato curry, and garnishes of tangy lime and spicy mango pickle. Beside every plate is a spoon, but Arjun ignores it and starts eating with his right hand. The twins are eating Indian-style, too.

Ravi catches Gracie's eye. Immediately, they both put down their spoons and start using their right hands, too. Once again, in sync. What's he going to do without her around?

That weird have-I-done-this-before feeling returns to Ravi as his fingers form small balls of rice and lentils and pop them into his mouth. PG and Kat and Mira stick with spoons, but Ravi guesses their hostess has provided those only to help her guests feel at home.

"I'm sorry you girls have to leave us," Mira says. "But it's wonderful you can help the new mothers. They're just children themselves."

So that's what they'll be doing, Ravi thinks. *Taking care of babies. Exactly what Gracie DIDN'T want to do.* She grins at him across the table.

"How were the babies for you, Kat?" PG asks.

Kat shrugs. "Okay. Turns out they're not so different from cubs or pups at the zoo." Ravi can't help noticing that she seems much more relaxed than she did this morning.

"You work at a zoo, Kat Didi?" one of the twins asks. Bijoy, Ravi thinks.

"Sort of," she answers. "I take tickets for a train ride. But someday I want to study zoology."

"Cool!" says the other. Anand, probably.

"You'll have to visit *our* cheer-ee-ya-kha-nah," says Mira. "It's the oldest zoo in all of India."

"Nice work, Mira," Arjun says. "Our family has decided to throw in as many Bangla words as we can to help you succeed in your Bangla ish-cool."

"Ish-cool. School. What's the word for *baby*?" Gracie asks.

"Bahch-cha!" the twins answer, in unison.

"What's going to happen to them?" Ravi asks, trying to sound casual. "The babies, I mean. Will Asha House let them stay there?"

Arjun shakes his head. "For a while, at least. We are struggling to care for these babies of babies. Our goal for rescued girls is repatriation with grace to their families and villages. Bringing a baby along who was fathered by a customer or pimp makes that much more difficult."

"It's not the baby's fault," Kat says immediately.

Silently, Ravi agrees. Are they going to be deposited in an orphanage in Kolkata? Sent far away to strangers? "Isn't there any way they can stay with their mothers?" he asks.

Gracie looks at him, her eyes wide.

"We're doing our best," Arjun says. "So much need. So few resources. And there's another due soon, too."

"Kavita's," Kat says. "When is her due date?"

"Quite soon, I think," says Arjun. "I'm waiting until the baby comes before I ask her to testify."

Suddenly, Kat leaps to her feet.

KAT

Kat can't believe what she's just heard. "What? You're going to ask her to go to court? After what she's been through already?"

"It's hard, but that's what she must do to get this man behind bars."

"She can't do that! She needs to move forward now, not relive her past! She made that fund-raising film for you guys. Wasn't that enough?"

"Time out, Kat," PG says, and his usually calm voice has a warning edge.

"Kavita volunteered for that opportunity," the man says. "Shireen made sure she was ready. The trauma counselor told us that it actually helped her."

Kat's going to have to rename him. He's more like a Spotted Hyena than a Pheasant. "Testifying will just bring her more trauma," she says, ignoring the expression on PG's face. "It's easy for you to suggest, but she's the one who'll have to face her abuser."

Gracie gives the hem of Kat's blouse a small tug. "Easy," she whispers.

"Arjun and Shireen are the experts here, not us," PG says.

His tone is steely. "They know these girls. They've been doing this for years. Sit down, Kat."

Kat sits. Her butt lands with a loud thud on the wooden chair. She leans back and folds her arms across her chest.

"First abuse, and now childbirth," says Mira. "Poor girl. I can understand why you're upset on her behalf, Kat."

Arjun reaches over and lightly touches his wife's shoulder. The food that seemed so delicious before this conversation now tastes like dust. Kat pushes away her plate. Gracie elbows her, but Kat doesn't say anything.

"Thanks for a delicious dinner, Mira Auntie," Gracie says. "It's been a long, challenging day. Sorry if we seem . . . tired."

Not tired, Kat thinks. *Pissed off.*

PG pats his stomach. "Our church is hoping I'll lose a few pounds while I'm here. At this rate, Mira, I'll get back to Boston with even more of me to love. I hope the food at the seminary dining hall isn't this good."

He's trying to lighten the atmosphere, but it doesn't work. The tension in the room is as heavy as the humidity in the air.

Kat stands up again. "Let's go, Gracie. Those babies need feeding every three hours. It's going to be a long night for us."

"I have to go, too," PG says. "It's going to be a long auto-rickshaw ride for me."

"No rickshaw rides for any of you," the Hyena man says. "I'll drive you. Ravi, will you carry a few suitcases?"

RAVI

After the girls, Arjun, and PG leave, Ravi helps the twins clear the table, responding on autopilot with "that's right" and "maybe" to their video game argument. Why did Kat react so fiercely to Arjun? Her anger seemed out of proportion. Nefertiti, back with full force.

If he had his phone, he would have texted Gracie, and they would have gone back and forth to process the evening. But there was no way to do that now. And she'd hurried off so fast Ravi didn't even have a chance to say goodbye.

He hadn't told her about Bontu. Or shared details about Shen.

Her rows of pink hearts always encouraged him. How is he going to make it through the summer without them—*and* without her hugs?

KAT

INT./EXT. MISS SHIREEN'S COTTAGE—NIGHT

"Did that conversation bring up memories, Kat?" Gracie asks gently after the Maruti drops them off and the guard locks the gate behind them. "Is that why you got so upset?"

Kat takes a big breath of night-blooming jasmine. "I shouldn't have lost it like that, I guess. I just don't think Kavita should testify. She's already gone through so much."

"Maybe you're right. But we have to trust our Indian hosts. We signed PG's contracts, remember?"

Kat sighs. "I know. I just hate it when men tell a girl what to do. Especially after other men do terrible things to her."

They haul their suitcases to Miss Shireen's lighted cottage in the back of the enclosed garden. As the older woman gives them a quick tour of her place, Kat feels herself start to relax again. This door secures with a lock, bolt, and chain. A small spare room has been set up with two mattresses on the floor, two cots, and two sleeping (for now) babies. Miss Shireen shows them the small kitchen where they can mix formula and heat up bottles, and the bathroom, which is full of scented shampoos, perfumed soap, and other girl-only products. It locks, too.

"Good night, girls," Miss Shireen says. Putting earplugs in her ears, she disappears into her bedroom.

Gracie and Kat decide to stick with their original assignments—Logan for Gracie and Diana for Kat. Logan wakes once in the night with a soft cry. Diana screams like a banshee four different times, bringing Kat to her feet with her heart racing.

That means they both get woken up five times. The good news is that Kat can already bottle-feed on autopilot by the time the sun rises.

INT. BENGALI EMANCIPATION SOCIETY
HEADQUARTERS—DAY

Kat and Gracie fall asleep during the rickshaw ride to the office, and the driver has to raise his voice to wake them up when they arrive. The buzzer lets them enter and they stumble into the classroom where Mrs. Bengal Tiger and Ravi are waiting.

Their teacher starts with phrases that she thinks they'll probably use every day.

Kaw-thoh dhahm? How much does it cost?

Rickshaw koh-th-aye? Where is the rickshaw?

Kat's tired brain struggles to keep up as the three of them repeat the sounds of the words. Their teacher explains the difference between the "yous" in Bangla. Ap-nee for adult strangers and people who are older, thu-mee for friends and people your own age, and tu-ee for your closest friends and younger brothers and sisters. So, ap-nee for the Partridge,

Mrs. Tiger, and Miss Shireen. Thu-mee for Ravi and Gracie. And tu-ee for Baby Diana, Kavita, and the other Asha House girls.

Nothing at all for Hyena man.

RAVI

"I won't be here tomorrow for Bangla class, Mrs. Gupta."

Tomorrow is Thursday. The day he's been waiting for his entire life, even though he didn't realize it until a few months ago.

Mrs. Gupta tips her head to the side. "Teek ach-che."

"We won't be here, either," Gracie adds quickly.

"We won't?" Kat asks.

"No . . . I'm exhausted," Gracie says. "I could use a morning to sleep in. Jet lag's no joke."

"Well, then, I shall see you all again on shombar dheen. Monday."

After Mrs. Gupta exits, the three of them find a table in a corner of the common room. Today Gopal offers flat circles of wheat that he calls chapati, along with eggplant, potatoes, and more lentils.

Ravi's ravenous. Must be all that working out with Shen Every muscle is crying for fuel. Food's been decent here, thank goodness. A little spicy, maybe, but tasty. And weirdly familiar.

"How were the babies last night?" he asks, spooning more eggplant onto his plate.

"My girl eats enough for three babies," Kat says, sounding proud.

"Mine sips his formula like a hummingbird," Gracie says. "But I'll fatten him up, don't worry."

Ravi glances at Kat. Should he ask why she got so upset at dinner? Maybe that would be too intrusive. Besides, she's with Gracie. It doesn't get better than that when you need to talk to someone.

"I think I've made a new friend," he says. "Bontu, the guy who's 'working out' with me." Ravi puts "working out" in air quotes. "He's Shen's nephew. Doesn't really want to be there, but his father's making him."

"Do *you* want to be there?" Gracie asks.

"Yeah," Kat adds, "why is that bossy man making *you* train, anyway?"

"Arjun's not bossy, Kat. He just wants me to change Shen's mind about Americans."

"So you have to prove to this other hater that all of us aren't crap?" Kat asks.

"Basically. Not sure Shen's a hater, though. He acts tough, but I think he's one of the good guys." *Like Arjun*, he thinks, but doesn't risk saying it.

"What's your schedule going to look like?" Gracie asks, reaching for another chapati. "Ours is Bangla, babies, and then more babies—five afternoons plus three nights. Every week."

"Intense. I'll do an hour or so of data entry here after lunch—which looks like it might actually be interesting—and then head to the training center Mondays through Thursdays."

"How long is one session?" Gracie asks.

"Two hours. Sure glad Bontu's there or I might not survive this 'act of service.' Wait till you see that kid—he looks kind of like a giant toddler."

Kat tears a strip of chapati and wraps it around a piece of potato. "Maybe he's a mutant, like me," she says. "Miss Shireen's tailor's delivering my jumbo-sized uniforms this afternoon." She pops the savory bite into her mouth.

"The Asha House girls think you're a goddess, Kat," Gracie says. "Just wait until they see you in a shalwar kameez."

"Is yours going to be yellow, too, Kat?" Ravi asks, fingering the soft material of Gracie's sleeve.

Kat chugs some water; she must have accidentally included a piece of chili pepper along with the potato. "My Asha House uniform will be. But Miss Shireen's turning me into a human rainbow. She ordered four other shalwars for me—lavender, aqua, lime green, and pink. I haven't worn pink since I was seven."

Kat in a pink shalwar kameez? Ravi will have to see it to believe it. Maybe wearing colors is *her* "act of service."

KAT

"So . . . tomorrow's your big day, Ro—Ravi," Gracie says.

"Yep," he says. "My appointment's at ten."

Gracie catches Kat's eye.

"You want company?" Kat asks.

"No, thanks," he says.

"Maybe PG *should* go with you, Ravi," Gracie tells him.

"Or Gracie, by herself," Kat adds quickly. "I can handle both babies on my own for one afternoon." *Has the lack of sleep made me lose brain cells?*

"I'll be fine," Ravi says.

"Wish we had our phones," Gracie says. "Then you could text us if you need anything. Are you *sure* one of us can't go with you?"

Ravi swivels his head in a figure eight, as if he's been saying no-yes like that for years. "Don't worry about me. You guys take care of those babies. Pass the lentils, will you, Kat?"

Kat hands him the bowl. Obviously, Kal-El doesn't want to discuss his search for planet Krypton. She can't help feeling worried. What's he going to find? Something that might hurt him? Or nothing at all, which might devastate him even more?

RAVI

INT./EXT. KOLKATA POLICE TRAINING
CENTER—DAY

Ravi hails an auto-rickshaw by scraping the air with his palm down. *Take that, Shen*, he thinks. Only a few days in Kolkata and he's already gesturing like a Bengali. Three auto-rickshaws stop for him and he jumps into the nearest one.

"Police training center, please," he tells the driver.

The man looks closer at Ravi's face. "Mr. Amit Biswas? Why no lee-mo gari?"

A limo. Right. That's what Bollywood stars cruise around in.

"No. Sorry. I'm not him."

Heavy drops are falling again, steamy monsoon rain that comes and goes, drenching the makeshift shelters on sidewalks where children are resting beside their mothers. It's nap-after-lunchtime everywhere in the city. Everywhere except in the police training center, where Ravi's out-of-shape body is about to generate a personal monsoon of sweat.

Just as the auto-rickshaw pulls up to his destination, Ravi sees Shen dismounting from an über-cool KTM motorcycle. He's wearing reflective sunglasses and a black leather jacket over his uniform. *How does it feel to maneuver a KTM through this busy Kolkata traffic? Must be like playing a driving game in five dimensions.*

As Ravi pays the driver and walks up the stairs, he indulges in a mini-fantasy. *Shen loans him the bike. Ravi's wearing silver aviators and his biceps are bulging. He stops the KTM in front of the office and a beautiful girl in a yellow shalwar kameez with long black hair runs out. She jumps on behind Ravi and wraps her arms around him, her embrace so familiar* . . . Wait! What was going on inside his muddled brain? *Everything* about that fantasy was off, especially the bulging biceps part.

He's brought tennis shoes and fresh undies along this time. He changes into the shorts and T-shirt in the locker room slowly because he's so sore.

When he walks into the gym, Bontu's face splits into a watermelon smile. "Ravi! I ate six chapatis and a big bowl of lentils for lunch, so my tummy may be troublesome. Apologies in advance."

Shen nods in Ravi's direction. "Start with laps." He blows the whistle twice.

Ravi takes off, stiff legs shrieking in pain. Bontu, too, starts jogging around the edge of the gym. Ravi manages nine laps this time and Bontu pants alongside for three before collapsing, cheering Ravi on from a floor mat.

The whistle blows once. Ravi stops, trying to catch his breath. His shirt is so drenched he could probably water a garden by wringing it out. And kill everything growing in it, judging by his stench.

BEEP! "Push-ups," Shen barks.

Ravi does six today instead of five. He strains to lift barbells with both arms that Shen can lift easily with one. Next come the dreaded crunches. Bontu's upwind of Ravi and foul post-lentil smells do start coming his way, just as predicted.

Bontu fans the air around his bottom and grins at Ravi through his legs.

Two hours of sweating later, the last whistle of the day—three short *beeps* in quick succession—dismisses them to the locker room. Bontu trots off to shower, but Ravi needs to tell Mr. Badass that he's not showing up the next day.

"I won't be here tomorrow, sir."

"Quitting already? I'm not surprised. Americans can't survive training in our Kolkata heat."

"I'm not quitting, sir. I have an appointment. But I'll be back on Monday."

"Ehh," Shen grunts. "We'll see."

That syllable of disgust grates on Ravi's nerves. Even though it means he'll lose quarts—or liters—of sweat over the next nine weeks, he isn't going to quit.

KAT

INT. ASHA HOUSE—DAY

Kat mixes her baby's third bottle of the afternoon. At this rate, Baby Diana might grow up to be as big as her Kat Auntie. She's eating twice as fast as Logan. Kat puts her in a vertical position for another Wonder Woman burp.

"Come on, little Logan, drink, drink, drink," Gracie says. "You need to grow. Sure hope Ravi's going to be okay tomorrow."

"He's tougher than he looks," Kat says.

"Logan or Ravi?"

"Both."

"That's why I canceled our Bangla class," Gracie says. "I thought we could kind of lurk around outside the orphanage and keep an eye out for him."

Not a bad idea. "Do you want to go by yourself?"

"This isn't about *us*, Ravi and me," Gracie says. "This is about *him*. My gut tells me he might appreciate both of us being there."

"Okay, then. I'm in."

Miss Shireen comes in holding a folded stack of yellow, lavender, aqua, pink, and lime-green fabric. "Katina, here are your shalwars. Take the yellow one and put it on, please. I'll hold the baby."

As soon as Diana leaves Kat's arms, she starts to cry. "She likes her head a little higher," Kat tells Miss Shireen.

"Kat's a baby whisperer now," Gracie says.

Miss Shireen smiles and shifts the baby's head a little higher.

Kat takes the yellow shalwar kameez into the bathroom and changes out of her black jeans and shirt. This time the outfit fits. She walks to the mirror, bracing herself for the sight. But it's not bad. Loose and flowy, not restrictive and clingy. But so dang yellow. Instead of the long yellow orna, she decides to keep wearing Grandma Vee's chiffon scarf. *Red and yellow, kill a fellow,* the herpetologist told her when she was visiting the snakes. *Yellow on black, venom lack.*

When Kat emerges, it's time for tea and biscuits, and the girls are returning from their afternoon activities. It's their favorite part of the day, when they gather in the common room to relax and chat. They surround Kat immediately, oohing and aahing over her in the XXL version of their uniforms.

Kat looks around at them, taking stock of their bodies, assessing their BJJ potential. Some are so small, they might not even make the minimum weight required to grapple in any category. Amrita might be a good candidate, but her baby's only three months old. How long after childbirth can a body begin to fight?

She catches sight of Kavita sitting wearily on the sofa. Carrying two cups of tea, Kat goes over to sit beside her.

"You look so Indian in that shalwar, Katina Didi," Kavita says, taking one of the cups.

"Thanks," Kat says, then hesitates. "How are you feeling?"

"I'm a bit frightened about the future, to tell you the truth. I'm not at all certain I'll be able to protect this baby. Not when I wasn't able to protect myself."

My point exactly, Kat thinks, a bit surprised by the honest answer. She doesn't say anything out loud, though. Lost her cool the night before at the Bose flat, but she has to stay in control now. Plan B depends on Miss Shireen trusting her.

"I only hope it doesn't turn out to be a girl. Life can be so much harder for a girl." Kavita's hand curves around her belly. "Some people find out and choose to stop the baby when they learn it's a girl. But I did not want that."

No questions, Kat tells herself sternly. But she can share about *her* life, can't she? "My mother was sixteen, one year older than you, when she became pregnant. She chose to have me, too. And raised me by herself, with no relatives to help."

"A strong woman," Kavita says. "Like her daughter."

"She's always taken good care of me."

"That is my wish, too, Katina Didi. To protect and provide for my child. That is why I am working hard at sewing and studying in school."

"You can do it, Kavita. I know you can."

Gracie and Miss Shireen come out of the baby room, holding Diana and Logan.

"Does it fit?" Miss Shireen asks. "We've been waiting."

Oops, Kat thinks. *Forgot about modeling for them.* "What do you think?" She jumps up and puts her hands into a namaste—she's starting to like this no-touch greeting—and swishes her hips so the yellow fabric swirls around her body. "I'm Bollywood ready, Miss Shireen."

One of the girls hoots and another whistles, making everyone laugh.

"Wow, Kat," Gracie says. "You look stunning."

"Fits perfectly," Miss Shireen adds. "I'll give the tailor your thanks."

"Definitely," Kat says. Time to plant a seed. "Can your girls play sports in these shalwar thingies?"

Miss Shireen hands her baby Diana and looks around the room. "Thomra kee khaa-lah khel-the pah-row, jokh-ohn shal-war poh-row?"

"Badminton!"

"Football!"

Football?!

"Soccer, you call it in America," Miss Shireen explains.

"What about fighting?" Kat asks. "Wrestling? Boxing? Judo?"

Miss Shireen raises her eyebrows, but she translates this, too.

The girls don't answer as readily this time. "Indian girls like us—from the village—do not learn to fight, Katina Didi," Charubala says finally. She isn't smiling. None of them are.

Miss Shireen claps her hands. "Dinnertime. Give the babies to their mothers, Katina and Gracie. They need breast milk. Time for us to head home."

RAVI

INT. KOLKATA POLICE TRAINING CENTER—DAY

Reality hits in the shower. Ravi's arms are so sore that scrubbing himself with soap is another mini-workout. The cold water feels incredible, though.

Tomorrow, tomorrow, tomorrow, he thinks. The chant almost sounds like music in his head. A song of hope that brought him here.

Even moving slower than usual, he's dried off and back in his jeans and blue button-down shirt while Bontu's still in his stall belting out a Bollywood song. "Hey, Bontu!" Ravi calls. "I won't be here tomorrow, but I'll see you on Monday."

Bontu sticks his soapy head out. "I hear other Americans are visiting with you? Two beautiful girls. Am I right?"

"How did you hear that?"

"I have spies in many places," Bontu says. "Including the headquarters where Arjun Uncle works."

"Oh, so you know him? He's the one who told you, then. Wait—he said they were *beautiful*?"

"Oh, no. Mira Auntie told me that. My parents are their friends. But Arjun Uncle suggested I take all three of you on a tour of our city this Saturday. I happen to be the best tour guide in Kolkata."

"The best, huh? That's a big claim."

"I'll be launching my tour company shortly," Bontu says. "Taking you people around will be excellent practice for me."

"Is that your big dream?" Ravi asks.

"Yes! Wait just one minute and I will tell all." He ducks his head back in the stall and rinses himself off, and then steps out with a towel wrapped around his waist. Sort of. It definitely doesn't cover all of him. "As soon as Baba gives up on this idiotic police plan, I shall have a sign painted on my car. 'Bontu's Bengal Barano,' I'll be calling my business. BBB for short."

Ravi feels a twinge of envy. Bontu's only a year or two older than he is and knows exactly what he wants to do for a career. All Ravi knows is what he *doesn't* want to do—go to law school. Or take over the family business as the next figurehead president.

"What does 'Ba-rah-no' mean?" he asks.

Bontu has to think for a moment. "Outing, I think is the best English translation. I plan to take tourists around West Bengal, including the Sunderbans, where wild tigers still roam, and Darjeeling, our lovely Himalayan mountain town. Our home state is a marvelous place, Ravi. Starting with the city of our birth. Will you let me take you and your companions on a tailor-made tour on Saturday?"

Ravi hesitates. He has no idea what he'll be doing Saturday. So much depends on what happens tomorrow at the orphanage.

"That might work. I'll borrow a phone to confirm, okay? What's your number?"

"No mobile?" Bontu says, fumbling in his bag for a scrap of paper and pen.

"We agreed not to have them with us this summer. Hard to live without mine. Don't tell your uncle. He'd probably say 'Ehh' again."

"He's kinder than he sounds. Here's my number. Hope to see you Saturday, Ravi."

KAT

INT. MISS SHIREEN'S COTTAGE—NIGHT

Miss Shireen serves a simple supper. "This is called duudh, bhath, kawla. Milk, rice, bananas. Mixed with a lot of sugar. How we Bengalis love our sweets. Have you tried roshogollah yet?"

Kat listens with half a mind as Miss Shireen describes some other Bengali treats. The other half is wondering if and when to bring up her Plan B.

The phone rings, and Miss Shireen picks it up. "Yes, I know that boy's family well," she says. "If it is permitted by their pastor and Mira, it is okay with me."

"What was that about, Miss Shireen?" Gracie asks.

"That was Arjun. Sergeant Shen's nephew, the boy who's training with Ravi, has offered to take you sightseeing on Saturday. If you want to go, it might be a good way to see our city."

Kat hesitates. This must be the giant toddler that Ravi described. "Do you know him?"

"I've seen him two or three times. A nice, jolly young man."

Gracie looks at Kat. "We'll think about it, Miss Shireen," she says. "I'm off to take a shower."

Now Kat and Miss Shireen are alone at the table.

"I hear you were upset about Arjun's intent to ask Kavita to testify," Miss Shireen says immediately.

Stupid, tattletaling Hyena. "Yes, I am. Why is he so eager to get her in that courthouse? If it were up to me, I'd talk her out of it."

"You'll do no such thing, young lady. Leave her to us."

Kat launches her move. "Well, I think she should at least learn how to defend herself. And so should the other girls. Miss Shireen, I've studied Brazilian jiu-jitsu for five years. That's a martial art. I'm an adult blue belt now. If you let me, I could teach them a few ways to fight off an attacker."

Miss Shireen drains her water glass and puts it down—it lands on the counter with a sharp rap. "Do you think we Indians are so backward that we don't know martial arts?"

Maybe, Kat thinks. She shifts her approach. "No, of course not."

"Fighting sports originated in Asia, remember? This part of the world. Do you think we don't care about teaching our vulnerable girls self-defense?" She's reminding Kat even more of a Bobcat in this moment than when they first met.

"Well, I don't see you teaching them—"

"You're wrong about that, too. Kolkata police launched a project some years back to empower school- and college-going girls with self-defense techniques. It is running successfully, I've heard, with several hundred girls enrolled."

"Oh. I didn't know that."

"Clearly not. Also in our city, we have several successful self-defense academies that train girls in karate, judo, tae kwon do. I'm certain they must offer the Brazilian method that's your specialty. Martial arts coaches are training hundreds of schoolgirls there at a nominal cost. And even that cost is waived for those from economically disadvantaged families."

I should have done more research, Kat scolds herself. She hadn't thought that the Asha House girls would know so much English, or be up to speed on movies, like *Wonder Woman* and celebrities like Halle Berry. And now, apparently Kolkata's bursting at the seams with self-defense teachers. Feeling a twinge of shame, she softens her tone. "What about *your* girls, Miss Shireen? Shouldn't they get a chance at defending themselves? We were told they might be at risk again once they turn eighteen."

"Yes, that's a worry. But I don't think self-defense lessons are suitable for them. It's better to teach girls who haven't yet been traumatized."

"But why? Jiu-jitsu could help *them* feel empowered. And safer. For the rest of their lives. Don't they deserve it?"

Miss Shireen yanks off her glasses. "Of course they do! They deserve the world. But unfortunately, Kat, even if I did offer them such a course, our girls may not want to learn." She rubs her eyes wearily. "They are not as strong and tall as you. Didn't you see them admiring your muscles? These girls won't believe *they* will be able to fight a man because—well, sadly, most of them have tried. And failed."

Kat doesn't give up. Tapping out isn't an option. "I've seen girls their size demolish much bigger opponents. That's what jiu-jitsu is all about. I'm here. I'll teach them for free."

"I'm sorry, but no, Kat. I simply can't expend any more energy on this subject. I have girls who need treatment for STDs. Girls waking up with panic attacks. A waiting list for new arrivals. One of our trauma counselors is sick. On top of everything else, I'm worried about housing our incoming arrival—Kavita's baby. We're already so crowded."

Kat sighs. Plan C, then. Whatever that might be. She has an inkling of an idea already. "Okay, fine. But would you at least consider *seeing* me do a jiu-jitsu demonstration someday? If it doesn't take time away from taking care of the babies?"

"Maybe. Now, good night. I'm sorry if I sounded angry."

Maybe. That's better than a flat-out no. *Plan C, here I come.* "Good night, Miss Shireen. *I'm* sorry . . . I mean, I know you love the girls."

You'd have to be an idiot to miss that.

RAVI

Ravi hasn't slept all night.

How can you, when you're about to visit the orphanage where you lived from infancy to age three? And, if all goes well, start a journey to find your first mother?

He can't eat much, either. Thankfully, Arjun left early, the twins aren't feeling well, and Mira's running around with a thermometer and aspirin. Nobody asks questions as he calls out a goodbye and leaves the flat.

The auto-rickshaw ride through town takes a half hour even though the orphanage is only six miles away. As the driver steers him through taxis and cars and bikes and rickshaws, Ravi remembers the counselor's advice about moderating his hopes. But he's way beyond that now. His are so sky-high, his heart is pounding and he's drenched with sweat even though it's only nine in the morning.

He wonders if anyone will remember him.

He wonders what's inside his file.

Will it lead him to her?

The rickshaw stops outside a two-story building. The rain has abated, and Ravi can hear children behind the high gate shouting and laughing and playing.

He pulls out some money to pay his fare, but the auto-rickshaw driver shakes his head. "Free, Mr. Biswas. Free for you. I like your fillums very much. I take photo for wife?"

"I'm—er, not Amit Biswas," Ravi says, but that doesn't stop the driver from taking a selfie of the two of them and driving off with a big grin.

Ravi rings the bell. After a short wait, the gate swings open a crack and an old man peers out.

"Thumi keh?" he asks Ravi.

Ravi's glad he tuned in to his Bangla lesson the day before, because he knows he's being asked who he is.

"Amar nam Ravi," he answers. "I used to live here. In this place."

The caretaker squints through the thick, dusty lenses of his glasses. After he looks Ravi up and down a few times, the gate swings open wide enough to let a visitor enter.

"Office this way," he says.

He walks slowly. Extremely slowly.

Ravi follows him, feeling like he's in a slow-motion montage. The yard is full of children playing hopscotch, jumping rope, drawing designs on the pavement, and kicking soccer balls. Unlike the children who beg for money on the streets, these kids look taken care of—healthy, dressed in cute blue-and-white school uniforms, the littler ones supervised by kind-faced women in saris. Nobody pays much attention to Ravi. He figures he must look like yet another Bengali man coming through for some reason that doesn't involve them.

Inside the building, the caretaker creaks down the hall. Ravi wonders if any human being on earth could walk any slower. He actually has time to study each poster on the wall as they pass by. And practically memorize them.

STOP TRAFFICKING, says one. ADOPT LEGALLY. A man's hands are reaching out to snatch a toddler sitting on the grass in the shade of a coconut tree. Ravi's heart skips a beat. Was *he* trafficked? He remembers that movie about some Indian kid who got separated from his birth mother and ended up adopted in Australia. He hadn't wanted to see it, so his parents went without him. That boy was almost trafficked in one scene, Mom told him. Maybe that's Ravi's story, too. Lost or stolen, separated from a mother who never wanted to give him up.

They pass an open door to a room full of cribs. Two women in saris are each feeding one baby. None of the other babies waiting in the cribs are crying much, Ravi notices.

Back along the hallway, his eyes travel to another poster. MOTHER INDIA ADOPTS! it says, showing an Indian woman in a sari cradling a baby. A brown man stands beside her, gazing down at the baby with obvious affection.

A surge of missing his parents sweeps through Ravi. Mom never wears a sari, but in his baby book photos, she's holding little Ravi just as lovingly as this woman was holding her baby. And Dad's face always lights up at the sight of him, just like the man in the poster's.

"Here we are," his guide says, stopping in front of a closed door.

KAT

INT. MISS SHIREEN'S COTTAGE—DAY

Miss Shireen's gone by the time Gracie walks into the kitchen to join Kat for breakfast. In her all-white pajamas, she looks more like a dove than ever.

"No babies last night, no Bangla class this morning," she says. "I slept twelve hours. This just might be what I needed to get over jet lag. Or baby lag. But we have to get going to that orphanage soon. Ravi's probably already on his way."

Kat takes stock of her housemate with "Plan C" eyes.

Gracie's tiny.

No muscles in sight.

Light-featherweight, probably.

If Kat can prove someone *her* size can fight off an attack . . .

"Gracie!" she says. "Would you like to learn a few jiu-jitsu moves?"

"What? I've never fought anyone in my life. I'm too small!"

"That's why I want to teach you," Kat says. "If Miss Shireen sees that *you* can defend yourself, even from a big dude, she might change her mind and let the Asha House girls learn, too."

Gracie's quiet for a minute. "I had no idea you were thinking of doing that, Kat. Are you sure Miss Shireen won't be mad?"

"She said she'd be open to a demonstration, and then *maybe* she'd consider it," Kat explains.

Gracie hesitates, then: "Could you teach me how to fight off a man who weighs about two hundred pounds?"

"I think so."

"How long will that take?"

"I'd say you could learn three moves in a couple of months."

"Then I'm in. But let's not tell anyone about this until I actually believe I can do it, okay? I might be a total failure."

"You won't. We won't. We'll train."

"But when? Our schedule's so tight already."

Kat thinks for a moment. "If we get to the office by eight thirty, we'll have an hour before Bangla class starts and enough time to get cleaned up, too. That big room where we study is perfect. It even has mats. The first level of jiu-jitsu isn't hard to learn, but all of it builds on regular practice. It's about the body developing habits so that instincts kick in when we need them in a crisis." *I sound exactly like Saundra*, Kat realizes.

"Okay, okay. We can start all that on Monday. Right now, we have to get changed. I want to be in front of that orphanage when Ravi comes out."

RAVI

INT./EXT. SHISHU JATNA SAMITY ORPHANAGE—DAY

The old man knocks on the door, and after a few long minutes, it opens. A woman holding the doorknob peers out at Ravi. The caretaker turns and starts shuffling away.

"May I help you?" the woman asks.

"Yes. I . . . I used to live here once. I have an appointment at ten? I'm a bit early."

Her face breaks into a smile and she opens the door wide. "Ah! Come in, come in! I am Mrs. Banerjee, and I have been looking forward so much to seeing one of our children returning home. Welcome back, welcome back. Mr. Kamal!" The caretaker stops and turns. "Prepare tea, please!"

Great. Tea. That will probably take an hour for Mr. Kamal to brew. And Ravi's counting the minutes now until he can open his file. While they wait, Mrs. Banerjee takes the chair behind her desk and he sits across from her.

"I have only been directing the orphanage for twelve years," she says. "So unfortunately I was not here at the same time as you."

"I left fifteen years ago. For the United States."

"Oh, what a wonderful place to grow up!"

Easy for you to say, Ravi thinks. *You weren't forced out of your homeland without any choice.* "Mrs. Banerjee, do you have my file? I was told I could access it."

"Ah, yes. Of course. Let me find it for you right away."

A dozen tall, heavy filing cabinets line the wall. Ravi waits as she opens one and then another. Is he there? Have they lost him? The minutes are starting to feel like hours, which means Mr. Kamal will be back in a week.

Mrs. Banerjee is still opening and closing drawers, her fingers pulling and pushing through hundreds of identical-looking manila envelopes in file folders. Ravi thinks of the many children who've lost their first mothers, ended up here for a while, and then sent off to join another family, even in countries far away from India. Do they all have this ache of longing? Where are they now? For the first time in his life, he has an urge to find a few of them. They might be the only other people on the planet who can understand how he feels. *No matter what happens today*, he promises himself, *I'll find one or two other adoptees when I get back to Boston.*

Mr. Kamal arrives bearing a tray of tea and biscuits. He pours Ravi a cup while Mrs. Banerjee continues to rifle through files. Ravi mutters his thanks and forces a sip, but it's hard to swallow. He stills his foot, which has been tapping the floor as he watches Mrs. Banerjee's search.

At last, she stops and pulls out one manila envelope. "Ah, here you are! Baby Ravi. Thornton Family Adoptee."

But she still doesn't hand it over. Even though it belongs to him.

"I'll need to snap a photo of your identification first," she says. "Our policy is that adoptees may gain access only once they are eighteen years of age."

Thankfully, the reunion counselor told him to bring along his passport. Mrs. Banerjee opens it and takes the photo. "You've come back so soon after your birthday. Most of the people who return are quite a bit older than you. But still, if you're ready—"

"I am."

Finally, finally, she slides the manila envelope across the desk, where it stops in front of Ravi. It's sealed. He puts one palm on it, lifts it with both hands, and places it carefully in his lap. "Is there a place to open this in private?"

"Of course. But let us finish our tea first and hear more about your life after you left us. Tell me about your family, Ravi, and what you're doing now."

He manages to share a few details about Boston, Mom and Dad, and graduating from high school. His hands are so clammy he hopes the manila envelope isn't getting wet.

"Are you going on for further studies?" she asks.

"Er . . . I'm not sure."

She frowns. "Why not? Can your parents afford it? Are they supportive?"

Their faces flash in Ravi's memory—Dad laughing as Ravi showed them his "new" car, Mom giving him a kiss after he withdrew his college applications. "Oh, yes, they are. They definitely are."

"Good," Mrs. Banerjee says. "The gift of higher education is what we desire for our children."

He stands up. Enough is enough. "I want to open this now," he says. "Please."

She looks startled, but she gets up, too. He follows her back down the hall to a small, airless room where she deposits him in a chair. He braces himself for a last bit of advice, but all she says is "Good luck" and closes the door behind her.

Ravi puts the manila envelope on the table. Again, he can't help wishing that Mom and Dad were here, sandwiching him like they do in church. But he can almost hear their voices in his head: "You're the best thing that ever happened to us, Ravi." And: "We're with you, honey."

He opens the envelope.

KAT

INT. AUTO-RICKSHAW—DAY—TRAVELING

The auto-rickshaw's stuck in traffic. Gracie keeps checking her watch. Kat's getting anxious, too. What is Kal-El finding on his mission?

They have to make it there in time.

She leans forward. "Hurry," she tells the driver, hoping he speaks English. "We'll pay you double."

He floors it, so he must understand. Or else he's heard the urgency in her voice. Gracie grabs Kat's hand as he starts careening through carts and motorcycles and SUVs.

SUVs. In Kolkata. Just like the ones in Oakland that drop the full-tuition kids off at Sanger Academy every morning.

The world's getting smaller, Kat thinks.

Their spunky little auto-rickshaw careens over a pothole and gets cut off by one of those pricey gas-guzzlers.

RAVI

INT./EXT. SHISHU JATNA SAMITY
ORPHANAGE—DAY

Pulling out the contents of the envelope, Ravi stacks them on the table.

On top are dozens of letters and photos that his parents sent to the orphanage after they took him to Boston. He doesn't look through those now; he knows they're a record of days he can remember because his parents talk about them all the time. He isn't looking for anything after "Robin Thornton" came into existence.

Once he sets those aside, he's left with five documents.

The first has a photo of a minuscule baby lost in an enormous diaper. It's dated March 5, the day after his so-called birthday. Underneath the photo these words are typed: *An approx 1-day-old relinquished male child "Ravi" was found by local police in lobby of the Royal Diadem Hotel in Kolkata. The same day, he was admitted in civil hospital for care and deposited for protection and permanent rehabilitation in Shishu Jatna Samity Orphanage. Police made efforts to trace parents and relatives but in vain. Thus Ravi was considered free for adoption.*

The phrases detonate one by one inside Ravi's mind.

Relinquished. Given up.

Bang.

Found by local police. Dumped in a hotel lobby on his first day of life.

Pow.

In vain. No chance of finding anyone.

Kaboom.

He sits with the paper in his hands, looking at the tiny baby, reading the words again and again until it feels like his insides are on fire.

And then he puts his day-old self aside and moves to the next couple of documents. One is from the court, declaring Ravi as adoptable. Next comes a doctor's assessment informing potential parents or guardians that *this baby is expected to have severe neurological and physical needs based on extreme prematurity.*

Bam.

No wonder prospective parents passed him by. Not many people want to raise a kid they think isn't going to flourish.

A fourth piece of documentation notes that "Ravi," aged three years old, is eligible for international adoption due to "severe intellectual disabilities." What? Sure, he's struggled in school, but it's not a disability. How can they even diagnose that so definitively at such a young age?

And the last item in the stack is a paper with three lines typed on it: *No original birth certificate. All documents created after child arrived in care. Verdict: Not enough information to conduct search for birth family.*

Crash.

When hopes become dust and fall to the ground, the

contents in your stomach head in the other direction. Leaving everything on the table, Ravi barrels out of the room and tears down the hall to the bathroom. Of all the things he dreamed of happening today, vomiting on his knees in front of an orphanage toilet wasn't on the list.

Once his stomach is empty, he takes a few deep breaths and splashes water on his face. His skin feels achy, as if someone punched him from the inside out. He trudges back, gathers his papers, letters, and photographs, and puts everything back in the envelope.

Mrs. Banerjee opens the office door to his knock. Her smile fades after one look at Ravi's face. "Didn't find out much, I'm guessing?"

He swallows. Hard, so his voice won't shake. "Mrs. Banerjee, is there any chance, do you think, to find . . . relatives once your file is marked *not enough information to conduct search for birth family*?"

She takes a deep breath before replying. "No. I'm so sorry, Ravi. You could try DNA testing, I suppose. But here in India, that is still not a promising way to find relatives. You may keep that file, however. It's yours. We have our own office copies under lock and key."

He has to get out of here. Fast. "Thank you. And . . . to the orphanage for taking care of me while I waited for my parents."

"It is our pleasure," she says. "Please come back again. Some of the aunties who work here might still remember you."

He forces a smile. "I might, one day."

"Goodbye, Ravi. God be with you."

The children are still in the playground, but it's like Ravi is seeing them through different eyes. Nobody makes scrapbooks for these kids, puts up a special shelf for their comic book collections, runs behind them on their first training-wheel-free bike ride, loses sleep over whether or not they're going to college. Only parents do that.

Mr. Kamal opens and closes the gate for him, and somehow Ravi makes it out to the sidewalk. He's drained and tired. And numb.

Like he felt before he decided to come to Kolkata.

Before he was tricked by hope.

He lifts his hand to hail an auto-rickshaw but suddenly gets so dizzy he has to sit down on the curb. Resting his head on his knees, he tries a couple of Mom's deep inhales and exhales. They don't work.

This is terrible. How is he going to get back to the flat feeling like this? He should have brought his parents along. Or Gracie. Even PG. Anyone. Why in the world did he think he could do this alone?

Suddenly, someone sits down on his right.

He manages to lift his head a bit to see who it is.

Gracie.

Oh, thank God.

She rests her cheek on the back of his right shoulder.

Someone else is sitting on his left.

Kat.

Her right hand's hovering in the air. Slowly, carefully, she lowers it and pats his left shoulder twice. Two light taps that

Ravi can hardly feel. Quickly, her hand returns to her own lap.

He knows, even though she's never talked to him about it, that touching a guy is almost impossible for Kat.

But she managed it today.

For his sake.

KAT

EXT. SHISHU JATNA SAMITY
ORPHANAGE—DAY

There's a sudden thunderclap, and the sky starts dumping rain on their heads.

Gracie manages to get Ravi on his feet while Kat hails an auto-rickshaw. The two of them stay quiet, and Ravi doesn't speak until the driver stops in front of the Bose family's flat.

"See you later," he says, and pays the driver before climbing out.

"Wait, what are you doing tomorrow?" Gracie asks. "You have the whole day off, right? Do you want company?"

He shrugs. "I'm not feeling great. I'll probably try and get some rest." And then he gives his head a little shake. "Oh, I forgot to tell you. Bontu, my training partner, is supposed to pick us up here at ten on Saturday. Do you guys still want to go?"

Gracie looks at Kat, and Kat knows what she's thinking. If they go, Kat will have to spend the day with a strange man. But Ravi's face looks so tired. And hopeless. She thinks she can handle it for his sake.

"We'll be here," Kat says. "And listen, Clark, we've got your back. Two Lois Lanes at your service, right here."

No smile, dang it. He turns and trudges into the building.

"Do you think we should call PG and tell him to come back early?" Gracie asks as the rickshaw hurtles off again.

Kat thinks about it. "No. Let's give Ravi a day or so to recover. He's not ready to talk about it yet, obviously."

"That was awful. Terrible. He looked so crushed."

"Kryptonite. Poor Kal-El."

RAVI

Ravi tells a sympathetic Mira he isn't feeling well and heads straight to bed. Once the family is asleep, he fumbles through their medicine cabinet and helps himself to a double dose of heavy-duty nighttime cold medicine. When your hopes explode into dust, you don't wait for the gift of oblivion. You grab it with both hands.

He stays in his room Friday, pretending not to notice the twins tiptoeing in with glasses of water and bowls of soup. Another strong dose of medicine gets him through the night, but now he's emptied the bottle so he'll have to replace it.

KAT

EXT. KOLKATA—DAY

"If you don't want the front, Kat, I'll sit here," Ravi says as he holds the passenger door open. He has dark circles under his eyes and stubble on his chin, but Kat's glad he's going. Gracie's squeezing into the back seat.

"Good view from every part of Bontu's Bengal Barano vehicle," the driver says, grinning. "Sit anywhere you'd like, sister."

Kat glances at the smaller-than-Ravi-sized space next to Gracie. That nest back there is obviously designed for the two of them. Especially today. "I've got shotgun," she says, and hops in the front.

She can tell right away that Ravi's friend is a Duck. Big, waddling, quacking, he's no threat to her or anyone else.

The Duck's lilting, polite accent is soothing as he points out different landmarks and talks about his city. Kat glimpses a gray river. "Kolkata was built along the banks of the Hooghly River. We are the second-largest city in the country. We used to be the capital of India due to trade during the British rule. Until 1911, when Delhi became the capital. Bad decision there."

They pass a field of screaming boys kicking a soccer ball. "Football city, they call us," says the Duck. "Second-oldest league in the world. Used to have the largest football stadium in the world, too. Until we downsized."

"Sounds like Kolkata comes in second a lot," Kat says. Maybe she wants to get this proud native riled up so he brags a bit more about his city. She hopes Ravi's listening.

"We are first in beauty," the Duck says. "Kolkata has more trees and green spaces than most big cities in Asia. I'll take you to Botanic Garden to see the Great Banyan. Biggest tree in the world. Twelve hundred years old. Thirty-three hundred roots falling to the surface. And we are also first place in India when it comes to books. We are home to the third-biggest book fair in the world."

"Only third biggest?" Kat asks.

She glances in the side mirror and sees Gracie throwing her a what-are-you-up-to look. Ravi's still gazing out of the window, like he did coming from the airport, but this time he looks anything but excited and hopeful. Kat really wants to bring his smile back. What's it going to take?

They drive past a big green field where men riding horses are carrying mallets. "Oldest polo club in the world," the Duck says. "Let's park here. I want to show you the Victoria Memorial. It is a good place in Kolkata to watch people. Many couples meet there for romantic reasons without their families knowing."

"What about you, Bontu?" Gracie asks. "Ever meet a girl here?"

"Not yet," the Duck answers. "But I am wanting to ask my neighbor Amira. She is liking me and I am liking her. Sadly, she is Muslim. It will have to be a secret meeting. Things in India are changing, but too slowly for me. My parents are sure to want my marriage to a good Hindu girl. Meantime, though, Amira and I can have some fun, right, Ravi?"

"What?" Ravi asks. "Are we near a bathroom, by any chance?"

Bontu points to one across the way, and Ravi darts off. Kat knows what he's doing. She recognizes pre-vomit swallowing when she sees it.

"Ravi's not feeling well, Bontu," Gracie explains. "He's had a hard couple of days."

"He seemed happy on Wednesday when I saw him during our training. Probably a family issue, right?" Bontu sighs. "Families can steal happiness faster than pickpockets can snatch a wallet. I've lost three of mine to their sticky fingers."

When Ravi comes back, Kat can tell he's washed his face. Ignoring Miss Shireen's advice about appropriate behavior in public, Gracie takes her cue from a few bold young couples passing by. She grabs Ravi's hand and holds it as they lead the way through manicured gardens and well-kept paths toward the stately white memorial. The Duck points at their backs, brings his index fingers together, and winks. Kat smiles, but then catches sight of a pack of canines. Quickly, she rearranges her face back into its old scowl. She's been so focused on Ravi she forgot she's in the public eye. And she's not hidden in her usual black. Instead, she's wearing the lavender shalwar made by Miss Shireen's tailor, along with a matching lavender-and-white headband that Amrita, Baby Diana's mother, handed her as a gift after her sewing class yesterday. Strange how comfortable Kat feels in these outfits. They're loose enough to hide her curves and help her blend in.

Sort of.

She's still taller and stronger-looking than almost every other woman in sight. And many of the men, too. People stare, even with her resting Lion face in place, but she notices they're also staring at Gracie and Ravi. Especially Ravi, in fact.

A group of giggling girls skip up to him now. They look about eleven or twelve years old. "Selfie, please, Mr. Biswas?"

"I'm not—" Ravi says.

But it's too late. They elbow Gracie out of the way, snap the photo, and dash away, giggling even harder. And they're only the first of many. After a while, Ravi stops protesting that he's not who they think he is and poses wearily.

Gracie's scowling in an un-Dove-like way at the constant stream of girls asking for "selfies with Amit."

"*Who* do they think he is?" she asks the Duck.

"Amit Biswas. Famous Bengali fillum star. Very good-looking. Many fans. Mostly girls."

"I can see that," says Gracie as Ravi signs a girl's bus ticket. "Are you actually signing that as *Amit Biswas*, Ravi?"

Ravi shrugs. "Why not? Maybe that was *my* real name, too. There's no way of knowing now, right?"

Gracie and Kat look at each other. Maybe that's what happened at the orphanage. He came up with zero information.

"Let us find an Amit Biswas fillum and you two can decide if Ravi looks like him," suggests the Duck. "It is getting so hot the air-conditioning will feel tremendous."

"Sounds good to me," Kat says. When she's feeling low,

there's nothing better than sitting in a dark, cool theater and losing herself in a story. Maybe it will ease Ravi's mind a bit.

"I'm in," says Gracie.

"Fine," says Ravi. "Let's go see my twin in action."

Good, Kat thinks. Even the thought of a movie must be helpful for him to toss off something like that.

The "fillum" turns out to be fantastic. It's a pirate flick that features a mermaid in a sari. All singing and dancing and fighting and über-steamy almost-kissing. Amit Biswas—or is that Ravi on the screen?—is AMAZING. A swashbuckling, sword-wielding hero with a Gracie-look-alike princess of the sea swooning into his arms in the last scene.

Ravi's the one who suggests stopping for ice cream when they emerge from the theater.

"Typical Bengali boy," the Duck says. "Always thinking of sweets."

As Kat watches Ravi sit close to Gracie, relishing his cone, she's suddenly grateful for this bulky, friendly avian.

Bon-too is his name.

Bon is the word for little sister, she remembers.

And that's exactly how their tour guide treats Gracie and Kat like little sisters.

When the car stops outside the Bose flat, Kat realizes that Bontu's been driving them around for free all day.

"Let's give him some money for gas," she suggests to Ravi in a low voice.

But their guide overhears. "No need, no need. I told Ravi

I am practicing my tours with you people. Will you join me again? There is so much more to show you in this beautiful city of mine. Of ours, I should say. Because Kolkata is your city, too, right, Ravi?"

"It is, I guess," Ravi says with a small smile.

So good to see, Kat thinks.

"Where should we go next time?" Bontu asks. "Gracie, you choose our destination."

"Santa Teresa's mission," Gracie answers, without hesitation.

RAVI

INT. BOSE FLAT—NIGHT

PG is waiting for Ravi in the flat. "We need to talk," he says.

Ravi follows him into the twins' bedroom, and PG closes the door. He sits on one cot. Ravi perches on the other. He was feeling slightly better by the end of his outing with Bontu and the girls, but the sight of PG's grim face is making the sadness come flooding back.

"Mira told me you've been sick, Ravi. Is that true, or did something bad happen on Thursday?"

Ravi stares at the small carpet on the floor between the cots. "Option number two," he answers in a low voice. The reality of what he found—or didn't find—inside his file smashes into him all over again.

PG groans. "I should have gone with you. I knew it."

Ravi flees to the bathroom. After he's vomited up the ice cream cone and the other snacks he ate, he washes and dries his face and returns to the bedroom.

PG is still on the edge of the cot, hands clasped, head bowed. He looks up when Ravi comes in. "Want to tell me what happened?"

"Not much to tell. Opened my file. Abandoned on day one in some hotel. Claimed by nobody. Sent to the orphanage. Passed over by families. Sent to Boston."

PG's quiet. Then: "I'm so sorry, buddy. God's—"

Ravi jumps up and starts pacing the room. "You can stop right there, PG. I don't want to hear about 'God's will.' Being dumped by your birth mother could never be 'God's will.'"

He pictures a baby, alone in a hotel, crying out with every bone and cell for her lifesaving scent and sight and touch.

"But you were—"

"If you say 'chosen,' I'm going to start screaming, PG, and I don't think I'll be able to stop."

He thinks of the children lined up in cribs at the orphanage, waiting for the hands and faces of strangers to change, feed, and bathe them.

"I wasn't going to say anything like that," PG says.

But Ravi doesn't care what PG wants to tell him. He doesn't want to hear any lies about his life being a miracle. It's not a superhero story. All day long, he's been remembering the photo in his scrapbook of that terrified three-year-old on the plane. After Kolkata, how unfamiliar everything must have seemed in Boston when he arrived there. White faces. Strange language. Snow. But unfamiliar was what he was used to from the start. He had to accept it all.

"It's not fair, PG."

"I know, Ravi. You're right. It's not."

Maybe it's because PG finally, easily says "Ravi" instead of "Robin." Maybe it's because he's clearly turned off his teaching faucet. Whatever the reason, Ravi stops walking around the room and sits beside this friend he's known for so many years.

PG's arm goes around Ravi's shoulders. "Did you tell your parents?"

"No. How can I? You took my phone."

"Want to call them now? We could borrow Arjun's."

Ravi doesn't answer. What *does* he want from his parents? Not to show up and whisk him away again, just like they did fifteen years ago.

"I'll email them, PG. And don't say anything to Arjun or Mira, please, even if they ask."

"I'll have to tell them something," PG says. "But not too much, I promise."

Exhaustion floods Ravi's body. *Guess that's what happens when you run out of hope*, he thinks. "It's been a long day, PG. Let's call it a night."

KAT

INT. KOLKATA CHRISTIAN CHURCH—DAY

"Forgive us for what we have done and what we have left undone."

Kat likes the sound of this old British-sounding prayer read in unison by two hundred people with Indian accents. They say it first in English and then repeat it in Bangla, their voices so in sync they sound like trained chanters.

It's strange at first to see the Sparrow on the wall here in Kolkata. This time he's not made of stained glass. His dark face is hand-embroidered into a banner hanging in front of the large hall. It's the same scene, though—he's surrounded by children.

This church is overflowing with children. They aren't sent out before the sermon, like at Grandma Vee's church in Boston. Here, they stay near their parents, doodling, coloring, whispering, giggling. But mostly, Kat thinks, they're quieter and better behaved than American kids would be if they had to sit through a service as long as this one.

The chairs are so tightly arranged she can't tell if she's feeling Dipika's sweat or hers through their shalwar sleeves. Like almost everyone else, they're sitting shoulder to shoulder. Kat's on the aisle; more room for her long legs. She looks around for familiar faces. Gracie's attending Mass at another church with one of the housemothers who's also Catholic. She'll get dropped off at the Bose flat in time for lunch.

Kavita, Amrita, and a few other girls are here, sitting in the row ahead of Kat and Dipika, with Miss Shireen and two housemothers flanking them. The rest of the Asha House girls worship in mosques or temples, so they don't attend church. *We want our girls to become used to being around good men again, bit by bit,* Miss Shireen told her. *That's why we take them to houses of worship.*

Kat scowls at the sight of the Hyena in the back holding some kind of basket. *Sure hope these men are good,* she thinks. Just because they're religious doesn't mean they're safe. PG's in the back row, a lone white face in a throng of brown. Ravi's toward the back, too, jammed between the Bose twins. He hasn't shaved. His eyes look glassy and he has that blank expression Kat remembers from the first time she saw him. It's like his heart was awake for a while but now he's slipped back into some kind of emotional coma.

I want you to meet my friend Robin, Grandma Vee told Kat that first night before sending her off to small group. *Something's been troubling that dear child lately. I have a feeling you might be good for each other.*

But how can Kat be good for him? Suddenly, an idea of what she can do pops into her head. She has to scrutinize it at first because it's so out of character for her. But it's a decent plan, she thinks. She takes the bulletin someone handed her at the door and looks around for a stray pencil. Oh, perfect. Some kid's dropped a red crayon, and it's in toe-heel reach. Got it!

As the preacher drones on up front, Kat starts to write. She's not as good at pithy proverbs or advice-giving as Grandma Vee, but after listening carefully to Professor "Pantera" on the mat for so many years now, she can remember instructions almost word for word.

RAVI

Ravi's plodding through Sunday like he used to in Boston. He chews and swallows porridge for breakfast, half listens to the Bose family's easygoing banter, and rides silently in a rickshaw with PG to church. Here, instead of sitting sandwiched between two tall white people, Ravi is sweating between two short Indian twins who are leaning into him from both sides.

At first, he tunes out the sermon. But a Bengali translator stands beside the preacher, and suddenly Ravi realizes he can understand a word or two in his mother tongue, even before the phrases are translated. "Asha," for example. How does he know what that means? Mrs. Gupta hasn't taught them the Bangla word for *hope*. Was it stored somewhere deep in his brain? He buries the word again, putting it out of commission where it belongs.

After the sermon, Miss Shireen and Mira stand to sing with the rest of the choir. Like most of the older women, they don't wear Western clothes or shalwars to church. Ravi feels a pang at the sight of their flowing, pleated, colorful saris. Somewhere in this sprawling city, his first mother is probably wearing one, too.

Arjun is one of the servers, and the "collection plate" he passes down the rows looks like a handwoven jute basket. The worship band plays instruments Ravi doesn't recognize—a hand-slapped drum on its side, a long-handled guitar look-alike.

He glances up at the embroidered banner hanging on the wall. Jesus looks Indian, too, like everyone in the room except PG, who's sitting in the back. A brown Jesus? That's probably right. He was Middle Eastern, after all.

Where were you the day she left me? Why didn't you help her?

No answer. He should probably stop believing in a good, loving God. But he can't. Faith is so deep in his heart he can't root it out. And he can't imagine any other version of himself than the Jesus-loving Ravi who grew up learning the Bible. If his first mother had kept him, though, he would probably have worshipped Durga. Or Allah. Was she a Christian? Hindu? Muslim? He'll never know now.

The ache for her drums inside him like a constant homesickness. It always has, he realizes. He'd feel a strange loneliness at Christmas, once the presents were put away and the gift wrap tossed in the trash. Any guitar solo in a minor key made the back of his throat ache. Even the sight of Mrs. Rivera's swollen stomach had made him sad. And saris. He'd avert his eyes when desi mothers came to events wearing them. Looking back now, he recognizes these all as echoes of grief.

They were about missing her.

In Boston, he managed to keep the sadness to a low beat in the background.

At the orphanage, though, after he'd opened that envelope and read through the contents, it slammed through him like a crescendo.

He can't completely silence it, no matter where he goes. It's a never-ending soundtrack to the story of his life.

"I have decided to follow Jesus," the men around him sing first in Bangla, then in English.

"No turning back," the women reply. "No turning back."

No turning back, Ravi repeats numbly. *No turning back.*

KAT

After the service, Kat finds Ravi, takes him into a corner of the room, and points out where the Asha House girls are clustered toward the front. The two of them stay at a distance, but some of the girls catch sight of them. There's a lot of giggling and pointing, and Kat can hear the words *Amit Biswas*, even from where she and Ravi are standing.

"The pregnant one's Kavita," she whispers to Ravi. "She's the girl in the video PG showed us in Boston."

She can see Ravi's eyes take in the size of Kavita's belly. And then register the weariness in her face. He flinches. Good. That's exactly what she wants him to do.

As they're boarding bicycle rickshaws to head back to the Bose flat for lunch, Kat cuts in front of PG and climbs up into the two-person seat next to Ravi. He shifts over so that their thighs and arms don't have to touch. So considerate, even in his sadness. *No wonder he's one of Grandma Vee's all-time favorites*, Kat thinks.

"You coming to lunch?" he asks, lifting his eyebrows.

"Nope. Just keeping you company on the rickshaw ride." She's avoiding the Hyena as much as possible. "What did you think of Kavita?"

"She looks . . . a little sad to me," he says. "And pregnant. That's for sure."

Kat takes a breath. It's now or never. "Like someone else, maybe? Eighteen or so years ago?"

He's quiet. The rickshaw splashes through a puddle, drenching the trailing red scarf she always wears as an orna with her shalwar kameez.

Kat tugs it in. "Did Grandma Vee ever tell you about 'Golden-Ruling'?"

"No, I don't think so," says Ravi. "She's always loving her neighbor, that's for sure."

"It's amazing, but she's gone through some rough stuff."

"I know. That's what makes it even more amazing."

"Anyway," Kat says. "She told me that when the people she loves are 'out of reach,' she offers some kindness—"

Ravi interrupts. "Kat, I know you mean well, but I already heard one sermon today. Do you really want to preach another one?"

Well, *that* didn't go well. Maybe he isn't ready to hear it yet. His heart is still raw. That's why you always have a Plan B. She fingers the folded bulletin in her hand. Grandma Vee's words are there, waiting for when he needs them.

They sit in silence until the rickshaw stops in front of the Boses' building. Ravi jumps out and lands in the mud. "Here, take this," Kat says, handing him the bulletin. "I wrote down what Grandma Vee said. And it's not a sermon, I promise. It's a survival strategy. I'm trying it, too."

"Fine," Ravi says, jamming it into his back pocket. "Thanks, I guess. Sorry I was grumpy."

She tells the driver the Asha House address. As they start moving, she turns and peeks through the slit in the back of the canopy. Ravi's still standing there, getting drenched. Her heart aches for him. Left behind, again.

RAVI

INT. BENGALI EMANCIPATION SOCIETY
HEADQUARTERS—DAY

On Monday, Ravi sends his parents a note that sounds more like a telegram than an email: *Opened file. No information. Search over.*

On Tuesday, his parents answer. *Robin, we're so sorry. We spoke with PG on the phone right after we got your email. Are you okay? If you do want to come back, we're here for you. Or we can come there. We love you so much. Dad and Mom.*

He definitely doesn't want them here. Especially not Mom, with her worrying and advice. He shouldn't need her help anymore—he's eighteen now, a man. And he doesn't want to go back to his life in Boston, not yet, anyway. *I'm staying,* he writes. *You don't need to come. PLEASE DON'T WORRY. I'm doing okay.*

But he's not sure he's telling the truth. It's only his second week in Kolkata. How is he going to make it through the rest of the summer?

Duty, loyalty, obedience.

Bengali values, according to Shen.

But they're already familiar to Ravi. They've been moving his feet and hands in Boston for years.

Duty was a decent motivator.

It turned down the volume of grief some.

So he tries it now.

He's supposed to be learning Bangla. Every day that week, Ravi concentrates hard in class. Amazingly, thanks to his three-year-old self who might have been fluent once, he's good at this. After only a few lessons, he's absorbing phrases, words, and grammar like a human Rosetta stone. He starts reviewing and practicing his lessons in the evenings with the twins, who are eager to help. In contrast, Kat and Gracie doze off in class after their nights of baby care. Mrs. Gupta keeps shaking her head at their mistakes and smiling at Ravi. For the first time in his life, Ravi Thornton is a teacher's pet.

Loyalty used to move him, too.

He puts it to work.

Slow steps, but still.

He sends daily emails to his parents. Brief notes and no phone calls, but he keeps writing them. He writes to Grandma Vee, too, and Martin and Ash. He keeps it light and brief, but they're on his loyalty list. Along with Gracie.

And Kat, even though he was short with her on Sunday. He's not sure why. Maybe it's because she dragged him over to see Kavita. It didn't seem right to focus on a vulnerable girl like that. A pregnant girl, like—he stops there.

It bugged him, too, when Kat sounded so excited about the Golden Rule. Had she never heard it before? He can recite the verse in his sleep: "Love your neighbor as yourself." But now, like a lot of stuff he's memorized from the Bible, it doesn't seem to make sense. The folded bulletin Kat gave him is on his nightstand, unopened. How can you love yourself when the person who's supposed to love you most dumps you?

He pushes that thought away, too.

Obedience keeps him trudging along.

Arjun asked him to do data entry. Okay. Training sessions with Shen? Fine.

So, after lunch, once the girls leave for Asha House, Ravi works for an hour or so in a small room at the back of the office. Weirdly, it's not boring work. As he inputs data from court reports about perpetrators who were caught and jailed, he realizes that most were caught thanks to Shen's heroes. And because a few brave trafficked girls gave their testimonies in court, like Arjun wants Kavita to do. In some of the reports, the girls are named, so he's required to shred those after entering them into the secure system. He's beginning to understand why everyone doing data entry needs to sign a confidentiality statement.

He inputs data from older internal office memos detailing rescues that took place in Sonagachi, one of the biggest red-light districts in Asia. A more recent document describes how the "enterprise of selling underage children for sex has been forced to spread out through the city." Apparently, "traffickers are now using a number of hotels throughout Kolkata."

Hotels.

Places where people come and go anonymously.

Where bad things can happen without anyone noticing.

The name of the one in the file from the orphanage is etched so deeply in his mind he knows he'll never forget it: Royal Diadem Hotel.

After enough data has been entered for the day, he takes an auto-rickshaw to the police training center. The silver lining to this act of obedience is that Arjun was right, and so was Kat: Exercise does relieve stress. You forget everything when you're gasping for breath, running sprints across a gym floor, or straining to push up a barbell.

Ravi forces himself through a sweaty, tough couple of hours. With each training session, and Bontu cheering him on, Ravi grits his teeth and runs a bit more distance, does two more push-ups, and a few more crunches than he did the day before. The two-hour sessions fly by, with Shen blowing his whistle constantly.

Ravi still hasn't earned a smile or a word of praise. But that's not why he keeps showing up. Now that hope has failed him, he's doing his duty, just as he has his whole life.

Loyally.

Obediently.

Meekly.

KAT

INT. BENGALI EMANCIPATION SOCIETY HEADQUARTERS—DAY

On Monday, when Kat and Gracie get buzzed into the office, only Gopal is standing there.

"Where is everybody, Mr. Gopal?" Gracie asks.

"In daily prayer meeting. It is finishing at eight thirty. You may join for last five minutes. But no noise, please."

Inside the large room where they have Bangla class, about fifty people are sitting cross-legged on the foam mats. Kat had wondered what those were for; they seemed too perfect when she thought about using them for jiu-jitsu lessons. But she'd been hoping to find the room empty. Instead, men are on one side, and women, some with their ornas covering their heads, are on the other.

Every head is bowed.

There's not a sound in the room.

Quietly, Gracie and Kat slip off their sandals and join the last row of women. Gracie bows her head, too. Kat takes one more look around and closes her eyes. She has no idea how to pray. *Hello*, she says in her head, picturing the brown, embroidered Sparrow on the banner at the Bengali church. *Help, I guess? To train Gracie. Thanks, too. For helping me touch Ravi when he needed it. Help him, too, maybe?*

"Lord, hear our prayers." It's the Hyena's voice. Kat's eyes fly open. There he is, standing at the lectern like he owns the place. "May God bless your hands, minds, and bodies as you serve and protect his beloved children. Go in peace."

She and Gracie stay seated as people exit in silence. Some see them and smile, others don't. Kat doesn't look up as the Hyena walks past.

Last to leave is Miss Shireen, who stops to greet them. "We don't require foreigners to join our 'family' prayer time, but I'm glad you found your way here. Come anytime. See you this afternoon back at home."

After she leaves, and the room is empty, Kat turns to Gracie. "She might not mean that if she knew we came early to fight, not pray."

"It's kind of the same thing, isn't it?" Gracie says. "Let's get started."

Kat's decided to keep it simple. She's going to teach Gracie three moves: Kimura, triangle choke, and mount escape. All three look impressive to a viewing audience.

"We bow before we step on the mat, like this. And then we high-five, fist-bump, and kneel, facing each other."

Gracie imitates her.

"You'll need a Portuguese nickname," Kat says.

"What? Why?"

"It's *Brazilian* jiu-jitsu; roll with it. Mine is 'Filhote,' which means 'cub.' 'Pantera'—Saundra, my BJJ professor—gave it to me when I was eleven." Kat narrows her eyes and studies

Gracie's face. "How about 'Fogo'? There was a little guy at our academy named 'Fogo' who made boys twice his size surrender."

"Wait—that sounds like 'fuego.' Does it mean 'fire'?" Gracie thinks for a second. "I like it."

"Great. Too bad we don't have gis; these shalwars will have to do."

"What's a gi?"

"Belted kimono outfits we wear on the mat. But since we're trying to demo a realistic attack, it's probably good to be in street clothes. We start warming up with somersaults. Like this." Kat demonstrates.

Gracie follows her down the mat; she's not bad. She can do backward somersaults, too. Even in a shalwar kameez.

"You're really good at that," Kat tells her.

"Four years of gymnastics."

"Good. That's going to pay off. Next, we shrimp."

"No, I'm shrimp. You're not shrimp." Gracie laughs at her own dumb joke.

"Hilarious. I mean we warm up like this." Kat flops on her back, lifts her hips, turns her body to the side, bends at the waist, pushes off with one foot, and does it again. She repeats this on the other side, scooching all the way along the length of the mat.

Again, Gracie imitates her. By the end of this exercise, she's out of breath. And starting to sweat. "Tomorrow I'm wearing a T-shirt under this shalwar and taking the top layer off before we start."

Kat decides they need a physical break. She doesn't want her student to burn out.

"Let's kneel again and go over some terms," she says. "The first thing to learn is 'position before submission.' You rely on trained instincts and your head to get your body in the right position, and hold your opponent there until he submits, or surrenders. You move slowly, position by position."

"Oh, I get it," Gracie says. "Like Lucha Libre, right?"

"*Not* like wrestling. You'll get exhausted if you keep constantly moving and fighting. You have to *think* more in BJJ, conserve your energy, wait for the right opportunity. In wrestling, you stay off your back. In BJJ, you can fight *and win* while you're on your back."

"Cool. What about if someone presses you up against a wall?"

Kat flashes back to the stairwell. "Yes, even then. You can definitely use BJJ in an upright position. You ready?"

Gracie nods.

"I think we'll start with a mount escape," Kat says. "Get on your back."

Gracie obeys, and Kat straddles her.

"This works when an attacker's sitting on you, like this." Kat puts some of her weight down on Gracie's chest. "I like this move because it shows how a girl can end up dominating even though she starts in a tricky position—on her back, pinned down."

"Wait—how am I supposed to get you off?" Gracie asks, looking up at Kat. "I weigh one hundred pounds, Kat."

"You'll learn. That's why BJJ is so great—it can help you defeat a much bigger opponent. Oh, and one more thing; if I'm in pain, I'll tap you a couple of times, or yell out: 'Tap!' You do that, too, okay?"

"Pain? Dios mío." Gracie takes a deep breath. Or tries to, anyway. Kat can tell it's hard with someone sitting on her chest. "Okay. Let's go, Professor."

RAVI

INT./EXT. ROYAL DIADEM HOTEL—DAY

Ravi sleeps in on Friday, and when he wakes, the flat is empty.
The twins are at school. Arjun is at the office. Mira's gone, too.
The girls are at Asha House. PG is an hour away, teaching.
Ravi has the whole day to himself, with no duties to fulfill,
no people to support, no instructions to obey.

He lies in bed remembering, letting the pain rise to the
surface. She left him in a hotel. When he was one day old.

Suddenly, he knows exactly what he wants to do today. He
gets dressed and grabs an umbrella. Even now, thunderclouds
are gathering overhead.

"Royal Diadem Hotel," he tells an auto-rickshaw driver.

"Are you certain, sir?" the man asks. "That place is not so
good. Let me take you to nice hotel."

"I'm sure," Ravi answers.

He's going to the place where she left him.

It was the last time they'd been together.

He wants to see it again.

Rain begins slanting in through the open sides of the vehicle, and passing cars splash them with muddy water. By the
time the auto-rickshaw pulls to a stop, the driver and Ravi are
both sopping wet. Ravi's umbrella becomes an unnecessary
accessory.

"There is the hotel, but nobody stays there," the driver tells him. "It must be closing down soon, I am thinking."

Squinting through the downpour, Ravi spots a Victorian-era mansion tucked between two modern buildings. An ancient sign etched with gold, cursive letters identifies the hotel: ROYAL DIADEM SOCIETY GUESTHOUSE.

He wonders at the "society" part.

"Very good tea just there," the driver tells him as he takes Ravi's money. He lifts his chin in the direction of a chai shop across the street.

But Ravi has no interest in tea right now. Holding his unopened umbrella, he runs through the rain to the front door of the hotel and walks inside.

The lobby's deserted. Frayed, elaborate lace curtains, faded carpets, carved teak furniture, and cobwebs—actual cobwebs—in the corners of the ceiling. A wooden staircase curves up from the lobby, and a vintage player piano is pouring out off-key music that sounds familiar. What is that song? Ravi recognizes it after a couple of rounds: "Amazing Grace." High-backed wooden chairs circle around a few small tables set with flowery china as if guests are about to arrive. There's nobody around, though, not even behind the reception desk.

It looks like the set for a horror movie. The driver was right—this place is a dump. Why did Ravi come? What was he hoping to find? A ghost with arms open, waiting for his return?

He turns to see if the rain is still bucketing down and spots a teak bench in a corner near the front entrance. He walks over to it and sits on the faded red cushion.

Here's where she might have left me.

He closes his eyes and tries to imagine the scene: a recently pregnant young woman, about Kavita's age and size, slipping into the hotel with a bundle in her arms. Suddenly, his eyes fly open again. At the Bengali Emancipation Society, he'd read about girls leaving unwanted babies in train stations—that seems a likelier place to him than a hotel. Why did his first mother bring her baby to the Royal Diadem Society Guest-house, of all places?

KAT

INT. BENGALI EMANCIPATION SOCIETY HEADQUARTERS—DAY

On Friday, even though they don't have language class, Kat wakes Gracie up to go to the office anyway. And in time for the prayer meeting. "It's a good way to start our day. After that, we get THREE FULL HOURS of training."

Gracie isn't bouncing out of bed anymore. This is her fifth day of training, and she's moving like Grandma Vee—carefully, with low groans as she sits and stands.

The sessions haven't been going so well. When Kat evaluates her student's progress, she has to admit that it's been slow. Well, truthfully? Almost nil.

At this rate, Plan C might end up failing, too.

But it's Kat's only hope. Gracie's been having a rough time with the mount escape. Maybe they should switch to the Kimura. It's the one Kat used on the Wolf, so she knows exactly how it works.

Inside the gathering space at the office, once the place clears out after prayer, Gracie lies on the mat and groans. "I'm SO SORE."

"Okay, today we'll try a Kimura," Kat says. "You hold your attacker in a double joint armlock to apply pressure on his shoulder. That way, if he struggles, he dislocates his own arm or tears his rotator cuff."

"Gosh, Kat, that sounds violent! I don't think I could actually hurt anyone. I thought this was *self*-defense."

"You hold him in place with the Kimura. He does the damage to his own body. Get it?"

Gracie looks doubtful. "I guess so."

"Ready to try?"

Big sigh. "Maybe I'm just not cut out for this, Kat."

"Don't give up now. We still have time. Imagine the day we do our demo and wow Miss Shireen! I think Bontu might be a better sparring partner than Ravi. His size will make your defense seem more impressive."

"Don't ask anyone yet, Kat."

"Okay." Kat straddles Gracie. "Close your legs around me. Establish your guard."

Gracie locks her ankles around Kat's waist. "Whoa. This is kind of cool. I'm under you, but I don't feel as trapped as I did in that first 'mount escape' position."

"Great. Now grab my neck with your hands and pull my head toward you—push my body forward with your legs, too—but make sure you keep my arms and hands *outside* your arms. Don't let me get them inside, next to your body."

Gracie grabs Kat's neck, but she can't pull Kat's head forward. She tries again. It doesn't budge.

"Pull hard, Fogo. Okay, I'll come in. There you go. I know . . . it's counterintuitive. Your instinct is going to want to *push* an attacker away. But if you hold on when you've got my neck, and I sit up, I actually pull you up with me. That's when you put a foot down for leverage, get up on an elbow, and grab my right wrist with your left hand."

Gracie squirms and twists her body but can't get up on her elbow. "This is impossible!"

"Okay, let's pretend you got there." Kat lifts her weight off Gracie for a minute and lets her get up on an elbow. "Now tilt your hips to the side. Yes, like that. Okay, reach through and grab my wrist. And then unlock your legs and put your right foot down on the mat."

"Like this?"

"Yes. Perfect. All you have to do now to trap my arm is grab your own left wrist with your right hand."

Gracie grunts and groans as she tries to reach her wrist. "I . . . can't . . . get there. Arms are too short."

Again, Kat lets her get in the right position. "See how you have my arm trapped now? Press your right foot against my left hip and scoot my hips back. Then throw your left leg high over my upper back."

Gracie tries that, but Kat breaks her hold almost instantly.

"You have to maintain control, Fogo. Let's set it up again so you can see how this move ends. Okay, here I am, trapped in your hold. Now twist, and drop your right shoulder back to the floor."

Gracie flops back but loses her grip on Kat's wrist.

"Remember, your goal is to keep my arm in this painful position so that if I don't surrender I'll do damage to my own body." *Like he did*, Kat remembers. "Let's go through it again."

Gracie tries the first step again: pulling Kat's neck forward. She can't do it. Once more. Another fail. Kat breaks it down into steps, letting her get into each position. But Gracie can't seem to grab anything—Kat's head, Kat's wrist, her own wrist.

Finally she falls back in exhaustion with Kat still on top of her, one arm thrown over her face. "I can't do this. I'M. TOO. WEAK." And then she starts to cry.

RAVI

INT. ROYAL DIADEM HOTEL—DAY

The piano starts playing again. It's stuck in a loop of "Amazing Grace," five-minute pause, "Amazing Grace." An elegantly suited man with silvery hair walks out of the door behind the reception desk. He catches sight of Ravi and his eyes widen. *Probably shocked by the presence of another human being,* Ravi thinks.

The man comes around the desk and walks over. "May I help you?" he asks, glancing around nervously. His crisp British-sounding voice makes Ravi feel even more like they're in a movie.

"I stepped in to get dry for a minute. Mind if I sit here?"

"Sorry, no. Loitering is not permitted on the premises. Please move along." A badge on his suit announces that he's Mr. Michael Francis, Hotel Proprietor. *What kind of an Indian name is "Michael Francis"?* Ravi wonders. *And aren't hotels supposed to be part of the hospitality industry?* This "proprietor" is the opposite of hospitable. No wonder they have no guests.

Ravi picks up his umbrella. "Okay, okay, I'm leaving."

The man hurries back to the reception desk as if he has a thousand tasks to complete for two hundred guests.

Ravi holds the front door open for a second and pauses at the threshold.

Goodbye, he tells two sad ghosts.

One brokenhearted baby.

One suffering young woman.

Just before he steps out into the rain again, he glimpses a dusty portrait on the wall near the corner of the lobby, partially hidden behind a pillar. Something in the old, wrinkled face reminds him of Ms. Vee.

As he moves back inside and lets go of the handle, the door bangs shut.

Up close, he can tell the woman is Indian, not African. But the dark skin, flat nose, crinkles around her eyes, and especially the kindness in her smile do resemble Ms. Vee. The placard beneath the portrait identifies her as "Miss Martha Das, Royal Diadem Housemother, 1947–1967." He reads the small description that follows.

Royal Diadem Society Guesthouse was established by foreign missionaries in 1902 for unfortunate unmarried girls who found themselves with child and had no other housing arrangement. The Society's mission was to nurture these desperate souls and their babies. After Partition, Miss Das took the helm and faithfully served young women who arrived at the Guesthouse for over two decades.

Ravi reads it again, and this time his eyes blur as the truth sinks in. He's found some information that wasn't in his file. Eighteen or so years ago, a "desperate soul" made her way to the Royal Diadem, hoping for a welcome that might be better than the one her newborn would get in a train station. The reputation of this building clung to it through the generations, and somehow, she must have heard of it.

Well, at least she tried, Ravi thinks, his eyes stinging suddenly.

That's something.

Suddenly, a loud clatter behind him interrupts his thoughts. Shoes are coming fast down the wooden staircase. Two pairs of them, at least.

KAT

INT. BENGALI EMANCIPATION SOCIETY
HEADQUARTERS—DAY

Once Kat releases her, Gracie stalks off and disappears into the ladies' room.

As Kat wipes down the mats with a towel she's brought along, she has a flashback to her angry little self at age eleven with Pantera making her push, bridge, grab, twist, and roll her way out of holds. It was controlled fury that finally led to her first escape, after which Saundra threw her arms around Kat, and Mom gave them both a standing ovation. How she wishes they were here! Especially Saundra, who'd know exactly how to teach Gracie. And do it fast.

Kat straightens the mat, making sure the room looks as ordered and peaceful as it did when the girls came in. At least she gets to hear Mom's voice today. When Gracie asked about calling home, Hyena man said he'd arrange it so they could borrow an office phone. And Kat had emailed her mother to say she would call after Mom's late shift on Thursday.

After a few minutes, Gopal hands Kat a mobile. "Mr. Arjun says you will be calling your mother today? Please use this phone."

"Thank you, Mr. Gopal!"

Kat sits on the mat and dials her mother's number. To Kat's relief, the call goes through quickly and the reception is good.

And the best part is that Saundra's there, too, listening in as Kat explains Plan C to Mom.

"Just be sure Gracie also wants to do this for herself, Kat. What's that?" There's a pause. "Saundra says those three are your signature moves, and she knows you can teach them."

"Tell her thanks, Mom. I'll do my best. I'd better hang up; PG said to keep it under five minutes. Talk next week."

"Love you, Kat."

"Love you, Mom."

Inside the lunchroom, Gracie is staring glumly at a full, uneaten plate of food.

Looks like Plan C's landing pretty hard on Kat's pupil.

"Listen, we don't have to do this," Kat says. "I can always come up with a new plan."

Golden-Ruling Plan D? What in the world could that be? She doesn't want to surrender. Again.

Gracie reaches for a tissue and blows her nose. "My abuelo says, 'Gato con guantes no caza ratones.' A cat with gloves can't catch mice. Sometimes you have to get your hands dirty to get the job done."

Kat has no idea what she's talking about, but it sounds like she's not quitting. "Are you *sure*?"

"As long as you think I can learn this, I'm in. Look out, Tío. This 'linda niñita' is staying on the mat." Now Gracie's eyes are flashing and she's *sneering*. The lifted right upper lip on that sweet face looks so out of place that Kat has to blink a couple of times. *Gracie's still an avian. But she's no Dove. This bird's on FIRE.*

Kat's never made a first move to hug anyone other than her mother, but valor like this deserves a response. She gets up, throws her arms around Gracie, and pulls her into a tight Filhote-Fogo embrace.

RAVI

INT./EXT. ROYAL DIADEM HOTEL—DAY

Ravi peeks around the marble pillar and sees a man hurrying down to the lobby. He's holding tightly to a girl's hand and dragging her with him to the front desk. His face is twisted into a snarl that makes Ravi catch his breath.

"Where were you when my customer arrived, Mr. Francis?" the man demands. He's speaking English. "This girl told me nobody came, so I rang him up. He was furious. There was nobody here to direct him."

"I am so sorry, Mr. Sarker. Fridays are a Muslim holiday, you know. Our new bellman left to go to the mosque and didn't inform me. Please forgive me. It shall not happen again, you have my word."

The girl tries to pull her hand away but the man gripping it yanks her even closer. "Make certain it doesn't," he says. "We can easily move to another one of our locations on Fridays. Perhaps we should."

"No need, no need. I already sacked the bellman. We count on your business, Mr. Sarker. Please, kindly take your money back for last night's booking. With interest."

Sticking his head out a little further, Ravi watches the proprietor pull out a stack of bills and push it across the counter. Sarker's hand reaches out, grabs the cash, and whisks it out of sight into his pocket. "And you'll also give me the next booking without charge," he growls.

The proprietor pulls out a handkerchief from his pocket and presses the folded square against his forehead. "Most definitely, sir, I will. I shall keep your reservations as they are, in perpetuity. We are most grateful for your business."

Ravi pulls back behind his marble shield as the man heads to the front door, still dragging the girl along. She's stumbling and tripping, trying to keep up. Just as Sarker pulls her out of the hotel, she swivels her head for a quick second.

She sees Ravi.

She looks into his eyes.

Hers are big and round. The pupils are dilated.

They remind him of his own, staring out of those long-ago pictures.

They remind him of someone else's, too. He takes a step and reaches out for her, but it's too late.

The door slams. She's gone.

Oh, God.

This child is scared.

The realization of her terror electrifies him.

Now he races out after them, but Sarker has already stowed the girl into a waiting sedan that screeches away. A blue Skoda, Ravi notes. He watches the taillights disappear, trying his best to see the license plate, but it's raining too hard.

Anger detonates inside his chest. He hurries back inside and marches up to the proprietor. "What was that man doing with a little girl?" he demands.

The hotel owner presses his hand against his heart. "Oh my God! You are still here? I . . . I thought you had left."

"Who was he? Give me his full name immediately."

"I don't . . . know it. She is . . . she is his daughter." He's backing away, his hand on the door handle behind him.

Still fueled by rage, Ravi slaps his palm hard on the high desk, making the bell vibrate. "You're lying! Where does he live? Is he coming back?"

But the hotel owner steps back into the room he came out of and slams the door.

Ravi hears the fastening of a bolt and chain. He runs behind the reception desk and pounds on the door. No answer.

Dashing out into the street again, he hails an auto-rickshaw. "Police training center," he tells the driver. "And make it *fast*. Joldi joldi!"

KAT

INT. MISS SHIREEN'S COTTAGE—NIGHT

On Friday, after Gracie's done with her phone call home and supper's all cleaned up, Kat and Gracie collapse on the sofa.

"I talked to all six of them," Gracie says. "But PG's right; once a week is probably a good idea. Hearing their voices only makes me more homesick."

Kat takes a deep breath of the pungent night-blooming jasmine aroma wafting in through the windows. She, too, misses home even more after hearing Mom's voice. But though they've only been in Kolkata a couple of weeks, this cottage is starting to feel a bit like home, too. Her list of homes away from home is growing. It's up to two now. She's been emailing Grandma Vee in Boston regularly, keeping her up to speed.

Miss Shireen joins them on the couch, turns on the television, and toggles to the channel that streams nonstop Bengali music videos—or Bangla gaan, as she calls them—and Gracie and Kat watch with her. *Feels like we've been doing this for years*, Kat thinks. At home in Oakland, though, she'd put her feet up on the couch. Here, she knows how rude that would seem to Miss Shireen, so she keeps them on the carpet.

On-screen, a sari-clad woman leans back into a man wearing tight pants and a shirt unbuttoned to his navel.

"Steamy," Kat says.

"Oh, yes," Miss Shireen says. "But they rarely kiss or take off any clothes."

"It's actually more romantic that way," Gracie says, fanning her face with all ten fingers.

Next, they watch a soap opera that's Miss Shireen's favorite. Lots of over-the-top gestures and big dramatic pauses make it easy for her to translate and the girls to understand. *A much better way to learn Bangla than studying it in the classroom, if you ask me*, Kat thinks.

After Miss Shireen says good night, Kat does her usual routine of burpees, push-ups, planks, and crunches. Gracie watches, her eyes narrowed. "You do that every night," she says. It's a statement, not a question.

"Yep. I change it up to challenge my body."

"Maybe I should join you. It might help me on the mat."

"Okay, but don't get too ripped. We need to show Miss Shireen and the girls that you can fight off an attacker without muscles like mine." Gracie gets on her knees and manages three push-ups.

"Oh, Kat." Gracie sits back on her heels and sighs. "I hope I can actually learn those moves."

"You will! I promise. We'd better get to bed; tomorrow's another Bontu outing, remember?"

Gracie shrugs. "I don't know if I like being in public with Ravi. So many girls come after him. It's going to be nice to be back in Boston, where nobody's heard of that dumb Amit Biswas."

"It's only a matter of time for the two of you, Gracie. Be ready. He'll get there."

"I don't know," Gracie says. "He's acting like his old zombie self again. After he stood up to Brian that day—your first day with us, remember?—and decided to go to India, it was like he . . . woke up. I think that was when I fell hard, even though I've always liked him."

"I know. He does seem sort of . . . back in a daze. He's grieving, like Grandma Vee said."

"It's heartbreaking. I wish he'd talk to me about it. He used to tell me everything, Kat. I miss texting him."

Kat sighs. "All we can do is be there for him—and be ready to help if he needs us. Now come on, one plank and then we'll call it a night."

Gracie manages a plank but her whole body starts trembling after about ten seconds. After twenty more seconds, she collapses facedown on the rug. "I'm so tired right now, I don't think I could fight off a baby."

"All you have to do is fight off a big dude who looks like a baby."

"He does, doesn't he? You're okay being around Bontu, Kat?"

"He wouldn't hurt a fly. Literally. I watched him roll down the window and let one out of his car last Saturday. We'll have to help him act mean for the demo."

RAVI

INT. KOLKATA POLICE TRAINING CENTER—DAY

Ravi takes the stairs of the police training center two at a time and bursts into Shen's office.

Shen looks up. So do the two uniformed men who are meeting with him.

"Thornton! What are you doing here? You don't train on Fridays. And don't they teach you to knock in America?"

"Shen—"

"Sir."

"Sir, I've discovered a trafficking center! It's in a hotel. The Royal Diadem. You have to send some men there to catch a perp named Mr. Sarker. I just saw him—"

Shen stands and comes around the desk. Slowly, menacingly, he walks over until he's about a foot from Ravi. "Keep. Away. From. That. Hotel. Do you hear me?"

Ravi doesn't step back; anger is still powering him. "But why? I know what that man looks like. He had a girl with him, she looked trapped—"

"Stay away. If you go near that hotel again, I'll have Arjun put you on the next plane back to America. Do you understand?"

The two other men exchange looks. "This boy's an American, sir?"

"Can't you tell?" Shen asks.

Ravi doesn't give up. "But that hotel's a trafficking location—I promise you. I saw how he treated her. We have to help that girl!"

Shen sneers. "Ehhh. So is that why you came to Kolkata? Typical. Americans come for a short time, know nothing about our culture, and want to become heroes to tell their friends how they saved the 'poor Indians.'"

"That's not what I'm doing—"

"That's *exactly* what you're doing. Now leave this office. Immediately."

"But—"

"I gave you a command, Thornton. Did you hear me?"

It's no use. The man's not listening. "Yes. Yes, sir. I did."

Ravi shuts the door, stumbles out to the sidewalk, and hails another auto-rickshaw. But as he climbs in, rage makes him thump the leather seat so hard with both fists that the driver twists his head to see what happened.

"Sorry," Ravi mumbles. "I'm fine."

But he isn't. He wants to turn over every table in Kolkata.

INT. BOSE FLAT—NIGHT

Ravi can't sleep.

He can't get Sarker's face out of his mind. Or the girl's terrified eyes.

Evil, evil man. Damaging something so valuable—a child!

A girl who deserves kindness and safety and a life of loving and being loved.

Ravi gets up. Paces the room.

Anger lashes through him, again and again.

By midnight, the depth of what he's feeling is scaring him. At first he thinks this is nothing like the brief flash he felt when he yelled at Brian in small group.

It's full-on FURY.

But after a while he sees it isn't new. This rage he's feeling at Sarker, his anger at Brian—they're louder expressions of an emotion that's been around for a long time. Just like the grief he'd recognized after visiting the orphanage.

Sitting on the edge of the bed, Ravi puts his head in his hands. Anger and sadness. Sadness and anger. The sorrow he understands now. But who has he been mad at for all of these years? God? Maybe a bit. But Ravi knows Jesus too well to think that being God's child means you never suffer.

No, if he's going to be honest, for his entire life he's been angry at two people.

First, the person who gave him life. The question had always lurked beneath the static of numbness: How could she abandon her own flesh and blood? But now—maybe because he imagined her desperation so clearly in the hotel—Ravi can guess why she made that choice. She might have been too young, like Kavita. Or in some kind of trouble, like the girl under Sarker's control. How can anyone be mad at them?

And second, there's himself. Somewhere even deeper inside, he's suspected that something about *him* made her give him up. Did he cry too much? His file said he was premature; maybe she had thought he wouldn't survive. With a shock he sees the truth: His entire life, he's blamed himself in secret. *If you hadn't been so weak, she might have kept you.* No wonder he could hardly look at the infant version of himself in that first photo from the orphanage.

The sky is finally starting to lighten, and Ravi empties the glass of water on his nightstand. He goes to the window. It's not raining, but the air is fresh and cool, and the sun is rising behind the tall coconut trees. As the first rays pour over the city of his birth, he takes stock of the emotions that are still lingering. The grief's still there, of course; the loss of her will always be with him. But after this long, sleepless night of confession, he's not really angry at her anymore, even in the unseen corners of his heart.

And you can't be mad at a baby, either. Ravi deserves love, too. *It's not your fault,* he thinks, feeling a rush of compassion for the big-eyed baby he used to be.

Love your neighbor as *yourself.*

Maybe *that's* why Kat was trying to talk to him about the Golden Rule.

Ravi picks up the folded bulletin on his nightstand. She's written something there in red crayon. *GOLDEN-RULING by Viola Jones. "When people I love are out of reach, I offer some kindness to another that I can't give my dear ones. It brings peace to me."*

He reads it again, through blurry eyes.

The Royal Diadem Society Guesthouse is the last place on earth Ravi was with his first mother, and now it's being used to hurt others.

He has to act. He's not mad at her. He's not mad at himself. But he's still angry. He has to do something, no matter what Shen said.

He reads Kat's note for a third time, and it's almost like he can hear Ms. Vee's voice saying the words out loud. *"When people I love are out of reach, I offer some kindness to another that I can't give my dear ones. It brings peace to me."*

Even if his first mother is out of reach, he can still offer kindness in her honor. Maybe Golden-Ruling means trying to help that girl, and others like her. Maybe it even means overturning tables.

Sarker said he'd return on Fridays to do his evil work.

Shen told Ravi not to go to the hotel.

But the chai shop across the street's not forbidden. And it's the perfect place to keep watch on the Royal Diadem.

KAT

EXT. KOLKATA—DAY

"Next stop, Mother House and the Missionaries of Charity," Bontu says, holding the back door open as Ravi and Gracie climb in. Kat's already in the passenger seat.

"These women still spend their time serving the dead and dying?" Kat asks.

"They do," Bontu answers. "And it's a lot tougher than beating up bad guys in Gotham, if you ask me."

"This city seems to have as many bad guys as Gotham," says Ravi. "I've been reading through files in the office."

"Sadly, all big cities come with their fair share of villains," says Bontu. "But your American bad guys seem to use guns more often than ours."

"True," Ravi says. "Most of your police don't even have guns. Your uncle might need one to stop these traffickers."

"He has already captured quite a few—without the use of guns," Bontu retorts.

"So I hear," says Gracie. "Miss Shireen says he's legendary when it comes to taking down bad guys."

"You have to come after them *hard*," says Ravi. "Jesus said that anyone who hurts a child should have a MILLSTONE hung around his neck and be THROWN into the ocean to DROWN."

Kat turns and looks at his face. *He certainly said THAT with passion. What's going on?*

"If you hurt a child, Jesus said a millstone would actually be better than facing God," Gracie corrects him gently.

There's a pause.

"You sound . . . energized about it, anyway, Ravi," Kat says.

"You *do* sound different," Gracie says. "Did something happen yesterday?"

He doesn't answer right away. "Ummm . . . No, not really. Maybe it helped to have the day to myself. What did you guys do?"

It's Gracie's turn to hesitate. "Not much. Just . . . well, Kat and I spent time at the office in the morning. And I called my parents again last night. At least they're not laughing at me anymore. When I first told them about my baby assignment, they laughed so hysterically I thought Mom might go into early labor."

"Sticking with baby care this summer is your 'act of service,' I guess," Ravi says.

"That's not all Gracie's doing to serve," Kat says.

"Hush, Kat," says Gracie. "We're here. Mother House. I can't believe it."

As they climb out of the car and walk to the four-storied, gray building, Kat notices that Ravi does seem much more animated than he has all week. His steps look more purposeful, somehow.

She follows Gracie into the quiet building and takes off her shoes.

RAVI

EXT. MOTHER HOUSE—DAY

Bontu and Ravi sit in the car outside the Missionaries of Charity building, waiting for Kat and Gracie to finish up.

After everything that happened yesterday, Ravi's worried Shen will kick him out of his training sessions. He's still mad at the guy for not dispatching his team in pursuit of Sarker, but Shen's a master at getting recruits ready to hit the streets. Ravi can tell his own body is starting to respond after only six sessions. And if he's going to watch for Sarker in that chai shop, Ravi needs to stick with Shen's regimen.

"Have you heard from your uncle?" Ravi asks Bontu casually.

"He came to dinner last night," Bontu says. "When Baba asked about my training, Uncle told him I was improving. Then he winked at me when Baba wasn't looking. Thank God he understands."

"Did he say anything about my stopping by yesterday afternoon?"

"You saw him?" Bontu answers. "He didn't tell us that. But I'm glad you're beginning to trust him, Ravi. Uncle likes you. I told him we were going out today, and he wanted me to tell you that he always keeps his word and repays his favors, whatever that means. And that he'll see us both on Monday."

Relief floods through Ravi. And determination. Shen's not firing him after all. If that perp shows up again at the Royal Diadem, Ravi's body needs to be in badass shape.

"Hey, Bontu, what kind of an Indian name is 'Michael Francis'?"

"Why? Did you meet someone with that name? Must be Anglo-Indian. Someone of British and Indian heritage. Legacy from colonial days. Older Anglo-Indians still speak only English, no Bangla, but that's changing, too."

"Oh." That explained the pseudo-British accent of the hotel owner.

Kat and Gracie come out of Mother House, and Ravi notices that Gracie's face almost looks like it's glowing.

"She knelt for a half hour by the tomb," Kat whispers to Ravi as she climbs into the car.

Beautiful Gracie, Ravi thinks as his best friend slides in next to him. *Kind to me, kind to everyone.*

Maybe he should tell her about his plan to stop Sarker. She's certainly been a safe place for Ravi's secrets in the past. But this is different. She might try to talk him out of it, saying it's too risky. He's not going to tell Kat, either. Or PG, that's for sure. He doesn't want to get sent back to Boston on the next plane and have his parents enroll him in intensive counseling sessions.

No, to execute this mission, he's on his own.

KAT

INT. CINEMA HALL—NIGHT

They end their Saturday outing at the movies again, where the real Biswas plays a heroic police officer rescuing a raven-haired actress from the clutches of an evil movie mogul. The Bengali officer is Hindu, the Bengali actress is Muslim.

"Like you and Amira," Kat hears Ravi muttering to Bontu.

"Amira is much prettier than this actress," Bontu answers loudly. His passionate declaration booms through the theater.

"This movie was on that billboard we saw coming from the airport," Kat whispers to Gracie.

But Gracie's not listening. She's entranced.

Bollywood might just be better than Hollywood, Kat thinks. It's probably because of the music and dancing—singing, dancing, love scenes, love scenes while singing and dancing, fight scenes, heroes battling villains while singing and dancing.

RAVI

In this "fillum," even Ravi has to admit that Biswas resembles him. *Especially if I keep working out with Shen*, he thinks, picturing himself in a white uniform with a black belt and boots. Toward the end of the movie, the black-haired beauty rides into the sunset on the back of Biswas's motorcycle, her orange sari billowing in the wind and highlighting her curves. It's strangely close to his own fantasy.

"Doesn't she look like Gracie?" Kat asks, leaning forward to catch Ravi's eye.

"Maybe a little," he says. *Gracie would look much better in that orange sari than Biswas's girl.*

He whispers into Bontu's ear. "Does Biswas ever kiss on-screen?"

"No, never," Bontu answers.

Too bad, Ravi thinks.

In the car on the way home, Ravi sits shoulder to shoulder with Gracie. He can't help inhaling the fragrant, flowery scent emanating from her hair.

"Why do you smell like a garden?" he asks. For some reason, he's keeping his voice low so the two in front can't hear him.

She turns her head to show him her braid. "Miss Shireen

gave me a string of jasmine flowers for my hair this morning. Guess the fragrance lasts all day."

Oh, so that's it. He takes another deep breath. "Smells amazing."

Just then, before Ravi has a chance to worry if he's developing some kind of hair-sniffing fetish, Bontu spins around a curve and Gracie smashes into Ravi's side.

"Sorry," she says. "Not much space back here, is there?"

"Here, let's try this," Ravi says, draping an arm around the back of the seat. "Gives us a bit more room."

"Fine by me," Gracie says, and leans back.

Why is his pulse racing? His skin feels electrified, his mouth is dried up, and his entire body starts trembling. What's happening? He has no idea. Good thing the road is bumpy; Gracie doesn't seem to notice.

But maybe this has nothing to do with his body.

Maybe it's about his heart instead.

What are you feeling, Ravi? he asks himself.

As they bounce over a pothole, Gracie jolts up an inch or two, and then nestles even closer against him on her landing. Wisps of her hair are dancing in the breeze coming through the open window; her kind eyes are gazing outside, taking in everything that's passing by. Every detail of her is familiar, and yet finer. Like she's coming into the sharp focus of a camera lens.

Oh . . .

He sees it now—as clearly as he saw the anger and the sadness the night before.

It's love.

And it's more, much more, than best-friend love. It's a motorcycle-riding, orange-sari-wearing, disappearing-into-the-sunset, leading-man-leading-lady kind of love.

Ravi Thornton—Edward Thornton V—is in love. With *Gracie*.

Ba-boom!

What now?

KAT

INT. MISS SHIREEN'S COTTAGE—NIGHT

Just as she's drifting into a luscious baby-free sleep, Kat's jolted awake by a loud banging.

Gracie flies to open the door. It's one of the housemothers from Asha House.

"It's Kavita! She's in labor—bleeding heavily!"

"Where is she?" Miss Shireen asks.

"Gone to hospital! Come quickly, Miss Shireen!"

Shoving her arms into a long sweater that covers her nightgown, Miss Shireen pushes past Kat and Gracie and dashes out with the housemother.

The girls watch from the window as a waiting car whisks off into the darkness.

They turn to each other but Kat can't think of anything to say. What can they do to help? Nothing.

Gracie hits her knees, crosses herself, and bows her head.

Kat paces back and forth, fighting her fury.

Kavita is fifteen years old. Fifteen. Her father is dead. No idea where her mother is. She was rescued, yes, but she can't go home. None of the Asha House girls can; that's why they're here. All that violence, and now her body has to go through this. Will she survive it?

Too many villains. Not enough heroes. The real world's nothing like the movies.

Make that Wolf pay for this. Take him down. Don't let him hurt her again.

This is prayer, too. Not on her knees, not with her head bowed, not using her hands because if she did it might mean raising a fist.

Storming back and forth across the room, Kat shouts at God inside her head while Gracie stays on her knees. A car carrying Miss Shireen returns just before dawn.

"What happened?"

"Is Kavita okay?" Gracie adds at the same time.

"She's alive, and so is the baby. It's a girl. Another sweet, beautiful girl." She plops onto the sofa. And hides her face in her hands—Miss Shireen is crying!

Kat feels like punching a fist through a wall.

Miss Shireen manages to keep talking through her tears. "Years of doing this, and still the heart breaks. That child almost died from loss of blood. And what will she do now? She won't give the baby up, and I don't think she should. But how will she take care of both of them?"

Kat doesn't have an answer. Neither does Gracie.

"When is she coming back?" Gracie asks after a while.

Miss Shireen wipes her wet face with her orna. "A week or so. We've sent her to rest in one of our safe houses, along with the baby. It was a hard childbirth; the baby was in breech position. At times like this I wonder why God doesn't smite the men who do such terrible things to children."

That's what Kat's asked him to do, anyway. In the meantime,

this Kolkata Wolf is still prowling around. He hasn't completely destroyed Kavita. Not yet, anyway. But he might try again if she decides to face him in court.

"Maybe now everyone will stop wanting her to testify," Kat says. "The less she sees of that disgusting trafficker the better."

Miss Shireen sits up and moves into Bobcat mode. "Kat, you can't say anything to Kavita about testifying. She *must* make up her own mind."

Kat doesn't give in, even though she's wrecked, and she knows Miss Shireen must be even more so. "What if Kavita brings it up first?"

"Well, in that case, we share experiences from our own lives. But please, refrain from telling her what to do. Will you promise me this?"

Bobcat versus Filhote. There's a mental tussle, but after this long, draining night of sadness, Kat surrenders. "Okay, Miss Shireen, I promise."

RAVI

INT. KOLKATA POLICE TRAINING CENTER—DAY

The news about Kavita's baby galvanizes Ravi into action.

"Is there a camera shop anywhere nearby?" Ravi asks Bontu after their training session. As usual, he's dressed and ready while Bontu's just stepping out of the shower.

"Yes, on Park Street."

"Do you know if they sell security and surveillance cameras?"

"You mean spy stuff? Why would you need that?"

"Oh, it's an interest of mine."

"Gadgets and gizmos, eh? Like Iron Man?"

"Yes," says Ravi. "Er, Bontu . . . how would I say, 'I want a girl' in Bangla?"

Bontu stops toweling his head. "Why would you say that? That is a terrible picking-up line, my friend."

"No! That's not why I want—I just need to learn to say it."

"Good. Because that lovely Gracie is the right one for you."

Ravi flashes back to the feel of a black braid against his skin. Gracie's face looked so lovely after praying in Mother House. But he doesn't say any of that out loud. He needs to tell her how he's feeling first. If they ever have any time alone together, and he can gather his courage. "You're as bad as those 'auntie' matchmakers who want to fix you up with Hindu girls and keep you from Amira. Now could you translate for me, please?"

Bontu pulls a clean shirt over his head. "What is that line again?"

"'I want a girl.'"

"Terrible. But here it is—ami ak-ta meh chai."

"Ami ak-ta meh chai. Is my accent okay?"

"Not bad. But I pray you are never saying this again in your life."

KAT

INT. ASHA HOUSE COMMON ROOM—DAY

During teatime, Miss Shireen walks into the common room and switches off the television, where music videos are playing nonstop.

"Kavita's coming in just behind me," she says. "Be gentle, girls. She needs rest."

The girls, who've been demonstrating steps for Kat and Gracie, immediately stop dancing and quiet down. But when Kavita enters the room, they swarm around her, cooing over the baby.

Kavita's shape looks more like it did in the film. But to Kat, she seems even more fragile than the tiny avian she's holding in her arms. Kavita's lips are cracked and dry, and she has dark shadows under her eyes. Her hair, usually so neatly combed and braided, is in a loose, messy bun on the nape of her neck.

"Nam kee diyecho?" Charubala asks.

"Shiuli," Kavita answers. "Her name is Shiuli."

Kat knows that word thanks to Miss Shireen. Jasmine flower. Like the one Kavita was holding in her palm for the camera.

"Let's take the baby into the changing room, Kavita," Kat suggests. "She looks a bit wet to me." *And you look exhausted.*

Miss Shireen gives Kat one of her eyebrow-high looks. *Don't worry*, Kat thinks. *I promised, didn't I?*

Inside the cozy baby room where she's been spending so much time, Kat takes the baby from Kavita's arms. "Rest," she says, pointing to one of the empty rocking chairs.

Kavita sinks into the chair. "How are you, Katina Didi?" she asks wearily.

"Not good," Kat answers, taking off the diaper and starting to clean the baby up. Amazing that she can do this so easily now.

"Why? What has happened?"

"I've been worried about you. Your future."

"Oh. That is kind. Thank you."

Kat folds a fresh cloth diaper into a triple absorbent fold, but she doesn't put it on the baby right away. The new human kicks her scrawny legs around and thrashes her little arms, so happy to be naked. She better not start peeing. Kat leans over and drops a couple of kisses on her tummy. Shiuli. The name fits perfectly.

Kavita keeps rocking. "Katina Didi, they have asked me to testify in court," she says.

Kat stops kissing the baby. "*Who* asked you?"

"The police. And Arjun Uncle."

That Hyena! So out of line. Powerful men like him KNOW NOTHING about girls facing Wolves! "And what will you say?" Kat asks, pinning the diaper in place carefully, so Shiuli doesn't get poked.

The chair stops moving. "I am not yet certain."

Kat bites her lip and manages not to spew out her opinion. *Have to wait for Kavita to ask first.*

The baby is dry and diapered now, but when Kat picks her up she starts to cry again. "Must be hungry," Kat says, and hands her back to Kavita.

Kavita tucks her baby under her orna and the sucking noises begin.

Kat rocks beside her in silence. There's nothing more she can do now. Maybe Kavita will ask for advice, maybe she won't. In the meantime, she's going to teach Gracie with all her might how to do a Kimura, a mount escape, and a triangle choke.

RAVI

INT. CAMERA SHOP—DAY

Despite his busy schedule, Ravi squeezes in a visit to the camera shop. He needs to make his purchase before Friday.

"I need to record a conversation without the other person knowing," he tells the woman working there. "Audio and video. And the device has to look natural, as if it's something I usually wear."

"What about a pen?" she suggests.

"Hardly anyone carries pens anymore, especially not people my age."

"Watch?"

"Same issue."

The saleswoman pulls out a camera hidden in a wallet, a hat, even a credit card. Ravi's amazed by the array of choices when it comes to secret recording gadgets. *Privacy's dead and gone*, he thinks.

The woman hands him a pair of glasses with a mini pinhole camera built into the frame. Ravi tries them on. *Perfect*, he thinks, looking in the mirror. They're even sort of a disguise in case he runs into that Anglo-Indian proprietor again.

He's growing a beard, too. It should hide his face even more, and make him look older. And manlier. Anyway, he hopes Gracie thinks so.

KAT

INT. BENGALI EMANCIPATION SOCIETY
HEADQUARTERS—DAY

Gracie bows and takes the mat. Shrimps. Bridges and flops. Does a few backward and forward somersaults. She's getting stronger, Kat notices. Their nighttime strength-training routine is paying off.

But as Gracie gets on her back to practice a mount escape for the umpteenth time, she sighs. "Ravi's keeping something from me. He was so sad after visiting the orphanage, but did you notice how quickly he got past that? He looks . . . so different now, and he's acting so weird."

Kat, too, has been warming up. Now she straddles her pupil. "Yeah, he did seem to bounce right back. Secrets make you weird." *I should know*, she thinks.

"Let's go," Gracie says. "I've got the Kimura down, and I've almost got this, but we still need to start practicing that horrible triangle choke."

RAVI

INT. CHAI SHOP—DAY

All week long, Ravi rehearses the phrases he'll need to convince "Mr. Sarker" that he's a customer. Bontu's "Ami ak-ta meh chai." How to ask the price of something—"Kaw-tho dhahm?"—which he learns from Mrs. Gupta. And while he plays video games with the twins, they translate for him in their sweet, high-pitched voices. "Is that man a bad man?"— "Oy lok ta goon-dah na kee?"—and "Are they keeping you a prisoner?"—"Thomake kee johr ko-reh rak-che?" He practices and practices the phrases and accent until he thinks he sounds almost like a native. The twins agree.

By Friday, the hidden-camera glasses are stashed in Ravi's backpack. So is the stack of cash Dad gave him. He heads to the chai shop, tense but ready. He takes a seat by the window. Peering across the rain-wet pavement, he can make out the sign: ROYAL DIADEM SOCIETY GUESTHOUSE.

HER hotel—not Sarker's.

When the chai-wallah comes over, Ravi orders a cup of hot cardamom-spiced tea.

He drains it. Orders another.

And then another, keeping a constant eye on the street. The chai-wallah brings a plate of biscuits, and then hot, crispy triangles of dough filled with chickpeas that he calls samosas.

They taste so different from the boxed ones stashed in the freezer in Boston that Ravi can't believe the two food items share the same name.

"I didn't order these," Ravi tells the chai-wallah. "But I'll have one more plate, please."

"No worries, Mr. Biswas," the man replies, smiling. "We are so happy to have you here. It's our pleasure to give you this."

"I'm not Biswas," Ravi protests, but he can tell the man's not buying it.

"I am Mr. Lakshmi," the chai-wallah says, grinning. Meanwhile, the rain comes and goes outside, and Ravi keeps an eye on the forlorn, dilapidated building across the street. Nobody goes in, nobody comes out.

"Is that hotel still open?" he asks Mr. Lakshmi.

"Oh, yes. But it's not a nice place, Mr. Biswas. I can give you a fine, five-star recommendation for lodging."

"No, thanks. I don't need lodging. And please, please, believe me—I'm not Biswas."

"Oh, pardon me, sir. I forgot about your Park Street penthouse here in Kolkata."

Ravi gives up and accepts a third complimentary plate of samosas.

By the end of the afternoon, there's still no sign of Sarker across the street. Leaving cash on the table that more than covers the tea he ordered and the food he didn't, Ravi heads back to the Bose flat.

KAT

INT./EXT. SHOPPING MALL—DAY

"I like your beard," Gracie tells Ravi.

"It's filling in nicely," Bontu adds. "But guess what? Amit Biswas grew a beard recently, too."

"That guy," Ravi replies. "Always trying to look like me."

"So . . . we're going to a comic book store, Bontu?" Gracie asks. "What's there for a non-comic-book person like me?"

"Amira likes romantic graphic novels," says Bontu. "You might browse that section. Hey, which Batman movie do you Americans think is the all-time best?"

"*Batman Returns*, 1992," says Kat. "Michelle Pfeiffer's Catwoman was incredible."

"*Batman Begins*, 2000-something is far better," says Bontu. "Christian Bale's Bruce Wayne was so perfectly tormented about his past."

"*Dark Knight*, 2008," Ravi chimes in from the back. "Obviously. I mean, Heath Ledger as the Joker? It doesn't get better than that."

All three agree on one thing: *Batman v Superman: Dawn of Justice* is the absolute worst. Bontu parks near the mall and leads them to a store with a great collection of vintage and new comic books.

As Gracie wanders in the graphic-novel section, Kat and Bontu start a heated argument over DC versus Marvel villains, debating who would destroy whom in hand-to-hand combat. Ravi's not joining in, Kat notices. What's Kal-El worrying about this time?

RAVI

Ravi's eyes keep going back to Gracie. She's walking with more confidence, he notices—is it his imagination, or does she look stronger, tougher, bolder? Maybe it's the pink shalwar kameez with white embroidered flowers that makes her look so different . . . not much like the middle-school version of Gracie that Ravi met seven years ago. But that Gracie's still there, too. He can see her. Sweet, easy to be with. Her face feels like home every time he catches sight of it.

As she walks toward them, her purchases swinging beside her in a brown bag, Bontu stops mid-argument. "You carry yourself differently these days, Gracie," he says, echoing Ravi's silent observations. "Kolkata's turning you into a superhero. You remind me of Bonita Juarez."

"Who's she?" Gracie asks.

"Firebird. Also known as 'La Espirita.'" He looks from Kat to Ravi, but they both shrug. "You don't know Firebird? She's . . . magnificent. She declined offers of full-time Avengers membership because she's so devoted to her church work. But she has powers over flame, and fought with them in the Kang Dynasty war."

"Wait—WHAT?" Gracie looks stunned. "There's a MEXI-

CAN GIRL SUPERHERO? Why don't the two of you ever talk about HER?"

"Er . . . I didn't know about her," Kat confesses.

Gracie turns to Ravi. "Well?"

"I've heard of her, but I didn't make the connection. Sorry, Gracie. My bad. Maybe we can find a comic book now—"

He's interrupted by a girl passing by. "Please, may I take a selfie with Mr. Biswas?"

"I'm not him," Ravi answers on autopilot.

"I don't care," the girl says. "My friends won't be able to tell on social media."

Ravi sighs. "Okay. Fake Biswas it is." He folds his arms across his chest and pouts into the girl's smartphone, trying his best to resemble his doppelgänger.

"You looked just like him," says Bontu, once the selfie-taker moves on. "Let's get some of that Kentucky-style chicken from your country for lunch, shall we?"

As they stroll to the food court in the mall, Ravi notices that Gracie's frowning. Is she still mad about Bonita Juarez? *I'll have to find those comics*, he thinks. *I'll check out Firebird myself first. And then they'll make a perfect birthday present.*

In the meantime, he decides to stop trying to convince people of the truth of his identity. It's a losing battle, anyway. Now that he's seen the real object of their affections on the big screen, he tries a series of smolders, scowls, and smiles for people's cameras. After each pose, Bontu and Kat rate his imitations: "mildly Amit," "moderately Amit," or "extremely Amit."

Gracie doesn't comment. In fact, she doesn't seem one bit impressed. *Maybe she thinks I'm being dishonest*, Ravi thinks. "Once I get my phone back I'll search for hashtag-amit-biswas and add hashtag-not-amit-biswas to every photo that shows up," he tells her, but all she does is shake her head.

KAT

INT. BENGALI EMANCIPATION SOCIETY
HEADQUARTERS—DAY

To perfect the mount escape, Gracie has to trap her opponent's arm and foot, bridge her hips, roll, and get to her knees.

"Keep your elbow tucked into your side," Kat instructs. "Your heels have to stay close to your butt. Okay, don't let go of my arm. Now thrust your hips up, Fogo. Great! All that's left is to roll over on top of me, jump up, and run away. You're so close. One more time."

After more than a month of practice, Gracie's finally making progress. Her body's starting to control her mind and the moves are turning into instincts. The triangle choke—which requires being on her back and trapping her attacker's neck in a triangle shaped by her legs—is hardest for her, so they've put that on hold until now.

"I think I've almost got this one, Kat. But that triangle choke—it makes me feel more . . . violent than the other two moves."

"Just picture the faces of those girls fawning over 'Amit Biswas,'" Kat tells her. "Let's try it again."

Gracie's next mount escape is perfect. She's on her feet and Kat's on her back in no time. "Ah, love," Kat says, smiling. "It's so motivational. But when are you going to tell Ravi what we're up to?"

"He's keeping his secret; I'm keeping mine," Gracie says. "Which means it's time for my quick bathroom change. Makes me feel like Superman heading back to his phone booth."

She reaches for the small towel and deodorant she brings along to hide any traces of the hard hour they've put in. Ravi usually shows up right at ten when Mrs. Gupta arrives, and by then, Gracie's changed back into her shalwar kameez and sitting demurely in her chair.

"We'll have to tell him soon," Kat calls after her. "Once we schedule the demo, we'll need Bontu's help."

While she's waiting, Kat brainstorms their next training session on a piece of paper, breaking down the triangle choke into easy steps. Planning these lessons has been so helpful to take Kat's mind off her worries about her own future back in Oakland, where she'll have to see the Wolf again, get back on the mat with male sparring partners, apply to colleges, find another job. All that's on hold now. Teaching Gracie is her focus.

It's thanks to her student, really. She's so grateful that Gracie's been sticking with it, day in and day out, even though it's been so challenging. When Bontu commented on Gracie's changed stature, Kat felt so proud. She knows how confident BJJ can make someone appear on the outside. It's been helping her for years.

The door opens, and Gracie comes back in, smiling at Kat, walking with that new bounce in her step. *Forget "Paloma,"* Kat thinks with a smile. Plan C still has a chance, thanks to Firebird.

RAVI

INT. KOLKATA POLICE TRAINING CENTER—DAY

About halfway through their time in Kolkata, Shen's training sessions are starting to pay off. The humidity has intensified and the gym feels like a sauna, but Ravi doesn't let that stop him. His stomach is gradually tightening into a defined group of muscles, though not quite a six-pack. Calves, arms, shoulders, thighs—slowly but surely, they're rippling into shape.

Is Gracie noticing? He sure hopes so. But she's not the reason he's working so hard. He needs every muscle he's developing and more in case he sees Sarker again.

Shen's still keeping his word to Arjun and training "the American," but he, too, is intensifying the workouts, almost as if he's seeing if Ravi will quit. Once or twice Ravi thinks he glimpses a fleeting expression of admiration on the older man's face. But after a blink, the stony expression is back.

They never discuss their argument at the police station.

Bontu's still coming to their workout sessions, but not exerting any more effort than he did the first day. Instead, he tells jokes to try and lighten the tense atmosphere inside the gym. Even though he's clearly given up on his own training, his uncle never says anything to him.

Every afternoon, it's another round of Shen asking more

and more of Ravi, Bontu cheering from the sidelines, and Ravi not giving up.

The days start flying by now, like they always do after a half-way point. Sundays bring PG, church, lunch—where he and Gracie can at least talk, even though the twins are never far away—and an afternoon nap once she's gone. Monday through Thursday, he has Bangla lessons and a few more hours with Gracie—along with Kat, and Mrs. Gupta, and Gopal, and other staff members of the Bengali Emancipation Society who pop in and out. After Kat and Gracie leave, he does data entry, pushes through another brutal training session with Shen, eats dinner with the Boses, and plays with the twins.

Fridays bring his solo outings to the chai shop opposite the Royal Diadem Society Guesthouse. He sits alone, sipping Mr. Lakshmi's tea, pretending to study his Bangla textbook and keeping an eye on the hotel across the street. But there's still no sign of Sarker. No sign of anyone, really. The hotel seems vacant. Even so, Ravi shows up, Friday after Friday.

On Saturdays, Bontu is turning out to be even better than his brag when it comes to taking them on outings. The four of them visit a host of other tourist spots: Belur Mat, Howrah Bridge, the Indian Museum, Shaheed Minar. They enjoy tea and scones at a fancy hotel after a trip to the zoo, where Kat wants to stay for so long Bontu drags Ravi away to get a snack.

He takes them to coffee shops where young Bengalis step up to the mic to share their original poems. He introduces them to cricket—"every Bengali must know about arm balls, backlifts, and bowling averages"—and they cheer as they watch intensely competitive games on the Maidan.

And every Saturday night, they finish with a "fillum," with Gracie sitting next to Ravi in the darkened theater. *Cool it*, he tells his skin when her forearm brushes against his and sets it aflame. With every passing day, his desire to hold her close—even kiss her—is growing more intense. If only they could have some privacy so he can gather his courage, tell her how he's feeling, and ask if she feels the same way. But they're never alone. All he can do is enjoy the sight of her graceful movements, settle for occasional accidental touches of her skin against his, and when they're in Bontu's car, put his arm around the back of the seat and take deep, weird whiffs of her hair.

KAT

INT. ASHA HOUSE COMMON ROOM—DAY

One midsummer afternoon during teatime, Amrita and Kavita come out of the kitchen carrying a cake. They put it on the table in front of Gracie.

Surprised, Kat manages to join in the chorus. "Happy birthday, dear Gracie, happy birthday to you."

"Feels like yesterday when I turned seventeen, Gracie," Miss Shireen says. "Your pastor called to remind us of your birthday."

"Now we each are feeding you a piece of cake and telling you something we admire about you," Amrita says. "Ready, Gracie Didi?"

Gracie nods and opens her mouth.

The Asha House girls bubble over with compliments as they take turns feeding Gracie. *You are kind, Gracie Didi. Good. Beautiful. Loving. Happy.*

When it's Kat's turn, she puts a piece of cake in Gracie's now-chocolaty mouth. "You are . . . fierce, Ms. Rivera," she says. "And powerful. Like fogo. Why didn't you tell me it was your birthday?"

Gracie chews, swallows, and loses the smile. "I wanted to see if Ravi remembered," she says in a low voice. "But he didn't say a word during Bangla class this morning."

"You've got to stop testing him like this, Gracie. He obviously adores you, but he's got a lot on his mind."

Charubala interrupts them. "Are you wanting to learn some more Bollywood dance moves?" she asks.

"Sure," Kat says.

"Definitely," says Gracie.

A wail comes from the baby room. Kavita stands up wearily. "That is sounding like Shiuli. She is eating nonstop."

"A growing girl," Kat says. "I'll be in soon to change her."

Charubala switches on the television to the music video channel. Amrita and a couple of other girls demonstrate how to move hands, hips, eyes, and heads in time with the music. Gracie and Kat try to imitate them. *Gracie's learning fast*, Kat notices. Meanwhile, she feels like an oaf. BJJ and bhangra dancing don't seem to have much in common.

One of the housemothers comes in carrying a huge bouquet of red roses and a big manila envelope. She hands her load to Gracie. "For you," she says. "Gate guard gave them just now."

Gracie inhales the scent. "Mmmmm . . . they're amazing. But who sent them?" She silently reads the card, her cheeks turning almost as red as the flowers.

"Open it, Gracie Didi!" The girls are clamoring, clustering around Gracie, curious about the envelope.

"I know who they're from," Kat says as Gracie pulls out three Avengers comic books. "Gracie's Biswas!"

The girls burst into loud cheers and start dancing again.

"He remembered," Gracie tells Kat. "All he said in the card was 'Feliz cumpleaños, Graciela' but look, he signed it . . . *Love, Ravi*."

"Of course he did." Kat's thumbing through the comics. All of them include scenes with Firebird. "Check this out. You're his Bonita Juarez."

"Maybe. Well, he's my superhero for sure. And he's looking so fit these days, have you noticed?"

"Not really. But now that I think about it, maybe he is. You should tell him."

"I would if he said something about these," Gracie answers, flexing her bicep. Kat gives it a squeeze, feeling pride in her work. "And where is he going on Fridays?"

"I have no idea," Kat says. "Why don't you ask him?"

"No way. You can't make someone tell you their secrets."

"You'll have to tell him yours soon. You're getting so much better at your moves, it's almost time to schedule our demo."

"I *am* getting kind of Fogo-ish, aren't I?"

"Your Kimura sizzles now. And your mount escape is perfect. All that's left is a—"

Gracie groans. "I know. That triangle choke. Can't seem to get that one down, can I?"

"You will. Happy birthday, Fogo. Okay, the girls are waiting, so back you go to the dance floor. Meanwhile, it's baby time again for Katina Auntie."

RAVI

"Thanks for the flowers, Ravi," Gracie says shyly, the morning after her birthday. "And the comics."

"Glad you liked them. Dad always sends Mom red roses on her birthday, so I thought—Anyway, Firebird is awesome. It's good you helped me rediscover her."

Their Bangla lesson's over, and Gopal is leading them into the lunchroom. Ravi watches Gracie's confident stride as he follows her. *Bontu was right*, he thinks. *She really does look like Bonita Juarez. Only much more beautiful.*

He's still wondering if Gracie's noticed the changes in *his* body, but she doesn't say anything. Ravi likes how he looks to his own eyes, and especially how he feels—stronger, healthier, more energetic. He doesn't flinch when he catches glimpses of his naked self in the mirror. The twins laugh hysterically at him, though, when they burst into the bathroom without knocking. Ravi throws on his clothes and chases them through the flat, trying to tickle them both at the same time.

He's relishing living with a Bengali family so much that it makes him feel guilty when he thinks of his own parents. In the Bose house, he can learn what it means to be Bengali just by being around the family, watching them interact and picking up on the different nonverbals. A head waggle for no; a head tip for yes. He's learning the meaning of sounds like "eeeesh"—which means "oh, no"—and phrases like "bap-re-bap"—"oh, wow."

He's even taking in the way Mira and Arjun flirt with each other, using eye contact and small gestures so their boys don't notice. It's different from the over-the-top affectionate way his parents relate to each other.

In the afternoons, he and Arjun often get back at the same time. As they take off their shoes at the door, the twins race up to throw their arms around their father and Ravi.

"Ravi Dada, can you beat the next level now?" one of them asks.

Mira shakes her head. "Homework first, boys. Then your game guru can show you the way."

As Ravi looks around the dinner table, he sometimes wonders what it might have been like to have been adopted, or even fostered, here in Kolkata.

He certainly wouldn't have had to work so hard to reclaim his Bengali-ness.

But he misses his parents, too. They attach funny, goofy selfies to every email they send, and each one makes him smile. How can he not be glad that the three of them ended up in the same family? Besides, even if Ravi wanted to rewrite his story, there's no going back.

KAT

INT. KOLKATA CHRISTIAN CHURCH—DAY

Instead of listening to the songs or sermon, Kat is sitting in church worrying. Not about herself and her future. That can wait.

She's thinking about Kavita instead. *Hope she won't cave in to the Hyena's request to testify.* And what's going to happen to Shiuli? And Baby Diana? Logan? And these beautiful girls at Asha House, sitting quietly around her in their yellow canary outfits?

She's worrying about Ravi, too. There he is, a few pews behind them, letting the twins lean into him as usual, but something inside him seems . . . *angry.* He doesn't aim it at her, or at Bontu, or anyone else, and laughs and jokes and is as kind as ever, but Kat's always been able to recognize anger. She hasn't said anything about it yet, but she sees it. *Guess that's what happens when your hopes get dashed,* she thinks, glancing back again at her friend's face. *They turn into anger.*

Who is he angry at? Not his parents. He adores them. And not his birth mother, she hopes. If he is, then the "sermon" she preached that day in the rickshaw didn't make any difference at all. But why not? She repeated what Grandma Vee had told her, almost word for word. Had she left something out?

As the choir sings the closing hymn, something about "take

it to the Lord in prayer," Kat goes over the conversation she and Grandma Vee had so many weeks before. Suddenly, she remembers the tears that traveled down those ancient cheeks.

Thou wilt find a solace there, the choir sings.

Oh. Now Kat sees it.

Grandma Vee shared her *story* with Kat.

All of it. The suffering and sorrow, too.

To really *get* it, to want to take on the Golden Rule as her own, Kat had to hear Grandma Vee's story first.

She's going to have to tell Ravi hers.

RAVI

As usual, Ravi looks around for Gracie at church, and as usual, she's nowhere in sight. She's been attending Mass at Saint Teresa's memorial chapel on Friday afternoons, so every Sunday he thinks she might turn up here. But she never does.

"The woman they hire for baby care doesn't know Logan and Diana and Shiuli like we do," she explained, when Ravi asked about it. "And besides, I like to keep the girls who aren't Christians company on Sunday mornings."

"And I take her shift when she leaves to meet you for lunch," Kat added.

Any excuse to avoid Arjun, Ravi thinks, dropping cash into the collection basket and passing it down the row.

At first, Gracie invited Ravi to join her at Mother House on Fridays, but he told her he was busy. He didn't say why; she didn't ask him again. At least he has Sunday lunch to look forward to. She never misses that.

He spots Kat sitting in her usual place next to the Asha House girls. She goes to Mass on Fridays with Gracie *and* comes here on Sunday mornings. Two worship services, every week. *For someone who didn't grow up religious*, Ravi thinks, *she's sure taking church seriously.*

After the closing hymn, it's starting to rain, so the congregation disperses quickly. Ravi's shocked when Kat climbs into his rickshaw for the ride back to the Boses'. She hasn't joined them at the Bose flat since that first Sunday.

"Glad you're coming to lunch," he says.

"I'm just along for the ride. I'll head to Asha House after you get out." Kat isn't looking at him. Her body is tense. She's almost Nefertiti again, but not quite.

Ravi tells the driver the address of the flat and they start moving. It's pouring now, and with the canopy up, a rickshaw feels like an intimate place. *Probably too tight of a space for Kat to be sitting next to a guy*, Ravi thinks. They've only ridden like this that one time before. Just as he did that time, he keeps his body carefully plastered against his side of the rickshaw.

"How's Kavita?" he asks, to break the silence.

"Kavita's tired," says Kat. "But the baby's fine. Beautiful, actually. Perfect. Her name is Shiuli."

Ravi listens to the rain pounding the canopy and the wheels splashing through puddles. Poor rickshaw driver's sopping, but he's humming a song as he pedals.

"You okay, Kat?"

Kat turns to him and takes a deep breath. "Yes, and no. Kavita's why I came here. To 'love my neighbor as myself.' When I arrived in Boston, Ravi, I was messed up. Angry. *Really* angry. But then Grandma Vee told me her story, and how she survived it . . . by 'Golden-Ruling.' I tried to tell you some of that before, but . . . well, can I tell you why I left Oakland?"

"Sure, Kat. I'm listening."

As she recounts the details of how she was attacked in the stairwell at her school and the aftermath of her suffering, he wants to reach over and take her hand. Her light touch on his shoulder outside the orphanage meant so much. But he doesn't do it. Somehow he knows she isn't ready for him to make that kind of move.

The rickshaw hurtles along. Kat balls up a corner of the red scarf into a fist and releases it. And then, in a low voice, she says: "The worst part is that he changed everything for me. I'm sort of damaged now. With men, I mean. There's no rewind button in real life. I wish I could go back to life before everything happened!"

That's when Ravi sees the tears streaking down her cheeks. Kat! Nefertiti! Months ago, he glimpsed her heart in the dimple, but he hadn't known about the broken parts. Kat can't say anything more, he realizes; she's too choked up.

"I know about wanting to rewind," he tells her. "I've been wanting to go back my whole life. Back to the moment when she left me. Maybe . . . if she'd had enough money, or help, or care, she'd have decided to keep me instead of . . . throwing me away."

In spite of her tears, Kat looks at him with so much tenderness she reminds him eerily of a miniature Ms. Vee.

And then, to his total amazement, tears of his own show up from somewhere deep, deep inside.

He can't remember the last time this happened.

His eyes have gotten moist a time or two, even recently, in the orphanage and when he was in the Royal Diadem Hotel, but here in this musty-smelling rickshaw, he's straight-up *weeping.* And he can't stop. It's like a subterranean pool of sorrow has built up for years.

Tears, and more tears. Here they come, and here they keep coming.

He lets them. A waterfall of sadness like this was made for remembering that your mother had to give you up. And that you can't go back in time to make life easier for her, even if you long to.

Kat's still crying, too. The two of them, side by side under this canopy, not touching, are weeping like a couple of . . . *What's the antonym of "superheroes"?* he thinks. *Microwimps?*

After a while, she hands him a corner of her scarf. "Don't blow your nose on it."

They smile at each other through the tears. He presses the soft chiffon against his cheeks. She's using the other end to dab at her own eyes.

"Look at us," he says. "Boy Wonder and Kat Girl. I'd cut this scene right out if I were editing this film."

"Not if tears are our superpower," she answers, and her voice is still shaky.

They might be, Ravi thinks. Because now the bottom of his heart feels lighter, drier, easier to traverse, like Kolkata's streets after a rare day of sunshine.

KAT

INT. BENGALI EMANCIPATION SOCIETY HEADQUARTERS—DAY

Ravi shows up early for Bangla class and walks in on the girls practicing. He boggles at the sight of Kat straddling Gracie. "*What* are you two doing?"

"Gracie's learning jiu-jitsu," Kat tells him, getting off her. "I've been teaching her for weeks. She's pretty good. We were about to practice a mount escape."

He looks at Gracie. "You are? Why didn't you tell me?"

Gracie doesn't answer. She's still on her back, and her face is blank.

"We're going to ask Bontu to do a demo for Miss Shireen," Kat says. "I'm hoping she'll offer BJJ training to the Asha House girls . . ." Her voice trails off.

Ravi isn't listening. His eyes are still on Gracie. "You kept this a secret, Gracie? From me?"

Awww, Kat thinks. *I knew we should have told him.*

But Gracie's face isn't blank anymore. She's glaring at Ravi. "I'm not the only one keeping a secret. Where have *you* been going on Fridays?"

Fogo, Kat thinks. *Uh-oh.*

Ravi blinks. Averts his eyes. "Nowhere."

"Yeah, right," Gracie says.

There's a silence. Kat looks from one of her friends to the

other. Is their time in Kolkata driving them apart instead of bringing them together? Suddenly, she gets an idea. Mrs. Gupta won't be here for another half an hour.

"It's good you showed up, actually, Ravi," she says. "I was just thinking Gracie needs someone to spar with so I can guide her through this tricky move. Will you help us out?"

He takes another look at Gracie's angry expression. "Er . . . I can try."

"Okay with you, Gracie?" Kat asks.

"Fine." She says it without a glance in Ravi's direction.

"Okay, Ravi," Kat says. "Sit on her like I was. Trap her legs."

Ravi looks flustered. "I can't do that."

"Yes, you can," Kat says. "Don't worry, she's going to escape. Go on."

He still doesn't do it. "Are you sure? Is that okay with you, Gracie?"

"Fine," she says again, but she isn't looking at him. "But you're supposed to bow before you start."

"He doesn't have to, Gracie. Okay, straddle her, Ravi. Just like I was."

So he does it. One knee on either side of her hips.

"Geez, Ravi. You need to put some weight down on her for this to work."

But he's not listening. He's looking down, straight into Gracie's eyes. Kat can almost hear the Bangla gaan playing in the background. She rolls her eyes. *When are these two going to wake up and smell the night-blooming jasmine?*

"Okay," she says. "Escape!"

RAVI

But Gracie doesn't move.

And Ravi's feeling awkward. Very awkward. What's going on? What's happening? This feels like it could be . . . a romantic position, but his heart isn't letting his body go there. He's shocked—and crushed—that Gracie's been keeping this a secret. If she loves him, she would have told him, right?

"Okay, Gracie!" Kat says. "Do your thing. Go!"

Gracie doesn't budge. She's looking up at Ravi, and her eyes look as sad as he's feeling.

Kat's still in training mode. "Come on! Get up on your elbow. Do it, girl!"

Underneath him, Gracie doesn't move a muscle, and neither does Ravi. "Why didn't you tell me?" he asks again, his voice low.

For some reason, Gracie's expression changes suddenly—*is that FURY?* With a loud grunt, she bridges her hips. He can feel himself shifting forward on top of her. Her knees are pressing up behind him, keeping him there. Her foot traps his. With a quick roll of her body, she flips Ravi over, flat on his back. *WOW!* Ravi thinks as he lands on the mat with a loud SMACK. *When did she get so STRONG?*

"Great mount escape!" Kat says, clapping.

"You know *my* secret now." Gracie's standing now, one foot on either side of his torso, arms crossed, glaring down at him. "Why don't *you* tell *me* yours?"

Oh, so that's it. And she's right. You don't keep big secrets from a person you love. "Let me up and I will."

She arcs her left foot over his body and takes a step back to give him room to stand.

Kat clears her throat. "Uh, I think I have to use the bathroom," she says, and starts for the door.

"Wait, Kat," Ravi says. "Come back. I want to tell you both what I've been doing on Fridays."

"Okay," Kat says. "But can we sit down first? I feel a little light-headed after watching you two in action."

They sit in their usual seats at the Bangla lesson table. Gracie's staring at their textbooks. Kat's body and face, though, are in full receptive mode, focused on Ravi. He can tell she *really* wants to hear what he's about to say.

He takes a deep breath and starts by describing his first Friday at the Royal Diadem Society Guesthouse. When he gets to the part about guessing why his first mother brought him there, Gracie's posture changes. She leans forward, and Ravi can see the signature grace return to her eyes.

He swallows and moves on quickly. This is no time for more tears. With Gracie nodding, and Kat still listening intently, he ends by describing his plan to catch Sarker. ". . . And now there are only two Fridays left. That evil man has probably shifted his trafficking to another hotel. I'm still planning to show up at the chai shop, just in case I get the chance to nail him, so please don't tell PG or Arjun or anyone else."

KAT

After a long pause, Kat clears her throat. "This 'plan' of yours sounds a little too much like a movie, Ravi," she says doubtfully. "I'm hoping that criminal stays away so you don't get yourself in trouble."

"Yeah, I guess part of me is, too. But I've been dreaming all summer long of punching that guy in the face. Or at least making sure he's behind bars before we leave India. What do *you* think, Gracie?"

Gracie looks him right in the eye. "You really care what I think?"

Ravi takes another deep inhale. "More than anything in the world," he says, and reaches across the textbooks to take her hand.

"Sounds really risky to me, Robin," she says, and Kat notices she's slipped back into using his Boston name. "Your parents would be heartbroken if anything happened to you."

"Yeah. I know you're right. But . . . I can't seem to let this go, for some reason. Maybe it's about more than taking this jerk down. Maybe it's about rescuing that little girl he was dragging along. And others, too. Maybe . . . I want to save them all from abuse for . . . somebody else's sake, too."

He doesn't look directly at Kat, but she gets the message. "Golden-Ruling," she says.

"Yep," he answers. "I've been trying to figure it out."

Gracie raises her eyebrows. "What are you two talking about?"

"I told Ravi what happened in Oakland," Kat says. "And how Grandma Vee helped me by sharing a survival strategy—she calls it 'Golden-Ruling.'"

"You told *him* and not me? We both know Rob—Ravi's the kindest guy on the planet, but still, Kat."

The kindest guy on the planet. Sounds kind of hot the way Gracie says it, and Kat hopes Ravi hears the sizzle. Her matchmaking is looking more promising. "I'm sorry, Gracie," she says. "Guess I thought it might help him. The weird thing is after I shared it, it ended up making *me* feel better, too. Maybe that's how that whole 'love your neighbor as yourself' thing is supposed to work."

Ravi looks right into Gracie's eyes. "I know I should have told you, Gracie. But . . . I was kind of traumatized after my visit to the orphanage."

"I'm so sad that didn't lead to anything," Gracie says. "I'm so, so sorry, Ravi."

She eases her hand out of his, stands up, and opens her arms.

To Kat's relief, Ravi takes the cue.

RAVI

INT. POLICE TRAINING CENTER LOCKER
ROOM—DAY

"Will you do Kat a favor?" Ravi asks Bontu. "She's teaching Gracie self-defense and she wanted me to be a sparring partner for Gracie, but . . . well, I wasn't a very good sparring partner. She wanted me to ask if you'd do it, and be part of a film. Of a Brazilian jiu-jitsu demonstration. It's a martial art."

"I can try," Bontu says. "But I am a man of peace, not violence."

"You'll have to channel your inner Hulk instead of your inner guru."

"Are you sure you don't mean 'bulk'?" He grins and pats his belly, which hasn't shrunk at all. "What is this fillum?"

"Kat will explain. But if you agree, she needs you all this week for practice. She wants to do the actual demo on Friday. No pressure. You can say no, she said to tell you."

"And miss *my* chance to be a fillum star? Never. I'll be there."

INT. BENGALI EMANCIPATION SOCIETY
HEADQUARTERS—DAY

Bontu and Ravi both arrive at the office the next morning at eight thirty on the nose for Kat's practice session. Ravi wants to be there to . . . well, to make sure Gracie won't get squashed.

No more secrets between the two of them now, thankfully. Well, almost none. He still hasn't had the chance to ask how she feels, or to tell her how he's feeling. He knows she loves him—her hug told him that—but that could have been the old Gracie. Not Bonita Juarez.

She greets him with a hug again today; nobody's in the large prayer room except Kat and Bontu, who doesn't seem to mind, judging by his smirk. Ravi holds Gracie close for as long as he can without it getting strange and then lets go.

Kat's smile is almost as welcoming as Gracie's hug. "Bontu! Thank you so much for coming. Do you have any experience with jiu-jitsu?"

"No. Absolutely none. But I watched a few videos last night. It's about escaping holds, and forcing your opponent to surrender, right? Will I have to wear one of those kimono outfits? Because I think they will suit me quite well. Amira will—"

"No gis," Kat interrupts. "But if you dress the part of a bad guy for the demo, it would be great. And Gracie will be in a shalwar. I want our video to look as much like a scene from a movie as possible. The Asha House girls will respond to that. That's our goal—real BJJ with a light Bollywood touch. So act it up, you two. Bontu: thug. Gracie: victim. Got it?"

MITALI PERKINS

Bontu's eyebrows are so high, they're disappearing under his bangs. "But I have never hurt a girl in my life. I am not even sure I can play that role. Are you sure I'm the right man for this job?"

"I'm not asking you to *hurt* her," Kat says. "Just *pretend* you're an attacker. But be tough and strong; don't go easy on her. She's been practicing with me. I think she can handle you. Right, Gracie?"

Gracie nods. "I'll try."

Now that it's happening in front of his eyes, Ravi isn't too sure about Kat's idea to use Bontu. What if Gracie gets hurt? Their friend's a big dude.

"You always bow before taking the mat," Kat says.

Bontu imitates Gracie.

Gracie lifts her palm. "And then we high-five, fist-bump, and kneel, face-to-face."

They do that, too.

"Okay, girl on bottom, thug on top."

Ravi doesn't like the sound of that. What if something goes wrong? Or she feels uncomfortable? "Wait!" he says.

"What's the problem?" Kat asks, frowning at him.

"Maybe I *should* be the one to do this, Kat."

"No way," Kat says. "The two of you 'fighting' looked more like a slow dance than jiu-jitsu. Listen, I get that this might be hard for you to watch, Ravi, but we're running out of time."

"You can wait outside if you want," Gracie adds.

Ravi shakes his head. "No, I'm okay. Sorry."

Kat turns back to her students. "Bontu, I forgot to tell you to tap her twice quickly on the shoulder if you start to feel any pain."

362

Tap twice to ease the pain, Ravi thinks. *Like Kat did for me outside the orphanage.*

"Pain?" Bontu asks, sounding doubtful.

"Yes. *Before* you feel a lot of it. Ready?"

Bontu nods.

"Okay. Get on top of her, Mr. Thug. Get him in your guard, Fogo. That's Gracie's BJJ name," she says to Ravi.

"Fogo" raises her legs and wraps them around Bontu's waist. Or almost around it—her ankles don't lock at first, but she stretches, strains, and somehow manages it. Ravi can barely see her beneath Bontu's body—all he can see are her legs.

"Okay, Gracie," says Kat. "Kimura!"

Suddenly, to Ravi's total amazement, Gracie does something he can't see, gets up on one elbow, and in the next moment has Bontu's arm trapped between her thigh and other elbow. She twists back, pulling his arm with her. Now her back's on the mat again and he's on top of her, but he's in such an awkward position that it looks like his shoulder might pop out of its socket.

"AAAAAHHHHH!" Bontu yells, tapping Gracie twice with his free hand. She lets go, and he sits up, rubbing his shoulder.

"A perfect Kimura!" Kat says, applauding.

"You okay, Bontu?" Gracie asks.

"I'm fine, fine," he says. "Well, that was a surprise. You're so . . . small. But so strong."

"What did *you* think, Ravi?" Gracie asks.

"Wow!" That's all he can say. And then: "Bap-re-BAP, Firebird!"

Gracie flips her hand at him, but she looks pleased. "Oh, Bontu's a good actor. But that felt GREAT, Kat!"

"I didn't act one bit," Bontu says. "You kicked the cow dung out of me. I'm heading home now to put ice on my shoulder."

"You *have* to act for the demo," Kat tells him. "You have to look mean, and evil. And you can't leave now. We've got two more moves to practice. Can you come tomorrow and Thursday as well? I want to do the demo this Friday."

"I'll be here," Bontu says. "Ice packs and all. Will you be joining us, Ravi? You can cheer me on for once."

Ravi hesitates. "I have to be somewhere else. But I'm sure it's going to be a success."

Kat throws him a look. "Oh, that's right. Friday."

Gracie's expression is worried, too. "Be careful, Ravi. I really wish you wouldn't go—"

"I'll be fine," Ravi says. "I think I'll step outside and let you practice in peace. I'll let you know when Mrs. Gupta's on the way."

Bontu waves him off. "Fine, Mr. Biswas. Since you're not in this scene, go back to your luxurious trailer."

KAT

INT. BENGALI EMANCIPATION SOCIETY HEADQUARTERS—DAY

On Friday morning for the filmed demo, Bontu shows up right on time, once the room has cleared out after prayer meeting. He looks nervous but ready. He's dressed just right, Kat thinks—black pants, black, wide-collared shirt unbuttoned too low, and fancy fake watch.

"Did you bring your phone?" she asks.

He hands it over as Gracie starts her usual warm-up of somersaults and shrimping. She's wearing her yellow shalwar, and her hair is in two braids. No makeup or jewelry. She looks exactly like an Indian schoolgirl to Kat—about twelve years old.

"Is it all right if I wear this over my head?" Bontu asks. He pulls out a stocking to show Kat. "I wouldn't want any of the Asha House girls to be terrified if they meet me in real life."

"Let's see?"

He tugs it over his head so that it smashes his features into an unrecognizable mishmash. "Ugly bank robber?" he asks, and even his voice sounds different.

"It's perfect," Kat says. "Keep it on."

Miss Shireen has agreed to a "meeting" with the three of them at nine o'clock, even though she has no idea what it's about. Kat is about to leave to get her when Gracie stops her.

"I want you to know that no matter what happens, Kat, I've had an awesome time learning BJJ. You're a great professor."

"Thanks, Fogo. Let's do this thing."

When Miss Shireen comes in, she greets Gracie and then catches sight of Bontu with his stocking mask. "Who is this man? What is he doing here? And why is he wearing *that*?"

He pulls it off immediately. "I'm Bontu, ma'am. Remember me?"

"Oh, thank goodness. Shen's nephew. But why are you here?"

Kat clears her throat. "You told me you'd be open to seeing self-defense in action, Miss Shireen. Well, today we want to show you how a petite girl can break free from a much bigger man. Bontu has agreed to take the role of Gracie's attacker. Will you watch?"

"Why, Kat? I'm not going to change my mind."

"I figured you might say that. But I still want you to see this demo."

"Does your father know you're here, Bontu?" Miss Shireen asks.

"Er . . . No, ma'am, but he is a big supporter of self-defense for women. He helped to launch the department's project. It teaches schoolgirls to protect—"

"Yes, yes, I know what it does." After one long, appraising look at all of them, Miss Shireen shrugs and tips her head slightly to signify a yes. "All right, Kat. I'm very busy today, but I'll give you fifteen minutes."

"It won't take long, Miss Shireen—under five for the whole demo. Why don't you sit here, in this chair?"

The older woman sighs but takes a seat.

Kat takes a deep breath and opens the smartphone camera. "Okay, you two, take the mat."

Bontu pulls his mask back on, and he and Gracie bow, step on the mat, high-five, fist-bump, and kneel side by side, this time facing Miss Shireen and Kat.

"Act it out, you two," Kat instructs, and then starts recording. "First, a Kimura," she says into the phone.

As they practiced, Bontu sits on top of Gracie and Gracie wraps her legs around Bontu's body. Gracie's face takes on a terrified expression. She starts writhing and protesting. This helps Bontu remember his part, too. He snarls and lifts a threatening fist in the air, shouting at her in Bangla.

Kat hears a small "oh" of surprise from Miss Shireen. He *does* look evil, Kat thinks, but she keeps recording. The good thing is that it's clear he isn't making it easy on the girl underneath him. He's using all of his bulk and weight to keep her pinned.

But Fogo knows what to do. It doesn't take much time for her to get up on her elbow. Turning her body so that her right hip is out from under his, she grabs his wrist, clutches her own, and then twists and falls back. After a few seconds in that uncomfortable position—which he recognizes this time around—Bontu pats her back twice for release. Gracie lets go and stands up while Bontu hams it up for the camera, clutching his shoulder, and throwing himself around in pretend pain on the mat.

A Kimura, perfectly executed, just as it was so many months ago now in that Sanger stairwell. Kat feels like cheering, but one glance at Miss Shireen's stony face restrains her. Besides, she's still recording.

Okay, moving on. "Next, a mount escape," Kat says into the phone.

This time Bontu sits on top of Gracie, pinning her legs. The stocking over his head can't mask the expression of deranged rage on his face. Gracie is acting like she's going for an Oscar, shaking her head back and forth, shouting, and pretending to cry. Kat registers Miss Shireen's second sharp intake of breath, but she keeps circling and recording.

Gracie's legs are trapped, but she uses her foot to hook Bontu's, bridges her hips, and rolls. Bontu lands with a hard "oof" on his back, and Gracie's up on her feet and running to the far side of the room in no time.

A perfect mount escape.

Miss Shireen's expression doesn't change.

"Last, the triangle choke," Kat tells Bontu's phone.

This is the move that's given Gracie the most trouble—probably because she hates inflicting any kind of pain. *You can do it, Fogo!* Kat thinks, trying to send her student good energy. She keeps recording as they get in their start positions again—Gracie on her back, Bontu on top. For some reason, in this third pose, he really looks violent, even to Kat. Miss Shireen's shocked gasp resounds through the room.

That didn't sound good, Kat thinks. But her pupil is concentrating so fiercely it doesn't stop the demonstration. Gracie executes perfectly. Within seconds, she's squeezing Bontu's neck between a triangle of her thighs so tightly that he gasps for air and taps twice. Once again, she's on her feet in triumph, with Bontu on the mat massaging his throat and taking deep gulps of air.

Kat stops recording and turns to their audience of one. "Well, what do you think, Miss Shireen? If Gracie can defend herself from a big attacker like that, don't you think your girls will want to learn how, too? I've recorded the demo if you want to show it to them. You can tell them you saw it in real life, and that we didn't fake anything."

But Miss Shireen's rising to her feet.

She's frowning.

Her head is figure-eighting.

Could be yes, could be no, but something—that last gasp, maybe?—tells Kat her Plan C, her beautiful Plan C, is crashing to the ground harder than Bontu just did.

"I warned you that this wasn't a good idea," Miss Shireen says. "Do you really think a counselor would let me show something like this to abused girls? Some of them wake up screaming at the memory of men on top of them. I'm sorry you wasted your time, you two. I wish you'd heeded me, Kat."

And with that, she stalks out.

RAVI

INT. BOSE FLAT—DAY

No sign of Sarker at the Royal Diadem. Ravi's starting to feel like Kat was right—he's living in some kind of superhero fantasy world. Capturing a villain doesn't happen in real life. Not for Ravi Thornton, anyway.

Hopefully Kat's plans will turn out better than his; he can't wait to hear how the demo went. But on Saturday, while he's still in bed, the girls call early—*Kat's not feeling well and Gracie's staying with her*, Mira tells Ravi when he comes into the kitchen. Did something bad happen? Was the demo a total disaster? Bontu might be able to tell him, but he wants to hear about it from Kat. He'll just have to wait. He borrows Arjun's phone to text a message, telling Bontu that they can't make it to their second-to-last Saturday outing.

On Sunday, Kat doesn't show up to church. *Not a good sign*, Ravi thinks. As he rides back to the Bose flat for lunch, he remembers when she told him about what happened in Oakland. Poor Nefertiti. She had such high hopes that coming to Kolkata might help her recover. He knows exactly how it feels when hopes shatter.

"How'd it go on Friday?" he asks Gracie as soon as she walks in the front door.

"Terrible," Gracie says, sighing. "Miss Shireen nixed Kat's plan. I kind of figured she would. I should have warned Kat, I guess, but I was so eager to learn the moves myself I didn't want our training to stop."

"You're so good. Kat did an amazing job teaching you. Hope I get to see her soon." *Kat was there for me; I want to be there for her.*

"All that hard work didn't matter in the end. Not for her, anyway. She's crushed. It's probably good we're going back to Boston soon. Maybe Ms. Vee can work some of her feel-good magic again before Kat heads home to California."

"Lunchtime," Mira calls.

The conversation around the table doesn't flow like it usually does. The twins are out. PG keeps yawning. Ravi knows that Gracie's worried about Kat. So is he. But what's wrong with Arjun and Mira?

"Why so quiet, Arjun Uncle?" he asks.

"Court date's coming up," Arjun says. "Kavita still hasn't decided to testify. Shen thinks this man is going to slip right through our fingers without her as a witness."

"The courts let girls sit behind a screen, right?" PG asks.

"Right," Arjun says. "But time's running out, and I'm not sure what she'll decide to do. Shireen's letting her make up her own mind."

"As she should," Mira says.

"And what about the baby?" Ravi can't help asking. "What's going to happen to Shiuli?"

Mira sighs. "The babies. Most vulnerable of all, aren't they?"

"How will Kavita manage to support herself AND a baby?" Gracie asks. "Can the Bengali Emancipation Society help her?"

"Our goal is always family preservation first," Arjun says.

"Keeping the babies with their mothers?" Ravi asks.

"Right. We're discussing some possibilities: partnering with an organization that trains and funds foster families, renting another house somewhere for our mothers to stay and raise their babies in safety, finding sponsors to provide financial support so the girls can educate their children. But it's only in the visioning stage for now."

Suddenly Ravi flashes back to a square embossed envelope with his name on it. "Maybe we can still be a part of it after we get back to the States," he says. "Raise some money to help with any option you choose?"

"Great idea, Ravi," PG says. "Our people love to give; I'm sure they'll come through. Does that sound helpful, Arjun?"

"Definitely," Arjun answers. "I'd like to get our organization to the place where we can pay for programs like this without money from abroad, but we're not there yet."

"I hear you, brother. Besides, we need you just as much as you need us. Money's not the only gift that changes lives. Maybe we can launch a foundation to partner with BES."

Ravi thinks of the hotel—HER hotel. "What about naming it the 'Royal Diadem Foundation'?"

PG turns to him. "You've been reading your Bible, kiddo!"

"Er—I have?"

"That's in the Book of Isaiah. 'You will be a crown of

splendor in the Lord's hands, a royal diadem in the hand of your God.' And then the next verse says: 'No longer will they call you "Deserted," or your name "Desolate."'"

"It's a perfect name," says Gracie, smiling at Ravi.

KAT

INT. ASHA HOUSE BABY CARE ROOM—DAY

Kat stays in the baby room on Monday morning, sending the housemothers off for a rest. With three little ones in their care now, she spins through them systematically, taking turns feeding, burping, and changing them.

No more BJJ training with Gracie, she thinks, rocking Diana as she finishes her bottle. Without that, what's the point of going to Bangla class? She's not been a very good language learner; it's their last lesson anyway.

They still have a week or so left in India, but Kat's checking out early. At least mentally. This Kolkata match is over. She wants to get on the next plane and go home.

Home to Oakland, where she belongs. Or where she used to belong, before—

She gets up, puts Diana in her crib, and picks up Logan and his bottle. More rocking. *If the zoo doesn't hire me back, I'll have to find a job somewhere else.*

Shiuli's diaper needs changing. Kat does it on autopilot now. *No idea what I'm going to say in those stupid college essays.* Maybe she'll drop out of Sanger and finish her senior year at the neighborhood school.

Shiuli takes her time to finish her bottle. *I'll tell Saundra that*

I'm quitting BJJ—no use in trying to get to black belt. I'd have to spar with a lot of men to get to that level.

I tap out, she thinks, putting Shiuli gently down in her crib.

Looks like all three babies are finally asleep. Maybe she should head back to Miss Shireen's cottage and start packing her suitcases. Just then, Baby Logan opens his eyes. At the sight of Kat's face, he reaches up his arms with a happy gurgle. He doesn't need a feed, or a burp, or a new diaper. Must just want a cuddle. Kat picks him up and holds him close.

RAVI

Ravi is late to their last Bangla class of the summer, but it doesn't matter much. Kat is nowhere in sight. *Hope she's feeling better*, he thinks. Mrs. Gupta isn't there yet. Gracie is asleep with her head on the table. Must have been a rough baby-tending night last night. Or else she stayed up with Kat, trying to comfort her. That's something Gracie would do.

Ravi heads to his usual spot, trying not to wake her, but he accidentally jostles her chair. A book slips out of her lap. He picks it up and glances at the cover. She's been reading *this*? Bap-re-BAP. It's a graphic novelization of a movie. She must have bought it at that comic book shop, and the word *graphic* fits perfectly. *Island Rajah* is the title, and a buxom, sari-clad woman is leaning back against a shirtless hero, whose eight-pack abs glisten under a flower garland. The gleaming-skinned, muscular hero looks familiar. Yes. Starring Amit Biswas as "the Rajah," it says.

Ravi takes a closer look at the abs. Thanks to his workouts with Shen, Biswas and Thornton look even more alike now than at the beginning of the summer.

Gracie's head flies up. "Ravi!"

He hands back the book. "Spicy content, Ms. Rivera."

"Oh, you know . . . I only bought it because . . . well, he does remind me of you. Especially on that cover." She isn't looking at him now; her long eyelashes are resting on smooth, soft cheeks. Her lips are a dark pink color, even without any lipstick.

Exactly the same hue as her shalwar kameez.

They're finally alone. This seems like the perfect time to do what he's been wanting to do for weeks now. But his stomach is dancing like it's auditioning for Bollywood. His skin is sizzling again.

He takes a step closer.

She stands.

Their eyes meet.

He smiles, and decides to risk it. "I'd try to be your Island Rajah any day, but is Ravi Thornton good enough?"

She smiles back. "More than good enough. He's perfect."

He leans in, Gracie tips her head back, and he does what his look-alike never gets to do, at least on-screen: kiss a leading lady on the mouth, sweet, deep, and long.

Shazam.

Gracie's arms curve around Ravi's body.

He pulls her even closer.

This is Gracie, his friend.

This is Gracie, his beloved.

With her in his arms, Ravi feels like he can take on a hundred villains at once. Even if he never gets to in real life.

They look into each other's eyes. Neither of them notices Mrs. Gupta walking in.

"You two are looking exactly like a Bollywood fillum," she says, giggling like one of the girls who ask Ravi for autographs.

KAT

INT. ASHA HOUSE BABY CARE ROOM—DAY

"Our last Bangla lesson!" Gracie says, bursting into the baby room. "I can't believe we're heading home so soon. Everyone said to say goodbye to you, Kat—Gopal, Mrs. Gupta, everyone."

Kat's still rocking babies. She's been there the whole day. She can't seem to make herself leave. Holding small bodies in her arms, feeding them, keeping them dry and warm—these are the only things she still feels like doing.

She looks up from Baby Diana's face. Weird. Gracie looks even more like Bonita Juarez than usual. "What happened to you? You're smiling like this baby after one of her massive burps."

Gracie blushes and picks up Shiuli. "Ravi kissed me," she says softly, as if she's telling the baby, not Kat. "It was . . . incredible. One kiss, and then Mrs. Gupta came in."

"Took you guys long enough," Kat says.

Logan starts wailing, so Gracie bends over the cribs to switch babies.

Kat closes her eyes and rests her cheek against Diana's.

Is there a kiss like Ravi and Gracie's in her future? She doubts it.

If you can't stand a man's touch, he'd better not kiss you.

RAVI

Ravi hasn't seen Gracie after that amazing Monday moment. No more Bangla lessons, so she's been sticking around Asha House to keep Kat company. And Ravi hasn't seen Kat at all— not since the Thursday before her failed demo.

"You taking us out again this Saturday, Bontu?" he asks, toweling off in the locker room after powering through his thirty-fifth—and second-to-last—workout with Shen.

Bontu's head pops out of the shower stall. "Certainly. And tomorrow, if you're free, let's take a last 'men-only' sightseeing trip, Ravi. We can go to a comedy show, and—"

"Er . . . I have plans," Ravi says.

Bontu's poking a towel-covered finger into each ear to dry them off. "Where do you go every Friday, anyway? It's a big mystery. I've been thinking of all kinds of possibilities. Let me join you tomorrow. Please, Ravi."

"I go to a tea shop and study Bangla," Ravi says, sitting on the bench facing the panel of lockers. "Not too exciting."

"What's the name of this shop?" Bontu asks, pulling on his shirt and pants. Ravi can tell that he's shifting into tour guide mode.

"I don't really know the name. The sign's in Bangla, which

I can't read. Not yet, anyway. It's across the street from a hotel, and it serves really good cardamom-spiced chai."

"What's the name of the hotel?"

"Er . . . it's called the Royal Diadem Society Guesthouse."

"Oh! *That* shop. Their chai *is* quite good. I'd like to go with you."

As he watches Bontu tie his shoelaces, Ravi doesn't say no. His time in the city of his birth is dwindling. They're leaving India on Tuesday. Oh, how he hates endings and goodbyes. And there are so many to come. Bangla lessons are over; on Monday he and Gracie said farewell to Mrs. Gupta, Gopal, and a few other staff members in the Bengali Emancipation Society office. Over the next few days, he'll share only a few more meals with Arjun, Mira, and the twins. One more service in a Bengali church. And he'll finish up his thirty-sixth and final training session with Shen on Monday. He'll have to say good-bye to Bontu then, too, and he hates the thought of that.

That means tomorrow, Friday, is his last time at the chai shop. Ravi's been sitting there alone for seven Fridays in a row, keeping an eye on the Royal Diadem Society Guesthouse. One more watch. Stupid or not, the thought of stopping Sarker and rescuing that girl helped him survive this intense summer. Anyway, he needs to say goodbye to his biggest fan, Mr. Lakshmi the chai-wallah.

Bontu stands and hoists his workout bag over his shoulder. "Well, Ravi? May I join you tomorrow?"

Ravi stands, too, and looks up at his first friend in Kolkata. After so many hours in that shop alone, it might be good to finish out his Friday vigils in good company. "I'd like that, Bontu."

KAT

EXT. ASHA HOUSE VERANDA—NIGHT

It's so hot on Thursday that the only breeze at Asha House comes at twilight on the front porch. That's where Kat finds Kavita rocking in a chair with Shiuli on her lap. Kavita's sitting in exactly the same spot as she was in the video Kat saw so many weeks ago.

Kat takes the empty chair beside her, fighting a wave of sadness. She leaves India in a few days and she's managed to do zilch to help Kavita. Besides change a few of her baby's diapers.

"You've stopped wearing shalwar kameez, Katina Didi," Kavita says. "May I ask why?"

Kat's in her Oakland clothes again. And it's too hot for Grandma Vee's red scarf, so there's not a spot of color in sight. "I'm not Indian. Those clothes belong in your culture, not mine. May I hold the baby?"

Kavita hands over her daughter. "But we're so happy to share our culture with you. Why not a mix, at least?"

"I'll wear the headbands you and Amrita gave me, I promise." Kat kisses the baby's cheek. "I'm so glad you named her Shiuli."

"I am living for her now. Not only me. Maybe that is why thinking about testifying is making me so afraid."

Kat's whole body tenses. Maybe she hasn't decided yet.

Don't say anything. Don't say anything.

"What do *you* think I should do, Katina Didi?"

There it is! She's asking for advice. Kat's one last chance to help before she leaves. She hands back the baby, suddenly so excited she's afraid she might drop her. "Do you really want to know what I think?"

"Yes. What would you do if you were me?"

"Well, I was in a . . . similar sort of situation as you last year. A different and much smaller experience, but still. Someone attacked me. I managed to fight him off, but it was horrible."

Kavita stops rocking. She's listening closely now. "And?"

"Well, I . . . spoke out against him. But I shouldn't have. He lied. He's a good liar. Nobody knew which one of us to believe. But he was able to stay. I was the one who had to leave. His life didn't change. Mine completely changed. I lost. He won. I think they always do, Kavita."

Kavita props Shiuli up over her shoulder and pats her on the back. "But you told the truth?"

"Yes."

"And he lied?"

"Yes. He told the authorities that *I* was the one who attacked *him.*"

"You fought him off physically?"

"I did. I'd learned self-defense, you see. He gave up after a knee injury and a shoulder dislocation."

"What happened to you? To your body?"

"Not too much. He groped me, tore my clothes, and that's it. But my mind was a mess. *Is* a mess."

Kavita tucks the baby under her orna and starts feeding her. "How is it that you say he won? He was forced to lie. You told the truth. He was physically hurt. You were not, as much. It sounds like standing against him made *you* the winner, Katina Didi."

No. Wait. That's not right.

"But I had to leave my mother, school, and job, Kavita. He was able to stay right where he was. Keep everything he had." And then she says it again: "He won. I lost. Don't you see?"

"I see that because of what you chose to do, you came here to us. To me. I see that, too. Isn't that winning?"

Kat doesn't answer. *In a way, it is, I guess. In sort of a big way.*

"Don't worry about me," Kavita says, gazing down at her baby. "I'm strong, like you. And now I shall become even more strong, for the sake of this little one."

She hands the satisfied baby back to Kat. Little Shiuli.

"She's so beautiful," Kat says. "And yes, I know you'll protect her, just like my mom did for me."

"When you told me about your mother, it gave me hope. If she can raise such a good daughter as you, perhaps I can, too."

Kat's glad it's getting dark out here, because as she kisses Shiuli again and again, nobody but the baby sees her superpower.

RAVI

INT./EXT. CHAI SHOP—DAY

Bontu manages to find a place to park not far from the chai shop and hotel. The day is so hot already that Ravi can feel the sidewalk sizzling under his sandals.

"This cardamom-spiced chai is tasty," Bontu says, ordering biscuits with his second cup. "I'll put this shop on my BBB list."

"Sounds great," Ravi says, still keeping an eye on the deserted hotel through the window. *Force of habit*, he thinks. He's brought his backpack along with the glasses and has cash in his pocket. Just in case.

Bontu waves a hand in front of Ravi's eyes. "What are you staring at?"

"Oh, nothing. Just the street. I'm going to miss Kolkata, Bontu."

"Come back and visit. What will you do when you go back to America? Are you intending to become a policeman?"

"Me? Er . . . no. I've never thought of that, actually." Ravi notices a sedan pulling up outside the hotel. It's a blue Skoda. He keeps watching, but nobody gets out.

"Why are you gazing outside, Ravi? Am I missing a beautiful girl who keeps passing by?"

"No. It's nothing."

Mr. Lakshmi brings Ravi's second and Bontu's third cup to their table. "Here you are, Mr. Biswas."

Bontu grins. "I, too, am in Mr. Biswas's next fillum. We are rehearsing right now, actually."

Ravi glances across the street again. And almost chokes on his tea.

There he is—Sarker—climbing out of the sedan!

He leaps to his feet. "Bontu, it's him! The perp!"

Bontu spins around so fast he overturns his teacup.

The trafficker is standing on the pavement outside the hotel door, greeting another man. *His "customer"!* Ravi thinks. Sure enough, Sarker reaches out his slimy hand and gives the other man something that glints in the sun. *Room key!* Ravi guesses.

The disgusting "customer" walks into the Royal Diadem Society Guesthouse. Ravi starts fumbling through his backpack for his hidden-camera glasses.

"What's going on?" Bontu asks. "What's a 'perp'?"

"That man's a bad guy, Bontu! A trafficker! We have to stop him."

Where are those glasses? Why is there so much STUFF in this stupid backpack?

Bontu is staring like Ravi's got three heads. "You can't just storm in there. These criminals always keep guards nearby. With guns."

"I know he's got a girl in there! We have to do something!"

Ravi's fingers finally find the glasses, buried underneath four comic books and his Bangla textbook. Everyone in the shop is staring.

"Please sit down, Ravi. They're thinking Amit Biswas has gone mad. Let me ring my uncle if you really think something's going on."

"I already tried the last time this happened! He didn't believe me! I'm going in!"

Ravi's hands are shaking as he puts on the glasses.

This is it.

The moment he's been waiting for ever since he saw Sarker. Ever since he looked into the terrified eyes of that girl.

He puts on the glasses and activates the camera. Good, the thing still works.

Bontu puts his big hands on Ravi's shoulders and gives him a little shake. "Ravi, listen to me! You sound just like those Americans Uncle always complains about! If a girl *is* being sold in there, you'll put both your lives at risk by running in on your own like this."

But Ravi doesn't want to listen. He wants to feel his fist land on Sarker's jaw. Twisting out of his friend's grasp, he starts to make a run for the door.

He takes two steps. Suddenly, with a big *OOOMPHH!*, Bontu hurtles himself at Ravi from behind and flings both arms around his waist.

Ravi falls flat, facedown.

The camera glasses fly off.

Bontu landed hard, and now Ravi's pinned under his weight. "Get. Off. Me," he grunts.

Somehow Bontu manages to sit up, but he doesn't obey Ravi. Instead, he wriggles around until his butt is firmly planted on Ravi's back.

At least Ravi can breathe now.

"HELP! SOMEONE GET HIM OFF ME!"

Nobody comes to his rescue.

"What is happening?" he hears someone ask.

"It's Amit Biswas," Mr. Lakshmi answers. "He is rehearsing a scene from a new fillum with that big fellow."

All around them, Ravi can hear people oohing and aahing over their performance.

Ravi clenches his jaw. "Bontu—GET OFF!"

But Bontu doesn't budge.

He sits on Ravi like a Tata truck.

Ravi struggles hard to escape, pushing, twisting, shouting, even trying to remember some of the moves that Gracie used. He's almost in tears now. "Bontu! Please! We have to save those girls!"

And that's when he hears sirens, getting louder and closer.

Bontu climbs off him. "Ravi, come and see."

Ravi gets on his feet and walks to the window. Four police cars have pulled up in front of the Royal Diadem Society Guesthouse. Shen leaps out of one of them. Ravi spots Sarker sprinting down the street, but Shen catches up to the criminal in ten seconds and has him in handcuffs in another ten.

Two other officers escort the "customer" and hotel owner out of the front entrance. And after a few more minutes, as Ravi and Bontu and everyone else in the chai shop watch, two officers, both women, come out of the Royal Diadem Society Guesthouse, each holding two crying children by the hand.

Four girls.

Rescued.

Three perps. Including Sarker.

Captured.

The entire chai shop bursts into applause.

With a jolt, Ravi realizes that none of this would have happened had he raced in there fifteen minutes earlier. He turns to Bontu, who's clapping loudly beside Mr. Lakshmi. "I'm an idiot. Thanks, Bontu. Thanks."

"My pleasure," Bontu says with his trademark grin.

Not all heroes wear capes, Ravi thinks. *Some just have round, hefty bottoms.*

KAT

INT. MISS SHIREEN'S COTTAGE—DAY

Kat and Gracie are in their small alcove bedroom, holding babies again. The sun is rising after their last overnight baby watch—an extra one that they volunteered for when they heard the housemothers chatting about how much they wanted to see the new Amit Biswas fillum.

"I'm glad you told Kavita your story," Gracie says, after Kat shares what happened on the veranda. "That Ms. Vee knows what she's talking about. You look so much happier today. I'm going to have to try some of this Golden-Ruling myself."

"You Golden-Rule all the time, Gracie," Kat says. "It comes as naturally to you as walking or speaking Spanish."

"Thanks. I try, anyway. Hey, are you going with me today to meet Ravi and Bontu? It's so hot that we're skipping sightseeing and heading straight to the cinema hall."

Kat thinks for a moment. "No. I think I'll stay here and spend time with Miss Shireen."

"Okay, but Ravi's going to be sad not to see you, Kat. Mind if I tell him about your talk with Kavita? And that you're feeling better?"

"That's fine. And tell him I'm sorry I'll miss seeing his twin's newest 'fillum.'"

*   *   *

Miss Shireen and Kat are collapsed on the couch under the ceiling fan, listening to Bangla gaan and talking about the big rescue that took place at the Royal Diadem Hotel the day before. It made headlines in the newspapers this morning.

"They're saying Shen's the best police officer in Kolkata," says Miss Shireen. "He'll probably get promoted."

"I wish I could have met him while I was here," Kat says. "He sure got Ravi into shape. That kid's body looks totally different than when we got here."

"As does Gracie's," says Miss Shireen. "Thanks to you."

There's a pause. The two of them haven't discussed the botched demo since it happened.

"Kavita tells me her talk with you was very helpful," Miss Shireen says, breaking the silence. "What did you tell her?"

"Not much. Just shared my own story, like you suggested. It was helpful for me, too."

"Yes, you seem more cheerful today. Anyway, whatever you said to Kavita, it helped her make up her mind. She's decided to testify. Arjun's thrilled."

Kat's not surprised. After their talk, she guessed that's what Kavita was going to do. But still—she wishes Hyena man could know how much courage it will take for Kavita to walk into that courtroom.

"Arjun really cares about the welfare of our Asha House girls, Kat," Miss Shireen says, as if she can read Kat's mind. "He loves them like family." She hesitates again, as if she's weighing her next words. "One of them *is* family, actually."

"What do you mean?" Kat asks, sitting up.

"It's not a secret. They talk about it freely, but now that their boys are getting older, they are a bit more cautious."

Kat sees it now. "You mean . . . Mira Auntie?"

"Yes. She was one of the first girls to be housed here. And now, see—as a survivor, she's able to do wonderful work with our rescued boys."

Kat pictures the kind, capable woman who welcomed her that first day in Kolkata. Happy spouse. Loving parent. Plus, a success at her job. Maybe a traumatized girl *could* become a strong, successful adult. "Did Arjun help rescue her?"

"Oh, no, not at all. They met years after that, in our church. I was there, so I can assure you there was no exploitation—it was all proper. Mira left Asha House for college, returned to work at BES, the two of them met, and the rest is history. So you see, Arjun sees his beloved wife in every one of our girls. He sees what they can become in the future."

Guess everyone has a backstory.

They make us real, even if they do make us cry.

She glances at the face of the woman sitting beside her. "How did *you* end up at Asha House, Miss Shireen? You've never told me much about your life."

Miss Shireen smiles. "That's a longer story than I can share after only ten weeks' acquaintance." But she reaches out and pats Kat's hand. "I'm sorry if I was abrupt the other day. I've been ruminating on your 'demonstration,' and there is one thing I can agree to: Every baby who comes our way could receive this self-defense instruction. When Shiuli and Diana and Logan are old enough, will you return here to teach them?"

"I will," Kat says. "By then I hope to be a black belt, and a much better teacher."

"Is that a promise?" Miss Shireen asks.

"Yes. I keep my promises, Miss Shireen."

"That is why I'm inviting you to return. And when you do, *I* promise to tell you my whole story, from start to finish."

RAVI

INT. KOLKATA POLICE TRAINING CENTER—DAY

The Monday after his team rescues four underage girls from the Royal Diadem Society Guesthouse and arrests three thugs for trafficking children, Shen makes Ravi hit the floor for what feels like three hundred push-ups.

Bontu's nowhere in sight. Ravi found a note from his friend waiting on a bench in the locker room: "Meet at the chai shop once you're done."

He's on his own with Shen for his last training session. The whistle blows nonstop like it did during his first. No words, just that stupid whistle. Ravi pushes, and pulls, and runs, and sweats. His body manages to do everything he asks of it, even though by the end of two hours he's exhausted.

The closing whistle sounds—three short beeps in quick succession. Shen hasn't said a word other than grunting a few commands.

"Thank you for training me this summer, sir," Ravi says, and he means it. In spite of the focus required to survive the intense physical challenge—or maybe because of it—Shen's sessions carried him through the lowest points of the summer. Plus the man gave Ravi a big chunk of his time. And didn't give up on him.

"I understand you witnessed the rescue?" Shen asks abruptly.

"Yes, sir. I see now why you asked me to stay away."

Shen doesn't reply.

What else is there to say? "Goodbye, sir." Ravi turns and heads to the locker room for the last time.

"Stop!"

Ravi obeys.

Boots thud his way.

A hand of steel lands on his shoulder. It spins him around.

Ravi catches his breath. Has Bontu told his uncle about the stupid plan the American almost tried? Is Ravi Thornton about to get the scolding of a lifetime?

But Shen is smiling. Actually smiling. Ravi can almost hear the man's cheeks and jaw creak from the unusual exertion.

"You have worked hard and seen good results, Ravi Thornton," Shen says. "Maybe you should consider law enforcement as *your* line of work. Any police force would be lucky to have you. American or Bengali."

Ravi can hardly believe what he's just heard. "Thank you, sir. Thank you for everything you've taught me."

Especially how a South Asian badass can take down villains.

INT./EXT. CHAI SHOP—DAY

Bontu and Ravi talk everything over while they sip their chai—how stupid they must have looked on Friday and how angry Ravi was at Bontu.

"I finally put my inner Hulk to good use," Bontu says.

"And your outer bottom," Ravi says. "Ouch, Bontu."

"Wasn't my uncle's team impressive?"

"They must have been watching that hotel every day," Ravi says. "No wonder he told me to stay away."

"I could never do that job. I finally told Baba that this weekend."

"You did? What did he say?"

"Gave Bontu's Bengal Barano his blessing!" Bontu says, with a grin so wide Ravi can see it on either side of his cup of chai.

"That's wonderful."

They cross the street to take one last look at the hotel. As Ravi walks up to the door, he notices that both handles are secured with a strong iron chain and a padlock.

"Hey, Bontu, look—there's a 'closed' sign on the door."

Ravi presses his face against the glass, trying to see inside, but it's dark.

"Uncle told me they might shut the place down. The owner will probably have to sell."

Hmmmm. Maybe Ravi should mention that to Arjun.

"Are the rescued girls on their way back home?" he asks as they walk to the car.

"Not yet. They're in a safe house, getting counseling. The police have to make sure that their families aren't the ones who sold them to the traffickers. People get horribly desperate when their children are hungry."

So much work left to do. So many powerless people to protect. Here, in the States, in every corner of the planet.

They walk in silence to where Bontu's car is parked. Ravi

gives the hood a friendly slap. "Thank you for showing me around this great city," he says.

"Call it your 'desh,' brother," Bontu answers. "Your village. I'll see you at the airport tomorrow."

INT. BOSE FLAT—NIGHT

Ravi's last supper in Kolkata is just him and the Bose family. PG's students are feasting with him at some restaurant near the seminary. Kat and Gracie are eating with Miss Shireen and the Asha House girls.

Mira makes Ravi's favorites: lentils, rice, egg curry, cauliflower and potato curry, raita, and payesh, that classic Bengali sweet rice pudding, for dessert.

"Thank you for everything," Ravi says. "The home, the delicious meals, the Bengali lessons . . . everything."

"It was our pleasure, Ravi," says Mira.

"Don't forget the video games, Ravi Dada!" says Anand.

"And the Bengali lessons *we* gave you," adds Bijoy.

"You'll keep up with your Bangla, I hope?" Arjun asks.

"I will," Ravi promises.

"I spoke with Shen, by the way. He had nothing but praise for you. He's agreed to having foreign visitors again—if they're anything like Ravi Thornton, they're welcome, he said. Those were his exact words. My jaw literally dropped."

"Well done, Ravi!" Mira says. "Maybe we should have you speak to all our potential big donors. One conversation with you, and rich old people will certainly empty their pockets."

She and Arjun laugh. They don't know anything about the Edward Thornton V trust fund that's waiting for Ravi at home.

"What do you think about Shen's rescue on Friday?" Arjun asks. "We were celebrating today in the office. Amazing! At the Royal Diadem Society Guesthouse. That place has quite an interesting history. I found it curious that the foundation you're starting in Boston will share the same name."

Ravi holds his breath, but Arjun doesn't ask questions. The sentence hangs in the air for a second or two.

"Well, it looks like the police shut down the hotel today, Uncle Arjun," Ravi says. "It might be available for rent. Or even to buy, if you can raise the money."

"I'll check into it."

And Ravi knows he will. Turns out, South Asian badasses come in every shape and size.

"Last video game battle, Ravi Dada?" Anand asks.

"No," Ravi says, making the twins' faces fall. "LAST TICKLE CHASE!"

They run down the hall, squealing, and Ravi races after them, wiggling all ten of his fingers.

KAT

INT. ASHA HOUSE COMMON ROOM—DAY

Gracie and Kat haul their suitcases out of Miss Shireen's cottage. She comes out, too, dressed and ready for work as usual, and locks the front door.

"Thank you for hosting us, Miss Shireen," Gracie says.

Kat looks fondly at the small, unassuming cottage, and then turns to the small, unassuming woman—at least on the outside. On the inside, she's a Bobcat defending Canaries with all her might. "You gave us a home away from home. Thank you for everything."

"I'm not sad; I know you're returning one day," Miss Shireen says brusquely as they accompany her to the gate. She gives them each a namaste and climbs into the van that takes her to the office.

"Well, that was short and quick," Gracie says as they watch the van pull away. "She's probably glad to have her place to herself again."

But Kat's not fooled; she saw the fierce love in those feline eyes.

Kat kisses each of Baby Diana's cheeks at least five times. She's grown so much. Gracie's doing the same thing with Logan.

He's grown, too, even though he's still only two-thirds the size of Diana. Shiuli's waiting in her mother's arms for her turn. Kat and Gracie switch babies until all three of the little ones are kissed thoroughly.

The Asha House girls encircle them, giving them loving hugs and kisses. Amrita and Charubala promise to send photos through Arjun. So does Kavita. She and Kat hold each other for a long minute.

"Thank you for coming, Kat Didi," she says. "Thank you for everything."

"I'll try and visit again, Kavita," Kat answers. *Goodbye, my Canary.*

The Maruti is waiting outside the gate.

INT. KOLKATA AIRPORT—DAY

True to his word, Bontu's at the airport to see them off.

"Your business is going to be a huge success," Gracie tells him. "We'll write you great reviews and follow you on social media."

"Thanks again for doing that demo with Gracie, Bontu," Kat adds. "*You* were terrific, even though nothing much came of it."

"Want to see something curious, Kat?" Bontu asks, handing her his phone. "Firebird and I have gone viral."

"What? How?"

"I uploaded our demo on my channel, and it began getting hits and comments almost immediately."

Kat looks at Gracie, who shrugs and says, "I told him he could."

Ravi, Bontu, and Gracie gather around Kat as she presses PLAY.

"You blurred out my face," Gracie says. "Thank goodness. I was a little worried about that. And nobody can tell it's you with your mask on."

Kat sees that Bontu's also cropped, edited, and added a soundtrack of Bangla gaan. He's kept her voiceovers announcing each move: *First, a Kimura. Next, a mount escape. Last, a triangle choke.*

"This is incredible, Bontu," Ravi says. "Looks like a scene in a real fillum."

"But you can tell that it's real BJJ, too," Kat says. She reads the caption out loud. "'Tiny Girl Fights off Big Bad Guy with Brazilian Jiu-jitsu.' That's perfect."

"I don't feel as small as I used to," says Gracie. "But I guess if that wording gets us more views . . ."

"Look at all those comments," says Ravi. "Some are creepy, but most are from girls saying they want to learn how to do this. And they're not just Indian girls, people are commenting from all around the world. This is what *you* did, Kat Girl. You're Golden Ruling like a maniac here."

Kat's stunned. As she scrolls through the comments, she sees BJJ instructors and academies from different countries linking to their websites. The view count has already doubled since Bontu handed her the phone.

"Amira wants to sign up for a course," Bontu tells them.

"Not to fight me off, of course; only to protect herself when she takes the last bus back from college. And when I showed my baba the video, he couldn't believe it was me. He's planning on seeing if they can use it for their police self-defense workshops for girls."

PG comes up just then. "Time to check in," he says.

RAVI

Ravi's been dreading this so much. Leaving Kolkata with that dead-end manila envelope in his carry-on. Saying these last few goodbyes.

Kat smiles at Arjun. "Thanks for everything, Arjun Uncle. I'm sorry . . . that we argued this summer. And please give Mira Auntie my regards."

Ravi can't believe his ears. But the dimple's there; she must be saying what he's hearing.

"I will indeed," Arjun replies. "In fact, you reminded me a bit of her from the start. Loving, and a fighter. I like to see that mix, especially in a young person."

Ravi tries to make himself say something. He's so grateful to Arjun but he can't seem to put that into words.

Arjun seems to understand. He pulls Ravi into a brown-man hug. "You'll always have a home in Kolkata with us," he says. "Come back soon."

"I will," Ravi says, looking from Bontu to Arjun. "This is my desh, too, right?"

"Just as much as it is ours," Bontu answers.

Ravi tries to smile, but that's also too hard. He'd returned to his birthplace with such high hopes, and now he's leaving empty-handed. And then, as if she can read his heart *and* his mind, Gracie slips her hand into his. They head for the plane.

KAT

At the gate, PG unzips his backpack and hands them their phones. "You did good, people. Nobody died of cell phone withdrawal. So here, take your tech back."

Kat powers hers up. She's not expecting many texts because she's been emailing and calling Mom all summer. Sure enough, only a few come in, a couple from Mom, and one each from Amber and Brittany.

She starts with Mom's. The first one says, *I DID IT! Saved up enough to buy my ticket to Boston! Not going to tell you by email or phone so this is a SURPRISE when you get your phone back.* Many dancing ladies and laughing faces follow.

Her text from yesterday tells Kat that they're safe and sound in Grandma Vee's apartment. They're planning to meet Kat at the airport, followed by hearts, trumpets, and other celebratory emoji.

Kat is so excited she can hardly sit still.

"MOM'S IN BOSTON!" she shouts, and PG, Gracie, and Ravi cheer.

See you tomorrow, Mom! she texts. *I'm soooooo glad you're there.*

Mom answers right away: *Can't wait, darling! It's GREAT to hear from you by text. I've missed you like crazy cakes.* Fifteen small cakes appear.

Kat hearts that, and then takes a deep breath before reading the texts from her classmates at Sanger. Brittany sent hers weeks ago, just before school got out for the summer holiday. *Guess what, Kat? A ninth grader filed a complaint against your enemy, and her story sounded a LOT like yours. His parents yanked him out of school before the committee even began the investigation.*

Kat's heart starts beating faster.

She reads the one from Amber: *People are saying they wish they'd believed you. Brittany and I did! He's not coming back for senior year!*

Bap-re-bap.

Kat was ready to face that Wolf again after her talk with Kavita, but now she doesn't have to. She'll be able to walk through the halls of Sanger with her head held high. Well, she's always done that, but now she won't be acting. First thing on her list this fall, though, is to find that brave freshman. *Took two of us to take him down. I'll love her forever.*

Across from PG and Kat, Gracie and Ravi are reading texts, too.

"My parents' texts read like diaries," Ravi says. "They knew I wasn't getting them, and they sent loads of email, too, but looks like they wanted to share what was happening on a daily basis anyway. And check this out: I heard from Brian. *Made it down to Baylor. Be good to Gracie. She's a keeper.* How did he know about us, Gracie?"

Gracie smiles at him. "I think everyone knew. Everyone but you."

She kisses his cheek. Kat rolls her eyes. Those two.

PG looks over at Kat and raises his eyebrows. "They finally got together?"

"Yep," she says. "With a little help from Amit Biswas and Bonita Juarez."

"No idea what you're talking about," says PG. "But let's leave it that way."

And now it's time to board, to say goodbye to Kolkata.

Kat is the last passenger to enter the jetway, and Ravi and Gracie are walking ahead of her. Just before Ravi steps into the plane, he turns and blows a kiss.

Some people might look stupid doing that, but not Bird Boy.

He's as graceful as a leading man making an exit, a star.

Kat can almost feel his kiss breezing by her.

She pictures it flying out of the airport and swooshing along Kolkata's highways, streets, and lanes.

She hopes it gets to Ravi's intended destination.

And that a mother feels it land on her cheek, a thank-you from a stranger who adores her.

RAVI

Ravi throws his arms around his parents. They've been waiting outside customs over an hour for their first sighting of
him, Dad tells him.

"Your mother made me get here two hours before the plane
landed."

"I'm not the one who was so excited I woke up at four a.m.,"
Mom says.

"I missed you guys, too," Ravi says. "Let's go home."

They're dear and familiar *now*, he realizes, even though
they weren't the last time he arrived in Logan.

As they drive home from the airport, Ravi's parents start
asking questions. "Why is everyone calling you 'Ravi'?" Mom
asks.

"It was my orphanage name. Do you remember?" And
before they can answer, he asks, "Do you guys mind calling
me that, too?"

"Of course we don't mind," Dad says. "We called you 'Ravi'
before you started school. Still do sometimes when we pray
for you."

Ravi looks out of the window as they head home on the
Mass Pike. He sees the Pru. The Citgo sign. Fenway Park. The
thick, leafy trees of August block his view of the Charles, but

he knows it's there. He knows every curve of it. He rolls down his window. The Boston air is as humid as Kolkata's. He takes a deep, long inhale of it. This is home, too.

INT. THORNTON KITCHEN—NIGHT

As they sip the cardamom-spiced chai Ravi's brought back with him, his parents listen as Ravi talks. He tells them everything—his visit to the orphanage, what he discovered about his first mother at the Royal Diadem Society Guesthouse, and even about his botched, stupid attempt at a rescue.

When his mother hears about the four little girls who were freed at the hotel, she starts crying.

"Mom!" Ravi says. "It's good news. No need for tears."

"Thank God for tears," she says. "They're made for times like these. Painful memories. Happy endings. Lives saved."

Or no memories at all, Ravi thinks. *And sad endings.*

"So what was your big takeaway from the trip, Ravi?" Dad asks.

He notices how easily his father uses his reclaimed name. "I guess it was 'Golden-Ruling,'" he says.

They listen again as he describes what he wants to do in honor of his first mother.

"Oh, darling, that's perfect!" Mom says.

His father, though, asks him to wait awhile before donating a chunk of his trust fund to the about-to-be-established Royal Diadem Foundation.

"It's a big decision," Dad says. "A good one, but you want to be sure you'll have no regrets."

Ravi won't, he knows. He's made other decisions, too, but he doesn't tell his parents about those yet. Some small, some big.

Like join a gym so he can keep working out.

Find a Bangla teacher.

Visit Kolkata every year. Or more often. For longer stays.

Explore criminal justice classes at the community college. If you want to fight villains, you'd better figure out how to do it right. Teamwork, training, toughness—Shen modeled it all.

Schedule an appointment with a post-search counselor listed in that pamphlet he stuffed in a drawer before leaving for Kolkata.

Find out more about DNA testing. Maybe it's worth a try.

And he'll connect with other people who hear the drumbeat of grief that never leaves you if your first mother did. It's not going to stop; Ravi knows that now. It's still here with him in Boston, just as it was in Kolkata. The volume might turn up at times, and he might be able to lower it a bit, but it's never going away. That early loss means he'll have to work harder to feel his emotions, and even to act on them, but he's willing to make the effort.

For her sake.

For his own.

KAT

INT. THORNTON HOUSE—DAY

When Kat, her mom, Saundra, and Grandma Vee arrive at the Thorntons' for Kat's going-away party, Ash is mixing drinks for the adults.

Kat admires the new nose ring. "Some of the Asha House girls wear those, too," she tells Ash. "How were the last couple of college visits?"

"Awful. It's decided—I'm taking a gap year after high school like Robin. Ravi, I mean."

Kat introduces her to Mom—Saundra's met most of the church folks on her previous visits—and then finds Martin, who's handing around a plate of Grandma Vee's fritters. He's leaving for Brown in just a few days. With Mr. Boots, his therapy animal.

Mom shakes hands with everyone except Ravi and Gracie, who each get a big hug. "You'll have to come visit us in Oakland. Right, Saundra?"

"Definitely," Saundra says. She turns to Ravi. "You look in better shape than the last time I visited. Been working out?"

"He's been training with the anti-trafficking unit in Kolkata," Gracie says proudly.

"Trafficking's bad in our town, too," Saundra says. "Ever considered law enforcement as a career, young man?"

"Actually, yes," Ravi says, surprising Kat and almost everyone who overhears him.

Even his parents, she thinks. His mother looks like she's about to say something, but her husband puts a finger to his lips. Gracie, though, is smiling at Ravi knowingly. *The keeper of his secrets*, Kat thinks. *As it should be.*

Meanwhile, Mr. Rivera is frowning at how close Gracie and Ravi are on the sofa. He's the only one who doesn't seem 100 percent delighted to discover that they've become a couple. Ravi catches his eye and shifts his butt over a couple of inches away from Gracie's. Mrs. Rivera, whose stomach is reminding everybody that another baby is due in two weeks' time, gives Ravi an encouraging smile.

PG comes over to Kat. "I heard from Arjun," he tells her. "The trial's starting soon. They're preparing Kavita to testify."

So now it's Kavita's turn to fight. She's going to win, Kat's almost sure of it. No matter what happens in that court, though, Arjun Uncle, Miss Shireen, Mira Auntie, and the others at Asha House and the Bengali Emancipation Society will be on the mat with Kavita.

PG reaches into his bag and pulls out three sealed envelopes. They look familiar. He hands them to Kat, Gracie, and Ravi. "Open these in private, people."

His guess is that they'll want to be alone, but Kat wants to be with her friends. "Meet me in the Bat Cave in five," she tells Ravi in a low voice. "And bring Firebird."

INT. THORNTON GARAGE—NIGHT

Inside the Thorntons' garage, the small, decrepit vehicle looks like she's been counting the days until Ravi's return. He and Gracie lean against her, facing Kat, and they open the envelopes.

Gracie laughs as her eyes scan what she scribbled so many weeks ago. "*I hope to avoid babies,*" she reads. "Well, that was dumb. What's wrong with babies? I love them."

Kat does, too. Maybe that church Mom's been going to with Saundra has a nursery where she can get her fix.

"*I hope to learn something new that has nothing to do with babies,*" Gracie continues, reading her number two. "Oh, I definitely did that. Jiu-jitsu, thanks to you, Kat. Now I can enjoy every family party without having to hide from a two-hundred-pound lech."

Look out, "*Tío,*" Kat thinks. *One Kimura coming your way.*

Ravi doesn't open his envelope. "I didn't find my first mother, but at least I tried." He stops. Fights the choking sound in his voice.

Gracie scooches over so she's even closer to him. To Kat, the car they're resting on seems as annoyed as Mr. Rivera.

"Number two was I hope to *help* my first mother," Ravi says, and his voice is steadier now. "Couldn't do that when I didn't find her, right? But I *am* going to Golden-Rule in her honor." He flashes Kat an Amit Biswas smile.

It's her turn. She pulls out the paper and reads her number one out loud. "*I want to help Canaries fight Wolves.*"

Neither of them ask what she meant when she wrote that.

They're quiet, giving her a chance to take stock, so Kat does. Her own plans didn't work out at all. But maybe she was meant to make a difference in other ways, right from the start.

Helping Kavita to fight, but with her story, not her strength.

Teaching Gracie not to fear a big canine.

And in a few years, if she can keep grappling, going back to teach jiu-jitsu to Shiuli. And to Baby Diana, too. Maybe even Logan, if he wants to learn.

Kat reads her number two aloud. *"I hope I can get over my disgust of men."*

Again, Gracie and Ravi don't say anything. Kat looks at her friends' faces. Especially Ravi's. She remembers the time she was able to touch his shoulder outside the orphanage. Maybe she's a bit better. But she'll never be the person she was before the attack. It's changed her life forever, in bad ways and good.

When she gets back to Oakland, she's going to ask Mom to find her a woman counselor. Somehow they'll figure out a way to pay for it. She needs to spar with men to get her black belt, and she's not giving up jiu-jitsu. She thinks of Mom, Mira, Grandma Vee, Miss Shireen, Kavita, and the other Asha House girls. Maybe that's the way healing works. No surrender. You stay on the mat. You keep fighting.

RAVI

Kat and her mother are catching a late flight to California right after the party. Deputy Saundra, though, is staying with her great-aunt an extra week. She and Ravi have already planned to meet for coffee to talk about the vocation she loves.

After giving each person at the party a goodbye namaste, Kat takes off the red scarf and offers it to Ms. Vee. The old woman smiles and fingers the chiffon, but doesn't take it. "It's yours to keep, child."

Kat throws her arms around her, and then around Gracie.

Now it's Ravi's turn. He puts his palms together in a namaste. "See you soon, bon." Little sister, he's called her. Because that's what she's become.

"Goodbye, Dada," she answers. Older brother.

And then she steps forward and puts her arms around him. It isn't a full-body embrace, like the one she gave Gracie. It lasts only a second or two before she pulls away. But it's a hug.

Ravi can hardly believe it. *This is love, too*, he thinks.

Turbocharged, sixteen-cylindered, mega-horsepowered love.

Kat's mom's eyes are teary. Ms. Vee's expression looks like she wants to burst into the "Alleluia" chorus. And Gracie is giving Ravi that "you're-hotter-than-Batman-*or*-Biswas" smile of admiration that makes him want to fly.

He's never felt more like a hero.

ACKNOWLEDGMENTS

Thanks to Harold and Geneinde Jones, Bekah Mallory, Biju Mathew, Sally Petterson, Smita Singh, and Laura Sullivan for informing portions of this novel that depend heavily on their experiences and expertise. I'm grateful to my friends Dean and Jane Thompson for facilitating the opportunity to learn about anti-trafficking work in Kolkata.

I'm also in debt to International Justice Mission, Dear Adoption, Family Preservation 365, Jatiyo Kristyo Prochar Samity (JKPS), Mahima House, and Nancy Newton Verrier, author of *The Primal Wound* and *Coming Home to Self*. Please visit forwardmebacktoyou.com for more resources.

To my beloved agent, Laura Rennert, my kind and insightful editor, Grace Kendall, and the ultra-supportive editorial, publicity, design, and marketing teams at Macmillan—including but not limited to Elizabeth Lee, Joy Peskin, Nancy Elgin, Hayley Jozwiak, Jill Freshney, John Nora, Cassie Gonzales, Elizabeth H. Clark, Kristen Luby, Katie Halata, Lucy Del Priore, and Brittany Pearlman—bless you all.

Last but not least, I owe this story to Rob, my husband, our resilient and loving sons, James and Timothy, and my mother, who amazes me.